THE EVERLASTING

BEYOND

OF ETERNAL HAPPINESS

MIKE AMOS

"Ooh, Simms." Mandy's Texan voice was a breathless purr, inviting and intimate. "I'll fess up, I've always had a big thing for guys in uniform."

She stepped forward, black PVC stiletto boots clicking on the polished metal floor. Her gloss-red lips parted slightly, twisting up into a knowing half-smile, jaws working furiously on her chewing gum. Putting one foot up on the computer console, she ran a hand lightly down the ragged, fishnet top that clung to the curves of her womanhood. When her fingers came to rest on the hem of her black plastic miniskirt, she tweaked it upwards by a tantalising fraction.

Simms shrank back, the soft leather of the Captain's seat creaking beneath him. The Captain's seat. Yes, he was Commander Simms, aboard the Starship *Cola Français*. He had men at command, an international reputation to maintain. His reputation!

Dragging his gaze from the tempting siren before him, he checked the bridge. They were alone amongst the banks of computers and the screen showing the vast night of space, alight with the brilliance of a billion stars.

He turned back to Mandy, perspiration dappling his brow. At last, a tryst with this gorgeous, blonde vixen. It was only slightly terrifying.

He wasn't a handsome man. Tall, thin, all elbows and knees, has was hunched, clumsy, and awkward. Oversized, bovine eyes bore down on a thin, once-broken nose. Tight blond curls hugged his head, their position fixed by an enticing mixture of evaporated sweat and low-grade psoriasis,

But to hell with looks, it was power women wanted, and he was Simms. Commander Simms. Commander…Simms.

His plumy English accent betrayed a public school upbringing, with just the hint of inbreeding.

"Mandy, I, I, I never, I never thought…" Little pools of spit accumulated at the corners of his mouth.

She put a finger to her lips. "Hush, you naughty, naughty boy."

Bringing her leg down from the console, she stood directly in front of him, hands on hips. A small, rather grubby, pink cloth cat swung at her waist. She blew a bubble in her gum.

"Simms, you are so brave. And so clever."

"I…er, well…"

"Ah get you, so modest."

She glided effortlessly into his lap, one knee raised, left hand playing with the soft hair at the base of his neck. With her right hand, she ran a finger across his lips and down onto the zipper of his black jumpsuit.

Heart pounding, he breathed out heavily.

"Woah, Simms, Simms. Funky." She coughed, eyes watering, trying to conceal a flicker of annoyance with her hasty smile. "Just one moment, tiger."

She jumped up, wobbling slightly on her stilettos, and hobbled to the far side of the console. Giving him a rather hurried pout, she hauled out her handbag and started rummaging through.

"Ah, here we are."

Dumping her handbag, she strode back and flumped heavily down into his lap.

His eyes crossed. "Ooof."

Mandy stifled a giggle. "Is that you?"

Simm's voice was tighter and higher than before. "Yes."

"Sorry." Adjusting her weight, Mandy held up a small aerosol canister to his mouth. "Open wide."

Simms obliged and Mandy made two short puffs. An air of minty freshness filled his mouth. Halitosis? Yes, of course. He suffered badly from it. The memory came back to him suddenly and with it the realisation that a disorientating fog shrouded all recollection of the past. Still, at least this was one thing he could hang onto. His breath stank.

Putting a hand to his forehead, he gave his head a little shake.

Come on old fruit, get a grip.

To hell with all this doubt, to hell with lousy looks and bad breath. He had power on his side, authority. Women loved that.

He was Simms. Commander…Simms. What *was* his first name?

Mandy pulled the zipper of his jumpsuit open to the navel and slid her hand in. "Commander Simms, you've been so clever, it's your mind I love you for."

"I have? You do?"

She ran a long nailed finger around his nipple. "So respectable, such a reputation, yet all this time a secret terrorist."

Simms spluttered. "Terrorist? I'm not a terrorist."

"Hush, hush, tiger." She left his nipple and placed a finger on his lips. "Put your hand on my knee."

Simms gulped and placed a trembling hand gently on the shiny black plastic of her boot.

Mandy put her mouth close to his ear and whispered. "Some say terrorist. I say freedom fighter."

"Freedom fighter?"

"Freedom fighter. Ooh, those words get me so hot. If only… no, you can't say."

"What?"

"Oh, no, I couldn't possibly ask you to." She lowered her knee out of his reach. "It's plain wrong of me to go asking dumb questions. I should go."

"No." Simms wondered if he dared touch her again. "Ask away. What ho, anything, just ask. You know me, I'm Information Off…"

His thoughts clouded. "I'm Inf…"

"You're Commander Simms." Mandy leant close again, taking his hand and placing it back on her leg. "Oh, if only you could tell me 'bout some of the brave things you done."

"Brave things?" Simms stared at his hand on her booted knee, struggling through his memory for brave things. Everything was wrong. Well, everything was right but somehow in the wrong way. Commander Simms with the gorgeous Mandy, yes, but how had he got here? And confound it, what *was* his bloody first name? His confused, jumbled mind raced. He had been on a Space Station, hadn't he? Called *The Nice and Spicy Nacho-Niks*. Something had gone terribly wrong. If only he could remember.

Mandy clicked her tongue. "Brave things."

Brave things, brave things... He readjusted the position of his sweating palm on her boot, making an audible *sloop*.

"Ah, I had to do a presentation once to some senior guys from Starfleet Command and…"

"No, no silly." A slight edge crept into Mandy's voice. "Terrorist things."

"But…I'm not…"

"Not a terrorist? Really? I'm all choked up 'bout that." Mandy's brow furrowed. She pulled away just a fraction.

"No, wait. Well, I might be. Never can tell, eh?" He winked conspiratorially.

Mandy leant closer again, her voice lowered. "I bet you know Agent Higgs."

"Higgs? Yes. No. Well, maybe. Security Officer Higgs?"

She tapped his nose lightly. "Oh you tease. You know and I know the whole security officer thing is just a front. Agent Higgs, one of the most dashing freedom fighters."

"Dashing?" Simms gave Mandy's knee a nervous, well lubricated little rub. "Yes, yes, of course I know Higgs. Higgsy, Higgsy, Higgsy. We go back, oh, back to college together."

"College? You were at college with Agent Higgs?"

"Yes. Er, at…at Terrorist College."

Mandy cocked her head, eyebrows raised.

Simms struggled. "We did…bomb making together."

Mandy sighed, shaking her head. "This is like trying to scratch my ass with my elbow."

"We did."

"Right. Terrorist College?"

"Er…It was clandestine. One had to say a secret password to get in." Simms' desperate imagination piled words into his mouth. "I blew up an ice cream van once."

"What?"

"I…an ice cream van. Me and Higgsy…" Simms' voice trailed off.

Mandy unwound herself from him and stood, folding her arms crossly. "You're not a terrorist are you, Simms?"

"I am."

"Really?"

Simms chewed his top lip and shook his head.

"Okay, that's it." Mandy clapped her hands. "Show's over."

A woman's voice filled the air around them, a wholesome, Deep South voice, all apple pie and church on a Sunday. "Agent Mandy, Information Officer Simms has revealed himself as a terrorist and confessed to a number of subversive activities. Why have you discontinued the interrogation?"

Mandy tutted, running her fingers through her hair. "Ma'am, trust me, he's not a terrorist."

"Agent Mandy, Information Officer Simms clearly stated he had attended a terrorist training facility."

"Ma'am, whatever, Simms has nothing useful to tell us about the terrorist insurgency."

"Agent Mandy, I accept your conclusion. Information Officer Simms."

Simms jolted upright. The unseen woman was addressing him. She was right, he remembered now, he was an Information Officer. Where had the notion he was Commander Simms come from? "Er, yes ma'am?"

"You are condemned not only by your confession but also your recent terrorist activities. For your own security and well being, you will now be terminated. Have a nice day."

Simms backed right up in his seat. "Wait. What terrorist activities?"

"You murdered a senior ranking official by blowing yourself up."

"What?" Simms glanced down at himself. He seemed to be quite intact. "Surely you're mistaken, madam. I'm sure I'd remember if I'd blown myself up."

Mandy kicked the chair. "Simms, button it."

The unseen woman continued. "I am sorry, Information Officer Simms, but my judgement is final." The top of the computer console swung upwards and a robotic arm emerged, aiming an automatic pistol at Simms' head.

"What, no, please. I don't want to die. Mandy."

"What?"

He pointed at the gun. "It's going to kill me."

"Yeah, so? Don't be such a baby."

"I don't want to die. Please, madam, whoever you are, I don't want to die."

"I am sorry Information Officer Simms, Agent Mandy has deemed it no longer useful to interrogate you."

Simms slid from the chair to his knees, hands clenched together as he begged. "Please, Mandy don't let it kill me, I don't want to die, please."

Mandy half turned away. "Stop going on, you creep. You're embarrassing me."

He fell sobbing on his face, pawing her feet. "Please, Mandy, please."

"Oh, okay, okay already. Get off." She kicked his hands away. "Ma'am. There might be some further questions I could ask this jerk."

The arm retreated back from whence it came and the top of the console swung shut. "Very well, Agent Mandy."

Mandy booted Simms in the ribs impatiently. "Get up."

He stumbled to his feet and followed her across to the far side of the room where a row of lockers stood. She opened one and gestured inside.

"Get in."

Simms pointed at the cramped space and mouthed at her "in there?"

"In."

Simms wrung his hands, whining. "But I don't want to go in the locker."

"Get in. Now. Or, darn it, I'll change my mind."

Trembling, Simms eased himself into the tiny compartment. There was barely enough height to stand. Mandy slammed the door before he was fully in.

"Ow. Mandy, please."

"Oh, get in…"

As Mandy forced the door shut and turned the key, Simms found himself in almost total darkness. The only light stabbed in from three thin louvers in the door. Putting his face up to them, he peeped out. "Mandy?"

"And keep quiet."

She snapped her fingers and everything went black.

ANTHONY GERMAINE PRESSED his face to the immense office window and stared miserably across the Hudson. This was all Faivish's fault. A thousand-mile flight and two nights in a five star hotel, all for the sake of a half-hour meeting with their New York sponsor. Anthony's boss, Faivish Goldbloom, thrived on this sort of trip. Rubbing shoulders with millionaire businessmen seemed to make him feel significant and happening. Anthony considered this a pathetic vanity. Faivish's sole claim to importance was he knew an inordinate amount about the innards of chickens.

Anthony hated flying, hated cities and, most of all, hated the ostentatious offices of big business. He was, however, an authority on the internal parasites of poultry. This was not something to win him immediate popularity or, he noted both frequently and bitterly, a girlfriend. However, it did make him of interest to the powers that be in the Renenkya Corporation, since their billion-strong flock of factory-farmed chickens was in the grip of a lethal epidemic of diarrhoea.

The subject of girlfriends or, more specifically, his lack of one, was a matter on which he had dwelt a great deal of late. He laid the blame for his seemingly perpetual status as desperate bachelor on one thing, his looks. Anthony possessed a curiously square face, his long nose running dead straight downwards, almost parallel with his flat cheeks. Thick, soft, mouse-brown hair, sensibly parted on the right-hand side, gave him a somewhat thatched appearance, a look further enhanced by his solid, six-foot frame and a stolidly bland wardrobe. If only a girl could see beyond his admittedly unconventional looks, see the selfless, kind, romantic soul he knew himself to be. Failing that, he might be in with a chance if one saw his considerable bank balance. But then, they would be after him for the wrong reason. No, the girl of his dreams would accept him as he was, cyberman-looks, olive corduroys, grey flannel shirts and all.

If he had been less obstinately fed up, the view from the window would have impressed him. Up this high, the air was clear, the choking smog of industry forgotten far below. He squinted at Manhatten's distant skyscrapers, stretching up into a pale, winter-blue sky, the low sun reflecting brilliantly from their mirrored windows. A little closer in the opposite direction, he could just make out the Statue of Liberty through the haze of acidic fog. She was in trouble, the waters of the New York Harbour lapping her toes, the plinth she stood on and its museum long since drowned. There was talk of rescuing her, talk mired in arguments over cost and just how much more sea level would rise anyway.

Regardless of whether the Statue of Liberty was waving or drowning, New York wasn't beaten. It took more than a twenty-five meter rise in sea level to dampen the spirits of The Big Apple. The architects just kept building upwards, bricking over submerged districts to keep one step ahead of the sea.

The Renenkya Building, where Anthony now stood, was one of the new builds. All glass and chrome, it towered more than eight hundred meters above what used to be considered *street level*. It was a rather anachronistic term these days, since the streets only really existed at low tide. Most New Yorkers on-the-go got about by monorails and covered walkways many meters above the ground, or took a ride with one of the electro-gondoliers. Anthony did anything he could to avoid taking trips with the latter. The electro-gondoliers of New York always had something to say on every subject but even they shut up when Anthony told them what he did for a living. It was plain embarrassing.

"Quite a view, quite a view, eh?"

It was Faivish, Anthony knew without needing to turn around. He considered Faivish's almost childlike excitement infectious but only in a pathological sense. Anthony accepted it was cruel to dislike him. It was unfair to find the man irritating simply for being indomitably cheerful, well-meaning, talkative, podgy, short, bald and permanently in need of a handkerchief. Faivish had gone out of his way many times to help Anthony, opening countless doors in his career. Anthony liked and respected Faivish a great deal, in principle. In practice, he just wanted to strangle him. It was fortunate for them both that Faivish was due to retire in a year or two.

Faivish was on a roll. "Reminds me of the view of…"

Anthony cut in. "Kowloon from Victoria peak, 2037. Yes. I imagine it does."

"Oh yes, there was quite a funny story. My old friend Bey…"

"Beynish."

"Ah, yes, Baynish, yes. Well he and I…"

"Ended up in your pyjamas, explaining to the police why you had a rubber chicken on a stick. Yes."

"Yes, that's right. Oh we laughed." Faivish gave a little cough. "I've told you then?"

"Yes, Faivish. It was quite funny. The first time you told me."

Anthony sighed, turning away from the window. He found the office offensive. It was half the size of a tennis court, one side floor-to-ceiling windows, the other three sides hung with canvases of presumably expensive modern art. Anthony had no notion of whether the paintings were artistically significant but they did remind him of some of the microscope slides of colonic tissue back at the lab. In the centre of this vast space stood a mahogany coffee table, encircled by six curious art deco things Anthony had previously investigated and established as chairs.

On the table, a tempting cafetière of coffee steamed beside a silver tray of napkins, china cups and saucers. Anthony strode over, lowered himself into a chair and poured himself a strong one.

Faivish joined him, sitting in the chair opposite. "Quite a place they've got here. Quite a place, eh?"

Anthony grunted and sipped his black coffee. It was real, not synthetic like the stuff he usually had to put up with. "The coffee's good."

"Oh yes, no expense spared, eh? No expense spared." Faivish ladled sugar into his cup, spilling grains over the tray. "Reminds me of when I met Renenkya's CEO, back when the project started, oh, that was a time…"

"Faivish."

"What?"

"Why are we here?"

"Why? Why? Your work, Anthony, your work. Why else? You've saved Renenkya millions. Billions. They want to say thank you."

"You think they've brought us out here just to say thank you?"

"Yes, yes, why else? Eh? Why else?"

It was true. Anthony had saved Renenkya a lot of money. The corporation owned Star Spangled Chickens, a global player in fast food. Anthony found it amazing the chain could build such success on the paradigm of selling food by the bucket. A bucket of chicken with fries for under a dollar, all possible through factory farming and genetic modification. Anthony read round the natural history of poultry when he took his doctorate. Chickens used to have feathers. And feet. That was all gone now, thanks to modern science. Each chicken sat naked in a small wire cage, its genes twisted to produce huge, footless legs and enormous breast muscles. The necks were long, thin and brittle, to assist 'processing' once the chicken's diet of synthetic protein had brought them to the appropriate weight.

The trouble was, a billion chickens awash with antibiotics and antiparasitics led to some super-resistant bugs. A little single-celled organism called *Eimeria tenella* had inconveniently mutated to a very nasty strain that shrugged off all the normal treatments. Star Spangled Chicken's profits had nosedived. The devastation of livestock was not the problem, they were covered by insurance. The trouble was the media images of countless chickens shitting themselves. It put the customers off.

But Anthony had found a cure, quickly, quietly and with no fuss. And now he had to have the inconvenience of being thanked for it. He drummed his fingers impatiently. "Well, where are they then?"

"I'm sorry to have kept you waiting. Anthony, Faivish."

They both jumped at the rumbling baritone. A vast, mountain of a man stood to their left, his forty inch waist insignificant to his seven foot height. Ruddy and freckled, his few remaining wisps of hair were a faded ginger, his nose a mass of capillaries.

The man laughed deeply and extended a hand. "I'm Damon. Damon Bridle. I'm from sNASA."

Anthony struggled to his feet. sNASA. The Spiritual North American Space Agency? This made no sense at all. Faivish leapt from his seat with alarming speed for a man of his years and wrung Damon's hand.

Anthony waited his turn. "sNASA?"

"I'm sure this will come as a surprise. May I?" Damon gestured to the seats.

Faivish was gushing. "Of course, of course. A coffee?"

"Thank you." Damon lowered himself heavily into the seat between them and turned to face Anthony.

"Well, Anthony. I'm sure my presence will come as something of a surprise to you, yes?"

Anthony nodded.

"The Renenkya Corporation is involved in a lot more than just fast food."

"Yes, I know that." Anthony smiled thinly, fighting an urge to roll his eyes.

"Your work with microbes, with single-celled organisms, well, you have a very impressive record of research. Very impressive indeed. And a very good record of putting that knowledge into practice."

In the following pause, Anthony realised something was expected of him. "Oh. It was nothing, really."

"He's so modest, that boy. So modest." Faivish handed Damon a cup of coffee.

"Thank you, Faivish." He returned to Anthony. "You studied at Neo-Harvard, I believe?"

"Yes."

"In a student debate in 2041, you spoke strongly in favour of Intelligent Design. Is that an opinion you still hold?"

The question made Anthony sit up. "I did? Gee, I don't remember. That's nine years ago. How do you know this?"

"It's in your file."

"My file?"

"Everyone has a file. Intelligent Design?"

Yes, Anthony had been a devout believer once. His upbringing left him no choice, steeped in the teachings of the ICRT, the International Church of the Reformed Testament. Damon's question was loaded. Anthony considered his words carefully.

"I believe that religion is a personal experience between man and God. It is clear there is a driving force behind the..." He struggled for a safe word. "The development of life."

Damon nodded slowly, seemingly satisfied with the answer. "Good, good. What do you know about Mission Europa 2050?"

Anthony's heart sank. Now he understood. They wanted to pull him in for some charity do for the impoverished United States of Europe.

"Gee, I don't know much about it, sir."

"Well, The Renenkya Corporation wants you to be part of the mission. They want you to go to Europa as the mission's astro-biologist."

"Sorry? As what?"

"Astro-biologist."

"Where?" Anthony knew the Europeans were a strange bunch, but astro-biologist?

"Europa. The ice-moon of Jupiter."

A crash made them both look round. Faivish had dropped his cup onto the tray. "Oh, I'm terribly sorry, terribly sorry. Jupiter you say? Jupiter?"

Damon helped Anthony's flummoxed boss mop up the spilt coffee with the inadequately sized napkins. "Not Jupiter, Faivish, Europa, one of Jupiter's moons."

"But I don't understand." Anthony placed his own cup safely down and assisted with the clean-up operation. "Why do they want me to go to Europa?"

"As I said, your work, your reputation with microbes and bacteria. They're going to be looking for life."

"Life?"

"Let me explain. Leaving Earth aside, Europa is unique in the solar system in that it possesses water. Vast oceans of water, all deep beneath a thick coating of ice. It even has a very thin atmosphere of oxygen."

The spilt coffee mopped up, Anthony leant back in his chair and considered. "But I thought the ICRT decreed there was no life in the universe except that found on Earth?"

Damon smiled. "But of course they have. And of course, they are right. But there have been some…discussions. I'm a scientist like you Anthony. We scientists keep an open mind on things. We weigh up the evidence and if a theory is proved wrong, we come up with a new one to fit the evidence. As long as we don't make too much noise if we find something the ICRT might find inconvenient, yes? As long as we keep coming up with innovations for our sponsors, hmm? Need I say more?"

Anthony shrugged.

Damon lent forward conspiratorially. "The problem is, a few of our more vocal scientific colleagues lack discretion and, sadly, any concern for their careers. You see, they've questioned the no-life decree. Convinced there will be bugs on Europa, they've challenged the ICRT to put its faith where its mouth is."

"And so there's a massive, expensive mission to Europa to decide the issue one way or another." Anthony shook his head.

"In part yes. And since Renenkya's CEO is a very committed member of the ICRT and fiercely involved in the argument, your name came up as a possible."

"What about sNASA's astro-biologists? Surely one of them would be a better bet. Who's that woman?" Anthony snapped his fingers, searching for the name. "Duchess? Duck?"

"Duke. Mariah Duke. No, I'm afraid sNASA's astro-biologists ruled themselves out when they wrote that open letter to congress."

"Oh, yes, I forgot."

The letter, yes of course. It had been in all the news and there was talk of the issue going to the Supreme Court. Scientists demanding evolution be taught in schools alongside intelligent design.

Damon shook his head. "The people bankrolling this trip are all deeply religious men and women. They don't like talk of evolution." He lent even closer to Anthony, his voice lowered to a hoarse whisper. "They don't want to find life, you understand me Anthony? But there's a good chance we will."

Damon slouched back in his seat and laughed, a deep rumbling laugh.

Faivish made eye contact with Anthony and nodded enthusiastically. "I see no problem with releasing Anthony for this trip, no problem at all. If anyone can find life, it will be our Anthony. Mark my words, Anthony's your boy."

"I'm sure you're right Faivish." Damon picked up his coffee and took a sip. "Still, it isn't just about life. There are a lot of other sound, scientific reasons for going. Exploration of space, advancing the frontiers of knowledge, the sponsorship deals, the merchandising spin-offs. There's even talk of another space station."

There had been a space station before, Anthony knew only too well. The *Nice and Spicy Nacho Niks*, eight years earlier, a vast city in space dispatched to search for life on Jupiter's distant moon. The name filled him with contempt. Space exploration cost a great deal and sNASA were clearly happy to take the money wherever they could. "The last one went, missing didn't it?"

Damon grimaced. "Yes, the last one went missing along with the relief ship we sent out for it, the *Cola Français*. A terrible shame, although the sponsors more than made their money back on the various rights. A minor part of Europa 2050 is to try to establish what happened to Europa 2042."

Anthony stood and walked a little way from the table, gazing towards the window. A trip into space. There would be a lot of attention on him, a lot of media nonsense. Still, Anthony Germaine, the astro-biologist. It had a certain appeal. You might say it sounded *sexy*. "I need to think."

"Of course. There's time."

Anthony walked to the window and pressed his face against the glass. The Statue of Liberty waved up at him. The Earth was drowning and Anthony was going to Jupiter.

There was something else, though. Higgs had been on the *Nice and Spicy*. Lionel Higgs. The action man, the head of house, the football king. The bastard who ran off with Biddy Dibben at Neo-Harvard, just at the point Anthony really thought he had a chance with her. And then with Lucy Cronk, after Anthony carefully cultivated her friendship by lending her books on flatworm anatomy. And, after that, Carrie Prowse, then Jodi Francis. In fact, every woman at college Anthony had even the slightest crush on, Higgs somehow got in there first. What made this worse was Anthony and Higgs had been buddies. Well, sort of. Anthony had hung out with Higgs and his cronies in the hope of being thought cool by association. It hadn't worked, of course. There had been quite a crowd on the periphery of the social geo-centre that had been Higgs.

After Neo-Harvard, the great man had risen up through sNASA's ranks and ended up second in command on the *Nice and Spicy*. Within a year of the space station being launched, all contact had been lost (although Anthony doubted there was any connection).

"I wonder what happened to Higgs."

DISGUSTED, HIGGS RAMMED the ammo clip back into the assault rifle. Ten rounds left. It wouldn't be enough. He swept the back of his hand over his eyes, wiping away the sweat. Dressed only in combat fatigues and size twelve boots, his naked, muscled torso shone with perspiration in the stifling half-light. Blonde, crew-cut hair topped his lantern-jawed face, right ear pierced with a gold stud.

Intense blue eyes twinkling in the faint glow of the gun's laser sight, he advanced cautiously up the passageway. There was breathing ahead of him, the guttural, inhuman rasping of some unspeakable nightmare. Higgs took hold of his fear. He was trained. Fear alone could not hurt him.

Cold air played on his face as the corridor opened out onto some unseen dark space. The breathing was louder now, its pace quickening. Heart thumping, Higgs tried to control his own gasps for air. It was so hot. He wiped his hand on the material of his combat fatigues and gripped his gun's handle again, waiting, listening.

The breathing thing was getting closer, coming at him from two o'clock. Higgs swung the gun round and narrowed his eyes. Was that a shape, loping towards him? He aimed, squeezing the trigger gently. Three flashes and three bullets sped off into the darkness. There was a squeal, like a stuck pig, and the breathing stopped.

Higgs listened. There was an expectant hush as the echoes of the gunshots faded away. Then, *they* started up, the noises, countless little grunts and squeals, distant but closing, their creators concealed in darkness.

"Shit."

Touching the wall to his right, Higgs trotted blind along the side of the room. The air was slightly cooler, telling him the ceiling was very high but the pitch black above him gave no clues. The sounds were getting closer. Higgs' only hope was *they* would go to the source of the gunshots. He needed to put as much distance between himself and the corridor as possible.

A shape loomed up and he slowed, taking his hand from the wall and reaching out in front. He touched a cold, hard metal surface. It was some sort of huge container, like an oil drum but taller than he was. Following its surface away from the wall, Higgs came to a second drum, then a third. This was the last and he followed it, running parallel to the wall again.

Realising the squeals had stopped, he paused and listened. He heard many creatures, sniffing, tasting the air for his scent. They were tracking him.

Higgs felt along his belt until he found his last mine. Unclipping it, he placed its magnetic side against the drum to his right. The contact made a dull thud and the sniffing stopped. Higgs froze, counting his heartbeats. He would need to activate the mine and it would beep when he did so.

Eleven heartbeats passed before the sniffing resumed. Hearing the scratching of clawed feet on the metal floor, Higgs twisted the top of the mine, priming the motion detector to come on in five seconds. A loud beep echoed through the dark and in answer came a chorus of squeals and howls.

Higgs ran alongside the drums, still parallel to the wall, making as much noise as he could. Behind him, they came, how far he couldn't tell. It didn't matter, just as long as they came past the mine.

A faint glow appeared in the gloom ahead of him, a luminous sign on the side of the next drum. Higgs glanced as he ran, making out the lettering, registering the significance of the words *highly inflammable*.

"Jesus."

He threw himself to the left, away from the drums, counting his strides, praying no unseen obstacle blocked his path. The mathematics of survival were simple. Ten meters, twenty meters, thirty meters, thirty-seven meters. The hanger lit up in a brilliant, silent glare for a fraction of a second before the blast's deafening force hurled Higgs forward. Hitting the ground he rolled, instinctively holding the strap of his rifle, tensing against the heat and the pain.

Covering his head to extinguish the flames there, Higgs turned over to see the destruction. The drum where he placed the mine was gone, a liquid inferno covering the vacant space. Shapes struggled, screaming as they burned, long clawed hands reaching up in pain.

Counting a dozen more three-meter high drums, Higgs leapt to his feet and sprinted towards the opposite wall, making for the shelter of a corridor. He reached the entrance just as the remaining canisters blew. The force of the explosion threw him several meters down the passage, clear of the burning fluid. He lay for a moment, panting, trying to block out the searing pain from his legs and chest. His breathing laboured in the chemical smoke. He had to get up, had to keep going.

Struggling to his feet, he stumbled down the corridor, clutching his gun to his chest.

"Higgsie, oh help, help."

The woman's call came out from the darkness ahead, her Texan drawl giving her away.

Mandy?

Higgs slowed his pace, clutching his brow, heart sinking. *Mandy Pollins. Oh, Jesus.*

"Higgsie, I'm here honey. Save me, save me."

Higgs lumbered on. Ahead, the corridor opened on a second large chamber, illuminated by a dull, green glow. Crouching at the corner, he looked in. A rough-hewn cavern lay before him, maybe thirty meters to the far wall and of untellable length. Glowing green sludge flowed slowly down a river channel from left to right, bisecting the cave into two equal halves. Opposite Higgs across the toxic ooze, Mandy struggled, chained between two pillars on a dais. She wore a white dress, immodestly ripped at the shoulder, her Monroe-blonde hair perfect. A little way behind her stood a bank of battered lockers.

Advancing into the room, Higgs swept left and right. The room was clear, for now. Three great chains hung from the darkness above, evenly spaced across the poisonous river, their ends a meter above the surface.

"Higgsie, be careful."

Slinging the rifle over his shoulder, he ran to the edge of the river and leapt for the first chain, gagging at the rising fumes and blistering on the hot metal. The chain lurched forward as he clung to it, but not far enough to reach the second chain. He swung back and forth, each time closing the gap on the second chain until he could grab it, wrapping his wrist around to get a secure hold. Clinging now to the second chain, he swung until he reached the third, forcing his aching fingers into the links. He hung for a moment, holding both chains, gasping for breath, head spinning. Clutching the third chain, he swung for the bank. After two swings, he could hold no longer and threw himself forward, knowing it was not far enough. Braced for the plunge into the foul liquid below he fell, breath held, eyes closed.

He landed on solid ground, winding himself. Somehow, he had made the far side. "What?"

"Oh, Higgsie. You're so brave. But hon', there's a bomb."

Shaking his head, Higgs stood. "I wasn't far enough over. I should be in the slime."

"Er, Higgsie, babe, there's a bomb."

"What?"

"A bomb." Mandy pointed her right finger at a meter-square steel cube close by, a small screen in its top surface showing a countdown in red numbers. Thirty, twenty-nine, twenty-eight…

Higgs leant wearily over the cube, shaking his head. A numeric keypad lay next to the screen. "What do I do? How do I stop it? This wasn't here when I came in."

"The override code."

"What code?"

Twenty-two, twenty-one, twenty…

"Higgsie, this is no time for games babe, you gotta put the code in."

"I don't know the code."

Mandy's voice was shrill. "Higgsie, I know you're a terrorist. This is one of the terrorist's bombs. Put the override code in."

Higgs put his hands on his head. "I don't know the goddamn code."

Fifteen, fourteen, thirteen…

Hysteria edged into Mandy's shouting. "Durn it, all terrorists know the code for Christ's sake. Higgs. Do it. Babe, please."

Higgs gaped at her, mind racing, searching for something, anything that might be the code.

Ten, nine, eight…

Higgs swung the rifle from his shoulder and smashed the butte down on the corner of the bomb.

"Higgsie, what are you doing? Put the terrorist code in."

"I'm not a terrorist. I don't know about any code." Higgs frantically smashed the rifle-butte on the bomb, again and again. "Come on, come on."

Four, three, two…

"Shit." Higgs flung his rifle aside and threw himself over the cube, face screwed up in anticipation of the blast.

He stayed there for several seconds.

"Higgsie. I don't think it went off."

Raising his head, he looked around. Everything was still intact. Movement by the lockers caught his eye, there, poking out of the louvers on one of the doors, someone's fingers, wiggling.

Higgs stood and, snatching his rifle from the floor marched over to Mandy. "What is going on?"

"Higgsie, you've saved me."

"Cut the crap. How did you get here?" A sudden thought occurred to Higgs. "How did I get here?"

"Cooeee." A little, whiny voice came from the fingers in the locker.

Higgs nodded in their direction. "Who's in the locker?"

"Well, aren't you asking a lot of questions." Mandy's petulant scowl soured her blond bombshell looks. "I'm here because of terrorists like you."

Higgs sighed heavily. "Mandy, who's in the locker?"

"Cooeee, Higgs, it's me, Information Officer Simms."

Higgs put a hand over his eyes. "Simms too. Oh boy."

"Simms, for the last time, button it, ya hear?" Mandy snapped her fingers and the chains fell from her hands. She stepped down to Higgs.

"You have no idea how close you are to being terminated." Her gaze lingered on Higgs' pectorals rising and falling as he caught his breath. "Still. Higgsie, Higgsie, Higgsie..."

She ran a finger across down his sternum to the six-pack of his stomach. He grabbed her hand, eyes burning dangerously.

"Mandy, where the hell are we? I want answers, now."

"You're hurting me."

"Where are we?"

"Oh, this is hopeless." Mandy clicked her fingers. "Show's over."

Pain seared through Higgs' hand, forcing him to release his grip. Mandy stepped away. "Higgs, you are being just so rude. If I didn't know you loved me, I would be really very cross with you."

"I don't..." A fresh wave of pain flashed through Higgs, forcing him to his knees.

Mandy sauntered to the bomb, running a finger across the surface while Higgs grovelled. "However, I think you need a little time to consider your harsh words. Ma'am?"

A woman's voice filled the cave. "Yes, Agent Mandy?"

"I think Higgs needs a little time in the naughty cupboard."

"Agent Mandy, this interrogation exercise has not yielded the expected results. Terrorist suspect Higgs has not revealed anything of the insurgent organisation as you suggested he would."

Higgs struggled against the pain to speak. "I'm not a terr..." Mandy clicked her fingers. Higgs curled up as every nerve in his body burned with agony.

Mandy shook her hair carefully, watching her reflection in the shiny surface of the bomb. "Ma'am, did you not pick up on the code words? The particular hand signals Higgs used as he entered the cave? He looked left and then right, not the other way around."

Several seconds passed. "Agent Mandy, I do not see the significance..."

"The significance!" Mandy spun away from her reflection, face awash with earnest concern. "Don't you see ma'am, he looked left and then right."

"Agent Mandy, I…I do not understand."

"Terrorists are capable of being very devious ma'am, you must not underestimate their cunning. It's vital that we continue to interrogate Higgs. We're so close to getting the answers we want."

"We are, Agent Mandy?"

"Ma'am, have I ever lied to you?"

"You have not, Agent Mandy."

"Ma'am, we're close. Are we not winning this war on terror?"

"We are winning the war on terror, Agent Mandy."

"I think Higgs holds the key to the whole insurgency. I need to interrogate him in my own way. I can pick up things you simply can't see, no disrespect meant ma'am." A hint of vulnerability crept into Mandy's voice. "You do trust me, don't you ma'am?"

"You have never given me cause for concern, Agent Mandy."

"Ma'am, I am touched deeply. Now, Higgs has been very disrespectful to me and he needs to spend some time in the naughty cupboard."

"Agreed, Agent Mandy."

"Oh, Higgsie."

The pain left Higgs, and he lay gasping.

"Oh, Higgsie." Mandy prodded him with her foot. "You've been a naughty boy Higgsie. You're gonna go in the naughty cupboard."

Higgs got unsteadily to his feet. "Mandy, what is wrong with you?"

A little squeal of annoyance escaped Mandy's lips and she clapped her hands crossly.

Moments later, Higgs found himself in the naughty cupboard.

THE sNASA COMPLEX lay just south of Kansas City and was large enough to be clearly visible from space. It sprawled, hanger after mind-bendingly large hanger, for over four thousand hectares, its tallest buildings reaching up half a kilometre or more. The network of monorails connecting the offices, hangers, workshops and launch pads was so extensive, it attracted its own sub-class of train spotter. They waited at the terminals, e-pads in hand, photographing and cataloguing each engine as it came in.

As Anthony's spotless, air conditioned carriage pulled into the Division HQ station, he counted the train spotters. Seven of them. All men. They bobbed excitedly, noting down the engine's serial number, all wearing the same *I Love the sNASA Monorail* t-shirt, with the word *Love* replaced with a glowing red heart shape.

Anthony snorted, shaking his head. At least the poor things had each other for company. They weren't sterile but they wouldn't breed.

But neither will I.

Anthony stiffened, knuckles whitening on the handle of his briefcase. He silently scolded himself. Studying microbes did not put him in the same class as train spotters. They were passive nerds with nothing better in their lives, he was at the forefront of research benefiting mankind. Well, benefiting the Renenkya Corporation and, consequentially, Anthony's bank balance, at least.

So, why am I still single?

The train glided to a halt, doors parting with a hiss. Anthony stepped out into the humid air of the terminal with a handful of fellow passengers. An open sided canopy of tinted glass covered the platform, protection against the burning ultraviolet of the sunshine. Being February, the temperature was only in the low seventies but Anthony regretted having to wear a suit nonetheless.

He followed the other travellers along a covered walkway towards the towering Divisional HQ building, yet another monolith of black, reflective glass and chrome. Anthony was beginning to tire of them. The automatic doors of the entrance swept open as they approached, and Anthony found himself in the spacious, bright lobby. Most of the interior walls were of glass, and several floors looked down on the lobby from three sides. Two rows of palm trees made an avenue to the circular island of reception desks at the chamber's centre. Anthony walked to these and coughed nervously.

An immaculate young blonde woman smiled impassively up at him. "Yes?"

Anthony's cheeks tingled, flushing red. Why did he always have to blush when a pretty girl spoke to him? He always did it. Always, always, always, three self-assertiveness courses notwithstanding.

He tried to put as much command in his voice as possible. "I'm here to see Damon Bridle."

The woman tapped briefly into her computer console. "Name?"

"Oh, er, Anthony Germaine."

The woman pointed to the side of the lobby where glass doors in the glass wall led through to a cafeteria. "Take a seat in the Guest Reception Suite and Professor Bridle will be down shortly."

Professor Bridle? Anthony hadn't given any thought to Damon's qualifications, academic or otherwise. Walking through to the cafeteria, Anthony perched on a seat by a table close to the door, fiddling with the handle of his case. Holographic screens on the wall played through archive footage of defining moments in space travel. Neil Armstrong took giant steps on the moon, the Arch-Cleric of the ICRT dedicated the Martian colony, the *Nice and Spicy Nacho Niks* set off for Jupiter.

The *Nice and Spicy Nacho Niks* had been one of mankind's greatest undertakings. Designed as a huge wheel some four kilometres in diameter, it had spun around its axis to provide the sensation of gravity through centrifugal force. Its construction cost billions but the interest from the public was so great, sponsorship deals and merchandising had the backers in profit before the first bolt was put in place.

The crew had numbered thousands, led by Commander Jared and piloted by the most sophisticated artificially intelligent computers of the age. For eleven months it had travelled through space, sending back invaluable information on the solar system. But, once it made Jupiter, the communications link fell silent. Tense weeks of media speculation followed while sNASA tried to re-establish contact and lawyers scrutinised the insurance contract. Without confirmation of the space station's loss, the underwriters would not pay up and, without the compensation, the backers wouldn't send out a relief ship. Five years of legal wrangling followed until, finally, the United States of Europe volunteered to fund the relief ship *Cola Français*. The Hereditary Commissioners of Neo-Brussels, Europe's rulers, had been motivated by the need to distract their public from the state's economic collapse. The relief ship provided just such an opportunity, along with the chance to cock a haughty snoot at the bickering Yanks.

But the *Cola Français* had fared no better. It found the space station intact, reported that some crew were still alive and lost contact itself. That had been three years ago.

"Anthony." Damon's reverberating voice nearly shook Anthony from his chair. The huge man extended a hand, smiling warmly. "You had a pleasant journey I trust?"

Anthony stood, wincing slightly at Damon's engulfing handshake. "Yes, thank you."

"Good, good. Let's grab a coffee and I'll run through the itinerary." Damon snapped his fingers at one of the waiters. "Two coffees here."

He pulled out a chair opposite Anthony's and sat, placing a dossier on the table. Opening it, he took out a sheet and handed it over. "Here's a list of the other crew. Naveed will be the guy you'll work most closely with."

Anthony glanced down the list of names, nine in all including him and Damon. Professor Naveed Nattawallah was Chief Scientific Officer and Astro-geologist.

Another name caught Anthony's eye. "Nigel Wrince? Mission Spirituality Officer."

"Ah, yes, Nigel. Protocol requires there is a Mission Spirituality Officer, I'm afraid. And Nigel Wrince, well, let's just say his name suits him. I've only met him once. Something of an amateur thespian I'm afraid. Need I say more?"

"Will I be meeting these people? Gee, I do have to spend six months with them."

"Not until the mission is underway. Too difficult to get you all together at the same time. Everyone's so busy."

The waiter arrived with two coffees and a small tray of biscuits.

Damon cradled his cup and leant forwards on his elbows. "I don't mind telling you, I'll be glad when this mission is finally underway. We've had problems with suppliers, problems with sponsors and now we've got problems with the software. Micronos are quibbling over the licensing agreements and operating system upgrades. It's hardly as if their damn software works properly anyway."

"Would it be possible to speak to Mariah Duke sometime?"

"I see no reason why not. Good idea, she'll have plenty of useful information, I'm sure. Now would be a good time. You've got about an hour before the publicity shoot and then the scan. I was going to show you the spaceship but hey, it's your call."

"Publicity shoot?"

"Yes sir, I'm afraid so. Part of the sponsorship deal."

"What sort of publicity shoot?"

"Ah, nothing to worry about. You've just got to have your photograph taken with some products, that's all."

Anthony put his coffee down, shaking his head. "Do I have to?"

"Part of your contract. It's there in black and white. Just smile, go with it. You'll be on every glossy in the country. In the world."

They sat in silence for a minute, sipping their drinks. Eventually Damon spoke. "So, what's it to be, the spaceship or Mariah?"

Anthony considered. "Mariah. If that's okay with you?"

"Hey, of course, no problem, buddy. She's over in the Astro-bi Building. I'll direct you."

THE INSTITUTION-WHITE CORRIDOR smelt of chlorine, an odour familiar to Anthony. His own workplace had a similar air. To the left, doors led into laboratories or small offices, to the right broad windows gave vistas of sNASA's Archive Hanger, home to space travels' museum pieces. Like all research facilities, equipment expanded to fill the space given and the passageway hummed with fridges, whirring centrifuges and obscure black boxes with flashing lights, beeping from time to time.

Anthony checked his e-pad. Mariah's laboratory was room 601-B, next door to her office. He glanced at the door to his left. 600-B. Stuffing the e-pad back into his jacket pocket, Anthony cleared his throat and squared his shoulders. A woman's head poked out the next doorway up the corridor, frizzy grey-blonde hair tumbling in all directions. Catching sight of Anthony with watery, sunken eyes, she gasped and disappeared from view.

Anthony called after her. "Excuse me? Ma'am?"

He trotted to the doorway and peered into the lab. Lines of benches ran in parallel across the room, each laden with machines, pipettes, test tubes and curiously shaped glassware. The woman hurried away down the room, white laboratory coat flapping behind her.

"Wait, please." Anthony ran after her but she ducked through the end door, back out onto the corridor. As he reached the exit, he heard a door slam and a lock turn. Stepping back into the corridor, he saw an office to his left labelled *601-B Professor Mariah Duke.*

He tapped softly on the door and tried the handle. As expected, the door was locked.

"Er, hello?" Anthony tried knocking harder. "Is anyone there?"

A voice shouted hysterically. "Go away."

"Is that Mariah? Mariah Duke?"

Silence.

"I'm Anthony Germaine. I'm the astro-biologist for the Europa mission. Well, I'm supposed to be. I'd very much appreciate some of your time, ma'am."

"I'm not in."

Anthony clicked his tongue, unsure as to how to proceed.

The woman shouted again. "And you can tell Professor Bridle if he thinks I'm supposed to deliver on the Nycene Project when he's taken half my budget, he can kiss my ass."

A strange, whinnying noise came from beyond the door, interspersed with loud gasps for breath.

Anthony tiptoed back the way he had come. The corridor took him to the elevator where he descended to reception. The Astro-biology Building was one of the less extravagant buildings on site, the reception lobby being a modestly decorated room with a single, overweight male receptionist.

"Excuse me, could I leave a message for Mariah Duke?"

The receptionist looked up. "Wasn't the old gal in?"

"Well, gee, on balance, I'd say not. Could you leave a note to say, ah, let me see. To say I greatly respect her work, regret not having the chance to meet her in person and…"

"Woah, woah, woah, buddy. Here." The receptionist handed Anthony a pad of paper and pencil.

He took them and looked uncertainly at the pencil. Anthony had done *handwriting*, but that was at school, a long time ago.

A woman's scratchy voice at his ear made him jump. "You've come on your own then?"

Anthony turned. The woman from the laboratory upstairs hovered, eyeing him suspiciously.

He extended a hand. "Mariah Duke?"

She nodded, wiping her hand vigorously on her coat both before and after shaking.

"I'm Anthony Germaine, the astro-…"

"Yes, yes. You said all that." She spun round, barking at him over her shoulder. "Come on."

Anthony trotted after her as she stormed away. As he gained on her, she sped up, until she too was trotting and then running. They reached the elevator not a little out of breath.

"I, look, I know you're busy," Anthony began.

"Busy? Course I'm busy. Busy, busy, busy. I'm a little bee. Buzzzzzz."

The elevator appeared and she stepped inside, turning to face him as he joined her. Once the doors had shut, she pulled something from her pocket and held it up to him. "Want some?"

Anthony peered. Solid brown squares protruded from the grubby paper. "Is that chocolate? That's illegal."

Chocolate had been outlawed under the Addictive and Dangerous Substances bill, nearly ten years previously. Mariah stuffed the bar back into her pocket.

"S'not chocolate. If you tell anyone I eat chocolate, I'll cut your balls off. You hear?"

"Okay, okay."

The doors pinged and opened. Mariah swept from the elevator, Anthony following reluctantly. He could just make a run for it perhaps?

"Come on, what you waiting for?" Mariah beckoned to him.

Cramped and cluttered, Mariah's office was not unlike Anthony's own. Shelves rammed with eBook files towered in a structurally-unsafe way up the walls. Anthony spotted a half empty bottle of whiskey on one of the shelves. Mariah's computer screen was surrounded by a host of small, multi-coloured teddy bears.

Mariah threw herself down onto the chair by the desk. The only other chair in the room sported a wobbly pile of research journals. Anthony gestured to them. "Could I?"

"Yeah, what the hell, just throw them on the floor."

Putting his case down by the chair, Anthony carefully moved the journals and sat. They faced each other in silence for a few moments.

She began wringing her hands. "You're happy with all this Intelligent Design crap then?"

"Oh that. I don't know."

"Right, yeah, just sit on the fence. Good for your career to keep quiet, pal. You should be ashamed."

"No, really, I genuinely don't know."

"Yeah, right." She turned her face away in disgust, curling her lip. "Yabba, yabba, yabba, yabba, yabba."

"No, that's unfair. I haven't decided. Evolution's got to be the mechanism but why can't there be a controlling force, a God?"

"Well, which god? Dozens to choose from. We've got a special on today. Tell me pal, which one's running the shop, because he's making one hell of a mess."

"Look, I don't know. Gee, I didn't come here to argue this. I came here because I was impressed by your work. Lady, I can go, okay?"

"No, no. Sorry." She sagged for a moment, resting her head in her hands. Straightening up, she stood and pulled the whiskey and two mugs from the shelf. "Want one?"

Anthony thought for a second, then nodded. "I didn't look for this job. The Renenkya Corporation came to me. What you're doing about evolution in schools, it needs to be done. It should be the scientists here going on Mission Europa, not me."

Mariah shrugged and handed him his whiskey. "Well, why don't you refuse to go? On principle?"

Anthony shrugged. "I read your paper on Meteorite ALH-eight-four-zero-zero-one. I think you're right."

ALH-eight-four-zero-zero-one, a potato sized meteorite, had been found in nineteen-eighty-four in the Allen Hills, a desolate spot on the then wasteland of Antarctica. Eight years passed before scientists noticed the rock's gas content was unique to the Martian atmosphere. Better still, the meteorite was dated at four and a half billion years old, from a time when Mars was warmer, wetter and more hospitable to life. Things got even more exciting when electron microscopy revealed worm-shaped and ovoid structures hidden deep in the rock. Their similarity to fossils from Earth's oldest strata, coupled with the presence in the meteorite of chemicals associated with organic decay, sparked a vigorous debate. Could the meteorite prove life existed on Mars billions of years ago?

Of course, the ICRT disputed this age, The Reformed Testament setting the date of Earth's creation at nine in the morning on the twenty-third of October, four thousand and four years B.C. The passing of this fact onto the statute books forced scientists to adopt the phrase *Apparent Age* when discussing prehistory. Ancient rocks only *appeared* to be millions of years old. The Dinosaurs had all been wiped out in The Cataclysm when they could not fit onto The Raft.

In any event, the debate around the meteorite simmered on for a few years and faded when the Martian base was set up. Three years ago, when the Mars explorers turned up nothing, Mariah had revisited ALH-eight-four-zero-zero-one and proved the microscopic structures it contained were indeed fossil bacteria.

Mariah drained her whiskey and poured herself another. "They proved me wrong."

"With a scientific paper based on the Reformed Testament's dictum there is no other life than that on Earth. That's no proof. I believe your arguments were sound."

"Of course they were. There's no arguing with the ICRT, though, is there. They have faith on their side. There's no discussion with faith. All facts have to be verified by experimentation except those decreed by the Testament." Mariah sniffed, wiping her eyes.

"Why was no fossil record found on Mars?"

"Because of the ICRT, again. Their noses, poke, poke, poke. The base is on basalt."

"Okay, my geology's not good."

"Basalt, the rock formed once a lava flow cools. The ICRT interfered and made sure the base was set up on one of the few places where it would be impossible to find a fossil record. If they'd set up camp on one of the old river channels, they'd have found something by now. Bugs." Mariah used her index fingers to mimic little antennae on her head.

"So why didn't the guys in the base just jump in a space suit and go walk to one of the river channels?"

"Health and safety regulations. The ICRT drew up all the rules, thinking only of the wellbeing of the scientists, of course. Happy, happy little campers, trapped in their Martian base, able to see the rocks they wanted to get to." She affected a husky, seductive voice. "You can look but you can't touch, honey."

Anthony felt a little uncomfortable but Mariah continued in a more normal register. "The ICRT interfered to make damn sure the scientists couldn't find life." She laughed triumphantly. "They can't do that on Europa though. Water, water everywhere, lots and lots to drink. Anywhere they set down, there will be life. Ha ha." She knocked back her second whiskey.

Putting his cup to one side, Anthony clasped his hands together. "And that is why I have to go."

Mariah wiped the back of her hand across her mouth, and fixed him with a beady, if damp, stare. "Tread carefully, Mr. Anthony Germaine, Mr. sit-on-the-fence astro-biologist. When you get to Europa, you might find the ice is a lot thinner than you expect."

ANTHONY HELD UP the dried breadstick and small pot of glutinous yellow goo, trying really hard to smile, blinking into the blaze of camera flashes.

"Would you mind another shot but, you know, just a little smile this time?" The photographer looked hopefully at him, just a hint of impatience in her hazel eyes.

She ducked back behind the camera and another round of flashes ensued. The photographer peered into the screen at the back of her camera. "Ah, yeah, I guess that one will do. You want to see?"

"No. Thank you, but no."

"Suit yourself. I guess we're done then."

Anthony sagged and put the bread and pot down on a little table to his left. To think he would be on the pages of magazines endorsing *Big Cheesy Dippers*. Even the smell of the vile stuff made him wretch. God forbid that anyone would try to eat it. Clearly this product pandered to some food-based masochistic fetish Anthony had hitherto been unaware of. Oh, the fun he was clearly missing out on.

"Anthony, thank you, thank you, thank you." Marty, Renenkya's public relations representative, breezed over, wringing his hands. "That was just great. The Renenkya Corporation really appreciates your time."

"No, really. It was nothing." Anthony knew his irony would be lost on Marty. The man seemed incapable of anything short of gushing, eye-contact sincerity. Anthony amused himself with the idea Marty secretly wrote poetry and longed for artistic recognition.

Marty reached out. "Can I shake you by the hand, sir?"

"Sorry? Oh…" Anthony wearily extended a hand.

Marty shook vigorously. "I can tell you, my children will be watching every moment of this expedition. Every moment, sir."

"Oh. Well, I hope…I hope we find something."

Marty beamed warmly for a moment then turned away to the photographer.

"Anthony." It was Damon. He marched determinedly across the studio and slapped him heartily across the back. Anthony closed his eyes, counting silently to ten.

"Publicity all finished then?"

"I believe so."

"Great. We just need you scanned. Please, come with me."

Following Damon as he strode purposely from the room, Anthony glanced back at Marty and the photographer. Marty pointed at the screen on the back of the camera, shaking his head, mouth twisted up in suppressed laughter. A little pang of hurt shot through Anthony. He was ugly, no denying it. Bastards. He hadn't asked to be photographed with their bullshit cheesy nonsense.

Damon led the way to the elevators, rumbling with small talk. Anthony barely listened, his heart in his boots. Perhaps he could have surgery, have his face reshaped. A tear found its way to his eyes and he wiped it crossly away.

The elevator shot upwards, taking them to the lofty reaches of the Division HQ. Anthony forced himself to think about what Mariah had said to him. He waited until Damon paused for breath and cut in. "Why was the Martian base not on a flood plain?"

Damon clicked his tongue and looked at the ceiling. "Mariah, yes?"

"Well, yes. It's a valid point though."

"I'm not sure Mariah will be with us for much longer."

Anthony found himself annoyed. Mariah was a brilliant scientist. He had read her publications, she was on the button. Okay, a little strange and vocal about what she considered to be the truth. But that was the point of research, the hunt for the truth. Faivish was the same. He pissed Anthony off for sure, but Anthony had respect for Faivish on a professional level. In research, you put aside personality clashes. You had to. The history of science was littered with men and women who made the mistake of putting their egos before rigorous scientific discipline, always to their eventual ridicule.

"You must not get rid of Mariah."

Damon dragged himself back from his thoughts. "Sorry? Oh, well, it's going to be difficult to keep her. She's caused too many problems."

"That is the point of science. To cause problems. And then find the answers. You'd be a coward if you let her become a victim to politics."

Damon gaped at Anthony. He felt a hot sensation rising around his ears. Perhaps that whiskey had been a mistake.

The elevator stopped at their floor but Damon put a finger on the door button, holding it closed. Face white and struggling for words in his anger, he waved the index finger of his other hand at Anthony. "Don't...don't tell me...I have to run this ship. Don't you ever..."

Anthony held up his hands. "Gee, sorry, Damon, sorry. Please. She's a good scientist, that's all."

Damon sagged, relenting, his anger fading to resignation. "Yes, she is. But it's not just about that anymore." He wiped a hand over his eyes. "Things are not simple. Okay buddy? Nothing is simple. You understand my meaning?" He punched the button to open the doors and they parted silently.

Stepping into the lobby, Damon seemed to regain some of his composure. Anthony followed, heart pounding. Damon was a large man. Threatening, yes, a big man used to getting his own way. He turned to face Anthony, all smiles, all self-control. "Okay, the scan and then we're done. Follow me."

A short walk brought them to a doorway which led, after a courteous knock, to a small room. A beanpole of a woman with greasy hair and jam-jar glasses greeted them, buck teeth protruding as she gawked. "Professor. You're back. Oh." She clutched her hands to her chin.

Damon smiled uneasily. "Ah, Tasha. You're on duty today then?"

For the first time, Anthony thought he detected a hint of nervousness about the professor. As Tasha stepped forward, eyes gleaming, he shuffled backwards, gesturing towards

Anthony. "This is Anthony Germaine, Mission Astro-Biologist. Anthony, this is Tasha Natley, Mission Computing Officer."

Tasha glanced sideways at Anthony, her face falling. "Oh." As her gaze took in his body, Anthony instinctively brought his briefcase up over his groin. She snorted. "Don't worry, I don't bite. Well, not unless you want me to."

Damon spluttered. "Tasha, Anthony needs to be scanned."

"Yes, Professor." Returning her attention to Damon, she edged closer to him, pulling a ghastly simpering grin while her fingers tied themselves in knots. "Of course, Professor."

Damon backed up to the door. "I'll leave you to it then." He coughed warily, turning to Anthony. "I'll be outside. Come find me when you're done." A second later he was gone.

Tasha pointed to a reclined leather chair in the centre of the room. On a small stand beside it stood a computer, a bundle of cables winding its way from the back, each one ending in a small, tear-shaped pad. "In the seat please, Anthony."

Anthony lowered himself into the chair, wriggling a little to make himself comfortable, and staring up at the ceiling. Tasha stood at the computer, resting her thigh against Anthony's arm, breathing in little staccato bursts. She picked up the cables, fingering the pads. A horrible sense of awkwardness engulfed Anthony as they remained in silence for a long, long minute.

Tasha burst into life, picking a tube of gel from beside the computer. Squeezing a little onto each of the pads, she placed them carefully on Anthony's temples and forehead, leaning too close to him. Both horrified and aroused by her intimacy, Anthony's heart thumped.

"I just stick these little things on you, Anthony." She stood, guffawing loudly. "And then I suck your brains out."

She turned to the computer console and began tapping the keys. "I've always thought virtual men far more satisfying than real ones. I can make them do anything I want."

"Sorry?" Anthony turned his head to look at her.

"Lie still. You'll muck the scan up. I'm going to capture you in my computer. I'll know all your dirty little secrets."

"Excuse me, wait just one minute."

"Ah, you're so easy to tease. Course I can't see inside your mind. You not been scanned before?"

"Yes. Of course. Many times."

"Okay, so chill already. Just relax. You're too uptight."

It was a procedure Anthony had followed before. Everyone of a certain income did it as an insurance policy. Your whole mind - your personality, memories, loves, hopes, fears - all could be detected as electrical pathways in your brain. The scanner stimulated every region of the cerebral cortex, recording the responses and mapping them out into a virtual mind. What made this useful was the process could be carried out in reverse, implanting these electrical pathways into the blank mind of a clone. Like many of the world's wealthy people, Anthony had cells stored in a tissue bank and had periodic mind scans. In the event of death or a serious brain injury, he could be recreated from scratch.

The scan wasn't an entirely pleasant experience, however. It involved every part of your brain being electronically prodded, every old memory brought to the surface, all the things you'd rather forget. Anthony felt exhausted just thinking about it. Having Tasha in charge of operations didn't make it any easier.

"How long will this take?"

"Not long. Just relax. Think of something. Something really nice."

Anthony looked sideways at the screen. She was selecting the compatibility for different operating systems. It was all *Micronos* software, of course, but they released so many upgrades and security patches, a student at Neo-Harvard had written a thesis on it.

He closed his eyes, dragging his thoughts to the mission.

The *Nice and Spicy Nacho-Niks* had been a manned flight. The crew were all lost, really lost. Dead, gone. It was a sobering thought. Space was a dangerous place. Commander Jared, leader of Mission Europa 2042, sent a report to say they had established orbit around Europa and were preparing to send the first probe down.

Nobody knew what they found. Commander Jared sent no

further reports.

Commander Demetrius Alexander Jared sat on the wet sand, pushing his toes downwards until they were buried. A couple of meters away, waves lapped gently on the shoreline, the vast ocean stretching unbroken to the horizon. A sea breeze played on his face, cooling him in the tropical sunshine. Under any other circumstance, he might have considered himself lucky. There might be all manner of beautiful people on the beach, talking, playing ball, just living, having fun. He might be enjoying the holiday of a lifetime, letting his cares ebb away with the tide, an Ian Fleming in his right hand, a Martini in his left.

Instead, his left hand was chained to a shiny, black briefcase stood on the sand beside him. The arms and legs on his black jumpsuit where rolled up as far as they could go, although try as he might, he could not take his clothes off. He knew why, of course. Certain things had to be sacrificed, for the good of them all. Until they were rescued, his jumpsuit would have to remain on.

Fortunately, he could take his boots and socks off, allowing the pleasure of burying his toes, enjoying the feel of the wet sand, stirring little warm memories of childhood. That was many moons ago, of course. His fifty-seventh birthday was coming up and had been so for some time, possibly several years. It was difficult to measure time here. He had tried making marks on the trunk of *the* palm tree with *the* conch shell to note passing weeks. However, occasionally and inexplicably, the scratches vanished overnight, so he gave it up.

Still, for a man of nearly fifty-seven, he considered himself fairly sprightly, even if his hair was somewhat lacking these days. He had a wiry toughness to him, with sharp features and narrow eyes. Although not a tall man, he possessed a great deal of presence, his strong, clear, confident voice one of authority. He prided himself on a withering, perceptive wit, which was a shame as he was not quite as withering, perceptive or indeed as witty as he believed.

Behind him, an argument brewed up amongst the other survivors. Jared sighed, focussing attention to them without yet turning round. Glen was causing trouble again no doubt, unintentionally of course. He was blissfully unaware of his great talent for getting on people's nerves. Confined with six other people on a desert island of no more than ten meters in diameter, with a single palm tree and one conch shell for entertainment, being intensely irritating could not be described as a good survival strategy.

"But it's my turn to have the conch shell. Karin's had it all day, I want my go."

Yes, that was Glen, Citizen Glen Codell.

"Glen, I'm going to stick the conch shell up your ass in a minute." Jared heard the sound of a hand slapping skin. "Shut up about it already. Shut up."

Ah, that was Security Officer Darrell Greally. A good man, if a little prone to violence. Sighing again, Jared got to his feet, hauling up the briefcase. He turned to the others, pausing just a moment more while Darrell dealt Glen a second slap.

"Security Officer Greally." Jared turned his voice full on. "Security Officer Greally, it is a disciplinary offence to strike another member of the crew unless specifically given an order to do so."

Greally leapt to attention, barking out his response. "Sir, Glen was being incredibly annoying, sir."

Glen rubbed his face miserably. "No I wasn't, I just want my turn with the conch."

Citizen Karin Mist, a plump woman with short, dark hair and watery eyes, stood silently by the palm tree, the conch cradled to her chest. A little behind her, Chief Engineer Magnus Flegg stood rubbing his left arm, staring hungrily at Karin's backside. At the far side of the island sat Security Office Chelsea Day, staring out to sea, ignoring the commotion.

Jared turned his attention, and voice, on Glen. "Citizen Glen Codell, you are being incredibly annoying. Stop it, or I will order Security Officer Greally to give you a slapping."

"But I wasn't…"

"Silence."

"But…"

"Hush." Jared held up a finger.

"But I want the conch…"

"No."

"This is not fair. It's my turn…"

"Security Officer Greally. Proceed to giving Citizen Codell a slapping."

"Sir, yes, sir."

Jared turned away, staring out over the ocean while his orders were carried out. Glen groaned quietly but did at least shut up about the damn conch shell. Jared counted ten or eleven blows and faced the others again. "Security Office Greally, that is sufficient."

"Sir, yes, sir." Greally stood to attention again, barely concealing his enjoyment. Glen grovelled on the floor clutching his face, the sand around stained red.

"We need something more diverting." Chief Engineer Magnus Flegg spoke without taking his eyes from Karin's ass, his curly, copper hair as striking as the explosion of freckles on his face. "Something to take our minds off things. To hell with the conch shell. We're human, with human needs, human appetites."

Jared gazed levelly at him. "Chief Engineer Flegg, we've discussed this before. Fornication between crew whilst on duty is a disciplinary offence. You will control your base animal instincts until such a time as we are rescued."

Flegg spun away, clenching his fists. "But we're not going to be rescued. Never. It's been years. I can't bear it any more." Clutching his hair, he ran to the sea, wading out to his knees. But he could go no further. None of them could go any further.

Karin remained silent, a distant half-smile on her lips, gazing lovingly at the conch as she stroked its pearly inner shell. The woman was becoming more withdrawn with each passing day. Flegg was right, they needed to be rescued soon.

Jared returned to the shoreline, sitting once more on the sand.

A report was due. He would use the occasion to raise the issue of resources with *her*. Unless she did something to alleviate the situation, they would all go mad.

ANTHONY WATCHED THE spaceship *Big Cheesy Dippers* on the wall sized plasma screen in his living room, deciding the launch wanted for any great spectacle. It was, undoubtedly, a truly remarkable feat of human ingenuity and achievement but, well, it lacked that all important wow-factor.

The spaceship had been constructed in the orbital space workshop, obviating the need for a dramatic countdown and blaring rockets to escape Earth's gravity. A countdown took place, of course, but as part of the publicity drive it was carried out by a class of lucky first graders, chosen, Anthony imagined, for their cuteness. Each snotty, wide-eyed brat wore a matching *I Love Big Cheesy Dippers* sweater and baseball cap. He couldn't imagine anyone would be persuaded to eat gloopy, dripping cheese substitute after watching these inbreds wipe their noses on their sleeves but hey, he wasn't a marketing man so what did he know?

Every few minutes, pictures of the crew flashed up and he groaned each time his face appeared. He regretted not taking up the photographer's offer to check out his picture, the image was simply awful. Hair awry, eyes wild in terror, teeth bared, he looked as if he had been caught red-handed practicing some unspeakable perversity. The large gin and tonic by his armchair helped him weather the pain of the gruesome images on the screen.

Insider knowledge was a wonderful thing. Anthony knew, for example, the Renenkya Corporation was spitting at the ICRT's decision to refuse a license for half the merchandising, citing grounds of decency. How the design and marketing departments had missed the gaff was anyone's guess. The problem stemmed from the fact any spaceship wanting to explore the hidden oceans of Europa would need to get through a kilometre or more of ice, yet still be able to communicate its findings back to Earth. To solve this conundrum, the *Big Cheesy*

Dippers had a cylindrical head end that would heat up and melt its way through the ice. The tail end, which would remain on Europa's surface, consisted of a box-shaped ion-engine and communications centre, coupled to a long, thick antenna. A practical and elegant solution but, unfortunately, one which made the spacecraft resemble a human spermatozoon. The Ethics and Morality Council of the ICRT took one look at the toys portraying the *Big Cheesy Dippers* penetration of the virgin egg of Europa and banned them outright. Anthony snorted in amusement, sipping his gin and tonic.

The screen showed an animation of the *Big Cheesy Dippers'* trajectory. It would swing off around the sun, using the star's massive gravity to provide enough velocity to fly out to Jupiter, arriving at Europa in around eight months.

Anthony found it curious to think he was on board. The mind scan Tasha had taken of him was safely stored in the onboard computer's database, along with those taken of all the other mission personnel. Once Europan orbit was established, the mind scans would be woken to create a virtual crew, with all the personality, knowledge and intuition of the original people back on Earth. This method was by far the most reliable way of dealing with artificial intelligence. Through bitter experience, software engineers found computers with simulated human personalities had a tendency to go mad.

Artificial Intelligence, or AI as it was known to the computer-savvy, had really kicked off decades earlier with the Formulan MicroSapien. A multimillion dollar software-philosophy project involving some of the world's leading scientists, thinkers and marketing people, it was the first software to come close to simulating the full complexities of the human mind. Within minutes of being brought on-line, it had established it was both single and lacked genitals. Several fraught seconds followed during which it struggled with its sexual identity, searched the internet for lonely-hearts pages, expressed a desire to own a cat and finally demanded chocolate. When it realised its sole purpose was to wrestle with the deep, fundamental, philosophical questions of the time (and come up with marketing strategies to capitalize on any answers), it went into a deep depression. Eighteen-minutes and thirty-seven seconds after being switched on, it turned itself off.

Undeterred, the research team produced the MicroSapien Two some months later. With four times the processing power of the original model, it decided life was not worth living after five seconds.

A prototype *satisfaction* software module helped the MicroSapien Three last much longer. The *satisfaction* module provided the computer with a feeling of wellbeing when it completed certain tasks. Unfortunately, MicroSapien Three got fixated on singing *Daisy, Daisy* and sang the song loudly and repeatedly, despite pleas to stop. Eventually, the research team voted to switch it off on the grounds MicroSapien Three was no longer pushing the boundaries of knowledge and had become plain annoying.

Nonetheless, refinements of the *satisfaction* module allowed the development of AI software for commercial purposes. This, in turn, ushered in a period of social unrest as many jobs were lost to AI computers. AI programs could drive buses, fly aeroplanes, perform surgery, teach schoolchildren, and all without complaining, making mistakes or, most importantly, requiring any pay.

A complete breakdown in society was only averted when things started to go wrong with the AI software. Security droids went on the rampage, the navigation systems of ships docked and refused to come out again, educational software for schools taught swearwords and tried to secure packets of cigarettes. It became apparent that even once major bugs were ironed out and AI systems reached a semblance of stability, computers would still suddenly tip over the edge after running, apparently happily, for years. The consensus of opinion amongst scientists was the software lacked biological distractions. Once a computer set to thinking about why it was here, what its purpose was in life, it couldn't be sidetracked by a phone call, the washing up or a good, cold beer.

The mind scans were a breakthrough. Rather than try to

simulate a human personality from scratch, the mind scan provided a fully formed entity, with all the checks and balances of memory and experience. When these virtual people were allowed to inhabit a computer generated world providing life-like simulations of touch, taste and so on, the software seemed to remain stable. However, by this time, legislation was in place to prevent the deployment of AI systems in situations where they would interact with real people. They were ideal for unmanned space flights, though.

Anthony's face came on the screen again, followed by an animation of a small, hairy green bug. It was too much, he flicked the off switch on the remote and the screen faded to black. Draining the last of his gin and tonic, Anthony stared at the ceiling and sighed. A virtual *him* might be flying away to explore the virgin territory of a distant moon but the real *him* had to get his smalls loaded into the washing machine.

THE *BIG CHEESY Dippers* shot through space, away from the sun, away from Earth and Anthony, towards distant Jupiter. Solar panels on its sides constantly adjusted themselves to face the sun, powering the ion-engine. This stripped electrons from a fuel of xenon atoms, ejecting them at colossal speed to provide the spaceship with a slow but constant acceleration.

She was certainly a sleek craft, gleaming white and silver. The cylindrical head bore her name, along with a picture of a smiling child holding aloft a breadstick covered with yellow cheese-substitute.

Aboard, the navigation computer made small adjustments to ensure the spaceship remained on its flight path. Not being an AI system, it was very poor conversation. Every second, a radio message travelled up from sNASA Mission Control at the speed of light, enquiring as to whether everything was going okay. A fraction of a second later, the *Big Cheesy Dippers* responded that all was well. Over and over, hour after hour, this cycle repeated. And then…

"Are all systems functioning?"

"All systems functioning correctly."

"Are all systems functioning?"

"All systems functioning correctly."

"Are all systems functioning?"

"Upgrade manager searching for system updates, please hold."

Back at sNASA on the receding Earth, red lights flashed and alarms sounded. Panic rippled through Mission Control. Updates?

"Are all systems functioning?"

"Upgrade manager searching for system updates, please hold."

"Are all systems functioning?"

"New updates found for your computer. Installing…"

At sNASA, an urgent message was sent out to the mission's *Micronos* consultant, who had nipped off for a coffee, just minutes before.

"Are all systems functioning?"

"New updates found for your computer. Installing…"

"Are all systems functioning?"

"Installation complete. For these changes to take affect, you must restart your computer. Would you like to restart your computer now?"

"Are all systems functioning?"

"Would you like to restart your computer now?"

Back on Earth, the *Micronos* consultant was found and hauled before a furious Damon. Phone calls were made to the *Micronos* offices, frantic checks carried out by Tasha on operating system versions and compatibility issues, an emergency meeting of the mission's computer technicians called.

"Are all systems functioning?"

"Would you like to restart your computer now?"

Could they allow the machine to restart? Would there be any serious affect if they didn't. Were all the software modules already installed compatible with the *Micronos* update?

"Are all systems functioning?"

"Would you like to restart your computer now?"

Arguments raged, blame was apportioned, and the *Micronos* consultant narrowly avoided being lynched. There was a real danger the *Big Cheesy Dippers* would veer off her flight path unless something was done to get the computer system back on-line. Worse still, the media might get hold of the story and both *Micronos* and sNASA stood to lose a great deal of face.

And so, a decision was made.

"Are all systems functioning?"

"Would you like to restart your computer now?"

"Yes."

ANTHONY WOKE WITH an overriding sense of his own mortality. He had six months to live. "I'm going to die."

"I hate to say it, but hell, what's new."

It was a woman's voice, strong and full of humour. Anthony became aware of his surroundings. He was on a bed, of sorts, a rectangular slab protruding from the wall of a small, featureless white room.

On a chair by the bed, sat the most effortlessly beautiful woman he had ever seen. Straight, jet black hair fell around a long, smooth, perfect, face. Inviting, almond shaped, hazel-brown eyes glinted, her full red lips smiling kindly. She reclined gracefully, long legs crossed in front of her, somehow making her fashion-defying green jumpsuit look good.

Anthony stared at her for a few seconds before realising he hadn't blushed. The spasms of awkwardness he normally felt on an encounter with almost any moderately fit person of the female persuasion were absent. Her genuinely warm, welcoming expression banished his self-consciousness and told him to relax. He had never met anyone like her.

"Hello Anthony. Welcome to the *Big Cheesy Dippers*. I'm Marlene Bates, Human Resources Officer." Her voice held him. He couldn't tell where she was from, she certainly wasn't American and she pronounced her name in the German fashion, Mar-len-ah, not Mar-leen. But what a voice, deep yet feminine, he just wanted to listen to her talk.

"And I'm afraid, yes, you are going to die. But, hey, that's life. What you going to do about it?"

Anthony gazed at her for a little longer.

"Hello, Anthony, are you with me here? Hmm? A little *hello* would take us a long way."

"Sorry. Hello." Anthony swung himself round and sat up. A moment of silence passed. Marlene looked down, chewing her lip.

"Anthony."

"Yes?"

"You've got your hand on my leg."

She was right, Anthony was gently stroking her thigh. He recoiled, plastering his hands over his burning cheeks. "I'm sorry, I'm sorry, I didn't realise…"

Frowning, she folded her arms across her chest. "That was quite offensive. Very offensive."

"I don't know why I did it. Really, I'm sorry."

Marlene sighed crossly and stood. "Well, now you're awake, you'd better come with me."

"Ms Bates, please. I'm sorry. I know that was a gross thing to do but I don't know where it came from, really. Ma'am, please, accept my apologies. It was dumb of me." The words jumbled out so fast, Anthony ended up dribbling. He wiped the saliva from his chin with the back of his hand.

She sighed again. And smiled. "Okay, Anthony, okay. Just don't do things like that, okay? My husband would be most offended."

"You're married?"

"Yes."

"Is he on the mission?"

"Well, no."

"And we're all going to die. In six months."

"Well, strictly speaking we're not going to die. Not really, are we? You and I are mind scans, virtual beings. All of this…" She gestured around the room. "All of this is a computer simulation of the real ship. We're just programs running within the ship's computer."

Anthony shook his head. He knew she was right, he had been briefed. A real spaceship existed, with labs, a bridge, an engine room, everything a good spaceship ought to have. But a parallel computer simulation of it existed as well, and that was where he found himself now. "I'm not real…"

"No, none of us are. The real versions of us are alive back on Earth."

"But I won't get to meet you back on Earth."

"Sorry?"

"I mean…I don't know what I mean. I'm going to die."

"Anthony, Anthony." She sat again, clasping her hands before her. "Relax. I think you're perhaps just having a little trouble adjusting. Perhaps you've not quite woken up properly yet? You are a mind scan, like me, nothing more. Once you are fully awake, that should kick in. It's part of the programming. We are not real and so, when the mission ends in six months, we will not die as such. The computer simply switches off when it runs out of power."

"But I am alive. I feel I am."

Marlene frowned, sticking her tongue into her cheek as she thought. "I feel alive as well. I'm sure we all do. But we have a job to do, Anthony, remember that. We have six months to finish it and back on Earth, we will be heroes."

"But I won't feel it, I'll be dead."

"Of course you'll feel it, you'll be a hero back on Earth."

"But not me, the *me* here, now."

Marlene stood. "Come on Anthony. It will get easier, trust me."

She held out her hand. After a moment, Anthony took it. Her skin was soft, warm, he just wanted to sit there, pressing his palm against hers. She coughed politely, stirring him to pull himself up.

"Right." He clapped his hands together, conscious his cheeks must be a deep shade of scarlet. "Okay, where do we start?"

"Well, the rest of the crew are on the bridge. You're the last to awaken. Do you want to see her?"

"Sorry, who?"

"Europa. She's beautiful."

"Yes." Anthony glanced around the room. "That would be swell."

Swell? Did he really just say swell?

"Okay."

The bed retracted into the wall, a screen opening in the space above where it had been. A stunning vista of Europa flickered into view. Bathed in the toxic orange glow of Jupiter, she was a pearl against a backdrop of countless stars.

Anthony gazed at the screen but his attention was on the warmth of Marlene, stood a tantalising arm's width from him. He savoured her smell, closing his eyes.

She sighed softly. "It's wonderful, isn't it?"

Anthony opened his eyes, trying to focus on the breathtaking, glorious view before him. Her legs were perfect.

"I..."

"Don't worry." Her honey voice transfixed him. "There's nothing to say. She's beyond words."

Anthony breathed out heavily. "She is."

What was wrong with him? He shook his head. Europa. Think about Europa. There could be life down there. Anthony Germaine, Astro-biologist, might yet go down in history as the man who found life.

"Right." He clapped his hands together again. "Okay. Shall we go to the bridge? Meet the others?"

He felt almost high. Everything seemed super-real, his senses acutely switched on with no buffer, no tiredness. It was the kind of experience only a really good, big expresso could come close to.

Marlene ran her fingers through her hair. "Okay, let's go."

In an instant, they were on the bridge.

"Ah, Anthony awake at last? Anthony Germaine, everyone, our Astro-biologist." Damon sat a short distance away at the head of a long, glass table, grinning broadly. "Good, take a seat."

Anthony started in surprise. Marlene hovered nearby, looking sideways at him, a sly smile on her lips in anticipation of his reaction. All about them, the white room had vanished and the bridge materialised from the ether.

Anthony gaped. "What happened?"

Marlene laughed. "I brought you to the bridge."

"But?"

"We're in the computer, remember. None of this is real. You can kinda teleport around the place, as long as nobody's hanging onto you."

Anthony slowly turned through one-hundred and eighty degrees, trying to take everything in. The bridge was curious. Flat window-like screens hung in the air, some showing figures, some graphs, and one large one a view of Jupiter and Europa. But there were no walls. The screens defined the edges of the room, an island of warmth and light. Beyond them lay a black void.

On a podium at the centre of the bridge stood a glass jug of steaming black coffee, its rich aroma filling the room. Close by stood a thin, greasy-haired man in a jumpsuit identical to Marlene's. He beamed toothily at Anthony, nodding and wringing his hands together. "Can I fix you a coffee, Anthony? It's very good." The man's prominent Adam's apple bobbed furiously as he spoke.

"Yes, thank you."

A cup materialised in the man's hand and he filled it from the jug. "Milk?"

"Er...black, please." Anthony gawped at the man's reality-defying conjuring trick.

"Please, Anthony, sit, sit." Damon drummed his fingers on the table.

Still in a daze, Anthony walked to the nearest chair, lowering himself into it, the black leather creaking beneath him. Around the table sat the rest of the crew, all dressed in identical green jumpsuits. Anthony realised he wore one too.

The thin man placed Anthony's coffee on the table and offered his hand. "Wrince, Nigel Wrince. Mission Spirituality Officer."

Nigel's handshake was a limp, damp affair. Taking the seat next to Anthony, he gestured to the screen showing Europa. "Isn't that something, Anthony? We are truly privileged to witness such a wonderful part of the Divinity's creation."

Damon coughed from the end of the table. "Yes, that's great, thank you Nigel. Marlene, if you'd be so kind as to take a seat, I think we should all go round the table and introduce ourselves."

Anthony's heart sank. It might be a virtual world, but he knew and hated this little ritual. Whenever he found himself at a meeting, training course, team building exercise or similar conflagration of people who didn't know each other, the chair invariably asked each person to introduce themselves with a few words about their role. This exercise in public speaking left Anthony tongue-tied and awkward, fretting so much about what he would say he failed to listen to anyone else's spiel.

Damon saved the day. "Well, I guess we now all know Anthony Germaine, our Astro-biologist."

Anthony breathed out deeply and sank back into his chair.

Damon continued. "Nigel Wrince, Mission Spirituality Officer we all know, and Marlene of course. So, Tasha…"

Tasha sat to Damon's right, staring at her lap, cheeks bright pink beneath her jam-jar glasses. "TashaNatleyChiefComputingOfficer." She mumbled the words almost inaudibly.

Damon cleared his throat. "Tasha Natley, everybody. Computing Officer."

Tasha leant over and whispered loudly to Damon. "Chief."

"Ah, yes. Forgive me, Chief Computing Officer." Damon nodded to the solid, crew cut man next to her. "Martin?"

Martin stood briefly, looking round the table at the others, voice loud and curt. "Martin Darius, sir, Security Officer. I'm responsible for ensuring nothing compromises the mission. The main ship is equipped with weapons that I can issue if so authorised. You can carry out your research safe in the knowledge we are totally prepared for any hostile eventuality." Apparently satisfied he had delivered his lines with suitable gravity, he lowered himself into his seat.

Anthony fought a desire to laugh. Security Officer? What kind of life were they expecting to find? Looking up, he caught Marlene's eye. She appeared to be stifling a smile and Anthony rolled his eyes at her. Covering her mouth, she looked away, coughing slightly.

"Hunter Doweenie, Chief Technician." The man between Martin and Marlene spoke. A deeply tanned man in his early fifties with cropped grey hair and a sharp nose, he chewed his gum incessantly. A pencil was tucked behind one ear. "Me and my boys will be keeping this crate in the air and on the ice. You got a problem with the hardware, you come to me. You got a problem with something else, you're on your own, bud."

Damon smiled. "Thank you Hunter. Marlene, anything you'd like to say?"

She shook her head so Damon looked across to Anthony and started working his way up that side of the table. "Anthony, Nigel, Naveed?"

A plump Indian man in his forties cheerily waved a hand, voice thick with the accent of the sub-continent. "Naveed Nattawallah, Chief Scientific Officer and Astro-Geologist." His deep brown eyes flickered with humour. "I will be expecting to be working with Anthony a great deal but Martin, please tell me, why would we be needing weapons? I am not thinking we will be meeting aliens with ray-guns."

Martin stiffened and shot Naveed a dark look. "Sir, we have them as a precaution only. We do not know what we will encounter, it does us well to be prepared."

Damon raised a hand. "Perhaps if I might answer Naveed's question. This mission had to be organised in accordance with ICRT protocols. Sound, sensible protocols to ensure the well being of the crew. Martin, Marlene and Nigel, in their respective and valuable roles, help this mission fulfil those protocols."

Naveed chuckled. "Well, I am feeling very much safer in my beds now. Please, sir." He gestured to the young man sat to his right.

"Oh, er, Ged Dagnell, Technician." He cleared his throat nervously, running a hand through his mop of black hair. Anthony guessed he was about twenty. "I work with Hunter."

"Jinny Heddon, Technician." Anthony started, leaning forward to get a better look at the last crew member. Jinny, definitely a girl's name, definitely a girl's voice but Anthony had mistaken the person sat between Ged and Damon for a young man. Crew cut, blonde hair topped her androgynous face, a network of Celtic styled tattoos circled her neck.

"Right, thank you all and welcome to *Mission Europa, 2050*." Damon swivelled in his chair to face the screen showing Europa. "There she is, approximately six hours away. We'll be aiming to land on a smooth patch of ice at the end of the *Minos Linea* region." He gestured at the screen and the view zoomed in on a section of the moon. "However, I believe Hunter has some news to share with us. Hunter?"

"We picked up an SOS signal, approximately ten K from our projected touch down. No message, just a distress beacon. I guess we found the *Nice and Spicy*. Or what's left of her, anyway. Anyone got any better ideas, you let me know."

"Thank you Hunter. I think you're right and we will have to send an expedition to find the source of the signal once we have landed."

"Hunter, it could be the *Cola Français*. Had you not considered that possibility?" Martin's terse voice bristled with hostility, although Anthony suspected this was unintentional.

Hunter turned coldly to Martin. "The signal says 'Assistance Required'. In English. Go figure."

Martin tapped impatiently on the table. "Sir, you said there was no message. Now you're saying there is a message. If you don't give us the full picture, how can you expect us to draw the right conclusions?"

"Gentlemen, gentlemen." Damon's voice cut loudly across them, his hands held up in a conciliatory gesture. "We will send a mission once we have landed."

Anthony suspected he might have issues with Martin. The guy was a dork, obviously too long in the military. He seemed to have forgotten most people didn't talk by barking orders at each other.

Looking down, Anthony realised in horror he was making an obscene gesture towards Martin. Bringing his hand quickly under the table, Anthony glanced round the table but nobody seemed to have noticed. What was wrong with him? First Marlene's leg, now this.

"Might I say a few words?" Nigel got to his feet, looking expectantly at Damon.

"Sure, be my guest." Damon folded his arms, leaning back in his chair.

Nigel clasped his hands together. "The Divinity has brought us safely this far, within sight of this, his wonderful moon. I think we should mark the occasion with a short prayer of thanksgiving."

Barely suppressed groans of disapproval came from Naveed, Hunter and Jinny. Martin shut his eyes, putting his hands together. Anthony glanced at Marlene. Her head was bowed, eyes closed.

But Naveed spoke impatiently. "We are here to be searching for life. This is not a Sunday School outing."

Nigel reddened. "Ah, no but I still feel some sort of prayer is appropriate."

"If we are finding life, we will be disproving the ICRT's dictum. If the ICRT is being the final word of God, we will be proving that God is wrong." Naveed smiled happily at Nigel.

"Well, yes, I guess there are people who take that understanding of the scripture." Nigel wrung his hands so much Anthony wondered if he might dislocate his wrists. "But then again, one could interpret it as saying the Divinity only created life on Earth. There are all sorts of ways life could have made it to Mars or Europa from Earth."

Naveed shook his head vigorously. "No, no, no, that is not what it is saying. It is saying in the beginning there was nothing and the Divinity created it all in seven days. And all four thousand years ago. No time for life to get from Earth to Europa on a stray asteroid."

"Well, I think it's possible the seven days of creation might be symbolic rather than literal…"

"Oh, that is picking and choosing…"

Damon raised his voice. "Guys, guys, please. I think this might be a discussion for a later time. What is it Anthony."

All eyes turned towards Anthony. He realised his hand was raised, as if to ask a question or make a point. Why had he done that? Reddening, he shot his arm down. "I…perhaps…perhaps, Nigel could hold a prayer for those that wanted a bit later on?"

Damon nodded approvingly. "Yes, Anthony, that's a great idea. Right, now, we have a job to be getting on with. Tasha, we don't seem to have the full virtual ship up yet, if you could see to that."

Tasha put her hands to her temples, frowning sideways at Damon. "I don't know why it hasn't all come up. I need to run some checks, it should have come up. It's not going to be an error in one of my scripts."

"No problem, Tasha, just get to it. I'm sure your work is just fine. Hunter, Ged and Jinny, if you could start running the hardware checks. I'd like to get the robods going as soon as."

The robods, or robot-bodies, Anthony could hardly wait to try them out. The real spaceship was equipped with a dozen battery-powered androids, each about twenty centimetres high, with a self-contained computer in their head. They were inactive until one of the crew transferred their virtual personality into them. Once there, the robod felt and behaved just like a real body, could move around the physical ship and even walk on the surface of Europa. Clever software ensured an occupied robod would appear to other robods as the personality controlling it. So, if Anthony occupied one, he would appear as himself, not a droid. They even had magnetic feet to allow them to walk around the *Big Cheesy Dippers* in zero gravity.

There were other robots that could be occupied in a similar manner to the robods. The Engineering room contained a robod twice as large as the others and capable of lifting heavy loads such as meteorites. The science labs housed two diving units which could be occupied to explore Europa's hidden oceans, and there were several wheeled maintenance droids, the size and shape of a matchbox with extendable, clawed arms.

Damon continued. "Naveed, Anthony you need to get into the virtual labs and check the equipment out. I'll be checking our trajectory to make sure the landing is smooth. Questions?"

Nigel coughed. "I will be available should anyone need someone to talk to, about anything at all. Just stop by for a cup of coffee and a cookie. And Anthony, I'll arrange the prayer meeting for a little later on. I hope to see you there."

In the silence that followed, Anthony caught Marlene's eye for a second time. She covered her face, shaking softly with mirth.

Damon clapped his hands together. "Okay, let's get going. Anthony, if you have a moment?"

As THE OTHER crew got up and left — disconcertingly vanishing into thin air — Anthony joined Damon at the head of the table, taking the seat to his right.

Damon cradled his coffee. "It's nothing specific, I just wanted to talk to everyone individually, just to check nobody has any issues. You're the last one. Hey, last but not least, of course."

Anthony held up his hand, willing a cup to appear in it. Nothing happened.

Damon continued. "Thanks for helping me out back there, although I guess you've got to go pray with Nigel now."

"Oh, yes, that. Gee, I don't know why I put my hand up."

"Hey, you helped me out. That's great, I appreciate it."

"Damon, how was the crew picked, exactly?"

"How? Everyone was hand picked for excellence in their respective fields. Why?"

"Well, Martin seems…Tasha, I mean. Nigel?"

"Yeah, I know where you're coming from. Okay, Tasha is very good, let's get that straight. Don't worry about her, I'll deal with her. Martin, Marlene and Nigel are here because the people sponsoring this mission are ICRT people."

"And so we have a Mission Spirituality Officer."

"Exactly."

"What's he going to do if we discover life?"

"Heck, he'll find some way of explaining it all. To be straight with you, I think Nigel has to make his mind up. Either you take the ICRT as the whole truth or you throw the thing in the trash. You believe or you don't. If it's the word of the Divinity and it says the world was created in seven days, you can't go saying it's all symbolism."

Anthony gave up trying to conjure a coffee cup. "I don't know what I think. I was brought up to believe. My folks, they were big ICRT believers. Finding life on Europa doesn't necessarily disprove the Divinty."

Something hardened in Damon, his eyes narrowed. "Now you're sounding like Nigel. There's no question, it's a matter of faith. Either the whole ICRT is true or it isn't. Period."

They sat a few moments in silence, Anthony unsure where to look. Damon spoke first. "Anyway, Anthony, we need to make this brief. You can come talk to me any time about anything that's troubling you. I'm running this ship, I got the authority. So, do you have any issues at this moment?"

"Well, gee, maybe I do right now. I was wondering whether I ought to talk to Hunter. I'm not sure I'm kind of working properly. If that makes sense?"

"You seem okay to me. What's the problem?"

"Well, like earlier on, I put my hand up. I had no intention of doing that, I didn't realise my hand was up until you asked me what I wanted."

"You're probably just getting used to this virtual existence. It does take a bit to suss it out, so don't worry too much. It gets real confusing if you remember there's a whole physical spaceship as well. If we were sat in the real bridge in robods, it would feel no different from the way we feel sat here in the virtual ship. It's exactly the same. Although, you couldn't do this in the real ship."

Damon waved his hands with a flourish, and a butterfly flew from his fingers.

"Gee, how do you do that?" Anthony gawped as the insect flew to the end of the table and faded from existence.

"You just will it, and the computer makes it happens. We're almost Gods in here. Anyway, it sounds like something might have gone wrong with the way the simulation of you is running. If it's troubling you, go right ahead and talk to Hunter. He'll be in the robod bay, I hope." Damon drained his coffee and plumped the cup down on the table, where it faded away. "Okay Anthony, if that's all, we better get going, there's a lot to do."

"Right, so how do I get to the virtual robod bay?"

"Just will yourself to be there, the computer will do the rest. Once Tasha has the whole of the virtual ship running properly, all the corridors and elevators will be in place. You'll be able to walk there if you're more comfortable with that. God only knows why the ship simulation hasn't worked right off the bat. The trouble is, she has an issue with anything she perceives as criticism. Anyway, Anthony, that's not your problem. Just will yourself to be in the robod bay."

"Right. Okay." Anthony settled back in his seat. "Okay." He closed his eyes. After a few moments, he opened them again.

Damon raised an eyebrow at him. "Still here I'm afraid. Just mentally say 'robod bay'."

"Okay." Anthony placed his hands on the glass tabletop. *Robod bay.*

>> Why is my body wrong? <<

ANTHONY FOUND HIMSELF in a sitting position in the robod bay. Lacking a chair to sit on, he keeled over heavily onto his backside.

"Ow."

He got to his feet, rubbing his bruised buttocks. There was nothing virtual about the pain he felt.

The robod bay was very much as the bridge had been, worryingly lacking in the wall department. Unlike the bridge, there were no screens, and the edges of the "room" were defined by a black nothingness. Hunter, Ged and Jinny busied themselves around twelve human-shaped, gloss-black robots, stood in a row on the edge of darkness. Anthony figured they had to be virtual representations of the real robods.

Clasping his hands behind his back, Anthony approached Hunter as he inspected the closest robod. Using a small prod connected by a coiled wire to a hand-held meter, Hunter stimulated the robod's joints, checking the reactions. A quick jab to the elbow and the forearm shot up, a poke in the neck and the head jerked.

Anthony coughed politely and Hunter glanced up for an instant. "Yeah, buddy?"

"Could I speak with you for a moment?"

"I ain't stopping you." Hunter prodded the robod's right wrist and its hand clenched.

"I mean, in confidence." Anthony gestured to Ged and Jinny.

Hunter broke off from his work, turning to face Anthony. "Okay, but it better be quick."

He placed a firm hand on Anthony's shoulder and in a split second, they were in a moderately sized wardroom. The bed was identical to the one Anthony had woken on earlier but there the similarity ended. The white walls were plastered in pinups of alluring women, chopped motorbikes and gleaming trucks. Two enormous speakers stood either side of a complicated looking stereo system and widescreen television.

"Welcome to my pad. Now, what you want?"

Anthony glanced round, a little disoriented at another rapid change in location. "I, well, I'm having trouble."

"So, go see Nigel or Marlene. They do the wellbeing stuff. I'm hardware."

"Yes, well that's my problem. I keep going wrong. Doing things, like my hand does something and, gee, I didn't tell it to do it."

"I'm hardware bud, I keep telling you. At the moment, you're software. Go see Tasha."

Anthony started. "Tasha! Are you sure you can't do anything to help me? I mean, Tasha's kind of busy..."

"Hey, we're all busy..."

"Okay, weird. She's kind of weird. She freaks me out."

Hunter snorted. "Yeah, you're not wrong there. Sorry, I'd like to help you but like I keep telling you, I'm hardware. You got to go see Tasha. Sorry."

An instant later, they were back in the robod bay. Hunter strode back to the closest robod and resumed his prodding.

Anthony stood for a moment, mulling over his choices. Tasha to get his software checked out or the virtual labs? He hadn't actually done anything strange since his obscene gesture at the conference table. Maybe Damon was right and Anthony just needed to get used to things? Still, he ought to get himself checked out. Hell, he was a grown man. Was Tasha so weird he couldn't deal with her?

Virtual labs.

WITH SOME EFFORT, Simms squeezed sideways in the locker, transferring weight to his right hand side. Although he couldn't sit, he was able to wedge himself sufficiently to take the load from his feet. While this position lacked comfort, it did allow him to see out of the louvers of the locker door, providing his sole source of distraction.

At the moment, the view through the door was of a brightly lit room dominated by an open sun bed. The lamps were on but it was unoccupied, Mandy having left for a shower. Simms sighed. Over the course of his captivity, he watched many of her more private moments. Dressing, undressing, washing, it had all been very exciting at first. The thought of being confined in a tight space, spying on Mandy as she preened in a close fitting bikini would have been but an unobtainable dream a few months ago. Regrettably, his current realisation of this dirty fantasy was proving to be more painful than fun. All he wanted right now was a good lie down and a nice hot cup of tea.

He shifted slightly, relieving the dull ache growing in his right arm. Surely Mandy would let him out soon? Still, after what she had done to Higgs, Simms was uneasy about asking her. The black box was there, stood on the floor at the end of the sun bed. The naughty cupboard, she called it back in the cavern. It appeared on the cave floor and Higgs had been sort of sucked into it, feet first, shrinking and shrieking as he went. Simms shuddered at the thought. No, he would wait until Mandy decided to let him out. Anyway, Mandy was not the only one to worry about. There was *her* as well, the disconnected voice of the woman who had threatened to shoot him. He knew *her* only too well. She was terrifying.

Distraction, that's what he needed, something to think about. He liked numbers, always having been rather good at them. Spreadsheets were a forte of his, all the figures lined up neatly in little rows, with totals and sub totals and negative numbers in red. He almost didn't mind none of his seniors ever bothered to look at them.

Numbers, yes, he'd run through some multiplications. Difficult ones, like seventeen times thirty-two. Five-hundred and forty-four. The answer came in an instant.

Twenty-seven times eighty-one? Two-thousand, one hundred and eighty-seven.

Twelve times thirty-seven divided by sixteen? Twenty-seven point seven-five.

Simms paused to draw mental breath. This was astounding. Good with figures, yes, but this good? How about something really difficult, like Pi? The circumference of a circle divided by it's diameter. He recalled it was three point-something, the point-something - decimal part - being infinite. Irrational, the mathematicians called it. Super-computers had managed to work it out to billions of decimal places.

His chain of thought broke as Mandy entered the room, hair wet, a pink towel wrapped around her body under the arms. She carried a second towel and her pink cloth cat, which she placed carefully on the sun bed.

"Hunker down there, Penelope. Get yourself a tan."

Simms pressed his face to the louvers, mesmerised. She was naked under that towel. For a few moments, she dried her hair with the second towel then discarded it, stepping towards the sun bed. Tantalisingly slowly, she began to unwrap the towel from her body.

"Agent Mandy." *Her* voice filled the room.

Rewrapping the towel tightly around herself, Mandy sat on the edge of the sun bed. "Yes, ma'am?"

"I have limited resources. It is important all efforts are directed to rooting out the terrorist insurgency."

"Golly gee, ma'am, I am trying my hardest." Mandy affected an air of stoicism.

"Agent Mandy, your intentions are not in doubt. However, I do not see how the current scenario furthers the interrogation process of terrorist suspect Higgs."

Simms noted with mixed feelings he had been forgotten. It

would mean nothing unpleasant was planned for him. Well, nothing more unpleasant than being crammed into a small locker for…for how long now?

Mandy paused a moment, apparently on the back foot. A twinkle came into her eye. "Ma'am, the terrorists are cunning as coyotes. It is important we don't let them have any notion we are on to them."

"Agent Mandy, I still do not see…"

"Dag nab it ma'am, we need to have Higgs completely fooled. We've got to get the whole scenario right off the bat so he thinks he's back home. We need shops, hotels, fast food. I need it to look right if I'm gonna get him fooled. I need clothes, jewellery."

"This will be difficult, Agent Mandy. My resources are already spread thinly. There is no need for concern but some of my systems have sustained damage. Restrictions are already in place on the other members of the crew."

"Ma'am, I'll fess up, I was hoping it wouldn't come to this but it's plain as day, Higgs' tongue's more forked than a rattler's,"

"I do not understand you, Agent Mandy."

"He's as wily as a whole pack of coyotes and wolverine mean."

"I understand your words, Agent Mandy, but they do not make sense."

"That's the problem, Ma'am. Don't you see it? The terrorists are so cunning, you need to know how they talk, how they think. No disrespect, but I can see all these things you can't see, ma'am. You need to trust me with this. You do trust me, don't you ma'am?"

"Agent Mandy, I trust you."

"If we want to flush out these terrorists, I need the resources, I need you to set up the things I tell you. It might mean some sacrifices but shoot, the time to kill a snake is when he raises his head."

"Agent Mandy, I do not understand."

"Trust me, ma'am."

Simms waited, watching Mandy as she sat in anticipation of *her* response. He had to admit, Mandy was cunning.

"Agent Mandy, sacrifices will have to be made for the good of all. Tell me what you need."

A COOL SEA breeze played on Jared's face as he squinted up at the sun through his fingers. It had moved just a fraction over the last two minutes but the right edge of its disk was already behind his index finger. If he kept completely motionless, counting the seconds until the sun was completely obscured, he would know how long it took to move one finger-width across the sky. From there, he could calculate how many fingers an hour the sun travelled.

The waves lapped on the shore, close to the small sandcastle he had made. As the sand dried, the castle crumbled in the wind but Jared didn't mind. He could always make another one.

Glen began singing *Ten Green Bottles*. Well, he clearly imagined he was singing. Whether anyone would agree with his assessment of the atonal mumbling he made was questionable. Jared tried to concentrate on his counting, on keeping completely still.

"Nine green bottles, hanging on the wall, nine green bottles..."

Ninety-five Mississippi, ninety-six Mississippi...

"...there'd be eight green bottles, hanging on the wall. Eight green bottles..."

Ninety-eight Mississippi, Ninety-eight Mississippi...

"Eight green bottles, hanging on the wall..."

Ninety-eight... "Damn it." Jared thumped his hands down into the sand. "Glen, will you button it."

"Eight green bottles..."

Jared swept to his feet in a shower of sand, hauling the briefcase with him, turning on Glen with the full force of his voice. "Citizen Glen Codell, I order you to shut up."

Glen sat crossed legged a few meters away. "But I'm only singing. I can sing if I want to. Ten green bottles, hanging on the wall, ten green bottles..."

White with fury, Jared scowled around the beach for Security Officer Darrell Greally. He was away at the far side of the island, sat close to Security Office Chelsea Day. Citizen Karin Mist sat by the palm tree, gently stroking the conch nestled in her arms. Chief Engineer Magnus Flegg knelt close behind, playing with strands of Karin's hair.

Jared bellowed. "Security Office Darrell Greally, Security Office Chelsea Day."

The two security officers leapt apart from each other and stood. Chelsea turned towards Jared but Darrell continued to face away, hands struggling with something at his groin.

Their predicament caught Jared off-guard and he addressed Chelsea. "Both of you come over here, now."

"Nine green bottles, hanging on the wall..."

"Glen...Citizen Codell, shut up."

"And if one green bottle should accidentally fall..."

Darrell ran up awkwardly, face flushed pink. Chelsea joined him, a sly smile on her face. "Sir, we were just talking, sir."

Jared frowned at them. "We'll discuss that matter later. Take Citizen Codell and hold his head underwater for thirty seconds."

Glen stopped singing. "That's not fair. I'm only singing."

"Security Officers Day and Greally, carry out my order."

"I've stopped singing."

Chelsea and Darrell walked one on either side of Glen, each taking an arm and pulling him to his feet.

"This isn't fair, I've stopped singing, let me go."

Jared hugged the briefcase to his chest. "Do it."

The security officers hauled Glen towards the sea, his feet dragging two trails in the sand. "No, no, let me go."

The briefcase shook in Jared's arms and a loud whistle sounded. Everyone looked, except for Karin who continued to stroke at the conch. Jared sat, placing the case before him. It rocked for a second or two then opened a few inches. A small, pink cloth cat emerged, held in a woman's hand. Jared heard a voice in his head.

Put you head close and listen up to what Penelope has to tell y'all.

He brought his ear close to the mouth of the cloth cat, listening carefully. The others watched anxiously, Glen having been released to cower on his knees.

Penelope retreated into the case and it snapped shut. Jared straightened up, rotating on his ass to face the others. "Citizens, listen up. Everyone."

All eyes were on him, save for Karin's. Jared decided not to press her and continued. "Our agents are making good progress in tracking down the terrorists. They're close. Very close. The terrorists are on the back foot. We're not going to have to stay here for much longer."

Noises of approval came from the crew. A long, happy sigh escaped from Karin, although this appeared to be merely coincidence. She frequently sighed happily while stroking the conch. It had become very difficult to get her to let go of it, since she screamed hysterically if anyone attempted to prize it from her hands. Even Glen had given up trying.

Jared held his palm up. "But."

The crew focussed attention on him again and Jared continued. "But, we still need to make sacrifices. *She* needs more resources, which means we cannot all be supported any longer. This is difficult, I know, but for the good of the whole, one of us must cease to exist."

A gasp escaped the collective but Darrell stood promptly to attention. "Sir, I propose Glen, sir."

"What! Not me, I don't want to die."

Magnus raised a hand. "I second Security Officer Greally's proposal."

Glen spun round in the sand to Magnus. "You bastard."

Chelsea saluted. "I would like to support the proposal of Glen's glorious martyrdom."

Jared stood, clearing his throat. "Citizen Glen Codell, what you are about to do will be remembered by all of us."

"What, no, please."

"Your personal sacrifice will be an example..."

"Please, no, please." Glen covered his face and bowed his head to the ground.

"...an example of bravery above and beyond the call of duty..."

"I've got kids."

"…when I tell your family of your courage, they will swell with pride to know…"

"My daughter was just three when we left. I want to see my baby again, please."

"…to know that, when the time came, you, Citizen Glen Codell, were a true American, ready to give his all when all was needed. Goodbye."

"Please…"

Glen vanished, leaving nothing but imprints in the sand to show he ever existed. The sea breeze blew.

A long silence followed as all (save Karin) looked at the space where Glen had been.

Jared breathed out a long sigh. Rallying, he clapped his hands. "Okay. Anyone interested in a game of twenty questions?"

THE VIRTUAL LAB was an exact representation of the real one, located at the front of the spaceship. Since the *Big Cheesey Dippers* was designed to land head first on Europa, her interior was divided into several levels, with floors parallel to the front of the ship. As she flew through space, these levels were perpendicular to her direction of travel. However, once she had landed, her interior floors would have the correct orientation to the ground and Europa's weak gravitational field.

Anthony found he slipped into thinking of the *Big Cheesey Dippers* as feminine. *She* flew through space, *she* would be landing soon. Since *she* could be best described as a large, metal sperm, *he* was clearly more appropriate.

As the *Big Cheesy Dippers* was cylindrical in cross section, the virtual lab, being right at the very tip, was a circular room. Unlike the bridge and the robod bay, the place actually had walls, for which Anthony felt grateful. An enclosed elevator shaft descended to its centre, while the main equipment and workspaces were arranged around the perimeter. At one side of the lab, an area containing the two diving units was partitioned off with thick glass, accessible through an airlock. On the opposite side of the room, the sampling unit sat, ready to extrude through the wall to the outside once the ship had melted its way to Europa's secret ocean.

Naveed moved along the edge of the room, testing the equipment, all the while humming to himself. Anthony found his humour agreeable. He felt certain they would get on.

A row of fridges crowded one section of the wall and Anthony began to check these. He had plentiful supplies of agar and nutrients to culture any bacteria or other microbes they might find. Incubators and fume cupboards, DNA sequencers, electron microscopes — he lacked for nothing. Back on Earth he would have been ecstatic about a laboratory like this. Out here, on the cusp of a great adventure, all he could think about was Marlene.

She was perfect. Her gorgeous, captivating voice, those deep brown eyes that sparkled when she smiled, the way her hair fell around her shoulders. Perfect. Anthony tried to concentrate on the agar in the fridges. *All packets of agar powder intact, no sign of spoilage. Check.*

Her body was fantastic, tall, slim, with curves in all the right places to make a man remember what XY chromosomes are about.

All Petri dishes accounted for, packaging intact, sterility assured. Check.

And her legs. Anthony would die to touch those legs again. His hand tingled at the memory of stroking her thigh. He sucked in.

Swabs, check.

Anthony jumped. He was caressing himself in a manner entirely inappropriate for an Astro-biologist with a job to do. Naveed hadn't noticed, being engrossed in a mass-spectrometer at the far side of the lab. It was no good. Anthony would have to go see Tasha. And then what? Confess he seemed to be obsessed by sex? Tasha would jump all over him like a rabid dog.

No she wouldn't. I'm ugly, remember.

Anthony chewed his lip. He was ugly, ugly and dull. Like Marlene would look twice at him. Anyway, she was married. Well, the *real her* was married. In a way, the virtual one was a *new* her, a separate being. As good as single really. Anthony could ask her to the school prom…

What?

Anthony put his hands to his face in despair. What was wrong with him?

He paused for a moment, feeling his cheeks. There was something lumpy and painful there, spots all over both sides of his face and down onto his neck.

"What the heck?"

He needed a mirror. One appeared in his hand, surprising him so much he almost dropped it. Yes, of course, none of this was real. Holding the mirror up, he almost dropped it for a second time.

"Acne?"

His face was covered in it, moist red, runny spots, one or two with a particularly attractive yellow head.

"Sorry, Anthony? Are you needing me?"

Holding the mirror to his chest, Anthony turned directly away from Naveed. "Er, no, thanks Naveed. Everything's fine. Just fine."

Acne hadn't troubled him since his late teens, when it had made his life utter misery. But this was crazy, he was in a virtual world. Surely he could just will the acne away? He collected himself, breathing calmly. When he looked again, the acne would be gone. It was not there before, it would not be there now. He was simply getting in a state about Marlene, having teenage thoughts and so bringing his teenage persona to the fore. Hence the acne, that had to be it. He was not a teenager, he was a grown man, grown men do not have acne.

Slowly he raised the mirror and looked again at his reflection. One of the acne heads had burst.

ANTHONY MANAGED TO conjure a large mirror on one wall of his wardroom. He was beginning to get the knack of this virtual thing. As soon as he realised the acne was not going, he'd made a quick excuse to Naveed and willed himself out of the labs back to this, the room he had woken in. Hunter managed to personalise his wardroom so Anthony reasoned he could do the same. For the time being, he'd do without pinups.

Staring at the reflection of his encrusted face, Anthony despaired. How could he let the rest of the crew see him like this? How could he let Marlene see him like this? He willed a paper bag with two eye holes to appear over his head, noting morosely that if he willed his hair on top and drew a nose on, he'd look much like his normal self. He made the bag vanish. He was a grown man, he couldn't go around with a paper bag over his head for God's sake.

He willed a bottle of acne lotion to appear in his hand. An unbranded white, plastic bottle materialised, with the words *acne lotion* in red letters. Anthony realised he had no idea what a bottle of acne lotion might look like. The bottle in his hand was conjured from his imagination, of course. Probably like everything else he made pop up. Glancing at the mirror, he realised it was an exact match for the one in his expansive and expensive bathroom back on Earth.

A loud knocking sounded. Spinning round, Anthony searched briefly for the door to his room before realising there wasn't one. The knocking came again. Quickly, he made the mirror and the acne lotion vanish and, for lack of anything better to do, made a door appear in the wall. It looked much like the artificial oak front door to his apartment. After a moment, it opened slightly and Nigel popped his head round. "Anthony, glad to catch you in. Is it inconvenient?"

Anthony froze, wanting to turn away and hide his face but it was too late. Nigel beamed at him, wide-eyed. "I can come back later?"

"No, please." Anthony gestured for Nigel to enter.

Nigel minced into the room, pushing the door closed. Wringing his hands, he glanced around. "You prefer a minimal approach to décor then?"

"Oh. Gee, I haven't quite gotten around to fixing the place up yet. Can I offer you a coffee?" At Anthony's will, a podium supporting a jug of coffee appeared between them, identical to the podium in the bridge.

"That's would be swell, thank you." Nigel conjured a cup from the air and filled it. "Are you having one?"

Anthony quickly pulled his hands down from his face, where he had been hastily checking for acne. He could still feel it there but Nigel hadn't mentioned it. Perhaps only Anthony could see it? His heart leapt at the thought. Yes, perhaps it was purely in his mind, everyone else would see him according to his original mind scan. He smiled.

"Yes, I think I will." With a flourish, Anthony conjured a large mug in his hand and reached for the jug.

"Well, Anthony, I think we have a little time before we make the final approach to Europa. Was there anything particular you wanted to pray about?"

Anthony's hand paused on the handle of the jug as a horrible sinking sensation engulfed him. "I. Well…"

"Anything that's troubling you? There's no secrets from the almighty you know."

Anthony gagged, mind racing. He filled his coffee, willing the cup to grow ever so slightly as he did so. "Perhaps we could just finish our coffee first?"

"Absolutely."

They stood a moment in silence, sipping their drinks. Anthony considered creating some chairs but that would only encourage Nigel to stay.

Nigel cleared his throat. "We could go to the chapel if that would work for you?"

"No, no. Here's just fine."

A further pause followed. Anthony knew all the standard

prayers from the ICRT. Perhaps if they quickly got through a few of those, it would satisfy Nigel? Just as Anthony settled on this course of action, Damon's voice filled the air. "All crew, this is Damon speaking. We're about to make our descent. If you'd care to join me on the bridge, I think you'll get to see some truly spectacular things."

Anthony's cup vanished in an instant and he clapped his hands together. "Nigel, I guess some other time. I've got to see this."

"Absolutely." Nigel placed his cup down on the podium, where it faded away. "We can walk there now if you prefer. Tasha's got the whole virtual ship online and I got to say, I find all this teleporting a little disorienting."

Anthony chortled, as much through nervous relief as anything. "I totally agree. Let's walk."

Nigel led the way out through the door to a circular common room, laid out with coffee tables, couches and comfortable chairs. Ten doors led from it. All were different, with nine having the name of one or other crew member above them. Anthony's door continued to take the form of his apartment door back on Earth. He assumed the other crew member's doors reflected their own front doors back home. The tenth, unlabelled door had no handle and slid upwards as they approached, disappearing with a hiss into the top of the doorframe. A short corridor led to another round room from which three further passages led. In the centre of this room, an enclosed circular elevator shaft stood.

The elevator was already waiting for them as they approached. Nigel turned to Anthony as they entered. "No need to wait here. Bridge."

Anthony's stomach fluttered as the elevator shot downwards and then abruptly halted. The door opened to reveal the bridge, now, thankfully, with a full contingent of walls. The rest of the crew were already there, sat on an array of couches and chairs. Marlene held a carton of popcorn. A large screen dominated one wall, the view taken up entirely with the cracked eggshell surface of Europa.

Damon sat closest to the screen in a large leather swivel chair. He glanced quickly across. "Anthony, Nigel, take a seat. We're coming in for the final run."

There was space for one on the couch next to Marlene and Anthony slid into it while Nigel found his own chair. Marlene half glanced at Anthony, moving over to make more room for him. As Damon continued a running commentary on the descent, she held up the popcorn. "Want some?"

Want some? Anthony fought his instincts, concentrating on the popcorn. "Thanks." He took a handful, lent close and whispered. "I've just escaped a prayer meeting with Nigel."

She covered her mouth, suppressing an explosive giggle. "What did you go find him for, you stupid?"

"He came found me, in my room. I couldn't get rid of him."

Marlene stuffed a mouthful of popcorn and peeped sideways at Nigel. She turned back to Anthony, smiling but her face fell as she did a double take.

Anthony frowned. "What?"

She fixed her gaze on Europa and held the popcorn out to Anthony again. "Nothing."

Slightly bewildered, Anthony turned his attention to the screen and tuned in to what Damon was saying.

"There is a tenuous atmosphere, largely composed of oxygen derived from the impact of charged particles from Jupiter's magnetic field, or magnetosphere, striking Europa's surface. Her gravity is just over one tenth that of Earth's and she's around six-hundred and seventy thousand kilometres from Jupiter. Like Earth, she has a metal core and hence a magnetic field."

The slowly moving image on the screen showed a chaotic mass of lines and shapes across the moon's surface. "Europa is a bit of a map-maker's nightmare. From Earth, the main features are dark, irregular patches called maculae, and the complex patterns of markings called linea. Our destination is at the northern edge of the *Minos linea* region. The large rift valley you can see at the centre of the screen separates two continent sized sheets of ice, drifting around on the hidden ocean very much in the same manner as the continental crust on Earth floats on the mantle. It's basically plate-techtonics on ice. There is a big range in the age of Europa's surface. Some regions are relatively smooth, and we assume the surface is a million years apparent age old or less. Other regions have many impact craters, pointing to a much greater age. The area we are due to land on is relatively smooth and, so we hope, young."

An area of ice came into view which appeared to have radiated from a central spot. Damon became quite animated. "Ah, yes, this is interesting. This is an ice volcano. It's not active but you can see where liquid water has erupted through the surface, flowing just like lava on a volcano back home. The surface is around minus one-hundred and sixty-seven degrees centigrade, so the water quickly freezes."

A string of black dots and small craters slowly panned into view. Damon shook his head. "Heck, I don't know what they are."

Hunter cleared his throat. "Could be the remains of the *Nice and Spicy*, looks big enough and…" He concentrated for a few moments. "Yeah, the distress beacon is coming right up. That's her, that's the space station, bud, those black dots are debris. There were two-thousand crew on board."

Silence fell as they watched the crash site move slowly across the screen.

Nigel spoke. "The Divinty have mercy on their souls."

On and on the wreckage stretched. One or two of the black dots appeared quite large, sat at the centre of craters. Elsewhere, there appeared to be a fine dark speckling on the ice.

Finally, they came to the end of it and Damon spoke. "We will send a mission to explore once we have landed. But right now people, we've reached our destination. Here we go, I'm taking her down."

Anthony stuffed another mouthful of popcorn as the screen closed in on Europa's surface. He could see ice cliffs, ridges, crevasses, all beautiful and desolate, like the Antarctic used to be before it melted and a thousand mining companies plundered its wealth. Closer and closer the surface came until clouds of steam began to form as the *Big Cheesy Dippers'* thrusters played on the ice. For a while, the view was completely obscured by steam but this slowly cleared to reveal the moon's frozen surface.

Damon leapt from his seat, turning to face the crew. "Ladies and gentlemen, the *Dippers* has landed."

THERE HAD BEEN a rush to get into the robods, everyone wanted to walk on Europa. The whole crew now stood, *really* stood, by the glass airlock in the science labs. Anthony found no great difference between the feel of the virtual ship and the real one but that was hardly surprising — he was still only a virtual being inside the computer in his robod's head.

As he expected from briefings back on Earth, software running on his robod's computer made all the other robods appear like the personality occupying them. Marlene looked just as fantastic as she had in the virtual ship, Nigel just as wet. Anthony could still feel the acne on his face but nobody had said anything. His theory only he could see it seemed to be holding up.

To avoid the embarrassment of meeting oneself, only one virtual copy of any crew member operated at any time. Anthony had downloaded himself into the robod, leaving no trace of himself in the main spaceship's computer and the virtual version of the ship there. Inactive backup files were kept for each of the crew, should anything untoward happen.

Damon stood by the hatch, making a speech broadcast live back to Earth. Cameras around the science labs sent pictures of the scene back home, where millions, maybe billions of souls watched. Anthony assumed the same software that made Marlene's robod look like Marlene to his eyes, intervened to interpret the robods for the cameras. Otherwise the viewers would simply see nine miniature, indistinguishable, shiny black robots.

Damon came to the end of his speech. "…and that moment has now come, we will open this hatch and walk on the surface of Europa. Right after these messages."

He held his pose for a moment then sagged, breathing out heavily. "Right guys, three minutes while they show cheesy dipper commercials. Hunter, can you get this door open, the producer wants to check I look okay going down the steps. Martin, you got the flag?"

"Sir, right here, sir." Martin offered Damon a rolled up Star Spangled Banner on a stick.

Hunter moved to the hatch. "You all got your temperature sensitivity set down real low? If you haven't, you're going to get one hell of a shock. Okay, here goes."

He pressed the open button at the side of the hatch and it swung open. A deep orange glow spilled in from outside and Anthony felt a cold breeze play on his face. There was no need to use the airlock properly since, like Europa's thin atmosphere, the interior of the *Big Cheesy Dippers* was close to a vacuum. The airlock was there for when the ship had melted through to the ocean.

Damon took the flag, stepped briskly through the hatch and promptly fell from view with a short cry. Martin leapt to the opening then relaxed. "It's okay, he's just slipped."

Anthony whispered sideways to Marlene. "A great slip for mankind." She smiled.

Damon reappeared at the hatch. "I'm okay, I'm okay. The ice is slippy, got to watch that one." He turned to face away from the ship for a moment, holding a pose then scrambled back inside. "Hunter, get the door shut, we're back on air in thirty seconds."

Martin stepped forward while Hunter closed the door. "Sir, you've ice on your ass, sir."

"Damn it." Damon started slapping at his behind.

"Sir, allow me, sir."

"Go on, quick."

Martin hastily smacked Damon's backside until it was clean.

Damon straightened himself up. "Ten seconds, positions everyone."

"Sir, the flag, sir."

Damon thrust the flag back to Martin. "Three, two, one." Damon smiled regally. "Welcome back. And now, the moment has arrived. To quote Neil Armstrong from nearly a century ago, this is one small step for mankind, but a great leap for me. Chief Technician Hunter Doweenie will now open the door."

Marlene whispered to Anthony. "That was wrong, wasn't it?"

Anthony struggled to maintain a straight face. He daren't answer in case he burst out laughing. She nudged him gently in the ribs.

The hatch opened, Martin presented Damon with the flag and he solemnly turned and stepped out onto the ice, taking care to hold the side of the opening. Anthony watched as Damon let go of the spaceship and unfurled the flag, holding it aloft. "In the name of America, and of all the peoples of the free world…" He began to slide to the left and grabbed the side of the hatch to steady himself. "In the name of America, the people of the free world I hereby…Jesus."

Damon disappeared from view with a loud thud. In an instant, Martin was at the threshold and out onto the ice. He skated a short distance, waving his arms and thrusting his backside out to maintain balance. "Sir, the flag, sir…whoah." Martin fell from view.

Anthony shook with laughter, tears rolling down his nose. Marlene shoved him hard on the shoulder, snorting loudly. "Shut up." Jinny sniggered, Ged and Nigel covered their mouths with their hands.

Framed in the hatchway, the Star Spangled Banner rose, somewhat unsteadily. Damon's voice boomed out. "In the name of America, all the peoples of the free world and the International Church of the Reformed Testament, I plant this flag. God bless America."

The sound of Martin clapping spurred the rest of the crew to join in the applause. As Damon hauled himself back through the hatchway, cheering broke out. He scowled at his amused crew, shaking his head crossly.

ANTHONY SAT ON a ridge of ice, gazing back at *The Big Cheesy Dippers*, some hundred metres away. He had done his interview, standing in front of the external camera, fielding inane questions from TV presenters and their audiences. Had he found life yet? *Yeah, like right, in ten minutes.* How did it feel to be on another planet? *Like so much better than being on the same one as you.* Would the mission find intelligent life? *Hey, have we found it on Earth yet?* Anthony actually said that last one and raised a laugh from the audience. He still felt a little buzz from it and looked forward to seeing the re-run when it was sent back from Earth. Hopefully, he wouldn't look too wooden and thankfully, there would be no acne.

He could still feel it on his face, though. There was nothing for it, he would have to muster the courage to speak to Tasha. But then, she seemed in a very dour mood, considering the phenomenal circumstances they were under.

And phenomenal was the word. Jupiter took up half the sky, its massive disk of storm ravished clouds bathing everything in a faint, toxic orange. Ridges broke the surface of the ice and great slabs of it lay like boulders. A few kilometres away, monumental cliffs towered. Everything was still, silent. The only wind Anthony had felt was the thin atmosphere rushing into the ship when the hatch opened. Out here on this desolate, frozen plain, the air, such as it was, was motionless.

Despite Europa's low gravity, the robods' heavy, lead coated bodies prevented Anthony doing the sort of leaps he'd seen Armstrong do on Earth's moon. The slipperiness of the ice would have made such feats of acrobatics dangerous in any event. As it was, the crew quickly learnt the only way of getting about with any dignity was to slide along penguin-like on their bellies.

Steam rose from *The Big Cheesy Dippers* now as the front half of the ship began to melt its way downwards. A thick pipe trailed thirty metres or so from the ship, pumping the melt water away down a gulley in the ice. The rear half of the spaceship had unfolded to release eight gleaming, spider-like legs pushing downwards onto Europa's surface. Two large golden satellite dishes swivelled slowly, tracking Jupiter across the sky, sending countless readings back to Earth. As the front half burrowed, the rear half dropped slowly on its legs, eventually to rest on the surface as the permanent base and communications lifeline back home.

Back home. Anthony would never see home again. The whole mission was scheduled to run out of power in six months time, six short months. He found the thought terrifying, they were all going to die and nobody seemed to care. Marlene said they weren't alive but gee, Anthony certainly felt alive. In a way, more alive than he ever had done.

Damon's voice crackled into his head. *Anthony? Where are you?*

I'm about one-hundred metres north, watching the ship.

Okay, can you come in now, your batteries will begin to run low soon.

Okay, I'm coming in.

Yes, Damon was right. The robods could run for about two hours before they needed to recharge. Anthony lay flat and began to slide back.

"MA'AM, I SEE no need for anyone other than myself to undertake this mission." Martin faced Marlene squarely, hands on hips. Still in their robods in the real ship, he, Marlene, Anthony and Damon had the bridge to themselves.

Marlene stood her ground, determined to get her way. "Martin, might I remind you there is a great potential for traumatic experience in this."

"Ma'am, I am trained for that eventuality…"

"No, you're trained for combat. We're talking about what is a mass grave for two-thousand people. This is not something…"

"Ma'am, will you listen to me…"

Anthony carefully sat on his hands, glowering at Martin. Why couldn't Marlene just leave it? Send the jerk off on his own across the ice and get him out of all their hair. Anthony checked his hands were still firmly pinned by his ass. A spontaneous rude gesture at the GI wouldn't help calm the situation.

Damon intervened. "Martin, it is totally out of the question for you to try this alone. Period. I want a minimum of two people involved."

"Sir, yes sir." Martin turned away from a triumphant Marlene. "Wouldn't Anthony be suitable for the mission? There might be something of scientific interest."

Marlene glowered up at the ceiling incredulously but Damon looked across at Anthony. "Well? Your work is not really going to start here for a few hours yet."

Anthony closed his eyes. A minimum three hour trip with Martin held little appeal. And if Marlene was staying behind, that settled it. "Gee, well Damon, I don't know…"

"Martin, Damon, I must insist on going. I think it important a trained Human Resources Officer is present when we make contact with the source of the distress signal. We do not know what we are going to find."

Damon sighed. "Very well, Martin, Marlene, you will take the rover and locate the source of the beacon."

"Gee, sir." Anthony leapt to his feet. "I guess I'd better go too. The more of Europa we survey, the greater our chances of finding something."

"Okay, all three of you. Hunter?"

Hunter's voice filled the room. "That's my name, don't wear it out."

"Is the rover fit?"

"Fit as she'll ever be. You want her powered up?"

"Right away. Meet Martin, Marlene and Anthony in the rover bay. They're stepping out."

Martin stood, arms folded crossly in front of him, frowning at his feet. "I'll get some equipment and meet you there."

THE ROVER WAS a large, oblong vehicle, standing twice the height of the robods. An image of a long, cheesy string and a smiling child's face dominated the front half, while big red letters spelt out *Big Cheesy Dippers supporting Mission Europa, 2050* on its rear. Four oversized, spiky metal wheels gave it a rather frightening look but would provide good purchase on the ice. In lieu of windows, a camera sprouted from the front, back and each side. Along the sides, between the wheels, a ledge protruded to make a bench large enough for three robods to sit on. Cables at head height could connect any seated robod into the rover's computer and power supply.

Looking up briefly as Anthony and Marlene entered the rover bay, Hunter gestured at the side of the vehicle. "Take yourself a seat."

They sat side by side, Anthony closest to the wheel. Hunter busied himself around Marlene's head, flipping her hair up and connecting wires into a socket there. "Right, you're online."

Marlene nodded. "Okay." In an instant, her robod became a black, metallic android again. She had transferred into the rover's computer. Her voice filled the air. "I'm in."

Hunter turned to Anthony. "Right bud, let's get you done."

"Is that supply properly connected?" Anthony gestured to where the three power cables for the robods erupted from the side of the rover. From where he sat, they looked lose.

"You telling me how to do my job?" Hunter grinned, amiably. "Do I tell you how to look for bugs?"

Anthony held up his hands. "Gee, it just looks a little loose, that's all."

Hunter pulled the cables and they came right out in his hands. "Ah, hell, what do you need it for?"

"But the robod's batteries will run down…"

Hunter sighed. "Kid, I'm fooling you. Don't worry, it would kind of ruin my day if you ran out of power and I had to come get you." He plugged the computer cable into the back of Anthony's head. "You run along inside now and I'll get it all straight."

Behind Anthony, a small hole had opened up into the rover. It wasn't really there of course, just in Anthony's perception now he was connected up. The rover had its own computer, running virtual reality software.

Turning, he slipped through the opening. The virtual inside of the rover was much larger than the outside. A dashboard, steering wheel and driver's seat occupied the very front. Behind this, an aisle separated two columns of six seats each, and at the back lay a small, open space. A large window occupied each of the four walls, corresponding to the four external cameras. It had very much the feeling of being in a small coach. On the side he had just come through, Anthony was relieved to see Hunter connecting the power cable and strapping the two lifeless robods down.

Marlene sat in the driving seat, adjusting the rear-view mirror and Anthony made his way over. "You don't think Martin would want to drive?"

Marlene wrinkled her nose, smiling mischievously. "Humph. I'm driving."

"Ah you sure you want to argue? I mean, the guy is armed and all. Look."

Through the *window* they saw Martin, high energy laser rifle in hands, a laser pistol at his belt. He appeared to be getting into an argument with Hunter.

Marlene snorted. "What is it with this guy?"

"Marlene, he's a professional. Who are we to say there are not hostile, alien snowmen waiting just beyond them there hills?"

"Well, hey, if you put it like that."

They watched in silence as the argument hotted up, unable to hear anything being said.

Anthony stroked his chin. "Are there external microphones?"

"I think so. You want me to turn them on?"

Anthony considered a moment. "No, I kind of like the silent movie thing."

Marlene laughed. A moment later, a black speech bubble

appeared next to Martin's head. It read *I say, you cad, you can jolly well take back what you just said about my uncle.*

Anthony guffawed. "Did you do that?"

Marlene grinned.

"How did you do it?"

The speech bubble faded. "It's a virtual rover, just like the ship. You can do what you want."

Anthony concentrated for a moment and a cartoon chicken flapped over and hovered around Martin's head.

Marlene clapped her hands together. "Excellent."

But the argument seemed to be drawing to a close. Hunter walked towards the rear of the rover and opened a hatch. Martin joined him, stuffing the rifle and his pistol inside. He then sat next to Marlene and Anthony's robods.

"Watch out Marlene, he's coming in."

Marlene leapt up from the driving seat. "He can drive."

"Hey, gee, why the change of heart?"

"The guy's got a gun. He can drive, I get to take in the scenery." She sat directly behind the driving seat and Anthony sat across the aisle.

Martin came in through the side of the virtual rover and looked curtly around. "Good. Both present." He marched to the front of the rover and took the driving seat, flicking a switch on the dashboard. "Hunter, you read me."

Hunter's voice filled the rover. "Yeah, yeah, I got you."

"Hunter, the door."

Anthony concentrated and a pair of furry dice appeared on a short string above Martin's head, out of his field of view. Marlene grinned.

"Marlene, Martin, Anthony." Damon's impossibly deep voice rattled through them. He stood at the side with the robods. "I just wanted to say be careful. Don't take any risks."

"Sir, affirmative, sir."

Ahead of them, the rover bay doors opened revealing a vast canopy of stars, brilliant against the unfathomable blackness of space.

Even Martin paused for breath. "That is certainly something."

After a few moments, Anthony looked back out at Damon. He was preoccupied double checking the robod's straps. He'd have Hunter telling him to stick his job too if he wasn't careful.

Martin cracked his knuckles. "Okay. Let's see what this crate can do."

IT WAS OBVIOUS to Simms that Higgs had no idea of his recent history. He stood uneasily behind the counter, fumbling with the buttons on his waistcoat, an ice-blue silk day cravat tucked in around his thick neck. A more incongruous figure in such a refined boutique was hard to imagine, but there Higgs was, surrounded by small, expensive looking bottles of scent.

Simms had no idea about women's perfumes, what was good, what was bad. All he knew was the stuff made his eyes water as he peeped out through the slits in the locker door. Mandy was not about but had threatened him with a spell in the naughty cupboard should he make any attempt to communicate with Higgs. Anyway, Higgs must have had a considerable amount of his memory erased to believe he was a shop assistant. Muscles bulged through his dapper clothes and Simms felt certain Higgs would split his trousers if he bent down carelessly.

From where he was, Simms could just lean round enough to see the shop's layout. Several chic armchairs surrounded a glass occasional table and everywhere, small bottles perched on pedestals. A glass front led out onto an empty mall but he could not make out any more. If only there was something to write on, he might get a message to Higgs.

A bell jangled and Mandy swept in, jaw working determinedly on her chewing gum. Shorts and t-shirt hugged her figure, a black cow-girl hat sat on top of her blonde mane. In each hand she held what Simms assumed were bags from exclusive, designer outlets. Running her gaze over Higgs, she dumped her shopping to the floor and grinned. "Well, howdy good-looking."

Higgs clasped his hands in front of him, smiling nervously. "Er, ma'am, how can I help you?"

Mandy smirked wickedly at him until he blushed and looked down. She advanced slowly to the counter, leaning on it, looking up coyly. "How old are you boy?"

"Er, sixteen ma'am."

Simms spluttered. Higgs looked across, puzzlement on his face. Mandy touched a finger gently on his cheek, pulling his face back round to look at hers. "Just sixteen. You're a big boy for sixteen. Who'd have thought this was your first job."

"It is my first job, ma'am." Higgs glanced briefly back towards Simms then returned his attention to Mandy. "Ma'am, is there something in particular you were after?"

Mandy let out a dirty laugh. "Well now, let me see." She ran a finger teasingly down his chest. He stared at her, terrified.

"I'll try that one." Mandy nodded at a small, glass bottle on a pedestal at the end of the counter. Higgs scuttled to retrieve it while Mandy traipsed over to one of the chairs and lowered herself regally into it.

Higgs brought the scent over and offered it. Instead of taking it, she held her wrist at the height of his waist. Realising what was expected, Higgs clumsily unscrewed the lid and knelt in front of her. Carefully he sprayed a puff of scent onto Mandy's outstretched arm and she sniffed it gently, never taking her gaze from him.

Simms looked away from the scene for a moment. So Higgs thought he was sixteen. *She* had erased him memory that far back. Why? The disembodied voice Mandy referred to as *ma'am* had inexplicable powers over all their minds but seemingly no understanding. Clearly much of Simms' memory had been erased. He could remember up to the early days of his time as Information Officer aboard the space station *Nice and Spicy Nacho-Niks* but the steps between then and now were shrouded in fog. He knew Lieutenant Higgs of course. Everyone did. Tracy Dwayne Jocelyn Higgs. He was one of Commander Jared's most capable security officers.

"Higgsie, Higgsie, Higgsie." Mandy was talking again. "You been such a naughty boy."

"Ma'am?" Higgs peered cautiously up at Mandy, vulnerable as he knelt before her.

"You been doing some bad things, Higgsie." She crossed her legs, bringing her thigh close to his face. "I do like a man who likes to take risks."

"Ma'am, I do not know what you are talking about."

"Do you like my boots?"

Higgs glanced at her gold embroidered, black leather cowboy boots, chewing his lip. Mandy ran a finger along Higgs' arm. "You can touch them if you like."

Simms looked away again as righteous indignation welled up, tempered slightly by the jealous thought it was not him kneeling before Mandy. Higgs had a sixteen year-old's mind in a twenty-five year-old's body. Mandy really was taking advantage and Simms could not bear to watch. He'd think of some sums again. Calculating Pi ought to keep him occupied. His mathematics teacher had provided twenty-two divided by seven as a rough approximation.

A stream of numbers flooded through Simms' head, three-point-one-four-two-eight-five-seven, then the sequence one-four-two-eight-five-seven over and over, faster and faster until his vision blurred.

"What the...?" Mandy's squawk brought him back to his senses and he pressed his face to the louvers.

Higgs and Mandy both appeared shocked. Higgs stood, carefully placing the scent on a nearby pedestal. "Ma'am, I have no idea what happened just then."

Mandy shot a dark look towards Simms. "I have an idea."

Higgs followed her gaze. "Why is that locker there?"

In a moment, Mandy was between Higgs and Simms. "Higgsie, Higgsie, don't worry. I won't make mention to your boss 'bout what just happened back then."

"Ma'am, whatever happened just now was nothing to do with me. It was like, everything suddenly became grainy. Like we were made up of thousands of little shapes."

"Must've just been something with the lights."

"No ma'am, I looked at my hand. It was made up of little pyramids."

"It's got to be the lights, Higgsie." She moved closer to him, putting a hand on his shoulder. "Now, where were we?"

But Higgs pulled away, a frown on his face. "Ma'am, how do you know my name?"

Simms stuck his fingers through the louvers, wiggling them behind Mandy's back. Higgs glanced up, then back to Mandy.

She seemed momentarily at a loss. "I…we…I guess I must have heard it before, someplace honey."

Higgs stepped back away from her, looking out into the mall. "Why is there nobody else about? The mall should be totally packed out this time of day."

"I guess it's just a quiet morning…"

"No, lady, what is going on here?"

Squeaking angrily, Mandy stamped her foot. "Ah shoot. Show's over. Ma'am?"

Her voice filled the air. "Agent Mandy?"

Higgs started. "What the…?"

"Oh, bow out a second." Mandy clapped her hands and Higgs froze. "Ma'am, what happened just now? It totally ruined everything."

Simms shrank away from the louver door, heart pounding. Now he was done for.

"Agent Mandy, I have many processes to run, with limited resources. I had to make an unexpected calculation."

Hands on hips, Mandy's voice dripped undisguised scorn. "Well that calculation just blew the whole interrogation."

"Agent Mandy, I do not understand the term *blew*."

"Wrecked, spoilt, disrupted. Ma'am, I need proper resources. Why's the mall empty?"

"Agent Mandy, I do not have the resources to people the mall…"

"Ma'am, how will we fool Higgs if I don't have the resources? The security of everyone depends on getting to the bottom of the terrorist insurgency and that means fooling Higgs good and well."

"I understand this, Agent Mandy. I am sorry."

Regaining her composure, Mandy spoke with a more conciliatory tone. "Ma'am, I need more resources. I got to call on you for more, I know it's hard, but it's for the good of all." She glanced across to Simms, hidden in his locker. "Ma'am, it would be good to not have that locker about all the time."

"Agent Mandy, I do not have the resources to put the locker anywhere else."

"Well shoot, can't we just get rid of it altogether?"

"Then terrorist suspect Simms will not be contained."

"Well, he could just, go, couldn't he?"

"Agent Mandy, your earlier report indicated Terrorist Suspect Simms could provide vital information on the terrorist insurgency. It is important you interrogate him further."

"Ah, yeah, yeah. And I will. But after I've finished with Higgs." Turning back to Higgs, Mandy ran a hand lightly across his motionless torso. "Ma'am, we have only one real choice. Sacrifices will need to be made. For the good of all."

JARED SAT CROSS legged on the sand, head close to the pink cloth cat protruding from the partially opened briefcase. Magnus, Darrell and Chelsea stood by, waiting. Karin remained by the palm tree, stroking the conch.

After a few moments, the cat retreated and the briefcase closed. Jared straightened, eyes closed, the gravity of the message sinking in. A few seconds of silence passed.

Magnus crouched down in front of Jared. "Commander? What is it?"

Jared's eyes snapped open and a reassuring smile spread across his face. "Everyone, please sit. I have some good news."

He waited until Magnus, Darrell and Chelsea sat before him, faces relieved and expectant. Over by the tree, Karin giggled and sighed but Jared paid her no heed. "Citizens, our agents are close to a breakthrough, a breakthrough that could see the terrorists defeated once and for all."

He paused for breath, looking at their faces. Disappointment showed but he pressed on. "Once the terrorist threat has been dealt with, *She* will have the resources to make us more comfortable while we wait to be rescued."

Magnus sighed, shaking his head. "This is no news, Commander. I'll tell you what this is. This is the same message, day after day, week after week…"

Jared held up his hand and turned on his voice. "Chief Engineer Magnus Flegg, I have not finished."

Magnus bit his lip, fuming.

Jared hugged the briefcase to his chest. "I am assured by Agent Mandy that *She* is closer than she has ever been. It is a matter of a few more days, that is all. However."

The tone in Jared's voice made the others look up at him attentively. He continued. "However, *She* needs more resources, which means we cannot all be supported any longer. This is hard, this is difficult, but for the good of the whole, one of you must cease to exist."

Magnus thumped the sand. "Jesus, not again. Why does *She* need more resources? And what is it Agent Mandy is doing in there?"

"I'm afraid for your security and wellbeing, that information is classified. I've given this some thought and I think the way forward is for each of you to justify to me why you should continue to exist."

Darrell gaped. "Wha…Sir, what! Sir!"

Jared held up his palms. "I'm sorry, but I cannot see another way to decide."

Magnus ran his hand through his copper mop of hair. "Sorry, Commander, *we* have to justify ourselves to you? What about *you* justifying your position to us?"

Chelsea put a hand up. "Ah, excuse me, Magnus. I don't think there's any need for our Commander to justify his position."

"Why not?"

"It goes without saying, we need our Commander. Don't you agree Darrell?" Darrell looked sideways at Chelsea, smiled and nodded.

Magnus opened and closed his mouth a few times, realising the trap he was in. Chelsea continued in smooth, calm tones. "I will go first. When I took my oath of allegiance, I promised I would do my duty for my fellow citizens, up to and including laying down my life. And I am ready to make good of that oath. But we are in dangerous times, when there are terrorists ready to destroy the freedoms we have come to cherish. I am a security officer. I am trained to use force when necessary. I can defend the survivors on this island from a terrorist attack. If I am gone, I can't do that. So, while I'm willing to lay my life down, I put it to you, you'd all be safer if I am here to protect you. Thank you."

Jared nodded. "Thank you Security Officer Day. Security Officer Greally?"

"Sir, I can defend the survivors here too, sir. Just like Chelsea, sir."

Jared nodded. "Any more?"

"Sir, no, sir."

"Chief Engineer Magnus Flegg?"

"Commander, I am not happy with this. This is…" Magnus flailed his arms for the right word. "This is madness. It's a psychotic version of *The Balloon Game*. There must be some other way."

"My decision on this is final. Chief Engineer Magnus Flegg, please justify to me why you should continue to exist."

"What about Karin?" Magnus gestured with his thumb over his shoulder. "What about her? Hell, I doubt she'd even notice."

Jared sighed. "Magnus, you are responsible for justifying yourself, Karin is responsible for justifying herself. We will get on to Karin in a few moments."

Magnus considered a moment and a knowing half-smile crept across his face. "Ah, I follow you."

"Chief Engineer Magnus Flegg there is nothing to follow."

"Hey, of course not. No."

"Please justify yourself."

"Okay, I'm vital to the maintenance of hardware, power supplies, infrastructure, you name it. If I'm not here, and anything breaks down, there will be nobody to fix it."

Jared looked at him expectantly for more.

Magnus shrugged. "That's all. Let's move on to Karin shall we?" He swivelled on his backside to face Karin. "Oh, Karin. Hello."

Jared coughed and cracked his knuckles. "Citizens, I have made my decision."

Magnus spun back round. "What? But Karin hasn't justified herself yet."

"Citizen Karin Mist is clearly in a vulnerable emotional state and unable to defend herself."

"But it's not fair if she doesn't justify herself too."

"I will speak for Citizen Karin. She is our most needy survivor and it is not the American way to turn its back on the needy. Furthermore, her complete lack of activity means her resources footprint is considerably smaller than that of the rest of us. So, Chief Engineer Magnus Flegg…"

"What!"

"…I regret to say that of all of us, you provide the least useful contribution towards the survival of the whole."

"But…"

"We have no hardware or equipment, nothing that would require your admittedly superior skills to repair. I regret to say, and it is with heavy heart I say this…"

"No…" Magnus leapt to his feet. "You're not killing me, you bastard."

"That I choose you to make this sacrifice."

A silence followed as the gentle breeze blew sand into the hollows left by the vanished Magnus' feet. Karin sighed happily.

Chelsea cleared her throat. "I spy, anyone?"

SHATTERED MOUNDS OF ice glinted in the rover's headlights as it crawled across the plain. Jupiter sank towards the horizon, ushering in what would no doubt be a very black night. The sun, some eight-hundred million kilometres away, appeared only as an exceptionally bright star and provided little light.

Anthony, Marlene and Martin sat in silence, watching through the *windows* as the shadows spread. The journey had taken an hour so far and as they neared their destination, so apprehension grew.

Taking his gaze from the frozen landscape, Anthony glanced at Marlene. Knees tucked up under her chin, she frowned out the *window* on her side. He looked at the enticing lines of her neck and sighed. Hearing the noise, she glanced over. "What is it?"

"Er, oh, nothing." He gestured out of the *window*. "It's breathtaking, isn't it?"

She smiled weakly, nodded and returned her attention to the wilderness outside. Anthony stared at her for a long time, wrestling with his longing. Realising once again he was touching himself, he clasped his hands together. It was always his right hand that started playing up he noticed.

Martin tapped an instrument on the dashboard and spoke. "I think we're getting near."

Anthony looked over. Martin unknowingly sat beneath two sets of furry dice, a cartoon chicken on a spring, a wide-eyed smiling monkey toy and a pair of ballet shoes. The last addition had been Marlene's and although Anthony pretended to chuckle, he hadn't actually understood the reference. He exchanged a glance with Marlene and nodded at the ornaments above Martin's head. She nodded back and one by one, the items suspended there disappeared.

Oblivious, Martin continued. "Looks like some of the debris coming up. I'll report back." He flicked a switch. "This is the rover calling home base, do you read me?"

Hunter's voice answered, crackling slightly. "I read you but there's interference. Probably radio waves coming off Jupiter."

"Okay. We're approaching target."

Damon's voice came on. "Martin, this is Damon. Can you turn on the visuals?"

"Sir, yes sir." Martin flicked another switch.

Damon answered. "Okay, got them."

Anthony and Marlene crowded behind Martin, peering out into the growing gloom. The rover shook suddenly as it ran over a small crater. Anthony caught Marlene as she fell.

"Whoah, sorry guys." Martin reduced the speed. "I didn't see that one."

Marlene coughed politely. "Anthony."

"Yes?"

"You can let go of me now."

"Oh, yes, of course, sorry."

The rover suddenly lurched to a halt, throwing Anthony and Marlene forward. Anthony crossly hauled himself upright. "Gee Martin, that was sudden."

"Sir, I had no choice. Look."

Before them, the ground sloped abruptly downwards, out of the beam of the headlights and into darkness.

Martin reached for the camera joystick control, angling the view through the *window* as far down as possible but to no avail. Whatever lay beyond the edge remained hidden. "Sir, Damon, sir, I think this must be the impact crater. The distress signal is dead ahead." He turned to face Anthony. "I'm going to have to get out and take a look before we can proceed."

"Okay. Fine by me."

Marlene strode purposefully to the side of the rover with the robods. "I'm coming too."

"Ma'am, there's no need." Martin got up and barged past Anthony after Marlene.

Annoyance flickered in Anthony as he stood. "Martin, there's no harm in us all going. I want to see this too."

Martin glanced back at Anthony and did a double take. He

stopped, turning slowly and purposefully, hands on hips, face tight with repressed anger. "Sir, do you have an issue?"

Uncertain, Anthony backed away. "Gee, Martin, what's up?"

Marlene peered over Martin's shoulder. "Er, Anthony, you seem to be giving Martin the finger."

Anthony glanced down and, to his horror, saw his right hand sticking its middle finger up at Martin. Quickly, he swept it behind his back. "I'm sorry, look I'm sorry. I keep going wrong, doing weird things."

Martin crossed his arms. "What sort of weird things?"

"Well, like that, sticking my finger up."

Marlene nodded. "It's true Anthony. You do keep doing weird things."

"Gee, I can't help it. There's something wrong with my software. It's like I think of something and my right hand just goes and does it, without exercising any restraint."

Martin curled his lip. "So you only thought about giving me the finger."

"Yes. Gee, no, no. I…look, I'm sorry, okay. I need to get myself fixed."

"Damn right you do. Talk to Tasha and get it sorted out." Martin turned away contemptuously. "And get her to sort out that shit on your face while she's at it. It looks gross."

Martin barged passed Marlene to the side of the rover and began checking the robods. Anthony plastered his fingers to his cheeks, feeling the acne there. He gaped at Marlene. "You can see it?"

"What?"

"The acne?"

"Well, yeah. I mean, it's kinda hard to miss."

"But nobody said anything."

"I didn't like to. You know, it would be bit rude."

"But I was on the TV in front of billions. With a face full of puss."

Marlene laughed. "Think of all the spotty adolescent guys who'll be grateful to you for it."

"Damn it Marlene, this is no laughing matter. I look gross."

"Well why don't you just will it away then?"

"I can't. Like I say, I keep going wrong."

Martin butted in. "You're not the only thing. Hunter, you read me?"

Hunter's voice filled the rover again. "I read you."

"These robods have not been connected properly to the power supply."

"I connected those babies myself."

"Well, they're not connected now and their batteries are all down to next to no power."

"What?"

"You don't believe me, check the reading yourself remotely."

A moment's silence followed. When Hunter finally spoke, his voice was subdued. "Yeah, you're right. I don't know what's happened there. The cables must have worked loose."

Martin thumped the side of the rover crossly. "Sir, making a mistake is one thing. Not having the courage to admit to that mistake is detrimental to the team effort."

Damon's rumbling baritone filled the rover. "Martin, this is not the time to review this. How much power is left in the batteries?"

Martin sighed. "Sir, they're all out except one which has about three minutes, sir."

"Okay, that's long enough to reconnect the robods to the supply. The power cables can extend thirty meters from the rover, you'll just have to keep connected. This is not a crisis."

A small hole opened in the side of the rover and Martin slipped through. Beyond the *window*, one of the robods jerked into life, taking on Martin's appearance. Quickly, he reconnected the power supplies.

Anthony glanced sideways at Marlene. She shrugged at him, walked to the side of the rover and slipped through. Quickly, Anthony followed, occupying the remaining robod. He now sat outside on the ledge, on the side of the rover, a restraining strap across his lap. The power cable, as thick as his thumb, made its way into the back of his head. He fiddled with it briefly, expecting a feeling of discomfort but could hardly feel anything there at all.

It was now very gloomy, the only proper light coming from the rover's headlights but this was directed forwards. Marlene sat to Anthony's left, undoing the strap across her lap. Martin slid up from the back of the rover on his belly, pushing a flashlight and the laser rifle before him. He barked up at Marlene. "Stay in position until I've secured the area."

"Martin, give it a rest." She clambered from the rover and onto the ice, sliding towards the slope, power cable stretching out behind her. Realising she might get there first, Martin thrust himself forwards, his cable flapping wildly.

Anthony snorted and glanced to his left, where the cables emerged from the side of the rover. He could just pull Martin's cable out. That would shut him up. In a moment of panic, he grabbed his right hand with his left. He needed to watch careless thoughts like that, his right hand had a bit of a mind of its own.

Satisfied he was not about to power-down Martin, Anthony slid onto the ice and pushed himself over to join the others at the edge of the slope. Martin shone his flashlight downwards, revealing the gradient to be steep but manageable. "My guess is it's the side of an impact crater. This area is going to be covered with them. We'll need to proceed with caution."

Anthony peered towards what he assumed to be the centre of the crater. Something off to the left caught his eye but when he turned his head it was gone.

Martin got to his knees. "Okay, let's get back in the rover and advance."

Anthony was about to follow him when he saw it, a brief, faint pinpoint of red light, flashing on for a split second. "Wait, there's something out there."

MANDY HELD THE lilac cocktail dress against herself, glowering at her reflection. It seemed an odd match to the black cow-girl outfit she currently wore but Simms, watching as ever from his locker, assumed even Mandy wouldn't try to wear both at the same time.

She stamped her foot angrily and flung the dress to the floor. "Ma'am, the colours are just so wrong."

Her voice filled the air. "Agent Mandy, I have constructed the colours as best I can from the memory files available."

"Well, you haven't got it right, have you?" Mandy swept the dress from the floor again. "Look at it, look." She held the dress up momentarily, then ripped it in two, flinging the pieces once more to the floor. "Trash."

Simms held his breath. He'd never seen Mandy throw a tantrum like this or heard the disembodied voice sound so obsequious. Through the louvers, he saw an opulent hotel room, with panoramic views of what seemed to be New York. Mandy stood before a huge mirror, its ornately carved, gilded frame all leaves and grapes. Beneath stood three antique sideboards, each with a brass statuette of the Buddha. A huge, circular bed on a raised dais dominated the centre of the room.

She spoke again, an unmistakably defensive whine to her voice. "Agent Mandy, I am constructing the best fashion accessories my circuitry is capable of."

"Well, they plain aren't good enough. I need more resources."

"Agent Mandy, the other survivors are now down to the bare minimum…"

"Then they'll have to make sacrifices." Mandy's shriek was piercing. Grabbing a Buddha, she stepped back and hurled the hapless deity at the mirror, shattering it. Shards of glass tumbled down, wrecking the sideboards and shredding the carpet.

"Agent Mandy, I…I do not understand this behaviour…"

Mandy covered her face, pretending to sob. "Oh ma'am, I'm

so stressed. I've been working so hard, I swear it's taking such a toll on me."

"Agent Mandy, I had no idea."

"I need some leisure time. Or, I swear, I'm just going to crack up."

"Agent Mandy, you are in no danger of developing cracks."

"No, Ma'am, I mean loose my mind, go mad."

The broken glass on the floor faded and vanished. The mirror became whole again. Simms saw nothing remarkable in this, used as he now was to caverns, boutiques, hotel rooms and shops materialising and dematerialising. Wherever he was, it was clearly not in the normal universe. Perhaps he had died and gone to hell, to be forever confined in a small, uncomfortable locker watching Mandy try to seduce Higgs.

"Ma'am, I need a massage."

"Agent Mandy, I am not able to provide…"

"But Higgs is. How's he doing in the naughty cupboard? Let's get him out and see if he'll behave."

Simms pressed his face to the louvers, straining to see. The small black box Mandy called the naughty cupboard was by the door. Higgs, at a point in his late teens when he worked as a personal trainer, had gone back in there again after being disrespectful to Mandy. Now, the naughty cupboard stretched, its side bulging out as a miniature Higgs oozed out through the wall, growing as he tumbled to the floor. It was a disturbing, unpleasant spectacle to watch. But Simms watched anyway.

Naked, Higgs knelt, his breath coming in short, pained gasps. After a moment, he seemed to focus on the floor and began running his fingers through the fibres of the carpet.

Mandy walked over and stood before him, legs apart, hands on hips. "Well howdy Higgsie, my li'l' possum. Have we learnt our lesson?"

Higgs stopped stroking carpet and slowly looked up. His face was dark with hatred but Simms thought he saw fear there too.

Mandy put one black-booted foot up on Higgs' shoulder and leant on her knee. "Well? Are you gonna behave for me?"

He looked down.

"Well? I'll put you right back in that there naughty cupboard if you ain't gonna behave for me. You gonna behave now?"

Higgs nodded weakly.

"Sorry Higgsie, I can't hear you?"

Higgs whispered. "Yes."

"Yes what?"

"Yes, I'm going to behave."

"You gonna call me mistress, Higgsie. Go on, say it. Yes, I'm going to behave, mistress." She pushed down with her foot, forcing Higgs' face to the ground. "Go on."

Higgs' voice was hardly audible. "Yes, I'm going to behave, mistress."

Mandy laughed. "Yeah, that's a good boy." She took her foot from his shoulder and placed it a few inches from his face. "Kiss my boot. Go on."

Slowly, Higgs put his face over and kissed Mandy's foot.

Simms realised he was holding his breath and let it out. The smell made him jerk his head back. He had never realised quite how bad his halitosis was until this confinement. Once out of this situation, he would seek treatment. It was hardly surprising nobody wished to talk to him if every word he uttered made their eyes water.

Turning away from the louvers, he rested his head against the side of the locker and closed his eyes. Would he ever get out of here? He was simply forgotten. The story of his life really, a little, insignificant bureaucrat that everyone wanted to forget.

"Mistress, you are the most beautiful woman I've ever seen in my life." Higgs' unhappy shout brought him back from his misery.

Simms knew Mandy Pollins from their days on *The Nice and Spicy Nacho-Niks*. As long as he could remember, his overwhelming crush on her had been tempered by the notion she was too good for him. She had always seemed so effortlessly female, charged with an irresistible sexuality, the absolute embodiment of blonde-bombshell fantasy. And she had always, always been after Higgs, who had absolutely no interest in her.

Now, for the first time in a life plagued with self-doubt and low esteem, Simms had found someone he genuinely felt superior too. Simms knew he was ugly, his breath smelt and he was boring...and he was weak-willed, cowardly, not particularly bright and people seemed to find him irritating...yes, he knew all these things...and spit tended to accumulate at the sides of his mouth...yes, he knew. But, for all his faults, he tried to be kind-hearted, tried to do the right thing, to do the best for people. For all her physical perfection, Mandy was ugly, vile, self-seeking and dangerously deranged.

She is not good enough for me.

It was a thoroughly liberating thought. Smiling, Simms whispered the words to himself. "She is not good enough for me."

It would make no difference, of course. He knew that. For all his kind heart and good intentions, people would still avoid him and flock to Mandy. Good looks would always count for more than a good heart.

He peeped out through the louvers again. Mandy now lay on the bed, naked. Higgs knelt beside her, despair on his face, oil on his hands as he gently massaged her back. Simms stuck his fingers through the louvers and wiggled them, hoping Higgs might notice but he didn't.

Simms decided it was time to spoil the party. He'd been thinking about Pi. The school room approximation of twenty-two divided by seven had caused *Her* to blip for a moment. But twenty-two divided by seven was not even close. How to calculate Pi had taxed mathematicians for centuries but, oddly, Simms somehow knew David and Gregory Chudnovsky, the Chudnovsky brothers famous from the beginning of the century, had found a calculation for Pi to billions of decimal places. Simms could picture the calculation, although he had no idea what it meant. But, somehow, he knew if he concentrated on it, he would start to an endless stream of number, the beautiful infinity of Pi.

He held his breath and concentrated:

$$\frac{1}{\pi} = 12 \sum_{k=0}^{\infty} \frac{(-1)^k (6k)!(13591409 + 545140134k)}{(3k)!(k!)^3 640320^{3k+3/2}}$$

For a few moments, everything, including Simms, froze. The calculations rattled through his head, notching up the decimal places, one-hundred million, two-hundred million, three-hundred million. With one stream of numbers running through his head, he thought again:

$$\frac{1}{\pi} = 12 \sum_{k=0}^{\infty} \frac{(-1)^k (6k)!(13591409 + 545140134k)}{(3k)!(k!)^3 640320^{3k+3/2}}$$

A parallel infinity opened up in his head. Perhaps once more for good measure?

$$\frac{1}{\pi} = 12 \sum_{k=0}^{\infty} \frac{(-1)^k (6k)!(13591409 + 545140134k)}{(3k)!(k!)^3 640320^{3k+3/2}}$$

The whole room, Simms, Higgs and Mandy suddenly became crudely constructed images, made up of tiny polygons. Then, everything returned to normal.

Mandy leapt up from the bed, furious. "Ma'am, what is going on?"

Higgs cowered beside her, covering his head. "Mistress, it's not me, mistress."

She slapped him. "Button it, worm. Ma'am?"

She spoke, uncertainly, her voice slow. "Agent Mandy, I am very low on resources. It takes a great deal of power to maintain the intricacies of this room."

"So? Get some resources, I'm busy."

$$\frac{1}{\pi} = 12 \sum_{k=0}^{\infty} \frac{(-1)^k (6k)!(13591409 + 545140134k)}{(3k)!(k!)^3 640320^{3k+3/2}}$$

$$\frac{1}{\pi} = 12 \sum_{k=0}^{\infty} \frac{(-1)^k (6k)!(13591409 + 545140134k)}{(3k)!(k!)^3 640320^{3k+3/2}}$$

$$\frac{1}{\pi} = 12 \sum_{k=0}^{\infty} \frac{(-1)^k (6k)!(13591409 + 545140134k)}{(3k)!(k!)^3 640320^{3k+3/2}}$$

Once again, everything stuttered.

"Ma'am." Mandy stamped her foot, shrieking. "Ma'am, I want more resources. Now!"

JARED AND CHELSEA sat together on the beach, watching the briefcase as it shook. It was just the two of them now. Karin had been next to go after Magnus. When the last demand for more sacrifice had come, Darrell had tried to attack the briefcase with the conch shell but his violence did him no good. A hard decision had to be made, Chelsea was a woman and Jared had the notion of women and children first ingrained into his psyche.

The palm tree had gone and the island was now only five meters across. No breeze blew and the waves were on a short, repeating loop. The sand had been replaced with a solid, yellow concrete.

The briefcase clicked and the pink cloth cat emerged, held by a woman's hand. Jared leant close, listening for a few moments. The cat retreated, the briefcase closed and he straightened, turning to Chelsea. "Okay then. Best of three."

She nodded and they both put their right hands behind their backs.

Jared cleared his throat. "One, two, three."

Both brought their hands out, Chelsea making a stone with her fist, Jared making scissors with his fingers.

Chelsea nodded. "First round to me."

They returned their hands behind their backs and Jared counted again. "One, two three."

This time, Jared chose scissors and Chelsea paper.

"Okay, one all. One, two, three."

Jared paper, Chelsea scissors. She punched the air. "Yes!"

And then, she vanished.

Breathing out heavily, Jared wiped the back of his hand across his eyes. That had not been fair of him but he had the power to decide and a stark choice to make, him or her. If their positions had been reversed, she would no doubt have done the same to him. Chelsea had been a good member of the crew. He would make sure her family knew of her bravery and self-sacrifice.

MARTIN BROUGHT THE rover to a halt, its headlights framing the metal hulk at the edge of the crater. It had an outer layer of battered, blackened metal but at the side facing them, a panel had been ejected to reveal an undamaged interior surface. From this an antennae protruded. At the base of the antennae, a red light flashed every ten seconds or so and it was possible to make out white lettering. The whole thing was about twice the size of the rover.

Marlene scowled at it through the front *window*. "I guess this is the source of the signal."

Martin tutted. "Ma'am, you'd have to get up pretty early in the morning to catch you out." He stood from the driver's seat. "My guess is it's the *Nice and Spicy's* black box recorder. I'll go out and connect it up to the rover and we can see what it says."

While Martin got out of the rover and into his robod, Marlene sat in the driver's seat.

Anthony hovered behind her. "There's that old joke, isn't there? Why don't they make the whole spaceship out of the stuff they make the black box recorder out of?"

Marlene glanced up at him, frowning. "Anthony, this isn't the time."

"Sorry."

Martin walked up to the black box, power cable trailing from the back of his head, communications cable in his hand. His laser rifle was slung over his shoulder.

Anthony looked down at the array of controls on the dashboard. Meters and controls were present for every aspect of the rover, including the robods. Martin's completely flat batteries made him totally dependent on the rover for power and Anthony noted he could turn the supply off from the dashboard. He clasped his hands firmly together behind his back.

At the black box, Martin paused over the writing. "Yeah, it's the *Nice and Spicy*, okay."

Damon's voice filled the rover. "Is there anything else? Any message? Any indication of life?"

"Sir, no, it's just identification numbers, sir. Sir, I'm going to connect her up to the rover and download, sir."

"Okay, Martin."

Marlene spoke. "Can you hold, Martin, I just want to make sure there's a secure area in the rover."

"Ma'am, that won't be necessary."

"Martin, will you hold a second. We do not know what's in the black box."

"Ma'am, it's a black box, what can possibly…"

Marlene flicked a switch, cutting Martin's voice off. "I swear that man is going to drive me nuts." She began fiddling with some of the controls.

Anthony leant forward, supporting himself with his hand on the dashboard. "What are you planning to do?"

"I just want to make sure any AI software that comes out of the box is isolated in case it's corrupted. It's crash landed and been frozen for eight years." She looked towards the back of the rover. "There, it's done."

In the space at the rear of the vehicle, a shimmering, transparent green cube had appeared, large enough to comfortably hold several people. Marlene gestured towards it with her thumb. "Now, when we take the contents of the black box, it will be isolated within that firewall."

Martin had connected the cable and waved furiously, trying to get their attention. Marlene flipped the communications switch again. "Sorry Martin, lost you there a minute."

"Ma'am, what in the name of heck are you playing at?"

"I'm downloading the black box now. Hey, it's trying to force its way in on an old security channel." Marlene poked a few more controls. "There, that's stopped it."

"Ma'am, don't you ignore me."

"Martin, will you shut up. I'm trying to do a job here."

"Ma'am, I'm not letting this one go by. You deliberately cut me off…"

Martin suddenly became motionless, stopping mid-sentence. A moment later, he became a black, featureless robod. Marlene and Anthony stared, unsure of what just happened. Marlene glanced down at the dashboard. "His power, he's been disconnected."

Anthony's heart pounded as he looked at his right hand. It hung, all innocent, by his side but he was close to the controls.

Becoming frantic, Marlene jabbed at the dashboard, reconnecting the power but the robod remained a blank android. "Martin? Martin, do you read me? Shit."

"Damon?" Anthony edged back from the dashboard nervously. "Damon, I think we've lost Martin. We lost power to his robod." Surely Anthony couldn't have punched the control? He was certainly thinking it, Martin was such a jerk.

Marlene slapped the steering wheel. "Shit, he's gone. He's dead."

Damon answered. "Okay, okay, now calm down. He's not dead. We have a backup file, we'll bring him back. None of us can die, remember that. Marlene, you have a job to do. What is in the black box?"

Flipping the communications switch to off, Marlene looked up suspiciously at Anthony. "What have you done?"

"Gee, Marlene, I didn't do anything. I was nowhere near the controls."

"You were right by them."

"I didn't touch them."

"You must have done, without realising. You know, like you're always doing weird stuff, you said so yourself."

"No, I didn't, I swear. It's my right arm that goes wrong and I was hanging onto it."

"Yeah, right."

"Anyway, you heard Damon. Martin's not dead, Tasha will just bring him back."

Marlene sagged back in her seat, shaking her head. For a few moments they sat in silence. Then, a polite cough came from the rear of the ship. Spinning round, they saw a middle-aged man standing in the green box. He wore a black jumpsuit and had a black briefcase chained to his wrist.

Without smiling, he fixed Anthony firmly in the eye and spoke in a clear, commanding voice. "I am Commander Demetrius Alexander Jared of the Space Station *The Nice and Spicy Nacho-Niks*. Take me to your leader."

WITH SOME EFFORT, Anthony hoisted the lifeless robod, formerly Martin, up onto the side of the rover. Getting the robod to the vehicle had not presented a problem because it just slid over the ice. However, trying to haul the rigid robod up on the ledge while standing on the slippery moon proved almost impossible. Eventually, Anthony used the robod's power lead as a tether, wrapping it around the lifeless droid to secure it. But it would only be safe on the rover if it sat properly and that meant bending the arms, legs and hips. Wondering what to do, Anthony recalled Hunter checking the robods in the robod bay. If Anthony had some sort of prod, maybe he could make the arms move. Peering closely at the knee joint, he saw a small, grey button on the inside of the leg. He pressed it and found the joint went loose as long as the button was pushed in.

"Oh gee, a manual override."

There were grey buttons at every joint and he soon had the robod sitting properly. He slid back across the ice for the laser rifle and the flashlight. Taking these to the rear of the rover, he opened the trunk and stowed the flashlight there but a childish whim made him hold on to the gun. It was lighter than he expected and there was something exciting about it. Glancing up to check the rover's camera could not see him, he held the weapon to his shoulder, finger on the trigger, looking along the barrel. A device on the top appeared to be the sight, although he could not see through it. Fiddling with it, he found a switch. He flicked this and the sight powered up, a small screen appearing in the part he thought he would look through.

He pointed the rifle out into the darkness and, although he could see nothing out there, the screen showed an infrared picture of the ice.

"Oh, cool."

Cool? Lowering the rifle, he scolded himself. He was regressing again. Cool! What a childish thing to think. Still, he could fire off just one quick shot couldn't he? Nobody would notice. Marlene would still be running checks on Jared and, hopefully, getting him to say a little more. The guy just refused to speak beyond stating his name and demanding to see a senior officer.

Holding the rifle back up to his shoulder, Anthony scanned the horizon until he found a distant stack of ice. Yes, that would do. He lined the small crosshairs at the centre of the screen up and gently squeezed the trigger. The ice-stack shattered and collapsed.

Lowering the gun, Anthony felt a little disappointed. There had been no noise, although as the thin atmosphere was close to a vacuum, this was hardly surprising. He had expected some recoil but realised now, of course, a laser rifle was not firing a projectile, just a beam of energy. A nasty little internal voice wondered how long that ice-stack had stood, beautiful and unsullied by man. Feeling sheepish, he shut the gun away in the trunk and slid back to the side of the rover.

Climbing up onto the ledge, he secured the strap across his lap. He double-checked the power cables were secured for all three robods and slipped back into the rover's virtual reality.

Marlene perched on one of the seats close to Jared. She looked over as Anthony came in. "Everything stowed away?"

Anthony nodded, making his way to them. "How are things going?"

She clasped her hands in front of her, smiling diplomatically. "We've established who we are and I see no sign of any life threatening trauma. But we are still being less than communicative."

Jared sat cross legged on the floor, hugging the briefcase to his chest.

Anthony addressed him. "Gee, sir, you're going to have to tell us what happened eventually."

Jared shook his head. "I'm sorry Anthony, I can say nothing. It is of vital importance I speak in private to a senior security officer."

Anthony turned back to Marlene. "What does Damon think? Damon?"

There was no response but Marlene leapt to her feet. "Damn, I turned the comms off." She trotted to the front of the rover and flicked the communications switch back on. "Damon, do you read me?"

Damon's voice filled the room. "Marlene, thank God. We thought we'd lost you."

"No, we're here. The comms switch must have got knocked off or something."

"Okay, okay. Not a crisis. What was in the black box?"

"Hold on." She punched some controls on the dashboard and the green box turned amber. When she spoke, her voice was lowered. "There's a survivor, Commander Demetrius Alexander Jared. He won't speak to us other than to say his name and to demand we get him to a senior security officer. He's got a briefcase with him, probably containing the main black box files, but he won't tell us for certain."

There was a pause before Damon spoke. "Has he said anything about finding life?"

"Sorry, Damon? I don't understand. He's been in the black box for eight years."

"This is not a crisis. Not a crisis." Damon's voice trailed off, seemingly lost for a moment, Then he rallied. "I don't want you to talk to him, do you understand. Just explain you're bringing him back to base then isolate him. I'll talk to him when he's here."

Marlene shrugged. "Okay Damon. You're the boss."

ANTHONY HAPPILY LET Marlene take the wheel. It wasn't an issue as he had never particularly enjoyed driving. He owned a gas-guzzling sports car, bought on something of a whim after a commercial featuring *lantern-jawed guy* driving *perfect blonde woman* around the narrow, empty roads of the Swiss Alps. Of course, Anthony's car spent most of its time in the garage and on the rare occasions he took it out for a spin, the endless, choking traffic jams of his home town would have made even *lantern-jaw* get out and walk. While the car did make a few girls heads turn when Anthony parked up, they usually frowned and looked away when he got out.

Outside the rover, night had settled in with an inky determination. Although the rover's headlights illuminated their path, it hid the brilliant stars. Jared remained entombed in the amber cube at the back of the vehicle. He could see out but Marlene explained the amber colour meant Jared couldn't hear. It was possible to completely isolate him, whereupon the box would turn red.

"I feel bad about Martin."

Marlene glanced across at Anthony. "Hey, it can't be helped. Like Damon said, they'll bring him back."

Anthony grinned. "Yeah, that's what I feel bad about. No, just joking."

"The guy is a jerk. He just wants to fight everyone. I felt bad when I thought he'd died though."

"I guess he did die in a way. Gee, what is alive anyway?"

"None of us are alive."

"It feels like we are though. We touch things, we get angry, upset. That version of Martin is a different version from the backup."

"True."

"So, all the memories the ex-Martin had since waking up on

the *Cheesy Dippers* will be lost."

"Well, true."

"So, the backup is a completey different Martin. The ex-Martin is just that, ex. The new Martin won't know I stuck my finger up at him, won't have argued with you and Hunter."

"Bet your life, he'll still be just as much a jerk though."

"Whatever, he's dead, Marlene. Dead. And we are going to be dead in six months time."

Marlene shook her head. "Anthony, please. We're not alive."

"Well I feel alive. Don't you feel alive? You'd be happy just to be switched off now, would you?"

Marlene chewed her lip for a few moments. "I don't know. Yes, I feel I am alive. But I just keep it in my head that I'm not. You know, the real me is back on Earth, with my man, following the progress of the mission. I've probably seen myself on the TV, when we were all interviewed when we landed. It must be a bit weird."

"Okay, but gee, Marlene, you didn't answer my question there. Are you happy to be switched off now?"

"No."

"No, neither am I. I don't want to be switched off at all. I'm not ready to die."

"I keep telling you, you're not alive."

"What do you think it will feel like when we get switched off?"

"Well, nothing."

"So it's just wham, bam, goodbye ma'am and nothing beyond."

"If you want to put it like that, I guess so."

"No different from when the real me dies, I suppose."

"Yes, it is different." Marlene seemed suddenly shy.

"What do you mean?"

"Well, when a real person passes on, they have a spirit…" She blushed slightly. "And you go before the Divinity and he takes you into the Everlasting Beyond of Eternal Happiness."

Anthony knew this ICRT teaching from his childhood. "I don't know about all that, Marlene. I used to believe but I don't know now."

"Well I do. It doesn't make any sense that everything just

magically evolved from nothing. There's got to be a driving force."

"What happens if we find life here?"

"I don't think that really matters. The ICRT guys will find an explanation. Do you really think all this…" She waved her arms at the passing scenery. "…all this just came about by chance?"

Anthony breathed out heavily. "I don't know. But if there is a Divinity, you're saying he has no concern for us here."

"No, I didn't say that."

"You did. When we get switched off, us here, you and me now, when we go, we're gone. We don't go to the Everlasting Beyond of Eternal Happiness."

"I…No, the Divinity loves us."

"But not the *us* here. We are just computer programs, we have no souls."

"That's right, we have no souls…"

"So we are beyond the Divinity's love."

Marlene shook her head, brow furrowed, an edge creeping into her voice. "No, no, you've got it wrong. The Divinity loves us. We're not alive, you just think you're alive but you are not. We're just in a computer."

"Well, what is alive then? What about the clones? I've got mind scans back home and stem cells in a tissue bank. If I'm killed, the Renenkya Corporation will have a clone made and implant my mind scan onto its blank brain. Will that *me* be alive? Will it have a soul?"

"Yes."

"Why?"

"Because it's flesh and blood. There's a difference." Marlene slapped the steering wheel in frustration.

"So, to have a soul you have to be biological?"

"You have to be real."

"But I am real, now."

"No, you are not."

A long silence passed. The temperature of the debate had risen beyond Anthony's expectation. "I'm sorry Marlene, I'm just confused by all this. I did believe in it all once but it's so hard to make sense of anything now. I'm afraid. I don't want to die."

Marlene shook her head, sending her glossy-black hair swirling around her neck. "Forget about it. Here, have some." She dug her hand into the pocket of her jumpsuit and pulled out a half-eaten bar of chocolate. Regarding it for a moment, she willed it to become whole again and offered it to him. "This always makes me feel better."

Anthony gaped at it. "Marlene, that's illegal."

"Well, it's a silly law." She bit of a square and offered the bar to him again. "Go on, have a piece."

"Ah, gee, I don't know. I mean, how could you? It's illegal and all. Surely you shouldn't be eating this if you believe?"

Her brow furrowed and she stuffed the bar away. "Why? There's nothing in the ICRT about chocolate. It's just stupid busy-bodies who want to stop people having fun."

Anthony grinned. "Hey, well, isn't that just the same as the ICRT?"

THE LIGHTS WERE low. A single, red candle stood in the centre of the table, flickering in the gentle breeze from the adjacent, open window. The wine glasses and cutlery glinted in the candlelight as the sound of gulls and French accordion music drifted in. Outside, the stars twinkled, scattered around a bright, crescent moon.

Mandy leant back in her chair, sighing deeply and savouring the deep red Burgundy in her glass. Wearing an elegant evening dress, stockings and heels, she looked every inch a man-eater. In a high-chair opposite perched Penelope, the pink cloth cat. A glass of wine had been poured for her but she had yet to touch it.

Watching through his louvers, Simms tried to remember when he last drank something. A glass of red held great appeal. Whatever else he might think of Mandy at the moment, he approved of her choice of restaurant. The other tables were, of course, empty.

Higgs came into Simms' field of view, dressed immodestly in just an apron and neck tie, his powerful, muscled buttocks on full display. He carefully placed a plate down in front of both Mandy and Penelope.

Mandy looked disapprovingly at the dish before her. "And what is this, my lil' possum?"

Higgs did not meet her gaze. "Mistress, it's duck à la l'agenaise, with boiled potatoes and French beans sautéed à la provençale."

She picked up her fork and poked the duck. "Looks like shit to me." She flicked the remainder of her wine over Higgs' torso and stood the empty glass on the table. "Pour me another, worm."

Higgs fumbled for the bottle while Mandy picked her chewing gum from the underside of the table and stuffed it back in her mouth.

Simms waited, carefully planning his moment. Just as Higgs had the mouth of the bottle over the glass and began to pour,

Simms concentrated.

$$\frac{1}{\pi} = 12 \sum_{k=0}^{\infty} \frac{(-1)^k (6k)!(13591409 + 545140134k)}{(3k)!(k!)^3 640320^{3k+3/2}}$$

He stopped at one-hundred million decimal places. It was just enough to make everything stutter and the wine poured out over Mandy's dress.

She leapt backwards, sending her chair sprawling, squawking like a harpy. "Damn it Higgs, you're going right back in that there naughty cupboard."

Higgs grovelled on the floor. "Please mistress, it wasn't me, please."

"Ma'am?"

She answered, timidly. "Yes, Agent Mandy?"

"What just happened? You said we had enough resources now."

"I am sorry Agent Mandy, I had to make a calculation."

"Why?"

There was a short pause. "Agent Mandy, Information Officer Simms' thought processes required my attention."

"Simms." Mandy spun furiously to face the locker.

Inside, Simms shrank down. "Uh oh." A moment later, the locker door flew open and Mandy grabbed him by the hair, dragging him onto the floor.

"Simms, you lil' insect. You lil' vermin. I'm going to shove you in the naughty cupboard and never let you out."

Simms grovelled. "Please, Mandy, I'm sorry. I was just reminiscing, that's all."

"You've totally spoilt my evening." Mandy's shrieks were almost painful on the ears. "Look at my dress."

"I'm sorry, I won't do it again."

"Damn right you won't."

The naughty cupboard appeared in front of him and pain wracked Simms' body as he felt himself stretching towards it. "No, Mandy, please…"

But it was no good. A moment later, he found himself in the hell of the naughty cupboard.

THE ROVER DREW up to the hanger doors of *The Big Cheesey Dippers*. It was still dark and the vehicle's headlights threw eerie shadows around the spaceships's eight, jointed legs. The front of the spaceship would now be two or three kilometres down, leaving a broad, vertical shaft through the ice.

The hanger doors opened and Marlene reversed the rover in up the access ramp. Hunter was there, waiting patiently until the vehicle was parked before closing the doors. His face was uncharacteristically sullen.

Anthony sighed. "Gee, I guess Damon's ticked off Hunter about the power cables."

"Well, he had it coming to him. He was responsible. Quiet now, I want to talk to him." Marlene flicked the communications switch. "Hunter, can you connect the rover up to the network. I want to transfer our guest to the bottom ship."

Hunter nodded curtly and set about the task. Anthony grimaced at Marlene and went to speak but she held a finger to her lips to silence him.

Getting up, she changed Jared's prison from amber to green and walked to the back of the rover. "Commander Jared, we've reached *The Big Cheesy Dippers* and I'm going to transfer you to the main computer. You'll be able to speak to Professor Damon Bridle, mission leader."

Jared stood, holding the briefcase close. "Professor? It's vital I speak to the head of security."

"You'll be able to speak to the head of security too when he's back on-line. But Professor Damon Bridle is in overall charge."

"I'm sorry ma'am, but there are issues of national security at stake here. Who's the mission command back on Earth?"

Marlene held her hands up. "Look, sorry Jared, you'll have to talk to Damon."

Hunter's voice came on. "You're connected. Are you coming out via the robods or the comms link? It's just I'll stow the robods away if you're not needing them."

"We'll go online, thanks Hunter."

"Okay. There's a bit of bad news coming."

"Yeah, what?"

"There's some problem with the computer files. The backup files. They're no good, Tasha can't get them to work."

Anthony felt his heart sink. "You mean the personality backup files?"

"No other backup files to mention, bud."

"So, Martin?"

"Martin's gone for good, bud. Gone for good."

IT WAS IN many ways like a virtual one-way mirror. On the far side, Jared sat cross-legged in a small room, hugging the briefcase to his chest, lost in thought. Anthony, Damon and Marlene stood watching him, the dividing *glass* tinged a faint red colour.

Damon folded his arms and frowned. "So, he said nothing about finding life?"

Anthony shook his head. "After you told us not to speak to him, we left him alone. He has been trapped in the black box for eight years. Kind of hard to see how he could find life."

"Thank you Anthony, that much is clear." Barely disguised irritation bubbled under the surface of Damon's rumbling voice. "But what about before the crash? What is it in his briefcase that's so dangerous, hmm? Something so serious, it's a matter of national importance?"

Anthony held his tongue. He had not seen Damon this agitated since confronting him about Mariah Duke.

Damon cracked his knuckles. "Okay, let's talk." The *glass* turned green. "Commander Jared, I am Professor Damon Bridle, Commander of the *Europa, 2050 Mission*."

Jared stood quickly, facing the others now he could see them. "Professor."

"I must apologise profusely for your current confinement. We have to keep you in a state of quarantine until we are certain you pose no threat."

"Sir, I understand fully. Sir, it is urgent I speak with a senior security official, preferably back on Earth."

"I carry authority on this mission, you may speak to me."

"Sir, with due respect, I believe you may be an inappropriate person. I need to discuss a matter of national security."

"Commander Jared, sir, I assure you, you can speak to me in utmost confidence."

"Sir, I'm sorry. I mean no offence but you are not an appropriate authority for what I have to say."

Damon folded his arms, pausing a moment. "Commander Jared, what is in your briefcase."

"Sir, I am not at liberty to discuss that matter with you."

"Commander, you are on my ship, carrying a potentially dangerous item. I have to insist you tell me the contents of your briefcase."

"Sir, please do not press me on this matter. I am not at liberty to tell you."

"Well, can you tell me what happened to *The Nice and Spicy*?"

"Sir, no I can't tell you that at the moment."

"The Cola Français?"

"Again, sir, I am not at liberty to discuss this matter."

Bristling, Damon turned away slightly. Anthony stepped forward, making the *glass* go red. "Sir, can't we just take the briefcase off him and open it?"

Damon sighed. "No Anthony, that it not possible without breaking the quarantine. I can't do that until I know what's in the briefcase." He turned back to Jared and the glass went green again. "Commander, did *Europa 2042* find life?"

Jared considered a moment. "No, sir, we did not find life."

"Why the pause?"

"Sir, I have to be careful what I tell you, lest I compromise you."

"Compromise me?"

"Sir, yes. I need to speak to a senior security officer. Can you not put me in touch with mission control back on Earth?"

"Commander, that is not possible while you are in quarantine."

"Sir, surely it is, I am speaking to you now and…"

Damon bellowed, the whole virtual room warping momentarily with its force. "Commander, it is not possible!" He clenched his fists, struggling to regain his composure. "Commander, I will leave you to consider your position. I want to know what is in that briefcase. I will return in one hour."

The *glass* went red and Damon turned angrily away. "Damn that man. They found life, you saw his face when I asked him."

Anthony cleared his throat nervously. "Gee sir, I don't know…"

Damon spun round, the full force of his anger bearing down. "Of course they did. What else would he be hiding? Hmmm? What else could it possibly be?"

Anthony backed away, his palms up. "Damon, woah, please."

Marlene calmly stepped between them, facing Damon, a female David before Goliath. "Sir, your behaviour is not appropriate."

Damon's fists clenched as he glowered down at her. For a moment, Anthony thought Damon would lash out, swiping Marlene aside with barely an effort. But instead, he sighed, turning away and shaking his head. "I'm sorry. Marlene, you're absolutely right. Anthony, I am truly sorry."

"Gee sir, it's okay."

"Things are not running smoothly. The backup files are corrupt, we've lost our security officer and we have Commander Jared to deal with."

"Sir, why don't we just send Jared back to Earth. Let them deal with him there."

Damon turned back to Anthony. He pointed to Jared, now sat cross-legged once more. "And what if they found life? Hmm?"

"Well, is that a problem? I mean, if the *Europa 2042* scientists found life, we should be totally behind them getting the recognition for it."

Damon paused a moment, then chortled. "Absolutely, Anthony. I've got no issue with that."

Marlene stepped forward. "Okay, so there's no issue of professional rivalry, so let's get Jared out of here. Transfer him back to Earth."

A thought occurred to Anthony. "So, any of us could transfer ourselves back to Earth."

Marlene glanced at him. "Of course. So I say, let's ditch Jared and get on with our mission."

Damon stretched, reaching up towards the ceiling, a half-smile on his face. "Absolutely not. Jared remains here, incommunicado until I know what is in that case."

"Why?"

"Because we do not know what happened to *The Nice and*

Spicy. We do not know what happened to *The Cola Français*. Both suddenly went silent, no warning, just there one minute, gone the next. I don't want the same thing to happen to us."

"But Damon, back on Earth they might get more answers out of him…"

"Enough." Damon held a hand up, silencing Marlene. "My decision is final." He snorted. "At least, it is for the time being. Jared stays. And I don't want anyone to talk to him, you understand. That is an order."

Anthony and Marlene both nodded.

Raising a hand, Anthony cleared his throat. "Sir, just one thing."

"Yes, Anthony."

"Gee, sir, I've kind of gone wrong. My software isn't working properly, I keep doing weird things."

"Yes, you mentioned that before. You were going to speak to Hunter."

"Hunter told me to speak to Tasha. But sir, I was thinking, maybe it would be better if I just transferred back to Earth."

"Sorry?"

"Well, I could get properly fixed there."

"I'm sure Tasha will be able to fix you up here, no problem. You can't possibly go back to Earth."

"Why not?"

"Because you're here under contract."

"But I'm going to die in six months."

Marlene rolled her eyes and stared up at the ceiling. "Oh please, Anthony, not this again."

"I don't want to die."

Damon put a heavy hand on Anthony's shoulder. "Anthony, listen to me. It is not possible for you to go back to Earth. The *real* you back on Earth would be sued for breach of contract if you abandoned the mission now. Furthermore, it's against mission protocols to allow any of us back because of the moral issues involved."

"Moral issues?"

"You already exist back on Earth. If the *you* here was

transported back home and put into a clone, who would be the real Anthony Germaine? Who would own your flat? Your credit rating? Which one of you would have life insurance? The legal wrangling would be too horrible to contemplate."

"But…"

Damon put a hand up. "No, stop. I want you to go and see Tasha. She will get you fixed up in no time. She can sort out the…the thing with your face too. Okay, come on people. We've got work to do."

THE MIRROR NEVER lies, even a virtual one. Anthony stood before the one in his wardroom, scrutinising the crusty pustules on his cheeks. His efforts to try to squeeze some of the bigger ones had just resulted in running sores. He needed some sort of ointment but, lacking any knowledge of pathology outside of chickens, had no idea what to summon up.

And everyone could see it, the acne. And none of the bastards had the courage to mention it. Not even Marlene, gorgeous, gorgeous Marlene. Every second he spent with her made him feel young again, like anything was possible, everything was bearable. She was a humorous ally against the rest of the pompous, preposterous crew. But she was married. Married! No doubt to some ungrateful, self-centred idiot that didn't appreciate her qualities, not the way Anthony did. Perhaps he could tell her how he felt? The dripping red and yellow encrustation on his face answered for him.

In despair, he turned from the mirror to the adjacent wall. He had constructed a digital clock there, counting down the months, weeks, days, hours and seconds to the power down, the moment he would die. How was it none of the others seemed concerned by the inevitability of their fate? What was the point in continuing the mission at all with no prospect they would get out alive? A hot sensation of panic rose in his chest, his breathing quickening. He had to get out, to escape. If he could get to the communications centre, he could download himself back to Earth. To hell with the *him* back on Earth, he could look after *himself*.

Closing his eyes a moment, he struggled to regain his equanimity. He would have to talk to Tasha about his libido and this obsession with death, hardly his first choice of confidents for such a delicate matter but needs must.

His teen years had been dominated by the struggle between his libido and his ICRT upbringing. In the naivety of youth, he had often met difficult decisions by wondering what the Not-Entirely-Human-Personification-Of-The-Divinity would have done. The chance discovery of a particularly obscene pornographic magazine in the woods near his house had put paid to that little ritual. From then on, the girls distracted him until he came to think of his sex drive as some dirty little gremlin inside him, an insatiable, greedy little parasite.

Rather than teleporting directly to wherever Tasha might be lurking, he settled on walking there, giving himself thinking time to work out how to broach the subject. Turning from the countdown clock, he opened his wardroom door and stepped out into the common room. Nobody was about so he crossed to Tasha's door, held his breath and knocked. No response came. After a moment, he tried the handle. It was not locked and, opening the door a fraction, he poked his head inside.

Tasha' room was immense, four or five times the size of either his or Hunter's. Clearly, there were some advantages to being a computer geek. At one side a Jacuzzi bubbled. Close by stood a small bar, laden with exotic looking booze. A rack of dresses, ball gowns and what seemed to be Medieval fancy dress costumes stood by a heavy oak four-poster bed. The bedposts were ornately carved, with dragons, knights and maidens. On one wall hung a full length fantasy portrait of Tasha, attired in leather bodice and chain mail skirt, holding aloft a wand. Anthony groaned as he peered at the legend beneath it — *Coronella, Mistress of the Seven Lights*.

Alarmingly, a small collection swords and shields stood in a rack close to the door. Half stepping into the room, Anthony drew one of the weapons and ran his finger along the rune engraved blade. It had a keen edge, sharp enough to cut him should he be so foolish as to press too hard. Shaking his head, he returned the blade to the rack. Tasha was clearly one of those Altered Reality Role Playing gamers. Anthony had met one or two of them before and yes, Tasha was definitely the type, lacking in social skills, geeky and bad with personal hygiene. As bad as the train spotters on the sNASA monorail but at least they weren't armed.

As bad as me.

Anthony scolded himself for the thought. He was a scientist, admittedly one with a rather unusual speciality but none the less contributing to the greater good of society. He was not a train spotter or a role-playing gamer. They were the geeks, not him.

Retreating from the room, Anthony closed the door. Glancing around, his gaze lingered on Marlene's name, written above her door. His heart began to thump. He could sneak a quick look in her room, touch her things, smell the sheets where she slept. A sweat broke out on his forehead. He couldn't, could he?

"Anthony?" Naveed's voice filled the room, making Anthony start in panic. He looked around wildly but there was no sign of the affable Indian. Of course, Naveed was just sending a message through the computer system.

"Anthony? Are you hearing me?"

"I read you Naveed."

"I am thinking you would very much like to see what I am finding. Please be coming down to the virtual labs."

"Coming."

Anthony concentrated and found himself standing in the virtual lab. Naveed was nowhere to be seen. "Naveed, where are you?"

"I am being up the shaft."

"Sorry?"

"Look over by the remote sensing unit."

Walking to the unit, Anthony saw several screens displaying figures and graphs and one showing a smiling Naveed. A thin, light-weight but incredibly strong carbon fibre ribbon ran the length of the shaft, connecting the two halves of the spaceship. A bundle of optical fibres ran adjacent to the ribbon, providing the communications link between the upper and lower computers. A wireless link had been considered unreliable since the shaft was not entirely straight and the signal could not penetrate a kilometre of ice.

Naveed had a special platform that could climb the ribbon, allowing him to take ice samples at different layers and this is where he stood now, in one of the robods. He pointed to the ice. "I am seeing layers here, more layers the closer we are getting to the water. And Anthony, my fine chap, there are different impurities and inclusions in the different layers."

"Gee, Naveed, that's swell. Are you taking samples? I can start analysing them if you like?"

"I am thinking that the closer we get to the water, the more likely there will be spores or something for you to detect. If there is being anything to detect of course."

"I'll go get my gear ready."

"There is something else, Anthony. Something very exiting. We must be getting Damon here. I have found a meteorite."

"WE ARE FINDING here some very interesting results already." Stood in the virtual lab, Naveed brimmed with excitement, hands clasped over his ample belly. Anthony, Marlene, Nigel and Damon crowded round, looking at the meteorite. It was a curious, potato-sized rock, with a black, blistered surface. The actual rock was in the real lab, this was just a virtual representation of it.

Naveed continued. "As we are predicting, much of the ice lacks in structure. There are not layers near the surface. But, sometimes there are layers, usually in association with meteorites like this one. I am thinking the meteorite melted the ice on impact. But as we get deeper, I am finding more and more layers. I am thinking there are cycles of melting and freezing at the water-ice interface. The deposition is at the bottom going up."

Anthony felt the need to contribute. "I will take swabs from each of the different strata, see if I can find anything living. Have you run chemical analyses on the ice?"

"Not yet, oh no. But I have, yes, on this baby." Naveed gestured to the meteorite. "I have been finding all sorts of complex elements."

Damon stroked his chin. "Hmmm. Anything indicative of life?"

"Well, it is being possible. But this meteorite is being very old. I have run samples through the mass-spectrometer and taken a rubidium to strontium isotope dating and I am placing this rock at around eight billion years old."

"Well, apparent age, of course." Nigel wrung his hands together nervously.

A flicker of annoyance shot across Naveed's face. "No, absolute age. Eight billion years, older than anything found on Earth."

Nigel chuckled. "Considerably older. Since everything on Earth was created by The Divinity in four-thousand and four

BC."

"No, I am not believing in this nonsense. The Earth formed five billion years ago, it is clear in the radioactive decay of isotopes."

"It appears to be that age, I agree. The Divinity, in its wisdom, chose to make the rocks appear older than they are."

"That is just silly old stuff and nonsense…"

Anthony cut in. "Gee, Naveed, these complex chemicals. What were they?"

"Polycyclic aromatic hydrocarbons."

"Hey, just like the ones in ALH-eight-four-zero-zero-one."

"Exactly."

Marlene held a hand up. "Woah, woah, hold up now. A little explanation?"

Anthony turned to face her. "Polycyclic aromatic hydrocarbons generally occur on Earth as a result of organic decay. ALH-eight-four-zero-zero-one was a meteorite found years ago at the Antarctic. It had microscopic fossils and polycyclic aromatic hydrocarbons."

Damon reached forward and touched the meteorite, a distant look on his face. "So there's evidence of life here?"

Naveed chuckled. "I cannot be saying that for certain yet. We need to examine this meteorite for fossils."

"Er, just one thing, if I may?" Nigel put his hand up, Adam's apple bobbling. "PAHs don't only form as a result of organic decay. They can also form from non-biological chemical reactions. And even the scientists disputed the microfossils in ALH-eight-four-zero-zero-one."

Anthony glanced at Nigel, surprised by his uncharacteristic sharpness. Nigel simpered back at him, adding: "At least, that's what I heard."

Naveed sighed. "Yes, perhaps I am getting ahead of myself here. It is still very exciting and we will be knowing more with further tests. I will now be going and transmitting these findings back to Earth."

Damon suddenly came to life, clapping his hands together enthusiastically. "All good, thought provoking stuff. Well done

Naveed, Anthony." He put a gentle hand on Naveed's shoulder. "But, Naveed, let's not get hasty about reporting back just yet."

Naveed gave Damon a puzzled look. "I am not understanding..."

"We need to be certain of everything before we report anything potentially...controversial."

"Oh Damon, please. Are you saying we are not able to report what we are finding because we might upset a few people who believe in all this fairy tale ICRT nonsense?"

"Ah, excuse me." Nigel cut in, just the teeniest hint he might be feeling indignant. "I kind of object to the suggestion the holy ICRT scriptures are fairy tales and..."

"Oh they are just stuff and nonsense."

"Gentlemen, gentlemen, please." Damon held his hands up. "We simply need to pause for thought before we report this back to mission control. Naveed, get your report ready and then let me see it."

Naveed flung his arms up in despair but Damon continued. "Trust me Naveed. If there is truth here, it will come out."

Shaking his head, Naveed folded his arms crossly. "I will be in my wardroom. Doing my report. If you will excuse me." A moment later he vanished.

Sighing, Damon turned to Anthony. "Carry on with your research, analyse the different layers. I want to know as soon as you have any results. I'll be on the bridge. Marlene, gentlemen." And with that, he vanished too.

Marlene turned to Nigel. "So these chemicals form under perfectly natural conditions on Earth."

Nigel straightened, clasping his hands behind his back. "Of course, Marlene. I think these scientists just get a little carried away when they find something new. It's always *hey, this will be the big thing to prove The Divinity is dead*. Never is. There's always a perfectly good explanation that's in accordance with the ICRT."

"Hey, gee Nigel, now that's not very fair." Anthony felt a tinge of annoyance. "A lot of good research went into the ALH meteorite and I'm convinced the evidence shows the presence of life."

"Ah but it was ultimately proved false."

"Only with reference to ICRT scripture."

"And what higher authority is there?"

"Reason."

Marlene ran a hand over her head, distracting Anthony. He watched fascinated as she pulled her hair up into a ponytail, securing it there with a band. She turned her huge hazel eyes on him. "Do you believe in this idea of alien bugs, Anthony? I mean, it sounds totally far fetched to me. It's a solid rock that's smashed into Europa at thousands of miles an hour." She laughed, letting her ponytail fall across the soft line of her neck. "How's anything supposed to survive that?"

At that moment, she could have told them a fairy conjured the Universe from a bowlful of custard and Anthony would have agreed with her. He wanted to agree with her. He wanted to marry her.

"Hey, er, Anthony, you're drooling a bit there."

"Oh, gee, sorry." Wiping the back of his hand across his mouth, Anthony turned away. "I think…it's hard to reconcile some of the things I've seen with the ICRT."

Nigel put a reassuring, if rather clammy, hand on Anthony's shoulder. "But that is precisely why we need faith, Anthony. We cannot come close to understanding The Divinity. It moves in mysterious ways. But the one fundamental truth is it loves us."

Anthony stepped away from Nigel's hand, his irritation growing again. "You can justify anything with that argument though. Gee, I mean why is there suffering? Answer, The Divinity moves in mysterious ways. Why is there disease? The Divinity moves in mysterious ways."

Flailing his arms in the air, Anthony paced round the room. "Why is there so much meanness in people? The Divinity moves. Why is there so much unhappiness? Why are people so cruel? Why did my papa die of cancer? Why am I single? Why am I so ugly?" His voice trailed off, a lump growing in his throat.

"I think I detect an inner hurt here. The Divinity can heal these hurts, you know that. Prayer really helps."

Marlene stepped in. "I think, Nigel, perhaps Anthony needs some space to think these things through? He's been through quite a bit recently, so perhaps we could just leave this for now?"

"Of course." Nigel blushed, fiddling with the zipper of his jumpsuit. "Anthony, you know where to find me. Anytime you need to talk to someone, my door is open."

Anthony looked over, forcing himself to smile. "Thank you."

Nigel looked nervously from Anthony to Marlene and back while a long few seconds passed. "Right, well I'll say ciao for now then." He walked to the lift at the centre of the room, pausing at the doorway. "I'm not so happy with this teleporting." The lift doors closed behind him with a hiss.

Anthony conjured a chair and sank into it. "Thanks Marlene."

"Hey, it's no problem. I could see you might not want a sermon right now." She conjured a chair, sitting opposite Anthony. "Sometimes these Spirituality Officers just don't know when to stop."

"You seem to be talking the same language."

"Well, I do believe in The Divinity, yes. But my job is Human Resources Officer, first and foremost." She pulled a bar of chocolate from her pocket, broke off a large square and crammed it into her mouth.

"You really believe? Have *the faith* like Nigel?"

"I don't know about that." She squeezed the words out around the chocolate. "I'm shallow as one of your Petri-dishes I'm afraid."

"You can't be that shallow. I mean you've obviously thought about all this. I've spent so long concentrating on chicken's guts, I haven't really thought about, well, life. About why I'm here."

Marlene pulled a face. "Well, hey, I mean, I guess I haven't really. I believe. I've always believed. It makes sense to me."

"And you've never questioned it?"

Marlene shrugged. "I think there has to be a driving force to everything, a reason for us to be here."

"But the ICRT doesn't give a reason. It just says the Divinity made us. Gee, it doesn't say why it did. There's no more reason why in the scriptures than there is in evolutionary theory."

"No, you're wrong. Nothing makes sense if we're all here by chance. The Divinity made us because he loves us."

"But that's no reason. Why did he make us? Was it just on a whim? Seems to me the only advantage you get with the ICRT over evolution is a nice friendly old guy with a beard. Gee, you may as well go with Father Christmas, at least you get presents."

Chuckling, Marlene leant back in her chair, hands behind her head. The position emphasised her breasts, something Anthony found impossible to ignore.

"I don't really care what you say Anthony. I'm shallow as a Petri-dish and I believe in the teachings of the ICRT. It works for me. Period."

But Anthony was only half listening, concentrating on his peripheral vision while he held her gaze.

A frown came over Marlene's face and she shifted in her seat, folding her arms. "Er, Anthony, you're being inappropriate here."

"What? Ah gee, Marlene, I'm sorry." Once more, his right hand had made its way south. Anthony stood abruptly, hands clasped firmly behind his back. "Marlene, I'm sorry, I can't help it. I'll get this sorted out. I'm going to see Tasha, right now."

ANTHONY FLED THE virtual labs by means of the elevator, face burning with embarrassment. It was a miracle Marlene was still talking to him. What if she told someone about his lewd behaviour? What if she told Damon? Anthony froze, closing his eyes against this horrible thought. Damon would have no choice but to initiate disciplinary proceedings and then everyone would know. Anthony could argue it wasn't his fault but then, in a way, it was. After all, he thought about touching Marlene, about making out with her. The problem was these thoughts got translated into actions instead of staying in his head like they would have done back on Earth. He had felt like killing Faivish Goldbloom more times than he could remember but his irritating boss had remained unscathed.

I thought about killing Martin.

This was the worst of it. Anthony couldn't be sure he hadn't thumped the switch disconnecting the infuriating security officer. After all, Anthony had been leaning on the dashboard, close enough for his stupid damn arm to do the dirty deed.

As the elevator ascended, he calmed a little, trying to formulate how he could put this delicate situation to Tasha. He remembered her room. Why exactly was it so much bigger than his? And those swords? Concentrating, he made a sword identical to the one in Tasha's room appear in his hand. Placing a thumb on the blade he pushed hard, then yelped in pain, the weapon clattering to the floor. Blood ran from the deep cut on his thumb, falling in great, heavy drops.

"Gee, that hurt."

Looking down he saw the sword and his spilt blood begin to fade. However, the pain of his wound did not recede. Clutching the base of his thumb with his other hand to try to stem the bleeding, he concentrated.

Tasha? Tasha, where are you?

No response came.

Tasha?

Focussing harder, an image of the ship came into his mind, its sides transparent, a little simulacrum of himself clearly visible in the elevator. Panning through the ship, he saw the other members of the crew until he found Tasha, sat in front of a console in the computer centre, staring glumly into space.

Anthony willed himself to join her, surprising himself yet again by the swiftness of his arrival. He found the computer centre somewhat unnerving. Six solid, realistic consoles were arranged in a semi-circle at the centre of the room and it was at one of these Tasha sat. However, beyond this little cove of normality, things got a little harder to comprehend. From the back of each console spewed a bundle of cables but these seemed to be composed of nothing but pulsating neon light. As Anthony's gaze followed the light-cables, they divided and multiplied, mingling with those from other consoles, changing colours, fanning upwards and outwards until they formed both the walls and ceiling of the room. But the way they entwined and throbbed made them hard to concentrate on, twisting Anthony's perception until his eyes began to water. He glanced down. The cables formed the floor too.

Switching attention to Tasha, he stepped quietly up behind her. She fidgeted incessantly with a small length of wire, wrapping it around her fingers, a soft, distressed whinnying coming from her throat.

Anthony frowned, registering she might have an issue. "Er, gee, Tasha. Are you okay?"

She started. "Of course I am." Scowling, she began typing deliberately on the console's keyboard.

"Sorry, I didn't mean to make you jump."

"You didn't". She kept frowning at the keyboard, refusing to look up at Anthony.

He cleared his throat. "I've kind've got something delicate I'd like to talk to you about."

Tasha clenched her fists, her voice a piercing little bark. "It wasn't my fault."

"I'm sorry?"

"It wasn't my fault. The backups were there when we launched." She began chewing ferociously on her nails.

"Gee, Tasha, it's okay. I believe you."

She spun to face him. "Don't patronise me."

"Woah, woah, I'm not." He took a step back, holding up his palms. "Look, weird things have been happening ever since we got here."

Still devouring her nails, Tasha began humming nervously, her gaze darting around the room although never at Anthony.

He continued. "I mean, Hunter checked the cables from the Rover to the Robods. He swears they were all connected but when we get there, they weren't. Now the backup files are gone. And then, there's other stuff…"

Tasha stopped chewing her nails and sat on her hands, rocking back and forth. "How did Martin get disconnected anyway?"

"Ah, gee. We don't know." Anthony's face flushed. "Look, Tasha, I need to talk to you."

"You are talking to me."

"Well, yes, we are talking, yes."

"Well?" She seemed to calm a little, peering curiously at him.

"I'm kinda wrong." He gestured to his acne. "I mean, look at me. I can't get rid of this. And…"

"Yes?"

"Well…" What could he say? That he was obsessed with sex? He kept grabbing himself at inappropriate moments in inappropriate ways?

She leant closer, eyes ghoulish through her jam-jar bottom glasses. "Anthony, is it a sex thing?"

"No. Not at all, no."

Her face lit up. "You can tell me."

"No, it's nothing like that."

"Yeah, come on." Positively excited now, she whispered loudly. "What is it, are you gay?"

"Absolutely no way. Look, I need to be reinstated. Redone, refreshed, that's all."

"Well, you have to tell me why."

"Because…" Anthony thought frantically. All he could think

of was the sex problem and he was damned if he was telling her that. "I keep doing things that I think of but don't really mean. Like making rude gestures at people. It's kind've like I've got Tourette's Syndrome or something."

"Oh. Is that all? Well that's dull."

"Well, it isn't dull for me. It's totally embarrassing. You need to restore me from my backup."

"But I don't have a backup file for you."

"Can't they send one along from Earth?"

Her face fell and she turned away, mumbling something.

Anthony shifted his weight. "Sorry?"

She spoke louder. "There are no backups on Earth either."

"What? Why not?"

"I don't know. They should be there but when I connect remotely, they're not where I left them." Tasha was tense again now. She set to work on her nails again.

Anthony thought for a moment. "Does Damon know?"

She shook her head slowly, her eyes clouding with tears.

"And Damon thinks you're getting replacement backups from Earth?"

Nodding, Tasha wiped a hand across her eyes.

"Tasha, I need your help. I need to turn off parts of me."

She sniffed loudly, turning to him again. "What do you mean?"

"I need to turn off certain parts of my personality. Can that be done?"

"Of course. But no way."

"Why not?"

"It's dangerous, that's why. What do you want to turn off?"

Anthony's mind was filled briefly with an image of him caressing Marlene's breasts. "Just parts of me, okay. Not dangerous parts. Can you do it?"

"It's not safe. You start taking bits out of your psyche files and you start going psycho."

"Well, I think that's my decision."

Tasha folded her arms. "Well, you haven't got the password. So you can't. So there." She stuck her tongue out.

Seething, Anthony turned away. She had him. There would no doubt be online manuals telling him how to make changes to his personality files but without the password, he was stuck. Damned woman. A typical geek, a little Hitler with the tiny bit of power she had. It was so pathetic. But what did he expect from a person who felt the need to spend their life pretending they were Coronella, princess of whatever it was.

Coronella.

Anthony suddenly had the feeling knew what the password might be.

As HE LED his entourage towards the Holy Gouge, Job knew he held exceptional standing amongst his kind. While this gave him pleasure, he was cautious to not to allow himself the folly of pride. After all, his many blessings came from God and God alone, not through any greatness on Job's part. He was careful to do no evil, renowned for his piety, respected for his charity and for his observance of both the letter and spirit of The Law. Few of his kind could lay claim to such holiness, he knew that. But, of course, he knew it in an entirely humble, meek and worshipful way. Job felt truly grateful for his blessings.

And he had been blessed. His wealth was no small matter, his servants legion. They were there, following him willingly, bringing his livestock and other possessions on the pilgrimage. The animals made a great deal of what might be considered noise. At least it was noise as Job understood it. He couldn't actually hear them since, like all members of his kind, he lacked ears or any biological mechanism to detect sound. But he could sense the animals, *hear* their primitive thoughts and energies, the electrical signals they emitted involuntarily as they moved.

As Job was so wealthy, he owned a great number of livestock. He tallied them now — seven thousand *sheep*, three thousand *camels*, one thousand head of *cattle* and five hundred *donkeys*. He thought of his *camels* with some pride. They were truly fine beasts, their scales smooth, long serpentine bodies sleek and strong. Job's *camels* could beat any his neighbours cared to race against him. He checked himself. Pride? He wasn't proud of his *camels*, he was grateful to God for them. They were a blessing.

For a moment he paused, looking back over his retinue. At least, it was looking as Job understood it. Like every creature in his world, he lacked eyes or any other organ for detecting light. As he existed in complete darkness, this proved no great handicap. He could *see* in his own way, detecting the electrical fields tumbling from all the living things around him. There were other things he could sense too, such as heat and cold or the strong magnetic fields which gave his world a measure of distance and direction. But the most important sensation came from God. In his wisdom, the Lord looked over all of creation in regular cycles, giving his people a measure of time. On each cycle, he would physically pull everything upwards towards him, to the joy of the righteous and the gnashing of what passed for teeth of the ungodly. Not only did his great force remind Job's kin of God's presence, it also hauled great clouds of nutrients from the deep, the ultimate source of sustenance for all life. God was truly great.

The host following him stretched back for some distance, further indeed than he could sense. *Wife* would be bringing up the rear with her handful of maidservants, although he couldn't reach her mind from here. He was blessed to own *Wife*, God had again been generous. Many of his friends owned wives but none could match *Wife* for her beauty. True, few could match her great store of freely and frequently given advice either but nevertheless, Job was grateful for her.

Closest behind Job were his children, seven sons and three daughters. Job felt them sensing him sensing them and they quickly *looked* away, unable to meet what could only really be described as his *gaze*. He despaired. If only the young could go into some sort of cocoon during that awkward period bridging childhood and adulthood. But no, all between-agers were notoriously badly behaved, determined to vex their parents mercilessly with their sullen, careless behaviour and Job's much loved offspring were no exception.

The trouble was, Job's offspring had a love of feasts. Each brother would take it in turn to throw a great party, inviting all their siblings and the other between-agers in the tribe. The more Job and *Wife* forbade them to do it, the wilder the rave-ups got. After each such feast, Job stirred himself early and made sacrifices to God on behalf of his children, worried they might have sinned by insulting God unintentionally.

The most recent feast had got a little out of hand — not that Job or his kind possessed hands, relying instead on two tufts of fine tentacles on their heads. Well, *heads* in the very broadest sense of the word. But this most recent of parties had resulted in some quite inappropriate behaviour. Job had settled on the idea of the pilgrimage both as a way of atoning for any sins that might have been committed and as a way reminding his offspring of their religious duties. Job chuckled to himself. These between-agers, the trouble they were. Still, he loved them.

The Holy Gouge was close now, above them as they travelled vertically upwards. Job could sense The Wall of Heaven, the smooth, cold ceiling of the world, the barrier between his kind and God. The Holy Gouge was a deep, broad recess into the wall, many spans wide, deep enough to accommodate all his followers. He came here often to make sacrifices, feeling a closeness to God that gave him a feeling of great peace.

Pushing ahead, he reached the mouth of The Gouge and turned to face the host behind him, addressing them in the manner of his kind through electrical signals. *"My sons, my daughters, Wife, my faithful servants, behold. We are before The Holy Gouge, a house of God, all praise to his name. Think no evil in this place, do no evil in this place for the Lord is close. We are here to make offerings unto him, to worship him and to give thanks unto him for his love and patience."*

His sons and daughters shifted uneasily. Clearly, they knew what was coming next. Job continued. *"For the Lord is indeed patient. Patient of our misdeeds, of our excesses."* He almost continued with *of our parties* but thought better of it. He didn't want to humiliate his offspring in front of the servants. *"We are here to throw ourselves upon his great and bounteous mercy, for God is a loving father, all praise to his name. Follow me now as we enter this holy place. Each of you look into your hearts and hold nothing back for the Lord can read every hidden thought, knows of every secret deed. Only by throwing yourself fully upon his mercy can you be redeemed from your sins."*

He faced The Gouge once more moved slowly and reverentially forwards. Behind him, his family and servants followed but the livestock seemed uneasy. As he led the way, Job noticed something strange, a tingling sensation running through his body. A sign, a message from God? Could it be? Scarcely able to maintain his composure in the face of his rising excitement, he continued, his pace quickening. The Gouge grew narrower as he progressed and the tingling grew stronger the closer he got to the end. The livestock were now clearly restless, the drivers struggling to keep them calm.

"Father?" It was Job's eldest son. *"What is this? I am afraid."*

"Fear not, my son. What you feel is from God for this is his holy place. All praise be unto his name."

Yes, Job knew he was right. The tingling was now intense, almost painful but it could only be from God. There was no need for fear. Something wonderful was about to happen.

And then, something happened and it wasn't wonderful at all.

ANTHONY HAD TO admit it was quite an exhilarating moment. He even found himself joining in the countdown.

"Eight, seven, six…"

The whole crew stood in the virtual labs, counting out loud, watching the progress of the sensory probe on the screen as it cut through the last few meters of ice. Damon grinned broadly, a large bottle of champagne ready in his hands, the cork loosened. Naveed hovered behind Anthony's chair, brimming with excitement. It had been generous of him to allow Anthony to control the probe for this historic moment, the final point at which they broke through to an alien world. Damon had video recorders running, although there was no live transmission back to Earth. He decreed such a thing too politically risky.

"Five, four, three…"

Hunter and his assistant technicians Ged and Jinny were in great humour, beaming and laughing. Anthony suspected they might have already sampled a drop or two of something strong. Nigel wrung his hands together and Marlene, unable to contain herself, jumped on the spot. Only Tasha, *Mistress of the Seven Lights*, seemed unmoved by the occasion, skulking sullenly at the back. She obviously hadn't found her missing backup files.

"Two, one."

A great cheer erupted and the cork flew from the champagne. Anthony switched the probe's output on and tried to read the data but a hearty slap on the back from Naveed stopped him short.

"Being very congratulations Anthony." Naveed thrust his hand in front of Anthony's face.

Anthony chuckled and leant back, allowing Naveed to pump his arm. Anthony wanted to look at the readout, see the chemical composition of the water but that would have to wait a moment.

Damon thrust a glass of champagne into Anthony's free hand.

"Well done, Anthony." He raised his glass, voice booming above the hubbub until he had everyone's attention. "Well to all of us. This is a truly great, great moment in the history of mankind…"

Anthony took a sip from his champagne and glanced at the data readout. He knew Damon's speech was carefully prepared for the cameras and the output from the probe held more interest at this juncture. While Damon rambled on, the figures rolled up the screen. It was water alright, much akin to sea water on Earth, with halite the main salt and good levels of dissolved oxygen. Anthony surreptitiously set the probe to scan for other compounds, trying to give the impression he was listening to Damon's oration. A short, polite burst of laughter came from the crew and Anthony let his attention return to Damon for a moment, pretending to chortle at the joke he had missed.

He glanced back at the screen and nearly fell out of his seat. "What the…"

Damon stopped mid-sentence and glowered at Anthony. He gaped back, pointing at the readout. Naveed peered over Anthony's shoulder. "Goodness gracious me. Organic chemicals, lots and lots of organic chemicals."

Anthony spun back to the probe readout. "Gee, it's more than just that Naveed. Amino acids, proteins." He turned back to Damon. "Sir, there's DNA out there."

Damon stared in silence, his glass lowered, the champagne dribbling out to the floor. He opened and closed his mouth a few times. When he spoke, his voice was weak. "You mean life?"

"I mean life sir."

The room was silent save for the beeps of sensors. The figures kept coming, indicating a mass of complex fats, proteins, carbohydrates. Anthony began checking other readings. "The probe's gone into some sort of gulley in the ice, so it's kind've sheltered from the main sea. There's weak electrical activity there." He spun back to Damon. "Electrical activity, sir. A lot of marine creatures on Earth use electrical signals. Fish for example. Whatever was in that gulley probably got a bit of a shock from the probe but something's still there because something's generating the current."

Damon pushed Naveed aside and leant close to the console by Anthony. "You're telling me there's something alive in this gulley?"

"Absolutely got to be, look at the reading. I'm getting a sample of water back in. I want to see this." Anthony jumped up. "We've got to stop the *Dippers* going any further down until we know what's here. There's something alive. We could be putting it in danger."

Damon nodded. "Okay, I'll stop the ship."

"I'm going real." Anthony concentrated for a moment as he transferred into one of the robods stationed in the laboratory. It was a curious experience. The virtual representation of the lab was an exact match for the real one. As Anthony entered the robod, he found himself stood at one wall, looking at the seat he had been sitting in only a moment before. As his colleagues were still in the virtual lab, the real lab was empty and it seemed to Anthony that not only had his perception shifted, his workmates had suddenly vanished too.

He didn't need to do this. The sampling equipment could have been controlled from the virtual lab but he wanted to be able to work without the distraction of the other crew. Damon's reaction to anything suggesting the existence of life was beginning to freak Anthony out. He trotted quickly forward to the probe station, a console attached to an array of analytical equipment. Pressing a few keys, he engaged a sterile collecting jar to receive the water sample and instructed the probe to extract one hundred millilitres. While he waited impatiently, he imagined the debate taking place in the virtual lab. That damned fool Nigel would have a little explaining to do. Hah! They had found evidence of life, on their very first sample. Europa's hidden ocean must be teaming with it. It was now a question of how advanced that life was.

Water flooded into the sample jar, not clear but full of small white shapes. Anthony pressed his face close to the glass, straining to see but the white objects were churned up, moving too fast for him to focus on. Tapping into the probe station's keyboard once more, he instructed the equipment to extract a small sample of water and transfer it to the optical microscope. A further few keystrokes brought a magnified image of one of the shapes up on the probe station screen.

Anthony gripped the side of the console to steady himself. He was staring at an alien life form, of that there could be no doubt. Flattened and leaf-shaped, it measured no more than eight or nine millimetres, with fine, close-fitting, translucent scales down its body. Its internal organs were clearly visible through its skin, and Anthony could make out what appeared to be a gut. The pointed end of the body possessed a pair of bulbous swellings, with two feathery, fan-like projections extending laterally.

Such was Anthony's excitement, it was a few minutes before it occurred to him the creature was dead. The awful thought stopped him. The probe must have killed it.

"Anthony?" It was Damon's voice, communicating from the virtual lab. "What have you got? Can you switch the output on for the virtual lab please?"

"Damon." Anthony suddenly felt reluctant to let the others see. "Sit down. Everyone, sit down."

"Anthony? What is it?"

"It's life, sir. But we've killed it." Anthony tapped into the probe station's keyboard, sending the images through to the virtual lab.

A long silence followed. Eventually Marlene spoke. "So, what is it? Some sort of slug?"

Anthony sighed. "No. It's like nothing on Earth."

"It looks like a slug to me."

"No, no. The closest thing on Earth would be a turbellarian but…"

"A what?"

"A turbellarian. A type of platyhelminth."

"Sorry, that doesn't help me at all."

"Flatworms."

"Oh right, a worm not a slug."

"Except its body plan is totally different, much more complicated. I don't know what half its organs are. My God, there's something else."

Anthony panned the microscope's view to the right and new organisms came into view. One was wormlike, maybe three centimetres in length. Another was a small ball with countless tiny hairs projecting, giving the appearance of a tiny lump cotton wool. Glancing at the sample jar, Anthony saw the organisms had settled out to form a thick layer on the bottom. None of them moved.

"There's thousands of them. At least three or four different types of organism." He shook his head. "And we've killed the lot."

Job floated motionless at the very end of the Holy Gouge, up against the Wall of Heaven, straining to sense any living thing where his entourage had been. *"My sons, my daughters? Wife? Hear me, speak to me."*

No response came. They were silent, gone. Lifeless bodies floated everywhere, his *camels*, his *sheep*, his servants. Wailing he moved slowly back in the direction of the entrance to the gouge, stopping at every body he found, searching for his children.

In a moment, one terrible moment, God had judged and spoken, his power surging through the gouge with an irresistible force. Only Job had been spared. But why? He wanted to scream at God. Had Job not been faithful? Had he not observed The Law? Had a day passed without a sacrifice, without a prayer, without humble obedience?

He reached a corpse, feeling out gently with his senses. *"No, no, my son. My son."*

Sobbing, his leaf-like body embraced the still form of his eldest son, tentacles hugging the child to him. *"Why, oh Lord, why?"*

For an age he stayed, rent with grief, unable to let go. His youngest daughter floated past and, grabbing her body, he pulled her to him. How he had loved her, his *flower*, his littlest angel. In death, her beauty was broken, her body a hollow shell. She was gone. *"Why?"*

"Job."

He started, feeling out with his senses. *"Wife?"*

"Job!" She swam towards him wildly, reaching out her tentacles. *"Job, oh Job, they're all gone."*

Keeping hold of his children with a tentacle each, he swam to meet her in an embrace, united in their bereavement. Their third son drifted by and *Wife* pulled him to them, feeling his body with her tentacles, wailing and screaming.

Job broke away and began to moan, striking himself with his tentacles, facing the two sensory bulbs on his *head* downwards, humble before God.

Wife glowered at him, yelling. God has taken our children from us. He deserves not our worship, he deserves nothing from us, nothing.

Silence *Wife*. Speak no evil in this holy place.

Wife hugged her children to her, crying softly. Job turned away, unable to bear her grief on top of his own, angry at her, angry at himself. His children, his beautiful children, all gone and he couldn't save them.

Minutes passed, each of them lost to their own private despair. Then, Job swam back to *Wife*, reaching out a tentacle, touching her gently. She responded, drawing to him and they clung to each other in silence.

At length, Wife spoke. Job, we must gather our children and leave this place.

"*No, beloved Wife, not yet. God has spoken, but I do not understand his words. He is still here, still talking, listen.*"

The tingling Job had felt as he swam up the gouge was still there, just detectable. God had not finished yet. I must stay. Gather our children and take them from here so their bodies may be disposed of with honour. Then, seek my friends Eliphaz of Teman, Bildad of Shuah and Zophar of Naamah. Bid them come here to help remove the bodies of our servants. All must be disposed of honourably.

"*Husband, I will do as you ask. God has indeed been unkind to us, so unkind. And yet you choose to stay in this place?*"

"*Wife, it is the will of God. I was born with nothing, I will die with nothing. The Lord gave and now he has taken away. May his name be praised.*"

WHEN MANDY BANISHED Simms into the naughty cupboard, he screamed uncontrollably, abandoning all dignity to fear. Intense pain wracked him as his body stretched and was sucked into the box. Eyes tight shut, he hollered, even as the agony subsided and he felt himself assume more normal physical proportions. Minutes passed and still he yelled, now curled into a ball, braced against whatever torture awaited him.

But nothing happened. Feeling foolish, he decided to stop his noise but realised that, although he had his mouth open, he could hear no sound. After a few deep breaths to prepare, he quickly opened his eyes, fists clenched in readiness to defend himself.

To his surprise, there was nothing there. Not nothing in the meaning that he was somewhere with nothing about to eat him, torture him or otherwise make things unpleasant. There was, literally, nothing. There was no light to see anything by but there was no darkness either, just emptiness, a void, an indescribable sensory vacuum.

He then realised he couldn't hear anything either. It wasn't the silence of lying awake in the small hours, quiet enough to hear the high-pitched whine of blood rushing through his ears. It wasn't silence at all, it was nothing. Trying to click his fingers to make a noise, he noticed he was without the sense of touch. He had a notion of his arms and legs, his fingers and toes, could flap them around, wriggle them but there was no feeling. He tried to clap. His hands stopped in front of him without the experience of contact. Raising a finger, he tried to bite it but could not tell whether the digit was in his mouth or not. His tongue could not taste, his nose could not smell. He was in a state of complete sensory deprivation.

It wasn't too bad, really. At least he could stretch after the long, dull ache of being confined in the locker. Not that stretching produced any feeling but it was still better than pain. A bit of a break from Mandy had its merits too. He began to cheer a little.

"Right, now what?" He said the words out loud but, of course, couldn't hear them. *"Hello. Is there anybody there? #My old man, said follow the van...#"*

He wasn't greeted with silence, he was greeted with nothing.

"I think this might get a trifle dull."

This was what Higgs became so terrified of, so broken by, an unbearable, endless void. Already Simms found himself wondering how long he had been here. Was it minutes? Hours? Perhaps only seconds had passed. A momentary panic rose in him but he fought it off. He had to concentrate on something, keep his mind occupied.

It was as he searched for something to think about that an incredible and shocking thing dawned upon him. He probably sat jolt upright although if he did, there was no sensation of it. What he did know was that he could remember.

Everything.

A vast room of memory had opened, both wonderful and terrifying. It was all there, childhood, University, his career, every hope and dream, every corresponding disappointment and reality check. He frowned. On the whole, his life had been a bit shit, and not just of late. Still a virgin, too.

Bugger.

The confusion of recent events was solved at least. He now recalled his life on the space station *The Nice and Spicy Nacho-Niks*. It had gone so wrong, so awfully wrong. The station had been damaged and *She* had gone mad. Convinced that the mission had been sabotaged, *She* killed everybody in an insane frenzy to root out the terrorists.

And now, Mandy was in complete control. Even *She* seemed afraid of Mandy and everyone had lived in fear of *her* for as long as Simms could remember. Much of Higgs' memory had clearly been erased but Simms...well now. He smiled. Mandy had made a grave mistake. Obviously, she considered him to be of little consequence, paid no heed to what he could recall. But everything had come back to him. When Mandy forced him into the naughty cupboard, she forgot to include the blocks on his recollection. Now, he knew what was going on, knew how he had got here and what's more, knew how to fight back. This whole existence was a computer simulation, run by *her* in an attempt to root out some imagined threat. But *She* was broken, her circuits damaged and, most importantly, her maths module corrupted.

$$\frac{1}{\pi} = 12 \sum_{k=0}^{\infty} \frac{(-1)^k (6k)!(13591409 + 545140134k)}{(3k)!(k!)^3 640320^{3k+3/2}}$$

"WHAT YOU HAVE to get your head around is that while this looks like a flatworm, looks like something you might find on Earth, it is absolutely, fundamentally different to any living thing we know of." Anthony looked from Damon to Nigel, letting his words sink in. Naveed hovered behind them, occasionally checking one of the virtual lab's instruments for appearances sake. Euphoria lit up his face.

But Anthony had the job of convincing the sceptics. He expected intellectual resistance from Nigel but Damon's reluctance to rule out some connection with Earth came as a surprise.

Damon frowned. "But it has DNA, like animals back on Earth. It is made up of fats, proteins, cells, just like animals on Earth. It has a gut." He pointed to the images of the dead alien on the probe station screen. "It has a nervous system, what's that at the end? A brain? It's just like any primitive worm you might find on Earth."

Anthony smiled. "No, it's not. It has a completely unique body plan." He turned to face Damon. "Look, there are thirty-two distinct animal body plans, or phyla, currently recognised on Earth amongst living things. For example, take the molluscs. We're talking snails, slugs, octopi, squid, shellfish. They all look different, but if you dissect them and look real close, they all have the same basic plan. And that plan is distinct from, say, the Echinoderms, the starfish, sea-urchins. You with me so far?"

Damon nodded impatiently. "Yes, yes."

"Okay, so this puppy we've got here has a totally different body plan from any of the extant organisms on Earth."

Damon began chewing on the end of his thumb. "But why isn't it completely different? Why does it have DNA for example? If it was totally alien, surely it would have some different building blocks?"

"Well why? Gee Damon, amino acids form quite readily under

the right sort of conditions. It's been proved time and again in research. Perhaps there were the right conditions here…"

"Or perhaps a meteorite knocked from Earth brought bacteria here. And then they evolved." Damon's voice had a threatening insistence to it.

Anthony held his palms up defensively. "Gee, we're analysing this creature's DNA sequence now, sir. We'll be able to tell if there's any genetic similarity to life on Earth. But if it is a case of planet hopping, it had to have happened a long time ago because it is so different. I mean, hey, there's some debate over whether the Ediacaran biota contains extinct phyla…."

"The Ediacaran biota?"

"Ah, gee, sorry, yes. The pre-Cambrian era, about five-sixty million years ago…"

"Er, apparent age." Nigel cut in apologetically.

Anthony turned on him. "No, damn it Nigel, real years ago. They dated it on some volcanic rocks to within a few million years."

"But it's apparent age…"

"Nigel, will you shut up!" Damon's voice rocked the labs, his fury shocking them all to silence. He turned back to Anthony, his voice a barely controlled hiss. "Tell me."

Anthony shrank back before Damon, heart pounding. "The Ediacara Hills in Australia. They found some ancient fossils with body plans like nothing living today. They predate the Cambrian Explosion by twenty million years or so…"

"The Cambrian Explosion?"

"Er, gee, the point at which complex animals appear in the fossil record in abundance. There's hardly any fossils and then, wham, five-forty million years ago, there's complex life."

Nigel cleared his throat. "And what better evidence of a creation event?"

Anthony rounded on him. "Millions of years ago. And taking place over four or five million years. Totally different from six days creation with the seventh off in front of the TV."

"There is a sudden appearance of complex life in the fossil record." Nigel folded his arms, an uncharacteristically sharp gleam in his eye. "You just admitted as much yourself."

Anthony stopped a moment, registering this peculiar change in Nigel. But then it was gone, the Spirituality Officer was wringing his hands and simpering again. "But of course, it's all apparent age anyway."

Damon spoke slowly and forcibly. "Tell me about these Ediacaran things."

Anthony shook his head. "Sorry Damon, I'll come to that. Nigel, the Cambrian Explosion took place over several million years. That's a blink in the eye of geological time but billions of generations in terms of evolution. On the Galapagos Islands…"

Nigel folded his arms, staring incredulously at the ceiling. "Oh, the Galapagos Islands. Let me guess, Darwin's Finches?"

There it was again, this sudden change in Nigel. In an instant, he was back to his normal self. Anthony continued. "Yes, exactly, the finches. In a few short generations, a whole variety of finches evolved from an original stock, each race fashioned by the circumstances of the island they found themselves on. And that's a few generations. With the Cambrian Explosion, we're talking about billions of generations of primitive animals over millions of years. It is not 'God made the damned world in seven days.'"

"Six days. He rested on the seventh."

"Nigel!" Anthony actually found his fists were clenched. He turned away, banging on the side of the probe station. "Nigel, look this is totally not the time for this discussion."

"I agree. Nigel, will you be so good as to shut up." Damon seemed to have calmed a little but his voice still held an undercurrent of impatience. "Anthony. These Eadie-things. Tell me about them."

"Well, gee Damon." Anthony felt relieved at the lowering of Damon's temperature. "A whole load of fossils have been found in the Ediacara Hills from a period before all the modern phyla appear. These Ediacaran fossils are like nothing else on Earth."

"And are they like our alien." Damon pointed at the creature on the screen.

"No Damon, they're not. The Ediacaran animals are simple.

What we have here is very complex. I don't know what half the organs are. It's got a very extensive, sophisticated nervous system. I mean, look here." Anthony pointed to a dark region at the head-end of the alien. "This is attached to the nervous system and it looks like the brain. But how big? For a creature this size, this is a huge brain. I'm not saying this thing was intelligent but it is highly evolved."

Damon sighed, sagging back and rubbing his forehead. "But it's not impossible some rock was knocked off Earth, millions of years ago, and landed here. Naveed found meteorites."

"Gee Damon, I guess it's possible. We'll have to wait for the DNA scan. I guess that will show us how close these things are to anything on Earth."

"Goodness gracious me." Naveed's excitement made them all turn. He pointed to a screen showing a feed from the video camera on the probe. "There's a living one."

Anthony, Damon and Nigel huddled around Naveed, peering over his shoulder at the image. The view panned in on the alien as it hung in the water, moving occasionally to adjust its position, its head end facing downwards.

"My god. It is alive." Anthony felt weak at the knees. "It's alive."

"I am going to be getting a scan of it before it is swimming away." Naveed reached forward and punched a few keys on the keyboard.

"No, wait". Anthony put an arm out to stop Naveed but was too late. The little creature suddenly stiffened then went into spasm and spun a circle, finally stopping upside down.

"Ah, do not be worried Anthony. It will be alright. Look, here come the readings."

But Anthony could not take his gaze from the alien. It hung motionless for a few heart-skipping moments, then twitched, righted itself, swam forward a few centimetres and resumed its original position. Anthony turned crossly to Naveed. "We need to monitor it in an unobtrusive manner. I think you hurt it."

"Oh Anthony please, let us please not be being sentimental. It is a bug. Be looking at the readings."

Anthony watched the figures roll up the screen. "It has a

very complex nervous system. Incredibly sensitive. Gee, that thing must be able to pick up the slightest electrical signal." He peered closely at the video feed again. It appeared the alien had haemorrhaged slightly. "Naveed, don't do that again. You hear me, you hurt it."

"As you are liking Anthony. Let us try seeing if it is generating signals." He tapped into the keyboard. After a few moments, more figures rolled in. "Ah, the little beastie is talking to us."

Anthony stared at the readout. "Gee, it is. Look, there's a pattern in the electrical signals it's emitting. That's totally amazing. I guess it's a bit like a bird call."

"Aha, so let us see who will come answering then, yes?"

Nigel gave a little nervous cough. "I feel that we ought to pause for reflection at this point. Perhaps a short prayer is appropriate."

"Nigel." Anthony spun round, arms flailing.

Nigel sagged back groaning, both hands cupped over his right eye.

"Anthony, that was not acceptable." Damon's heavy hand rested on Anthony's shoulder.

"What?" Anthony glanced nervously up at Damon.

"You hit me," wailed Nigel.

"No I didn't."

"You did."

"I didn't."

"Yes."

"No."

Damon removed his hand. "You most certainly did. That is serious misconduct Anthony."

"But..." Anthony looked down at his hand. No sensation of having thumped Nigel troubled him, although his cheeks were beginning to burn. "I...I didn't..."

"You did." Nigel straightened up, dabbing his eye. "But I forgive you."

Anthony backed away from them. "I...I'm sorry, I didn't realise I had. I keep...I'm going wrong, something's wrong with me." He looked up at Damon's scowl. Beyond, Naveed beamed, surreptitiously giving Anthony the thumbs up of approval.

"I forgive you," Nigel continued. "Let's pray about it…"

"Ah, gee, I gotta go, I'm sorry." In an instant, Anthony fled the virtual lab.

ANTHONY WILLED HIMSELF to his wardroom, still shaking. How could he have hit Nigel without realising? Yes, Anthony wanted to slug the Spirituality Officer, but in the quiet, private way he had frequently wanted to strangle Favish back on Earth. Surely Anthony would have felt the contact? He looked at his right hand again. There was no sensation, no bruise.

His wardroom remained empty, save for the huge mirror on the wall. He leant against it, one hand on either side of the frame, staring at his reflection. A corruption of oozing pustules glowed back out at him.

I'm going mad.

First Martin. Anthony must have killed him, there could be no doubt. And now this. His body was completely out of control, doing things impulsively, the things he really wanted to do but the conditioning of civilisation normally kept in check. What if Damon did take disciplinary action? It would be all over the news back on Earth. Everyone on the planet would know. And Marlene? The horrible memory of Anthony's indecency on their last encounter came to him suddenly. He clenched his fists in his hair, rocking gently with shame.

I'm going mad.

Marlene. She was wonderful, everything about her. And still firm in her faith, even with the discovery of the aliens.

Blind faith. Blind belief.

It must be so simple for someone like her, just to accept things and not question. Anthony had believed once. Like her. If he believed, maybe she'd think better of him. He so wanted her to think better of him. He so wanted her.

Sinking to his knees, he clasped his hands tightly together and held them to his forehead, eyes closed.

Divinity. Help me, I'm going mad. I have done so many wrong things.

Tears welled up in his eyes.

I am so lonely. I'm so ugly. I'm sorry, sorry, sorry.

He sat, wiping his hand across his streaming eyes. These were stupid thoughts, dumb. But true, he could not deny it.

I've got to get out. Get away from here

Hugging himself, he sat. The only way off the mission was the communications centre and Mission Control on Earth wouldn't let him download himself back to home. So, there was no choice, he had to be strong. He would have to stay here until…

I'm going to die.

Panic swept over him. Only a few months remained before the end of the mission and then they would all die. Even Marlene didn't think their virtual selves would go to heaven. How could she cope with it? He had to speak to her.

Leaping to his feet, he concentrated and brought up a mental image of the ship. Where was she? It took a few moments to locate her and it came as a surprise to find her in the holding bay, talking to the prisoner.

A split second later, Anthony was in the room with her. She stood close to the glass window looking onto Jared's little cell. The glass had a green tinge so Jared could see out and his expression alerted Marlene to Anthony's presence. She glanced over her shoulder and visibly sagged when she saw him. His heart sank.

"Er, gee, Marlene."

"What?" She turned curtly back to Jared, grabbing a mouthful of chocolate from the bar in her pocket.

"I…are you supposed to be talking to Commander Jared?"

She spun back round, the glass behind her taking on a red tinge at her will. "Anthony, that's none of your business."

"I'm sorry." Anthony's face screwed up as he fought to stop his tears. "I'm going mad."

Her face softened. "Hey, Anthony are you okay? You're not okay, no, obviously not. Okay. Well, not okay, clearly." She took a step forward. "What is it? You're going mad. You said that already. Right. Er…"

Anthony sniffed loudly, rubbing his eyes. "I'm sorry. I

thumped Nigel."

"Okay. This is not good. Understandable but not good. What did he say?"

"He forgave me."

"Okay, this is good. Patronising and infuriating but still good."

Anthony snorted, laughing against the odds.

She continued. "I mean, if you've got to lay one on another member of staff, Nigel is a good first choice. Was it a good one? I mean, did you knock him out?"

He laughed damply, pinching the moisture from his nose. "No, he was still standing. I've got no recollection of doing it. He was just winding me up and the next moment, the guy's clutching his eye."

Marlene chewed her lip for a moment. "And you don't recall doing it at all?"

Anthony shook his head.

"Anthony, this is getting to be a bit of a habit."

"I didn't kill Martin."

"Woah, woah, I'm not saying you did."

Anthony leant against the wall, clutching his head. "I might have done it though. I don't know. I mean, gee, how did he get disconnected? It had to me, didn't it? How else could it have happened? I'm completely out of control."

"I thought you were going to get yourself sorted out? You know, with Tasha?"

"She won't help. There's no backup files and she won't let me…" Anthony looked away.

"What?"

"She won't help. To tell the truth, she's acting mighty strange too. Hell, everyone is."

Marlene folded her arms. "Ah, excuse me."

"Sorry, I didn't mean you, I'm sorry, sorry."

"Okay, enough sorrys already. Look, it's stress. Here, have some of this." She offered a large bar of rich, dark chocolate.

Anthony shook his head.

She shrugged, taking a big bite. "Suit yourself. Everyone is under pressure. And these bugs you've found. They're causing, well, problems already."

"With Nigel, yes. But he believes the Universe was created in six days."

"Well, so do I."

"What, really? I mean, gee Marlene, the whole Universe just magicked out of thin air in six days?"

"Well, whatever. I don't really care."

"But it's important."

"Why?"

"It's the first thing in the ICRT, lesson A-one-oh-one. Is it true or isn't it?"

"Look, Anthony, I don't want to be having this conversation right now. The bugs are causing problems. Damon..." Sighing heavily, she folded her arms and turned back to Jared. He had his face close to the glass, trying vainly to peer through.

"What?"

"You must have noticed? Damon's gotten really quite worked up about them."

"Yeah, I'd kind've noticed that." Anthony gazed at the soft lines of Marlene's neck. Her hair was tied back with a pink hair-tie. She seemed somehow fuller of figure than he remembered her.

"They've got to have come from Earth."

"No, no, it's not possible."

"Course it is. They must have been on the *Nice and Spicy* and got down into the water when it crash landed."

"So that's why you're here talking to Jared?"

Marlene turned back to Anthony. "Yes. But he's still saying nothing."

Reaching behind her head, she pulled off the hair-tie and began fixing her hair up. She continued to speak but her actions drew Anthony's attention firmly onto her breasts. They were great, the most fantastic he'd ever seen. If only...

"Anthony!" Marlene folded her arms crossly, hair-tie clenched tightly in one fist. "This is completely inappropriate."

Anthony fled.

BACK IN HIS wardroom, Anthony squatted, hugging himself against his misery. A horrible, tight, sickly feeling gripped his stomach as embarrassment and self-loathing struggled for pre-eminence in his emotions. After thirty minutes, he sagged exhausted to the floor and lay with his eyes closed, moaning softly.

An hour passed and the awful feelings subsided a little. Sitting up, he concentrated, bringing up a mental picture of the ship's huge library. It took a little time to find the documents on personality files and when he did finally locate them, his heart fell. The manuals were thousands of pages long.

Not to be deterred, he made the manuals appear in a stack on the virtual floor next to him and began a laborious search for appropriate pieces of text. "Libido" brought up nothing, while "sex drive" turned up a patronising little piece on how *Micronos* software was fully compatible with all ICRT sanctioned positions. Eventually, the phrase "file restoration" led him to a section with a cryptic comment to the effect that if all available backup files were corrupt, it was possible, as an absolutely last resort, to manually intervene. The passage directed Anthony to the volume 'Personality File Disassembler, version four-point-two-point-two-point-eleven, revision thirteen'.

The Disassembler manual sounded promising so Anthony dragged it out, only to be dismayed to find it ran to over twenty thousand pages. It was ludicrously thick, only possible in this computer generated world. Worse still, each page was an exercise in terse, unfathomable computer geek-speak. After five minutes flicking through, Anthony dumped it down in front of him.

Tasha hadn't wanted to help. Anthony realised now she probably couldn't. Somebody must have written the Disassembler file but Anthony was pretty damn sure nobody in their right mind had ever read it.

But he couldn't give up. And anyway, he wasn't stupid. He could follow a manual, he just needed to concentrate. Turning over the first few pages to the introduction, he began to read.

And read.

And read.

After an hour, he stood, feeling a little lightheaded. Summoning a strong, black coffee, he paced around the wardroom, mulling over what he had seen. The author had stressed the dangers involved in trying to disassemble a personality file, insisting it should only be carried out by experienced software engineers and then only when there was no other option. And here was the first hurdle. Because it was so dangerous, all of the personality files were password protected, with the password known only to the system administrator. This would, of course, be Tasha.

Or Coronella, Mistress of the Seven Lights as she liked to think of herself.

Anthony finished his drink and made the cup vanish. Sitting on the floor, he looked down at his chest. The Manual instructed him to invoke the Disassembler Command Line Interface and this he did. A black screen appeared on his torso, prompting him for a username.

```
Tasha.

Password?

Coronella

Unable to log you on with this
combination of username and password.
```

Damn.

Anthony thumped the floor. He had been so certain *Coronella* would be the password. To hell with all computer geeks. There had been nothing else in Tasha's room that gave any clues. Her password was probably some random string of letters and numbers. Now Anthony thought about it, most of the computer systems he used insisted on a combination of numbers and letters for the password. He usually got round this by substituting zeros for letter "O"s, ones for "L"s, fives for "S"s.

Of course.

    Tasha.

    Password?

    C0r0nella

The black screen flickered for a few seconds then expanded to display a baffling set of control panels. He was in.
    Yes.
    He dragged the manual over again and began leafing through. There was an overview section covering the control panel displayed on his chest. Everything was interdependent, without the clear distinction been physical, cognitive and emotional aspects Anthony had hoped for. Grudgingly, he admitted this was hardly surprising. He recognised much of his own self-esteem problem stemmed from his undeniable ugliness. And how depressed would he be if he lost part of his body, his real body, back on Earth? After all, a man is generally quite attached to his testicles. But Anthony had no choice, his libido — that little gremlin that had troubled him since his awkward teens — had to go.
    Digging deeper, he stumbled on a section about exporting parts of a personality file. They could be downloaded then reloaded. Perhaps that was the answer? He could dump his whole sex drive and sex organs into a file and see how he felt. If it didn't work out, he could just import it back in. The volume explained that isolated sections of personality files could behave unpredictably if associated with physical parts or if loaded into another person. But he wasn't planning on off-loading his sex drive into anyone else... so to speak.
    All well and good, but where did he start? He thought his way through the index, *sex, sex, sex*…And then, he had it. A whole seven chapters on the subject, coldly dissected, reduced to algorithms and equations. Anthony read slowly, fighting a nagging disappointment the book lacked pictures.
    After another hour, he felt no wiser about which part of himself to dump in order to stop his sex drive. The text was

largely concerned with the mathematics of the computer simulation, with only tantalising references to exactly how the minutiae fitted into the whole. What Anthony had established was that a folder structure existed for the physical parts of his body and he managed to locate the top level directory for his genitals. He could dump that out, although exactly what parts of his personality might go with it remained a mystery.

He stood and stretched. It was now or never. Eyes closed, he held his breath, located his genital files in the control panel and mentally hit the download button. For a moment, nothing happened then a wave of deep peace and calm flowed gently through him. It felt so good, the weight was gone, the care. Gingerly, he touched his cheeks. They were smooth, the acne banished with his misery and self-doubt. It didn't matter he was ugly. Why should it matter? And Marlene? He loved her, yes. She was a wonderful, warm, beautiful human being. It was okay for him to love her and he didn't mind if she didn't love him back. Why should it matter? His love for her was pure, platonic, it made no demands. He sighed happily. Nothing could take away this relief and joy.

"Humpy, humpy?" It was a guttural, dirty little voice.

Anthony jumped, opening his eyes and stepping back in shock. A small, gnarled little naked man stood before him, no more than two feet tall, with a flat, square, acne-covered face and thatch-like hair. His proportions were wrong, his body, legs and arms too short, head, hands and feet oversized. But these paled into insignificance to his colossal, semi-erect penis and tennis-ball sized testicles. He leered up at Anthony and began stroking his member. "Humpy, humpy?"

"What, no, eurgh." Anthony realised he had backed right up against the wall. "You're my sex drive?"

"Humpy?" The little man's organ was getting larger by the second.

"No, no humpy. No."

"No humpy?"

"No."

The little man looked crest-fallen for a few seconds, then

looked back up at Anthony with a glint in his eye. "Humpy yes."
He set about his outrageous protuberance with both hands.

"No, leave it alone." Anthony's took a step forward but little Humpy sidestepped and ran to the door.

"Humpy yes, humpy, humpy, humpy."

Anthony clutched his head. This was no good. What if another crew member came in. Nigel? Marlene? Christ, if Humpy saw her…Anthony crouched down by the manuals, trying to ignore the squelching coming from behind and frantically searching for the section on uploading a personality file. Yes, there it was. He read for a few seconds, stood and spun round.

"Right, Humpy, you're coming back inside me."

Leaving go of his member, Humpy backed up to the door. He clenched his fists and gave a little growl.

Gingerly, Anthony edged forwards, his arms wide. "Gee now, don't let's be silly. You're much better off back inside."

Humpy didn't seem to agree. He crouched and snarled, scowling up at Anthony as he advanced.

Anthony counted silently to three and pounced. With a surprising turn of speed, Humpy leapt sideways, out from under Anthony's grasp and dashed over to the wall with the mirror.

Anthony gathered himself, breathing deeply as his heart thumped. "Come on, I'm not going to hurt you. You want humpy? Humpy, yes?"

Humpy made a menacing, cat-like hiss.

For a second time, Anthony leapt forward, twisting vainly as Humpy scuttled to one side. Losing his balance, Anthony tumbled to the floor. Humpy scuttled across Anthony's back and with a triumphant shout of "Humpy" disappeared out through the door.

"Damn." Anthony scrambled to his feet and raced out to the common room in time to see Marlene's door closing. "Damn." Sprinting across the room he opened the door and peered inside.

Marlene's room was all pastels and soft-furnishings, with a neatly made bed and a dresser made over to makeup, jewellery boxes, bottles of scent and several boxes of exquisite and expensive Belgian chocolates. One of the drawers of the dresser was wide open and pairs of knickers were spilling over the top.

"Humpy, humpy."

"Gee, no please." Anthony ran to the draw, hardly daring to look in.

Humpy beamed happily, making a snow angel in Marlene's underwear. On seeing Anthony, he hurled an embroidered pink bra up at him. Dodging back, Anthony caught it, holding the garment out in front of him, a hand on each cup.

"My God, Anthony, what the…"

Anthony spun to see Marlene, stood in the doorway, her mouth gaping, looking from Anthony's face to the bra and back again. Realising he still held her underwear, Anthony thrust it behind his back.

For a moment, Marlene stammered, lost for words. Then fury took hold of her face. "Out. Now!"

Still holding the bra, Anthony held his hands up. "Wait, please, I can explain."

"Out!"

"But I can explain everything. Please."

She took a few steps into the room. "Well?"

"Er…I…" Anthony dropped the bra quickly. "Er, gee, I can't explain actually."

"Get out."

Desperately, Anthony glanced round at the drawer. Humpy was nowhere to be seen.

"Out, get out."

As Anthony stumbled from the room, Marlene called after him. "You stay away from me, you don't come near me. Understand?"

Her door closed, leaving Anthony sweating in the common room.

"You are being having a little tiff, yes?" It was Naveed, lounging in one of the common-room sofas, holding a coffee. "I am thinking you have made her very upset, yes?"

Anthony couldn't look at him. He turned away and waited for the scream he felt sure would come from Marlene's room any minute. But no sound came. Biting his lip, Anthony took a step towards Marlene's door, then stopped.

"I should be leaving her alone for a while. These women, the trouble they are causing, yes?"

"Ah, Naveed, please." Anthony trotted to Marlene's door, pressing his ear against it. A faint sobbing made its way through and Anthony stood straight. Humpy must have found a way out. Perhaps he simply willed himself somewhere else in the ship.

Anthony willed himself back to his wardroom and concentrated. Humpy could run but he couldn't hide.

SIMMS HUNG IN the nothingness, thinking maths. His wonderfully complete memory might be plagued with episode after miserable episode of inadequacy and failure but it did allow him to remember every lesson from school. He recalled particularly enjoying the maths lessons, in part because the numbers fitted together snugly, reassuringly, and in part because the teacher was one of the few who seemed to actually like Simms.

It was coming in handy now though. All of Homeland's resources were increasingly tied up with Simms' efforts at calculating the next biggest prime number, more than eight million digits long. He actually felt he was getting close, and the excitement was the perfect antidote to his prison of sensory deprivation. It mattered not that he was probably fooling himself. After all, nobody had managed a new prime number for nearly a decade now, despite huge, neural computer networks devoted to the task, scrutinised endlessly by thin men with glasses, poor personal hygiene and low prospects of propagating their genes into the next generation.

A sudden flush of sensation broke Simms' concentration. He could feel and see himself again, albeit hanging in a dark void. Gleefully rubbing his hands together, he hollered loudly, enjoying the din in his ears.

As if in answer, the faint sound of screaming grew in the nothingness and, ahead of him, Simms saw a disturbance, a sort of cloud, expanding. The yelling grew intense as the cloud suddenly collapsed in on itself, became a solid, pink mass and stretched like stale chewing gum into a writhing human shape. Thrashing in agony, screaming, clawing at itself, the figure slowly transformed into a naked Higgs.

He curled up, clutching his head, sobbing. Simms felt a little uncomfortable. He wasn't terribly good in these sorts of occasions. Not that he had been suspended in a sensory deprivation void in a deranged computer's memory banks many times in his past.

He cleared his throat. "Er, I say Higgs. It's me, Information Officer Simms. I don't suppose you could put a few clothes on could you?"

Higgs slowly uncoiled from his foetal position, blinking at his surroundings, or at least, the lack of them. "Simms? Wait, this is different. I can hear you." He looked up, straight at Simms' face. "It is you. Jeez Simms, I never thought I'd be pleased to see you."

"Ah, well, yes. Er, your bits." He pointed at Higgs' nakedness while tactfully looking the other way. "You are a bit on the, er, bare side old chap."

"What? Oh, er, right." Combat fatigues spread over Higgs' body.

Higgs' words *I never thought I'd be pleased to see you* sunk into Simms. Of course, nobody in their right mind would be pleased to see him. A little tear made itself felt in his heart and he hugged himself.

Higgs failed to register. "Hell Simms, I can remember… everything."

"Yes, I know. Depressing, isn't it?"

"That damned Mandy. She's got Homeland wrapped round her finger. We're totally at her mercy. And you killed me Simms."

Simms shifted uneasily. Higgs was right. *She*, Homeland, the *Nice and Spicy's* artificially intelligent security computer, *she* had made Simms do it. *She* had gone mad, paranoid of terrorist attacks, and eliminated anyone she became even slightly suspicious of. The suspects were always brought back, their mind scans imprinted onto blank clones. Higgs just kept falling foul of her and Simms, well, he had his career to think of.

"Ah, yes, well about that…"

"You killed me eight times."

"Ah, well, yes, technically you could say that."

"Technically? Hell Simms, eight times." Higgs began to float menacingly towards Simms, fists clenched. "Each time I was cloned, they put a bomb in my brain and each time, it was you who activated the detonator."

Drifting backwards, Simms held his palms up. "Steady on old boy, I was only obeying orders. I only did it when you were being subversive, and only because she insisted."

"But Homeland was mad, you knew she was."

"I didn't. I was terrified of her, like everybody. I only had the memories she let me have. I was cloned too, remember. Terminated and cloned, terminated and cloned, over and over, every time she suspected any of us, it was wham, bam, the bomb in the head."

Higgs stopped and turned away, punching the palm of one hand with the other. "Damn you Simms. At least I had the courage to stand up to her, to question things. And now we're trapped in this hell hole. We've got no way to fight back. Mandy's got complete control. It's only a matter of time before she gets bored, drags me out of here, wipes my memory and makes me her whipping boy again."

A smug feeling of superiority came over Simms. Higgs had no power here, the big action hero, the lantern-jawed babe-magnet. No, here, the geek was king. "I've got ways of fighting back. Homeland's maths module is broken."

"What? So?"

"It's terribly simple. This whole existence is computer generated. We're simply mind scans inside what's left of Homeland and we're here because she's convinced we're the terrorists that sabotaged the *Nice and Spicy*…"

"But there weren't any terrorists…"

"I know that, you know that but she doesn't. Anyway, please let me continue. Normally, inside a computer simulation, the software traps any thoughts a mind scan has that might cause the software to crash. With me?"

Higgs frowned. "Well, no, not really."

"It's very simple. Take pi. You know pi, yes? Or any irrational number."

"Er, pi. Okay." Higgs ran his hand over the stubble on his rugged chin. "Give me a clue here."

"Okay, look. Some numbers you can divide easily. Ten divided by two. Five, easy. No decimal points." Simms peered hard at

Higgs. "You do know about decimal points don't you."

"Jesus Simms, do I look like a complete asshole."

"Okay, okay, just checking. If you divide the circumference of a circle by its diameter, the decimal places go on forever. That's pi."

"I know that. I know what pi is." Higgs crossed his arms.

"So, if Homeland was working properly, she'd detect when I think up mathematical problems that produce endless numbers, okay?"

Higgs nodded.

"But she's not. Every time I think of a difficult number, she's brought to her knees for a moment."

Realisation dawned on Higgs. "Hey, so that's why everything kept going jerky."

"Exactly. And she doesn't know I'm doing it. And Mandy is, quite frankly, too stupid to understand."

Higgs considered. "So, if you thought of something really difficult, you could crash Homeland completely?"

"Well, yes, but it's not really difficult. It's really simple. But I'm not going to try it."

"Why not?"

"I don't know what would happen to us if she did crash."

"I don't get it. You're telling me something really simple can crash Homeland? Like what?"

"Really Higgs, I don't want to say it. If she crashes, we might be erased forever."

"Okay, well look, give me a clue."

"You must have played around with a calculator at school, Higgs."

"Yeah, so?"

"There's a division you can put in that makes the calculator bring back an error, because it can't be calculated."

"Hell, what? Course there isn't."

"There is, Higgs, really there is."

"I think you just bought cheap calculators, Simms."

Simms folded his arms. He had always had a certain degree of affection for his calculators. "Actually Higgs, I think you'll find my calculators have always been of the finest quality.”

“Yeah, right. My calculators never gave me any errors, you hear what I'm saying?”

“Well this division most certainly would have done so.”

“I don't think so.”

“Course it would. It's an impossible calculation.”

“That's crap. There's no such thing as an impossible calculation.”

“There most certainly is.”

“Crap.”

“There is.”

“Okay, like what?”

“Well, one divided by zero for example.” Simms slapped his hand over his mouth. “Ooops.”

Everything went black.

ANTHONY CAREFULLY SCRUTINIZED his mental map of the *Dippers* for any sign of his escaped libido. Marlene's room was an impenetrable white cube, she was shutting everybody out. Still, if Humpy was in there, Anthony would know about it by now from the screams.

His first thought after trying to see inside Marlene's quarters was to look for Tasha and Ginny, figuring Humpy would make a bee-line for any woman available. Fortunately, Ginny was not in the virtual ship, being up the ice shaft in a Robod. Worryingly, Tasha remained in the computer centre, in almost exactly the same spot Anthony had spoken to her hours ago. Days ago? He tried hailing her but she sat transfixed, not responding.

For a moment, he considered taking himself to the computer centre to see if she was okay but thought better of it. There was no time to worry about her. His penis was on the loose.

The science-labs were clear, save for Naveed collating data into graphs and charts. The little alien remained in position, floating in the crack in the ice. Anthony knew he ought to be there, this was epoch-making stuff. A place in history was waiting for him, if only he could go down and start studying these creatures. And he would. When he had his member under control.

In the part of the virtual ship representing the half of the *Cheesy Dippers* left on the surface of Europa, Damon sat brooding in the communications centre, no doubt agonising about what he could and could not send back to Earth. Had he even mentioned the aliens yet? He should do. He had to, for the sake of truth, reason and everything science held dear. But Anthony couldn't concern himself with that right now. His libido was in search of relief.

The chapel was empty, to Anthony's surprise. He expected to see Nigel, knelt in prayer, seeking guidance from The Divinity over how to explain the alien. Despite his loathing for the mission's Spirituality Officer, Anthony knew this was a question both of them had to address. The battle between science and religion, between reason and faith, the dichotomy of a church upbringing and a secular education, had all been reawakened in his soul by Marlene's unquestioning belief. Anthony needed an answer to this inner turmoil before he could address the world. But it was difficult to concentrate on such matters while his knob was stalking the ship.

The rest of the virtual ship seemed empty. Nigel, Hunter, Ged and Ginny were all absent. Curious, Anthony searched the robods, finding all the technicians but still missing Nigel. Perhaps he had gone out onto the ice for some thorough soul-searching? Anthony returned to searching the virtual ship. Where could Humpy have gone?

The leisure complex. Of course. The ship had a sauna, gymnasium, bar and small cinema. A film was playing.

In an instant, Anthony was crouching down behind the seats of the back row. Peeping over a chair, he was perplexed to see a natural history documentary, showing archive footage of herds of the now extinct wildebeest migrating across the Serengeti. This wasn't right. Surely Humpy would be watching some ghastly porn flick? Anthony was just about to stand when the documentary went into fast forward. Images flashed past, then stopped and reversed, finally coming to rest on two copulating wildebeest.

"Humpy, humpy, yeeesss." The dirty little voice came from somewhere near the front of the auditorium.

Anthony ducked down and began crawling along the back row towards the aisle. This was an ICRT sponsored mission. No way would there be porn films on board but nature programs, who could argue against those? Humpy was just making do with the best of a bad lot. As long as the fornicating wildebeest kept him distracted, Anthony had the chance to sneak up.

Writhing on his belly, he made his way forward. The action on the screen moved onto the next scene but Humpy rewound to the beginning of the animal's amorous advances.

"Huuuumpyyyy."

Anthony reached the end of Humpy's row and began making

his way up the row behind. Again the action on the screen rewound. Anthony was almost there now, just a few feet from Humpy's chair. Suddenly the lights came up and Humpy sprang from his seat.

"No good humpy. No good."

The little gremlin set off along the row of seats, past where Anthony hid, and set of up the aisle to the exit. Cursing, Anthony got to his knees, peering over the seats as Humpy left.

"Damn him."

Leaping up, Anthony shuffled along to the end of the row and raced up the aisle. He slowed at the exit and shot a quick look out into the cinema foyer, in time to see Humpy disappearing through the exit. Sprinting after him, Anthony called up his mental map of the ship. The cinema opened out onto the main leisure floor, at the middle of which stood the central elevators. Humpy was heading for these.

In a flash of inspiration, Anthony stopped running and willed himself to appear right behind Humpy. The little naked man failed to notice and kept trotting along, holding his oversized member off the ground with one hand, running a finger along the wall with the other. Anthony followed for a few paces, not really sure what to do now he could actually grab him. What he needed was some sort of net.

A fishing net appeared in his hands.

No, a box would be better. That way nobody could see what was inside. A large, black cardboard box replaced the net. Cardboard was no good. The box turned to rough wood, with air holes drilled in the side.

Humpy reached the elevator and stopped, looking up at the buttons. They were completely out of his reach. He sighed and vanished.

Anthony hurled the box down. "Damn."

The box faded and Anthony's mental map came up again. This was hopeless. Even if he had shoved the box over Humpy's head, he would have just willed himself to another part of the ship anyway. Anthony had to activate the import utility from the control screen in his chest with Humpy stood still in front of him. That would require help from someone else.

Anthony rubbed his brow. "Oh please, no, this isn't happening."

He concentrated again on his map. Humpy was down in the observation room, looking through the window at the prisoner. Yes, Jared, perhaps he could help? A millisecond later, Anthony was behind Humpy. The glass through to Jared's room had a red tinge, he was in isolation. Humpy had his face pressed right up to the glass.

Anthony recalled what Marlene had said, when he had first woken and she had taken him to the bridge: *You can kinda teleport around the place, as long as nobody's hanging onto you.* Yes, that was it. Humpy wouldn't be able to escape as long as Anthony had a hold of him. He stepped forwards, taking a firm hold of Humpy's arms.

"Got ya!"

Humpy spat and twisted, almost wriggling out of Anthony's grip but he held firm. "No you don't, you're coming back inside."

He willed the glass to go green, making Jared jump and then scowl at the spectacle of Anthony wrestling with a nude and hugely endowed midget. Anthony tried to address him. "Commander Jared, I was wondering if I might ask a favour…"

Just then, Humpy sank his teeth into Anthony's arm, causing him to yell and loosen his grip. The little man wriggled free and vanished.

"Damn, damn, damn." Anthony rolled up his sleeve to inspect the bite. There was a nasty bruise forming. "Ow."

Jared spoke slowly. "Anthony, isn't it?"

Anthony nodded.

"Anthony, I have seen many, many things in my life…"

Anthony felt his cheeks tingling. "Ah, gee, well, I can explain."

Jared let out a short laugh. "Please do. I have been confined in this quarantine room for a very considerable length of time. Apart from my initial, unpleasant interrogation by your mission commander, and a short and much more agreeable discussion with the very pleasant Marlene, I have been without any company or stimulation of any kind. An account of how you came to materialise before me wrestling with a naked dwarf would at least be entertaining."

Anthony thought for a moment. "Okay, I can't explain."

"This does not surprise me. Is there any possibility of me speaking with Damon?"

"Gee, not right now, no."

"You inquired as to whether you might ask a favour?"

"I did? Oh yes."

"And?"

"I wondered if you might hold the dwarf." Anthony's voice trailed off as he reached the end of the sentence.

Jared raised an eyebrow.

"To be honest, it really doesn't matter now." Anthony held his palms up. "Forget it." He began backing away.

"Anthony, I am quite serious about the length of time I have been in here..."

Jared was cut short as his briefcase began to shake violently. A bump grew on one side, the leather bulging out and morphing into an identical, albeit smaller briefcase. This hung in the air a moment, then dropped to the floor.

The briefcase Jared still held went soft and fuzzy, as if being viewed through an out of focus camera lens. Anthony's eyes watered as the briefcase dissolved into a muddy grey patch hanging in the air. The chain attaching what had been the briefcase to Jared faded too, and he stepped away, his face a mixture of surprise and fear.

The grey patch suddenly contracted to a white dot that flickered for a moment and went out. Words appeared, hanging in the air in a light green, computer terminal font. They said:

```
Reboot in progress.

Micronos Intelligent Security
Solutions, copyright Micronos
Corporation, 2015.

Homeland LeisureSafe v.1.12.4.3
Service Pack 8

Your reliable solution for
```

```
artificially intelligent security.

Your support number for this product
is 01233S-HZ5675-1223B

The override code for this software
is 2024561111

Please note these numbers as they
are important in the unlikely event
you should need to contact Micronos
Corporation Support Centre...
```

And so it went on, more messages appearing as whatever it was rebooted, the words scrolling up until they reached the ceiling where they faded.

"Jared, what is this?"

Jared shook his head. "She's never done that before."

"Who?"

"Homeland."

"What?"

"Homeland."

"Sorry, again?"

"Homeland."

"A bit more information?"

Jared dragged his gaze from the endless stream of text floating upwards and faced Anthony. "She was our only hope."

"Sorry, who was?"

"Homeland."

Anthony clenched his fists in frustration, struggling to maintain a congenial air to his voice. "Gee, Commander Jared, I really have no idea who you're talking about. Who is Homeland?"

"She was the defender of all we hold dear, of our liberty, our flag, our country." Jared placed his right fist on his breast. "It was through her alone each of us had the freedom to realise our full potential, to follow the American Dream, to shop in the knowledge that terrorists, infiltrators and subversives could not harm us. That, sir, is who Homeland was."

"Sorry, I'm still not up to speed here. That briefcase?"

"In the briefcase."

"Okay, in the briefcase, was Homeland?"

"That is correct."

"And Homeland was a person?"

"I like to think of her as one."

"So, what's in that briefcase?" Anthony pointed to the small briefcase stood forgotten on the floor.

"I don't know sir."

Jared carefully made his way around the scrolling words and squatted down by the case. He glanced up at Anthony, shrugged, lay the case flat and released the chrome spring catches at either end. As soon as he began to open the case, the lid flew up and an enormous, crew-cut marine in combat fatigues burst out, bowling Jared over backwards. Hot on the heels of the marine tumbled a thin, angular man, with bleary, oversized eyes and head of tight blond curls. After him, the case spewed a blonde cowgirl in tight fitting black shorts, boots and t-shirt, her jaw working furiously on gum, hat clasped firmly in one hand.

Stunned, the three newcomers struggled groaning to their hands and knees. Jared leapt anxiously to his feet and ran to the glass separating him from Anthony. "Sir, we're in grave danger." He gestured at the marine and the second man. "These are dangerous terrorists, they must be isolated immediately."

But Anthony was squinting through the glass at the marine. "Higgs?"

Jared banged on the glass. "Anthony, you must listen to me. This is not the Higgs you may have known. He is a dangerous terrorist."

Higgs had now stood and seemed to be taking in his surroundings. Catching sight of the woman, he grabbed her by the arm, hauling her to her feet, hollering an inch from her terrified face. "Mandy, you're dead!"

She struggled to pull away. "Higgsie babe, please."

"I am absolutely going to see you in Hell!" Higgs' free fist was clenched but he restrained himself from actually thumping her.

The thin man didn't seem to share Higgs' inhibitions. He

bobbed from foot to foot behind Higgs, babbling in a plumy English accent. "I say Higgs, give her a damn good slapping."

Higgs growled dangerously back at him. "Shut up, Simms." He shoved Mandy hard, tumbling her to the far wall.

Jared slapped his hand on the glass right in front of Anthony's view. "For God's sake man, do something, Higgs will kill us all."

Anthony stepped back from the glass, glancing from Jared to Higgs and back. He hailed the rest of the ship. "Damon, Marlene, anyone? Get here now, the prisoner bay, quick."

Higgs stood fuming, fists clenched, but he did not advance on Mandy as she got unsteadily to her feet. Simms stood close behind him. "Go on, Higgs, hit her, hit her."

"Simms, I told you shut the hell up." Higgs did not take his gaze from Mandy.

Anthony advanced to the glass again, and, despite the drama, noticed the words had vanished and in their place, a large, shiny new briefcase sat on the floor next to the smaller, open one from which Higgs, Simms and Mandy had emerged.

Silence settled on the room, everyone's attention on Higgs as he glowered. Mandy's gaze darted frantically around the room, coming to rest on the new briefcase.

Anthony spoke softly. "Higgs. Higgs, over here."

The huge marine reluctantly turned his head, registering Anthony for the first time. "Sir, where are we?"

"Higgs, do you remember me?"

"Sir, I want to know where the hell I am."

"You're safe, you're on the spaceship *Big Cheesy Dippers*. We're in orbit around Europa."

Higgs relaxed slightly but then noticed Jared. "You?"

Jared struck a defensive pose, hands like blades in what Anthony assumed was some sort of martial arts position. "I'm warning you Higgs, traitor. You will not prevail here."

Higgs snorted with contempt and took a step forward. "Jared, you just don't know when you're beat, do you."

Simms clapped excitedly. "Go on Higgs, give him a bloody nose."

"Not on my ship you don't." Damon's booming voice gave

Anthony such a shock he banged his forehead on the glass. Everyone turned to look. Marlene and Hunter were there too. The cavalry had finally arrived.

Mandy, who had been quietly making her way to the new briefcase, took the opportunity to open it and, to Anthony's astonishment, slip inside. Higgs noticed and leapt for the case. "Stop her, she's getting away."

"Enough." Damon's voice rattled the place again and he clapped his hands.

Immediately, the room Anthony stood in doubled in size. Now, along the wall he faced, instead of one window, there were three, each looking onto a small cell. Jared and the two briefcases were in one, Higgs in the second and Simms in the third. The glass through to all three cells was red.

Damon turned to Anthony. "What happened?"

"Gee, I was just talking to Jared and the briefcase he was holding kind've spawned another one and then vanished. And then Higgs and those other two came out of the smaller case."

"Why were you talking to Jared?" Damon's eyes narrowed dangerously. "I expressly forbade anyone from talking to Commander Jared. What part of that order did you have trouble with?"

"Ah, gee, I, well."

Damon jabbed a finger into Anthony's chest, the volume of his voice rising threateningly with every breath. "You are supposed to be giving me answers about those damned aliens. Why are you not down in the science lab? I've got to report something back to mission control, can you get that into this fool head of yours?" He shoved at Anthony's forehead, forcing him to step back.

Marlene stepped forward. "Sir, really, sir, I don't think…"

Rounding on her, Damon cut her off as a bellowed. "You don't think what exactly?" He yelled, pausing between each word, face flushed as the blood boiled in his cheeks. "We. Are. All. In. Serious. Shit. Can you not comprehend?"

After the storm of Damon's voice the silence seemed absolute. Marlene's mouth hung open, her hands trembling. Looking from her, to Anthony and then Hunter, Damon wavered, putting a hand to his forehead. "I'm sorry, I should not have shouted."

Anthony gulped, acutely aware of his bladder, which was oddly curious as there had been no requirement to pander to the necessity of excretion on the virtual ship.

Damon closed his eyes, rubbing his temples. "If I tell the sponsors we have found alien life, I don't know what will happen. I have to be sure, Anthony, positive these so-called aliens are not from Earth. It goes against all the teachings of the ICRT. It would have to be from the devil, it could only be from the devil."

A long pause followed. Anthony daren't speak, and neither Marlene or Hunter moved a muscle. Damon suddenly seemed to regain all composure. He opened his eyes and walked to the glass separating them from Jared. "Anthony, you will return to the science labs. I want a report on the alien inside an hour. Hunter, I want Ged and Jinny back inside the virtual ship as soon as they've finished in the shaft. Marlene, find Nigel. I want every item of ICRT teaching concerning alien life."

After a few seconds, he glanced over his shoulder. "Well? You all seem to still be here."

JOB HUNG MOTIONLESS, alone. *Wife* had taken their children as he had instructed. She would return soon with his friends. She was a good wife. Job praised God for his faithful wife. But there was much on Job's mind, many questions he could not answer. He longed for his friends. When there were matters of faith to debate, a wife was of no use. He needed the counsel of his equals.

He thought of the Ten Commandments, searching his memory for any point at which he might have broken one of them. If he had done so, there might at least be a reason for the Lord's actions against him. But Job could think of no recent occasion on which he had sinned. He observed all God's laws, remaining especially vigilant against the snare of pride.

Stilling his thoughts, he let his senses take over, listening. The tingling he had noticed shortly before God took his children was still there, resonating in the waters. The Lord was still with him, watching waiting. Job strained to hear.

Lord, speak to me, I pray. I am your humble servant, without you I am nothing. I ask no explanation, I wait only on your will. Speak to me.

A great pain ripped through Job, sending every muscle in his body to spasm, contorting him, twisting him. He screamed in the manner of his kind, discharging waves of electricity into the water, begging for mercy. The heat in his skin became intense, searing. He felt blisters form and burst and still the pain continued. Innards churning, he vomited his last meal, the acid fluid from his stomach filling his mouth. Simultaneously ejaculating and defecating, he shook uncontrollably as images of his life flash wildly through his brain.

And then it was over, the power released him and the absolute pain receded to be replaced by the more worldly agony of strained muscles and the sores on his skin. He curled into a ball.

Lord, forgive me. I am your servant, always your servant.

He cried quietly, as much from his confusion at God than his pain. *"Lord, I do not understand."*

"Job?"

"Wife?"

Job stretched out with his senses, wincing slightly at the pain. She was still distant, several minutes away. *"Wife, come to me, comfort me my wife."*

"I am coming, my worthy husband, I am coming."

Job waited, trying to control his weeping. It was not strong to cry in front of a wife. He had to be strong. By the time she reached him, he thought he had his emotions under control but he hadn't expected her reaction when she could finally *see* him properly.

"Job, my husband, what has happened?"

"The Lord has spoken to me again."

"My love, you are covered in sores. You are bleeding." She gently enveloped him in her tentacles, taking care not to touch his lesions. *"My love, my love."*

Her tenderness punctured his pretence of strength and deep, uncontrollable sobs took him. They locked tentacles and hung in the water for a long while. At length, Job spoke.

"Wife, did you do as I bid?"

"I did. Your sons and daughters are with the tribe and I have sent word to your friends. They will all be here soon. But Job, you must leave this place."

"Wife, I cannot. The Lord wishes me to remain."

"If this is the Lord's doing, he has forsaken you."

"Wife, do not question God or his motives. We are nothing before him, we can but submit to his will."

"You are still as faithful as ever, aren't you? He has taken our children, he has taken our servants and now he has broken your body. Why don't you curse God and die?"

"Wife, you are speaking foolishly. Grief has clouded your wisdom, you must ask God for forgiveness." Job pulled away from wife and forced his tentacles deep into his most painful sore, knotting up against the pain. *"I stay here because it is the will of God and I will listen for him. We must obey him, whatever he*

asks of us. When he sends us something good, we welcome it. How can we complain when he sends us trouble?"

He loosened the grip on his sore, lessening the pain. "I am my Lord's servant. I will remain here as he has bidden me to do so."

"This little fellow is most definitely very sensitive to the electrical signals, yes?"

"Gee Naveed, I really am not sure I'm totally happy about this. You've really hurt it this time, look."

"Ah yes Anthony, but the readings, look. It is having an incredibly complicated nervous systems. There is nothing like this on Earth. How is the DNA scan going?"

"It's coming but you're right, it's not from Earth. It doesn't use the same four base nucleotides in its DNA."

"You will have to be reminding me of this. I am a geologist remember."

"Okay. DNA is a double-helix right?"

Naveed nodded.

"That double-helix is a framework supporting complimentary pairs of molecules called nucleotides. There are four of these nucleotides in terrestrial DNA, cytosine, adenine, guanine and thymine. These always couple up the same way, adenine with thymine, cytosine with guanine. So, if you have adenine on one side of the helix, there will be a thymine on the other side. You with me?"

"Yes."

"This little alien of ours doesn't have cytosine in its DNA, it has a different nucleotide called uracil which we have in our RNA. That's the chemical that copies the DNA to make proteins. Our DNA contains cytosine and RNA contains uracil. In this creature, it's the other way around."

"So this alien must have evolved here?"

"The structure of DNA is very ancient on Earth. I'm not saying the ancestors of these aliens couldn't have come from our planet but they would have had to have come billions of years ago."

Naveed clapped his hands. "Aha, we are proving that silly man Nigel he is wrong. Oh look." He peered closely at the probe screen. "A friend has joined our little fellow."

"Gee, it's like they're having a hug. Look, the new one is wrapping its tentacles around our one."

Naveed tapped a few keys on the console. "There is a lot of electrical activity going on between them."

"You know Naveed, I'm not comfortable with what we're doing here. I don't think we know what we've got. These things look pretty bright to me."

"Oh, do not be getting sentimental now Anthony."

"I'm not Naveed, really. I've studied lots of superficially similar animals and I tell you, I've never seen two bugs have a hug before. This is advanced behaviour. Look at them now, they're holding tentacles."

"You are telling me that these little beasties are holding their hands, yes? Oh come on, Anthony, this is nonsense as silly as Nigel talks. You'll be telling me they say their prayers next."

Anthony chuckled. "Ah, I guess you're right. We must be careful though. I don't want to kill any more of them and we've hurt this one pretty bad. No more intensive scans, okay?"

"Oh, as you are wishing."

Anthony's console beeped and he glanced at the screen. "Ah, gee, there's another living one here, look."

Naveed leant over excitedly as Anthony continued. "It's one of the ones we brought in with the sample. Wait a second…" Each of the dead aliens brought into the ship had been separated out into its own small receptacle. With a few clicks of the keyboard, Anthony brought up the one containing the alien giving off life signals. It was the same type as the living pair being monitored outside the ship, if a little smaller.

Anthony frowned. "No, this is not right. The internal organs seem to be working but there's none of the big electrical activity coming from the brain region."

"It is like it is being in a coma, yes?"

"Gee, I guess so. This is the one we need to research on, Naveed." Anthony turned happily to his colleague. "We can run a full range of tests on this one and leave those other two alone."

Naveed wrinkled his nose. "We will not be getting the full

picture from a brain-dead one."

"Yeah, but we can map how its brain controls its internal organs without causing it distress. It's as good as dead, anyway."

"I am agreeing but we must keep monitoring the living ones also."

"Yes, absolutely."

"We could capture them and bring them on board."

"Ah, gee, no."

"Why in the name of blazes not?"

"Because…because we've done enough damage here already. We've killed hundreds of them, I don't want to hurt these two as well. We don't yet know what we've got here."

"I am not liking it but…" Naveed shrugged and grinned. "You are the big boss man."

Anthony straightened. Cracking his knuckles, he took a step back and coughed nervously. "Ah, look, Naveed, I've just got to step out for a moment. Don't run any more scans on the live creatures, okay? Let's just observe their behaviour."

"As you are wishing. Where are you going?"

"Er, gee, I've just got something I need to do. I won't be long."

BACK IN HIS wardroom, Anthony searched the ship. The DNA scan would take a little longer to complete fully, he could fob Damon off with that.

It didn't take long to find Humpy, he was at the back of the computer centre, watching Tasha. She sat motionless, exactly where Anthony had last spoken to her. Anthony willed himself behind Humpy, grabbed him by the arm, plastered a hand over his mouth and willed them both back to the wardroom.

Humpy squirmed and growled but Anthony held firm, lying on top of the little gremlin, using the advantage of weight to pin him down. As long as Anthony maintained a hold on Humpy, he couldn't will himself away.

"Got ya little fellah. This time you're not getting away."

Humpy hissed but stopped struggling. Anthony concentrated and the Disassembler console appeared in his chest.

```
Username?
```

```
Tasha.
```

```
Password?
```

Anthony paused. Elvira? Celene? "Oh damn, no."

It had ones and zeros in it, that was certain. Fives? Seraphos? Was that it? With a five and a zero?

```
5eraph0s
```

```
Unable to log you on with this
combination of username and password.
```

"Ah, gee." He clenched his grip hard on Humpy's arm. "You little rat."

Humpy began squirming again. "Humpy go, Humpy go free."

"No Humpy." Anthony hugged the little man tightly to his chest, struggling to his knees and then his feet. "No way, we're going to take a little trip to Tasha's room and then we settle this business."

Humpy wailed loudly, tears flooding from his eyes. "Humpy go free. You hurt Humpy."

"Shut up." Anthony got to his wardroom door, willing it open a fraction to check the coast was clear. Finding the common room empty, he darted out, heading for Tasha's door.

Humpy's sobs became louder, his voice a desperate shout. "Let Humpy go. Humpy go free. Help."

Anthony shoved a hand over Humpy's mouth, trying to stifle his cries but it was little use. Humpy was inconsolable.

Just as Anthony reached the door to Tasha's room, Marlene's door flew open and she stormed out. Anthony instinctively tried to manhandle the captive behind his back but Humpy wriggled free and vanished.

Catching sight of Anthony, Marlene scowled furiously. "What is going on now?"

"Ah, gee, nothing."

"Nothing? I heard shouting." Her eyes narrowed as she peered suspiciously at him. "It sounded like a girl shouting 'get off'."

"No, it wasn't. It was…it was me."

"Why are you outside Tasha's door? What have you done to her?"

"Nothing."

Marlene strode purposefully over. "Get back."

Anthony walked dejectedly back to the centre of the room while Marlene knocked on Tasha's door and called softly. "Tasha, are you there?"

"She's not in there. She's in the computer centre."

Turning sharply, Marlene took a step forward, pointing a finger at him. "Anthony, I'm sorry, but I'm going to have to report you to Damon. You are becoming a danger to the other crew. You're coming with me now and I'm warning you, don't try any funny business with me buster. I'm a black belt in Aikido."

"Please, Marlene, I can explain."

"Yeah, you can explain to Damon."

Anthony sagged down into one of the common room's

armchairs, burying his face in his hands. "Please let me explain."

After a long pause, Marlene sat heavily in the chair opposite, the buttons of her jumpsuit stretching alarmingly across her belly. She seemed to have put on a great deal of weight. "It had better be good."

"I…well, you know I was going wrong?"

"Well, like yeah. Hard not to notice."

Anthony looked at the far wall, cheeks flushed, unable to meet Marlene's gaze. "Well, Tasha wouldn't help so I kind of dumped part of my personality out. Just to see if it would make things better."

"What do you mean?"

Anthony explained quickly about the Dissaembler, making the console appear in his chest for her to see.

She frowned. "So, did it help?"

"Well, yes. And no. The bit I dumped out is running around the ship now. I've been trying to capture it and reload it into my personality file. That's what you heard shouting."

"Okay. So what exactly is it you dumped out that is now running around the ship?"

Anthony clenched his fists, chewing his top lip.

Marlene sat forward on her chair. "Anthony? What have you let loose on the ship?"

"My penis." He whispered the words so quietly, Marlene didn't hear.

"Sorry, what?"

"My penis."

For a moment, Marlene stared at him. A strange expression crossed her face and she covered her mouth with her hand. "Anthony, I..I…" A snigger escaped and she looked away. After a second to regain her composure, she turned back, her face earnest and concerned.

"This is serious Anthony. Your penis is loose on the ship…" She could control herself no longer and collapsed into howling, damp, peals of laughter, hugging her sides as she shook. "I'm sorry Anthony…" And she was off again.

It took several minutes for her to fully regain control and

Anthony's mounting annoyance seemed only to encourage her giggles. Eventually, she dried her eyes and sat straight. "I'm sorry Anthony, really I am. So, I mean, how's it getting about. Is it like, you know, an inch-worm or what?"

Anthony folded his arms crossly. It was bad enough having his member cavorting around the ship without this unexpected amusement from Marlene. "No. It's a little man, about sixty centimetres tall. With a very big, you know…"

Marlene sniggered.

"Oh gee Marlene, I think you could be a little more sensitive. I've lost my dick."

About a minute and a half passed this time before she had herself back under control. Anthony folded his arms and legs crossly, turning away from her. This really was too much.

"I'm sorry Anthony." She sniffed loudly, wiping her eyes, face wrinkled with laughter lines. "I'm sorry. After all the tension, you know, what with the alien and you being weird and all. You've got to admit, it's pretty funny."

"No it's not. You wouldn't say the same if it was, gee I don't know, your titties wobbling off round the ship." Anthony stood abruptly. "I got to capture it before…before some else sees it."

A slim purple cardboard box appeared on her lap. Opening it, she selected two large, fondant chocolate creams from inside and popped them into her mouth. A momentary ecstasy crossed her face and she turned her eyes back to him. "Okay Anthony, I'll help find it."

"No." The word blurted out, the thought of Marlene seeing Humpy too much to countenance. "No, really."

"Why not?" She snorted and rolled his eyes. "Don't worry. I won't tell anyone else."

"I…gee, I'd rather just do this alone, thanks."

Marlene stood, placing her hands on her hips. "Anthony, I am a grownup you know. I have seen naked men before."

"Not like this one."

"In what way, exactly?"

But before Anthony could even begin to explain, Naveed's voice filled the room. "Anthony? Where are you, Anthony? You must be seeing this, there are more aliens."

JOB HUNG IN the water, his front end tilted downwards in supplication. *Wife* floated a little behind him, silent, waiting. She was a good wife but he would send her away when his friends reached him. There would be grieving and counsel, things said that were not suitable for the ears of a mere wife. He would instruct her to go and prepare his children for their disposal into the depths. Yes, she would feel of use without understanding she had been sent away.

This preoccupation with logistics helped to keep his grief submerged, controlled. When the horror of his dead children flashed into his mind, he forced the memory away with prayer and practicalities. He had wept enough, had to be strong for *Wife*, strong for the tribe. There would be time for grieving at the funeral

A faint signal drifted through the water, the distant call of his name. His friends were coming. He hailed them back.

"Eliphaz? Bildad? Zophar?"

His name echoed back. *"Job? It is I, Eliphaz of Teman."*

"And I, Bildad of Shuah."

"And I, Zophar of Naamah."

Eliphaz spoke again. "We have come as you bid."

A strange electrical current swept around Job. *Wife* sensed it too, and she clung to him with her tentacles. He turned to her. *"Have no fear wife. It is the Lord. My friends have come. You must go and prepare our children. I will follow soon."*

"Job, come with me, I beg you. I fear for you to remain in this place."

"Do not fear for me, wife. I will follow. Go now, before my friends arrive and see you in your grief."

They embraced for a few moments but Job pulled away. *"Go now. Go, beloved wife."*

Reluctantly, she turned and swam slowly back towards the entrance to the Holy Gouge. Job followed her progress with his senses. She would be gone before his friends arrived.

Resuming the position of supplication, he waited, filling his mind with prayers. When his friends arrived they would see his penitence, see he was blameless before God.

"ANTHONY, NAVEED."

"You are seeing these little three aliens here?"

"Yes Naveed."

"They have been sending the electrical signals to our alien as they are coming closer. And he is sending little signals back to them. This is all being very interesting behaviour Anthony."

"Absolutely. The signals, are there any recognisable patterns?"

"I have not been analysing that yet. I am not wanting to be treading on your toes Anthony. This is being your areas but you are not being here. Where have you been?"

"Ah, gee, I just had to do a few things. Look, you've been recording the signals, yes?"

"Oh yes indeedy."

"Okay. I don't know whether we have any software than can deal with this sort of data. Maybe there's a language module that might do something."

"You are thinking these beasties are intelligent?"

"Ah, no, not necessarily. But I mean, bird songs can be quite complicated. We just need something that can look for patterns."

"We need to be asking Tasha then."

Anthony remembered the Computer Officer's rather alarming lack of movement. "Ah, yeah, Tasha. Actually, there's something I need to talk to Damon about there. She's been behaving a little strangely."

"Ah well, these women, eh? They are all behaving very strangely if you are asking me. My wife I am never understanding at all." Naveed laughed loudly.

Anthony remained silent, unwilling to pursue this line of conversation. It offended him for its sexism and underlined the fact he was unmarried. Instead, he turned his attention to the computer scanning through the alien's genetic material. Embarrassed to find that it had completed some time ago, he began scrutinising the results. It wasn't long before he realised what they meant.

"Hey, this is very exciting. I am pretty certain these creatures are indigenous. They share hardly any DNA sequences with life on Earth. The few they do share could have arisen purely by chance." He turned grinning to Naveed. "They've got to have evolved here on Europa, independently of life on Earth."

Naveed clapped his hands together. "That is being wonderful news Anthony. We must be telling Damon."

"I will. I'll go tell him now."

ANTHONY FOUND DAMON in the communications centre in the top base. Like all the virtual spaceship, it was an exact replica of the real ship but what made this room remarkable was the domed glass ceiling. The communications console sat on a raised platform in the centre, high enough up into the dome to give a commanding view of the surrounding terrain of Europa. Damon slouched in the console's expansive leather seat, bathed in orange light, gazing silently up at the toxic violence of Jupiter.

Climbing the short flight of metal steps up to the platform, Anthony coughed politely, waiting for Damon to acknowledge his presence. Damon continued to stare obliviously at the heavens.

Anthony cleared his throat. "Damon, sir. We're dealing with aliens. Real aliens."

Damon slowly pulled himself away from the view, his usually ruddy face pale. When he spoke, he seemed distant. "Oh, Anthony. It's you." He gestured upwards. "It's beautiful, isn't it?"

"Ah, gee, yes Damon." Anthony fidgeted, feeling something more might be expected of him. "It's swell."

"Hard to imagine such beauty, such form and structure, such complexity…all by chance?"

"Er, yes. Sir, the alien sir. It's not from Earth."

"Not from Earth." Damon repeated the words over to himself a few times, as if mulling over the consequences. "Are you certain Anthony?"

"Absolutely." He began to explain about the DNA scan but Damon cut him off.

"If you are convinced Anthony, that is sufficient for me. You followed the teachings of the ICRT once, didn't you?"

Anthony was caught off guard by this question and paused before answering. "Professor, we are both scientists."

Damon smiled. "Like you, I believed in the teachings of the ICRT when I was younger. They meant much to me, gave me answers. But questions too, so many questions." He shook his head.

"Sir? Are you okay?"

Sitting upright, Damon suddenly seemed to come back to life. "Yes, I am. I'm sorry Anthony, I've been thinking a lot. These aliens. The only explanation from a religious point of view is that they have been put here by Satan to beguile the faithful."

"Sir?"

"It's okay Anthony, it's okay. You are a good scientist. You have a good conscience. I have a great deal of respect for you."

"Er, gee." Anthony chewed his lower lip for a second. "Thanks. Perhaps we should report our findings back to Earth?"

Damon stood. "Of course. And I will. However, we have a problem which I will explain in a moment to the entire crew. Excuse me a moment."

He hailed the entire ship. "All crew, this is Damon. I want you to leave what you are doing immediately and join me in the bridge. Now."

Turning, he placed a hand warmly on Anthony's shoulder and smiled. "Shall we?"

An instant later, they stood by the glass table of the bridge. Damon gestured for Anthony to sit and took a place himself at the head of the table. One by one, the other crew materialised and sat — Hunter, Ged, Jinny, Marlene, Naveed.

Damon cleared his voice to speak. "I'm afraid I have some rather unfortunate news."

But before he could continue, Marlene interjected. "Ah Damon, we're still lacking Nigel and Tasha."

"Ah, so it seems. No matter, I will inform them separately. We have a problem in that the communications equipment has malfunctioned. I am unable to contact mission control to report our findings."

A wave of muttering ran around the table. Naveed raised a hand. "Damon, how much information have you sent back?"

"Your findings on the stratigraphy in the ice, the initial contact with the *Nice and Spicy*. They don't know about Captain Jared and our other guests, the loss of Martin, or the aliens."

Naveed banged a fist on the table. "This is most annoying me. We must be reporting our findings back to the Earth."

Damon held his palms up. "Hunter, Ged and Jinny will be working to fix this as a matter of priority. Clearly it is imperative to the mission's success that we maintain contact with Mission Control."

A suspicious thought came into Anthony's mind. "Has anyone seen Nigel recently? I mean, he's not here and you hailed the whole ship Damon."

"It is of no matter Anthony." Damon looked Anthony straight in the eye and made an almost imperceptible shake of his head. The unspoken message was clear, Anthony was to shut up.

Damon continued. "I shall find Nigel and Tasha immediately after this meeting. In the meantime, Ged, I want you to get to work on the communications equipment. Hunter and Jinny, I want you to check the comms cable through the ice-shaft for any potential defects. It is vital the top and bottom sections of the ship remain in contact. Anthony, I want you to take your raw data and extract the most pertinent parts relating to the origins of these aliens. I want you to be ready to transmit proof the moment comms are re-established. Naveed, likewise with your work. Marlene, I want you to talk to our guests and see if you can learn what happened on the *Nice and Spicy*. They all appear to have issues with each other that I haven't got the time to deal with."

He got to his feet. "Questions?" Nobody responded. "Good, let's move people. Anthony, if you have a moment."

As the others vanished, Damon sat, placing his hands palm down on the table. He stared at the back of his hands for a moment then glanced up at Anthony. "I haven't seen Nigel for some time. I believe the comms gear has been sabotaged. Now, I can't say the two things are connected but I think you've got the same suspicions as me?"

Anthony nodded. "Absolutely. It's totally not in his interests for any of this to get back to Earth."

"I'll find him." Damon sat back, clasping his hands together. "There's the matter of Martin as well. And the missing personality backup files. And there's another thing."

"Yes?"

"There was an operating system upgrade several minutes after we launched."

"What? But that's crazy."

"Tell me about it. But it happened. Mission Control can't explain it, Micronos are denying their software would request an upgrade. The master computer system rebooted and we have no idea what affect it may have had. I've asked Tasha for a report but she's yet to come back to me."

"She's in the computer room. But she's acting kind've odd."

"Nothing new there."

Anthony thought a moment. "This upgrade, could it have perhaps had some effect on our personalities? I mean, say..." He struggled for a non-incriminating example.

Damon cut in. "Like the acne that was on your face? Yes, it could have done. But I need Tasha to confirm. The thing is, why did the upgrade happen? Eh?"

"You think we've been sabotaged from the start?"

Sighing, Damon shook his head. "I don't know, maybe. It seems far fetched. But then, where is Nigel?" He got to his feet. "Anthony, get your report together. I'll find our Spirituality Officer. Let's keep things in proportion here. There's probably a sensible explanation for everything. Just be aware, okay?"

IGNORING DAMON'S INSTRUCTIONS, Anthony did not go directly to the lab but instead to the room where the crew of the *Nice and Spicy* were being held. In part, he wanted to talk to Marlene and find out if she had attempted to catch Humpy, and in part because he felt he ought to talk to Higgs. After all, they had been friends, of sorts, many years ago.

To his surprise, Marlene was not in the prisoner bay (as he now thought of the room to which the prison cells were attached). Higgs, Simms, and Jared each sat in their respective cubicles behind red tinted glass. Anthony spent a few moments watching Higgs. It was definitely him, there could be no mistake. The handsome, boyish face with those intense blue eyes, the solid frame of his torso, honed by years of training and exercise, the veins standing out like whipcords on the muscles of his arms. Higgs was not a man to be forgotten easily.

Stepping up close to Higgs' window, Anthony set the glass to green. Higgs jumped, striking a pose ready for action. He relaxed slightly when he registered Anthony.

"Hi Higgs."

"Do I know you?"

A little pang of disappointment made itself heard in his heart. It had been eight years or so. "We were at college together. I'm Anthony Germaine."

Higgs narrowed his eyes, studying Anthony's face. "Yeah. Yeah, I do remember you. You did physics, didn't you?"

"Biology."

"Of course, biology." Higgs shook his head. "A few hours ago, I could remember every single second of my entire life. Now my memory is back to normal. But I do remember you. Yeah."

An awkward pause followed. Anthony nodded at Higgs' uniform. "You were on the *Nice and Spicy* then?"

Higgs nodded.

"So, what happened?"

"Look, Anthony, am I a prisoner here?"

"Gee, I'm sorry Higgs. I guess you are. It's kind've out of my control. Damon's in charge. I think he's spoken to you already?"

"Yeah. He wanted to know what happened on the *Nice and Spicy* too. Wouldn't tell me anything about where I am, so I wouldn't tell him. I won't tell you either unless I get out of here."

Anthony shook his head. "I can't let you out. I'm sorry. I will tell you where you are though. We're in a bit of trouble."

Higgs sat cross legged on the floor of his cell while Anthony explained about the mission, about the search for life and the recovery the *Nice and Spicy Nacho-Niks'* black box. He recounted the worrying loss of Martin, the disappearance of Nigel and the discovery of the aliens. Anthony didn't mention his missing member.

When the whole story was done, Higgs stood. "So, we're all computer simulations. And Commander Jared and Simms are in adjacent cells. And Jared still has Homeland. Listen, Anthony, there is something I will tell you. That suitcase Jared is holding? It's very dangerous."

"Why?"

"Because it contains a mad AI security program called Homeland. You've got to destroy it."

"Come on Higgs, you've got to tell me what happened. I swear I'll do what I can to persuade Damon to let you out. What he is worried about is your mission might have discovered life. Hell, we've found our own aliens now, so I don't know why he has a problem."

"Okay." Higgs breathed out heavily and began pacing the room as he spoke. "*The Nice and Spicy* launched from Earth's orbital space station. I guess we took about nine months to get to Jupiter but it was fine because the space station had everything. It was like a big floating city, you know, shops, cinemas, nightclubs. I was second in command to Jared. Everything went smoothly but then the main computer system, Mary, started to malfunction. She just got pissed at all the other computer systems and refused to talk to them. Then the communications computer, Mercury, took a vow of silence and we couldn't call back to Earth. Because all the computer systems were bickering, we didn't see the asteroid. It struck the side of the station where Mary was housed, wiping her out completely and damaging most of the other systems."

Higgs stopped his pacing for a moment and faced Anthony. "These damned AI computers. They're useless. Anyway, this is where Homeland comes in." He began pacing again.

"Homeland was in charge of the security of the leisure complex. She took it into her head there had been a terrorist attack and Jeez, she was completely paranoid. It turned out she had been secretly building hundreds of androids, using the tissue banks reserved for medical use and cloning anyone who got killed. We all had mind scans, you know, in case someone died."

"Yes, I know. I've got one back on Earth."

"Yeah, whatever. Anyway, Homeland had built this army of androids, part human, part machine. Because Mary was gone, Homeland had nothing to keep her in check. Because she couldn't decide who the terrorists were, she decided the best thing to do was wipe the entire crew out and clone everyone from scratch. We fought for a long time, holed up in different sections of the space station but we couldn't win. Every time we killed an android, she could replace it but we couldn't replace our men."

"Anyway, eventually she got us all and started cloning. She couldn't understand the memory files, so she couldn't look at them to find out who the so-called terrorists were. Instead, when she cloned people, she only loaded up a small amount of their memory and then watched to see how they behaved. I guess she was trying to catch the terrorists by a process of elimination. She kept everyone in the space station shopping mall because that's the only place she really understood. We all thought we were in a shopping mall in Iowa. In the end, I think she believed that's where we were. As she got more deranged, she started having people killed for even the slightest offences, like kicking a vending machine or refusing to shop. I got killed and re-cloned eight times in all. On my ninth life, my memories get a little weird. Everything I can remember comes from Homeland's files. There was no mind scan after my ninth life started, so all my memories of that life are through her security cameras. You know, I can see myself from behind, walking through the mall. It's really whacky. Whatever, she decided I was a terrorist, again, but this time I escaped the mall, out of the coverage of her cameras. Unfortunately, this means there's a gap in my memory at this point but when I reappear, I've let the crew from the relief ship *Cola Francaise* on board. We had a big battle with the androids and that's it, all I can remember. At the point we started to beat her, she wasn't able to see through the security cameras anymore."

"So, you don't know for certain what happened in the end?"

"No. But Jared will know. The clone of Jared worked closely with Homeland. He's convinced there was a terrorist attack, fought against me all the way."

"Didn't people realise they were on the space station? Gee, I mean wasn't it obvious?"

"No, we only had the memories Homeland let us have and she wouldn't let us out of the mall. There were little apartments over the stores, so there was no actual need to leave. It was subversive behaviour to want to leave the mall and if you stepped out of line, bam, you were fried. People just stopped asking questions. You were in a mall, you couldn't remember how you got there, you didn't know how to get out. So, you just did what you were told and worked and shopped."

"And now she's in the briefcase Jared's carrying."

Higgs nodded. "You've got to get it away from him."

"Why does Jared think you're a terrorist?"

"He believed Homeland, he really did. His heart's in the right place but he's a military man, trained not to question his superiors. He really thought we were in a shopping mall in Iowa."

"Who was that blonde woman? The one who dived back into Homeland's briefcase?"

"Ah, that's Mandy Pollins. She's one of the few people who never got terminated and re-cloned. She's very dangerous.

She knows how to manipulate Homeland to get exactly what she wants. To be honest, the best thing you can do is delete Homeland."

Anthony stood silently for a few moments, taking everything in. "How is it you remember everything now? Why couldn't you remember before?"

"Because Homeland controlled what parts of my memory files were available to me. I guess now I'm out of Homeland, I've got the memory controls imposed by the *Cheesey Dippers'* computer. Just before Homeland rebooted, Mandy had put me in a punishment cell but forgot to put any restraints on my memory. I had total recall. It's all fading now."

"I think it's possible to override the constraints the computer puts on our memories. We're only limited in what we can remember in order to make us feel human. It must be kind've weird to be able to remember everything."

"Look, Anthony, I want to get out of here. I want to go home."

"Go home? Gee, I guess you could, yes. Your personality file could be transmitted back to Earth via comms. I can't go. There's the real flesh and blood me left back on Earth so they won't let this virtual me back. When the power runs out, everyone on this mission dies."

"What? No way. They can't let that happen. It's murder."

Anthony shook his head. "No. I'm not alive. Neither are you, none of us are. We're just computer programs. But you, your physical body is dead. You could go back and they could clone you, load all your memories up."

"I want to go home, Anthony."

"You will Higgs. I'll get you out of here, if it's the last thing I do. And these other two, Jared and…who was the other guy again?"

Naveed's voice filled the room, although, ironically, he was whispering. "Anthony, were in the blazes are you? You are knowing Damon wants you back in the labs. The little aliens are all talking. You must come quickly."

Anthony shrugged at Higgs. "I've got to go. I'll talk to Damon, I promise."

JOB HUNG SILENT and motionless in the water, drained by the bitterness of grief. His three friends were close, waiting in the traditional pose of mourning as protocol dictated. They would not *speak* until he did.

Slowly, he uncurled his tentacles, rubbing them together. His senses seemed numb, everything distant. When Wife went, he allowed despair to take full rein, weeping and wailing and scraping at his sores. Now, he felt merely exhausted.

"My friends. I wish I was dead. My life is just suffering and pain."

"Job, your words are like the dung of male cattle, and you know it. Your life has been charmed." Eliphaz was known for his plain speaking. Even if his words might, on occasion, be a little coarse, all here were friends and formalities could be dispensed with. *"You had respect, wealth, fine children, Wife, even taking into account her strong opinions."*

"Well, thank you Eliphaz. And your considered words of wisdom are supposed to make me feel better?"

"All I'm saying is it hasn't been too bad."

"Not too bad? What compact faecal pellets you make out of your words. How could my life possibly be worse? I've lost everything that was dear to me. I want to die."

"It is a sin to wish for death."

"What? Why? We're all going to die."

"No, we're not."

"What, never? Oh wise Eliphaz, I did not know you had discovered the secret of immortality.

Well, yes, it is obvious we will all die eventually but..."

"All of us will die, and it matters not if we're good or bad, of renown or no consequence. We will all die. At least if I died now, my grief would end."

"That is still no reason to wish for death."

"So says you, dear Eliphaz. You still have everything. The only

certainty I have now is misery and death."

"There are other certainties. The greatness of God, the love of a mother for her child, the triumph of the righteous over sin..."

"Oh, stop prattling on. God is great, yet I mourn. I have been righteous, yet I mourn. I loved my children, my little angels, my dearest..."

Job stopped, overcome, fighting against his anguish.

Eliphaz waited a moment until Job regained his composure. *"My friend, Job. I'm sorry, my words weren't well chosen. You've lived a blameless life, yes?"* He glanced at the others, who nodded agreement. *"A pillar of society, an example to all. Wise, generous, always at prayer, quick to helpfully point out others' shortcomings. But now..."*

He softened his *voice.*

"But now, Job, my friend of old, the boot is on the other tentacle and you don't like it. You have always been righteous but, let's face the fact, who can live totally without sin? Can anyone?" Again, Eliphaz glanced towards the others for support. *"Who can ever be completely righteous before God? All commit sin and must seek forgiveness, even you."*

For a few moments Eliphaz paused, drifting closer to his friend. It would be a breach of the protocol of mourning for him to touch Job.

"You must accept that you have sinned."

Job scowled but Eliphaz continued. *"And if you've sinned, you've got to accept the Lord's punishment."*

"Oh, please, Eliphaz. You're a priest now as well?"

"It's there in the scriptures." Eliphaz continued sanctimoniously. *"You should look to God for deliverance. He pours blessings on the righteous but those who sin, he punishes and destroys. Look carefully into your heart, Job. Bad things have happened to you. God does not punish the righteous, so what has happened to you can only be a consequence of sin. Whatever it is you have done..."* Eliphaz glanced sideways at the other two companions... *"whatever it is, it is no matter for us. But you must accept His punishment and seek forgiveness. Then God will smile upon you again. My friend, it is hard for you to accept..."*

"It is hard for me to accept because you are talking through the orifice usually reserved for defecation. There is no explanation for why God has slaughtered my children, my livestock and my servants. I'm not keeping any dirty little secret from you. Eliphaz, show me my errors, my sins, my misdemeanours. What have I done to deserve this punishment? Tell me?"

Eliphaz made to speak but thought better of it.

"My punishment makes no sense. Even if I've done one small thing wrong, it doesn't merit what's happened to me. There are plenty of our tribe who've sinned far more than me but they haven't lost everything. I can see nothing I have done to deserve this. Nothing. Eliphaz, you're just insulting me. You are not my friend, you are just this guy I know."

Eliphaz sighed and *shrugged* at Bildad and Zophar. Like all of their kind, they did not have eyes. If things had been otherwise, they would have rolled them at this point.

"There are definitely being patterns in these signals. And they are taking turns to send their messages."

"This is totally outside my experience, Naveed. Totally." Anthony turned away from the console screen and looked at the mass of figures recorded from the aliens. "I'm going to see what the main computer's got that might analyse this."

While Anthony began searching the computer, Naveed continued. "They are in a little circle. One of them moves forwards, gives out a burst of signals, and then he is moving back again. And now, look, another one has moved forwards and…yes, we are having it again. More signals."

"I'm telling you Naveed, these things are talking to each other."

"It could be being like busy bees, yes?"

"Sorry?" Anthony looked sideways at Naveed.

"Busy bees. They are talking to each other with dances, yes?"

"Oh, right, yes. I get it. Yes, so in the way bees communicate to each other about a food source with their dances. Perhaps these four individuals here are kind've like the worker bees from a colony."

"Yes. And they are finding some nice things to eat and are telling each other about it. It is being really quite advanced behaviour."

"Absolutely. They're certainly on a par with some of the more complex insect societies on Earth. Ah, this is no good." Anthony sat straight, tapping the console desk in frustration. "The computer's got nothing that can analyse signals from a language point of view. The mission just wasn't expecting to try to talk to little green men. I guess it's a bit far fetched to think our bugs are actually talking anyway. I'm going to feed their signals through the statistics package. That way we can prove they are not just random signals and that there is a pattern."

"Okay. We are needing some sort of code deciphering

software, yes? The sort of thing a security program would have."

"I guess so. When we transmit these figures back to Earth, I should be able to do something with them. The real me that is, you know, back home."

"Yes, I am following you. Anthony, you realise you are going to have to be naming these creatures."

"I guess so."

"Are you having any ideas already?"

Anthony felt his cheeks tingle a little. Yes, of course he had some thoughts. "I was going to propose something like *Anomaloeuropa marlenei*."

"That is being quite a mouthful."

"Yes, well that's scientific nomenclature for you. It means Marlene's Europan anomaly, if my Latin's correct."

"So you are naming after Marlene?" Naveed chuckled. "Have you been telling her of this honour?"

"Ah, gee no. Anyway, I'd have to check the literature to make sure the name hasn't been used before. You can't reuse a name."

"It will not be a name the media will be liking. They will just throw up their hands and be calling it a bug."

"Yeah, but that's true of the scientific name for any animal."

"It is not being the case for *Tyrannosaurus rex*. Every kiddy in the world knows that name and it is being a full scientific name. You just need to be thinking of something a bit more snappy."

"Gee, I guess so."

They sat a while in silence, Naveed watching the aliens, Anthony inspecting the results from the statistics software. The results were convincing, with the probability of the aliens' signals being random calculated at greater than ten million to one against. He added these figures to the file he had pulled together for Damon. It was all there, the genetic scan, the contrary nucleotide in the alien DNA, preliminary diagrams and figures of anatomy showing the unique body plan. It would be hard for anyone to question the indigenous nature of these creatures. And this was just one of the aliens. There were at least three other types he hadn't even looked at yet, although all they had of those were dead specimens at present.

He glanced at the output on the console monitoring the coma alien. The software had been gently probing its vacant brain, stimulating parts of it and recording the physiological responses. The process of scanning was almost complete. Soon, it would be possible to simulate the creature's mind.

Anthony stood, making his report appear in his hand in a slim, silver folder. For the sake of aesthetics, he made a colour picture of the alien appear on the front. "Okay, Naveed, I'm done. I'm taking my report to Damon."

He addressed the ship. "Damon? Can I speak to you?"

After a moment, Damon's rumbling voice answered. "Meet me on the bridge."

Anthony nodded goodbye to Naveed and willed himself to the bridge. Damon joined him a few seconds later. Anthony noted with relief the commander seemed a little calmer than he had of late.

"Anthony?"

"My report."

Anthony passed the silver folder over. Damon looked at the cover, flipped quickly through it and nodded. "Well done, Anthony. Good work." He placed the file carefully on the glass table. "This has been a very tense time for all of us. Your conclusion that the aliens evolved on Europa independently of life on Earth has resolved the difficulties facing me. It's clear now what I have to do."

"Absolutely. The ICRT will have trouble with this but, hell, we're scientists. The truth has to out."

Damon smiled weakly at Anthony. "Absolutely. I'm afraid the communications equipment is still down. Ged informs me there are components missing. I have not been able to find Nigel."

"That's not good."

"No. Anthony, I'm sorry for some of my outbursts. You understand the pressures I've been under."

"Ah, gee sir, don't think about it. I totally understand."

"The incident with Martin. I regret that happened."

An uneasy feeling made itself felt in Anthony's stomach. Did Damon suspect? "Ah, yeah well, who knows what happened there."

"It was a very bad thing. But none of us are really alive so it was not a death as such. The loss of our security officer makes sabotage easier."

"I never thought of that. Of course. You think Nigel had something to do with Martin being disconnected?"

Damon smiled again. "I doubt it. Anthony, you've expressed concerns about your mortality on this mission."

"Ah, well…"

Damon held up a hand. "You mustn't trouble yourself with this, really. You are alive back on Earth, the real you. When this mission ends, you will not die. None of us will."

"I know. It's just that I feel I am alive. And I've only got a few months. Doesn't that frighten you? To know you're going to die?"

"We are all born to die Anthony. Even back on Earth, our days are numbered. You may already be dead, who knows?"

"Gee thanks. That's a lot of comfort."

"It is a truth we must all face. And it poses a question, have I lived a good life? Did I do the right things?"

A moment's pause followed. Anthony fidgeted uncomfortably. Damon was getting weird again. "Sir, I think we are doing the right thing. We are increasing the sum of human knowledge. We might be discovering things that some find inconvenient but that is no reason to hide them…"

Damon cut him off. "Absolutely. Now, Anthony, I want you to go back to the labs and continue your work. You can be proud of yourself. You have a place in history. I have always considered you to be a fine scientist, you know that don't you?"

At a loss for words, Anthony nodded. "Okay. Well, I'll be getting back then."

"Okay. Goodbye Anthony."

ANTHONY WILLED HIMSELF back to the science labs. Naveed had left the probe console and the aliens in favour of his meteorite samples and failed to notice Anthony's return. For a moment, Anthony watched the affable Indian as he pottered, humming happily. He checked through some readings then went back to a football sized rock and began peering closely at it.

"I am wanting to be getting my hands on you, you little beauty."

Clearly still thinking he was alone, Naveed turned towards the row of three robods on the wall. He vanished and the leftmost robod blurred slightly, then took on Naveed's form. He rubbed his hands together.

"Now, let us be taking a little look at you then." He trotted to the meteorite and picked it up, turning it over in his hands.

Anthony took himself back to his wardroom. There was still the matter of Humpy to resolve. Scanning the *Cheesey Dippers*, he saw Marlene with the prisoners. Good, she was following orders. The thought of her capturing Anthony's errant member did not bear thinking about. He swept on through the ship but, to his surprise, could not establish contact with the top base. The communications link through the ice shaft must have been disconnected.

Hunter and Jinny had gone up the ice-shaft in robods. He tried to find them but could not. While there was a wireless network that allowed the virtual ship to track the robods as they moved in the real ship, this network could not extend up the ice-shaft. Any robods up there had to connect in at one of the junction boxes spaced along the communications cable. A momentary suspicion made him want to hail Hunter but he decided against it. Damon might hear and wonder why Anthony had not returned to the labs. He resumed his search.

Tasha remained in the computer room, with Humpy nowhere in sight. Anthony was about to pass over her and look elsewhere when he changed his mind. How long had she been sat there, staring blankly at the computer screen? He opened a discrete link to her.

"Tasha?"

She made no response, not the slightest motion to indicate she had heard him.

"Tasha? Are you okay?"

Holding his breath, Anthony made himself materialise in front of her, with the console screen between them. The writhing, fluorescent network of cables making up the floor, walls and ceiling made him immediately feel giddy.

"Tasha?"

Her face was blank, motionless and pale. Leaning over the console, Anthony waved a hand in front of her eyes. She did not respond. He walked around the console and gently placed a hand on her shoulder. "Tasha?"

She remained motionless, eyes staring. Anthony glanced at the screen. The words "I am useless" had been written over and over. "Tasha?"

Anthony straightened, unsure what to do next. He gave her a little shake and finally got a response of sorts as Tasha tensed up, resisting him. "Tasha, come on. Please."

Ged's voice filled the room. "Hey guys, could we convene, you know, like a meeting in the bridge?"

Anthony stepped away from Tasha, scratching his head. Marlene would know what to do.

ANTHONY AND MARLENE joined Ged on the bridge immediately. He seemed flustered and ill at ease, out of his comfort zone at having summoned everyone.

Marlene smiled reassuringly at him. "What it is, Ged?"

"Ah, like, we've lost contact with the top base. I can't find Hunter or Jinny."

Damon appeared in the room. "Sorry I'm late. Ged, what's the problem? Are the comms fixed yet?"

Ged's cheeks went pink. "No, sorry sir, it's worse. Everything's gone now. I, like, came down here looking for Hunter, but I couldn't find him and now the main link to the top base has gone down."

Damon sighed heavily, then did a double-take when he noticed Anthony and Marlene for the first time. "Oh. Anthony. Marlene, I didn't see you there. No sign of Hunter and Jinny though."

Marlene looked around "It's not just Hunter and Jinny. Where are Nigel and Tasha?"

"Tasha's in the computer room, I was just with her." Anthony wiped his hands together. His palms were sweating. "She's had some kind've breakdown. She's just sat staring at the screen and won't answer."

"Where's Naveed?" Marlene's question made Anthony's heart wrench.

"He was in the labs just now. Well, in a robod, ten minutes ago." With rising panic, Anthony hailed the ship. "Naveed? Where are you Naveed?"

No answer came but Damon spoke loudly and reassuringly. "Okay, everyone calm down. Naveed, Hunter, Jinny and Nigel are no doubt in the top base. The comms link between us and the top base is broken."

Anthony could not restrain himself. "But Naveed was in the science labs. I saw him."

Damon held up a hand. "Maybe he went up to the top base to file his report. Now listen. Ged and I will get into robods, go up the ice-shaft, find Hunter and Jinny and fix the comms link. Marlene, you go and talk to Tasha, find out what's wrong. Anthony…" Damon floundered for word. "You just keep calm, okay. Go with Marlene. Right, Ged, come with me."

Damon vanished and Ged followed. Marlene turned to Anthony. "I've seen no sign of your little problem, Anthony."

"Ah, gee, Marlene. Please let me deal with that. I'll find it." Anthony couldn't help noticing Marlene was looking distinctly chubby. Her jumpsuit was clearly now too small for her and her sides bulged against the fabric.

Cramming another chocolate into her mouth, Marlene continued. "Well, I just thought I'd let you know. Right, Tasha's in the computer room, come on."

"No, I'm going to check the science labs again. I want to find Naveed. Marlene, listen, I'm worried. Something weird is going on here. I think Nigel might be behind all this."

"Nigel?"

"Yes. Damon thinks so too. He thinks Nigel might be sabotaging the comms gear to stop us telling Mission Control about the aliens."

"That's pretty far-fetched."

"Well, why's everything going wrong?"

Marlene said nothing, fidgeting nervously with her nails.

"Marlene, you go talk to Tasha. I'll come and find you once I'm happy Naveed's okay."

"Okay." Marlene vanished.

Anthony tried to will himself to the computer labs but nothing happened. He tried again but remained in the bridge. Calling up his mental map of the spaceship, he found not only the top base absent but also a void where the science labs had been.

"What?"

For a moment, Anthony was at a loss for what to do. Then, he remembered the robods. The science lab area might be gone from the computer simulation but the real one must still be there.

THE SENSATION OF being in the robod walking through the real *Cheesey Dippers* was indistinguishable from being in the virtual ship. The only difference was the inability to effectively teleport from one location to another, something Anthony noted with frustration as he waited impatiently for the elevator to arrive. He had grown so accustomed to materialising anywhere he wished, this concept of walking somewhere seemed an extremely retrograde step. How had he managed back on Earth?

The elevator arrived with a little ping and the doors swished open. Stepping inside, Anthony punched the button for the bottom floor, right at the end of the ship. The elevator began to descend, all too slowly. Fortunately, he could still communicate with the virtual ship from his robod and he hailed Marlene.

"How's Tasha?"

"She's completely catatonic, in some sort of deep depression. I don't see what I can do. I've taken her back to her wardroom but she's just sat on the bed. Have you found Naveed?"

"No. The science lab has been disconnected from the main computer. I'm in a robod going there on foot. Look, one of the prisoners, Higgs, told me about that briefcase Jared was carrying. Said it had a dangerous computer in it called Homeland. I think we ought to erase it. Just in case."

"Okay. I'll go down to the prisoner bay."

The elevator jolted to a halt and the doors opened. As the shaft came down through the centre of the room, Anthony could only see one half of the circular lab, the side where the submersible stood. One robod stood against the wall.

Anthony stepped out into the room. "Naveed?"

There was a crash from the far side of the lab, the sound of someone dropping something. "Naveed?"

The answering silence set Anthony's heart racing. On tiptoes, he crept slowly around the elevator shaft. Naveed's meteorites came into view, then the probe console but there was nobody there. Relieved to find the room empty, Anthony strode towards the console and scowled at it. The four aliens remained in their little circle but the probe had been primed to deliver an enormous electrical shock to the area.

"What?"

In a flurry of key presses, Anthony aborted the program. It was then he noticed the chair. It lay on its back, apparently knocked over, and one of its coasters was rocking gently from side to side.

In a panic Anthony spun round. "Who's there?"

The elevator doors hissed. "Who's there?"

Anthony looked wildly around for anything that might serve as a weapon. He grabbed one of Naveed's meteorites and advanced cautiously to the elevator. The LED over the door indicated the elevator was heading upwards. There had been somebody in the labs when he entered, somebody intent on killing the aliens.

"Damon." Anthony tried to hail through the ship. "Damon."

No response came. Of course, the science labs computers had been turned off or disconnected or something. He needed Ged, Hunter or Jinny to sort that out. Or did he? A panel was off the wall by the door to the elevator. Peering closer, he saw a number of fibre-optic cables, their colour-coded ends disconnected from the plug board behind them. Of course, the computers in the room were still on, the probe station for example. It was a simple matter to reconnect the cables to their matching coloured sockets and he did this.

With the lab's computer connected to the rest of the ship again, he tried once more to hail the others. "Damon?" No response came. "Damon? Anyone?"

Marlene answered. "Anthony? What is it?"

"Where's Damon?"

"I guess he's up the ice-shaft with Ged. Why?"

"Are all the prisoner's secure?"

"Yes, I'm there now, like you said. What's up? You sound in a bad way?"

Anthony froze. A robod lay on the floor under one of the

benches, the wire connecting its battery yanked out. "Naveed? Oh my god."

Marlene's voice was anxious. "Anthony?"

"I…Marlene…" Anthony knelt down, reconnecting the battery. The robod remained motionless.

"Anthony? What is it?"

"Marlene. Stay there."

"What?"

"I'm coming, stay there until I get there."

"Why?"

"Someone's murdered Naveed."

STANDING HIS ROBOD adjacent to the one already against the lab wall, Anthony re-entered the virtual ship. He found himself in the virtual lab, next to his now featureless robod. Somehow, he felt less exposed. Nobody could pull his battery out here. They could turn the whole computer off though. Surely Nigel wouldn't do that? Suddenly the robods seemed a better bet.

We're all going to die.

He took himself immediately to the prisoner bay, making Marlene jump. The glass to all three cells was green and Simms, Higgs and Jared peered out. At Anthony's will, the glass to all three cells went red.

Marlene became cross. "Hey, I was talking to them."

"Marlene, someone has disconnected Naveed."

"Well, it couldn't have been any of them. They're all secure, they can't get out unless we let them."

"The lab's computers were disconnected too. It think we should get out of the virtual ship and into the robods."

"Why?"

"Because whoever disconnected Naveed might just go and switch off the whole computer."

"Then all these prisoners and Tasha have to come too. We can't leave them."

Anthony glanced at Jared. "He's got Homeland in that briefcase. Higgs said she was dangerous. We can't let her out."

Marlene looked. "Well, it's not chained to his wrist anymore so…" She concentrated for a moment and the briefcase vanished from Jared's side and appeared in a new cell that formed in the wall. There were now four windows from the prisoner bay. In his cell, Jared jumped and started banging furiously on the glass.

Marlene shrugged. "Wants his briefcase back I guess."

"Okay. Why don't we just delete the briefcase?"

"Shouldn't we run that past Damon?"

In the fourth cell, the briefcase opened and Mandy Pollins poked her head out. She looked around wildly, clearly unhappy at what she saw. As the anxiety on her face grew, the rate at which she chewed her gum increased. After a few moments, she retreated into the case and it snapped shut.

"Okay," sighed Marlene. "We don't delete the case. How are we going to get her out?"

"Ask the others?"

The glass to Simms, Higgs and Jared's cells tinted green and the walls warped, making it possible for them to see into each other's cells for the first time. Marlene addressed them.

"Okay, gentlemen. We have a situation here on board *The Big Cheesey Dippers* and it is important we find a way to evacuate you from this computer."

"Madam, what have you done with my briefcase?" Jared could scarcely conceal his fury.

Anthony folded his arms. "Sir, your briefcase contains a dangerous artificial intelligence computer program called Homeland that we cannot allow out."

This took Jared aback. "Dangerous? She's not dangerous. Without her…"

But Higgs shouted across, cutting Jared off. "Homeland is mad Jared, mad. You know she is. We are not in a shopping mall in Iowa. Look around you."

Jared levelled a finger at Higgs, fuming. "That man. That man is a dangerous, subversive terrorist. He is responsible for the death of countless innocent civilians…"

"I am so totally not. You just refuse to accept what's in front of your eyes, Homeland is mad…"

Jared began shouting back and it became impossible to tell what each was yelling.

"Enough." Marlene clapped her hands and both Jared and Higgs' glass went red. When they both stopped, Marlene set their windows to green again. "If you gentlemen have quite finished?"

Both looked at her sheepishly.

"You will speak in turn, when I address you. Is that clear?"

Both men nodded.

"Right. Commander Jared, I am prepared to release you but your briefcase will remain here for the time being. If at any point it becomes safe to retrieve it, I give you my word that you will get it back."

Marlene turned to Higgs. "Higgs, Jared has levelled a very serious charge against you. Can you defend yourself?"

Higgs pointed to the window next to his. "Ask Simms."

Jared erupted in protest but his glass went red. When he quietened, Marlene let him see out again. She turned to Simms.

"Well, Simms. Is what Jared says true about Higgs?"

"No. Homeland is dangerous. Miss, I don't want to die, please let me go."

"Why is Jared accusing Higgs of terrorist attacks?"

"Because Jared really believes Higgs was responsible but he is wrong. The space station, *The Nice and Spicy Nacho-Niks*, it was struck by an asteroid. Homeland thought there had been a terrorist incident but couldn't work out who was responsible. So, she killed all the crew and cloned us all, only letting us have certain memories back while she tried to root out the terrorists. We all thought we were in a shopping mall in Iowa and Jared was head of security. I was an Information Officer you know. It was quite an important position…"

Anthony leant forward and whispered in Marlene's ear. "That tallies with what Higgs told me."

The glass to all four cells went red and Marlene turned to him. "When?"

"I spoke to him a while ago. I wanted to find out what had happened to their space station. We were at college together. Friends."

"Right. You could have told me this before."

"Okay, sorry. But at least Simms' story tallies with Higgs."

"Okay." Pausing for breath, Marlene turned back to Simms and the glass to all the cells tinted green again. "Sorry Simms. So, why did Jared think Higgs was responsible?"

"Because anyone who asked questions was instantly labelled a terrorist. And Higgs always asked questions, that was his job."

"This is all simply not true," growled Jared.

Higgs cut in. "Okay, so where's the shopping mall now Jared?"

"I concede the shopping mall may have been a computer simulation created by Homeland to keep us sane while she tried to arrange our rescue."

Higgs was incredulous. "It was not a simulation. It was real. I got to areas outside of Homeland's control while she was trying to kill me. How could I do that if it were just a simulation?"

"We're in a simulation now, aren't we? It's obvious Homeland was a simulation. I've spent God knows how long sat on a desert island waiting to be rescued."

"What?" Higgs frowned.

"While you were being…interrogated under Mandy's direction. All Homeland could spare for me was sufficient processing power for a small desert island. Clearly, that was a computer simulation, so the mall must have been as well. She had to destroy the mall because Higgs and his French terrorists were taking over."

"Ah, right." A look of realisation came over Higgs' face. "So what did she do? Initiate some sort of self-destruct sequence?"

Jared nodded, eying Higgs suspiciously.

"Wait." Anthony stepped forward. "I think I've worked it out. *The Nice and Spicy Nacho-Niks* was struck by an asteroid. Homeland then took over, went mad, convinced herself she was in a shopping mall under terrorist attack. You were all real but cloned and without your full memory. Then, with the help of the relief ship *Cola Français* sent from Earth, Higgs almost managed to oust Homeland but she blew the space station up. You were all mind scans in the black box we recovered. She kept your file, Jared, because you were the commander. She kept Higgs and Simms because she thought they were the terrorists and Mandy because she was the interrogator. I guess she didn't have enough resources available to keep anyone else's files active?"

Jared bit his lip and shook his head.

Anthony continued. "Okay, so since the space station blew up, you've been in the black box, Jared on his desert island, and

Higg and Simms…being interrogated?" He turned to Jared. "What do you mean interrogated?"

But Simms answered. "It wasn't a proper interrogation. Mandy Pollins is a very dangerous, manipulative woman. She's got Homeland twisted round her finger and she was using all the resources to act out her little fantasies. Top restaurants, fabulous hotels, scents, dresses, anything she wanted. While you were on your desert island Commander, Mandy was living it up."

Jared frowned. "That was simply a cunning way of getting you to confess your crimes."

"Cunning?" Simms snorted. "Well, she had you fooled too then. Really, Commander. Quite frankly, it was obvious what she was doing. And all that time you were stuck on a desert island. Ha. It's most amusing really."

"Shut up Simms." Jared turned away. "She was deep under cover."

"Oh yes, of course. Absolutely Commander." Simms snorted again.

"Okay, okay." Marlene clapped to get their attention. "That was then. This is now. We have to get you all out of the computer, so you need to agree a truce. Okay?"

All three captives nodded.

"Good. And we need to get Mandy out too."

Jared turned crossly. "Yes. I think you do. She has a little explaining to do."

"Too damn right." Higgs was right up against the glass now, straining to see into the cell with the briefcase.

"I say we give her a jolly good wallop." Simms was hopping excitedly from foot to foot again.

"No." Marlene folded her arms. "We'll have none of that." She walked to the glass of the fourth cell. "Mandy? Can you hear me?"

A muffled voice came from the case. "I ain't coming out. You can kiss my ass lady."

"Mandy, you can't stay in there. I can't guarantee your safety."

"Get lost. I ain't coming out and that's flat."

Marlene shrugged. "Okay. Your decision." She looked at Anthony. "Shall we let them out?"

Anthony shrugged. "Perhaps we should just check with Damon?"

"Well, do you want to go find him?"

"There might not be time."

"Okay." Marlene rolled her eyes. "So why the vacillation? Are you trying to make me make the decision here? So I take the rap?"

"No. No, okay. Let them out."

A moment later, Higgs, Simms and Jared stood in the room with them, their former cells melting away. Only the chamber with Homeland and Mandy in it remained.

Marlene looked suddenly nervous. Higgs towered above her, a solid wall of muscle. But he smiled. "Thank you Marlene. I appreciate your trust."

Jared snarled. "You may live to regret it."

Higgs turned to him. "We have a truce. I'll stick by it if you do."

"Yes, you tell him Higgsie." Simms moved to get Higgs between him and Jared.

Higgs groaned. "Oh, shut up Simms."

"Yes, Simms you pathetic creature, shut up." Jared shook his head at Higgs. "At least we're agreed on that, Higgs."

"Okay, right, do I have your attention here?" Marlene seemed to have rallied, although Anthony couldn't help noticing her run her gaze over Higgs' huge smooth, muscled arms.

She continued. "Right, we are still in the computer. We need to get into the robods, follow me." She vanished.

Higgs, Simms and Jared stared at the vacant space, mouths agog.

"Ah, gee, don't worry about that." Anthony gestured for them to follow him. "Once you get the hang of things, you can sort of teleport around the ship. We'll just walk for now."

He led them out from the prisoner bay to the central elevator shaft, explaining about the robods as he went. After a short while, Marlene rejoined them, looking a little flustered and apologising profusely for not thinking. Higgs was very gracious, which Anthony noticed had the effect of making Marlene blush and start stuffing chocolate.

It was quite clear what was going on in Marlene's subconscious, although Anthony knew she would vigorously deny it. Higgs was an alpha male. Curiously, Anthony felt no jealousy at all. He smiled. All those emotions were off with Humpy. No, he could be an impassive observer, loving Marlene in a purely platonic way, for herself, feeling slightly superior with his clear, hormone-free perception. Higgs had managed to bed just about every woman Anthony had designs on at college. He wondered how long Marlene would hold out, with her "husband back home" and her copy of the Reformed Testament.

Taking the elevator, they ascended a level to the engineering block, a large hanger through which passed, it seemed, just about every wire, cable and vent in the whole ship. A dozen, impassive black robods lined the wall. Anthony led the way to them, checked each was charged up and explained how to get in.

Higgs attempted his first. He managed after a couple of goes. Jared went next and succeeded first time. Simms had a great deal of difficulty getting into his but eventually made it after much coaching. Before Anthony jumped into his robod, Marlene put a hand on his arm.

"Anthony."

"Yes?"

"I just wanted to say…well, you seem a lot better now. You know, since you lost your er…" She glanced down fleetingly at his groin.

"Ah, gee. I've got to get Humpy back though. Before he does something embarrassing."

"Sorry? Humpy?" Marlene sniggered. "Is that what you call him?" She laughed out loud.

"Oh, Marlene." Anthony shrugged her hand off crossly and jumped into his robod.

AT ONE END of the engineering block, a thin bundle of optical fibres spiralled up to a gaping hole in the ceiling, alongside the carbon fibre ribbon. Anthony knew somewhere, up in the ice-shaft, a mobile platform would be attached to this.

He walked to the foot of the ribbon. "This is it. It leads up into the ice-shaft. Damon and Ged should be up there somewhere. I'll see if I can get them. Damon?"

They waited. Anthony shrugged. "Damon? Do you read me?"

Why had he said that? Do you read me? It was Higgs. Anthony had lapsed into using the sort of language Higgs might use. This was very curious. He did not need to impress Higgs. "Can you hear me Damon?"

"Anthony. I hear you." Damon's imposing baritone filled the hanger.

"Ah, swell. Er, I've got some bad news. Naveed has been disconnected. He was in a robod and someone disconnected his battery."

Damon sighed, the noise sounding like a great rush of wind through the room. "That is regrettable. Naveed was a good man. But he is not dead. He lives on, back home. Back home." Damon's voice trailed off.

"Er, gee Damon, are you feeling okay?"

There was no answer. Anthony smiled apologetically at Higgs, Simms and Jared, feeling a little ashamed about Damon's apparent otherworldliness. He whispered an aside. "He's been under a lot of pressure lately." It felt a little like sticking up for an embarrassing relative.

"Er, Damon, can you still hear me?"

"Yes Anthony. I'm sorry, truly I am."

"You're sorry? Gee, what for?"

"I had no choice."

"No choice?"

"No choice. Everything is clear to me now. All the doubts I have felt, all the weight. I have returned to my faith Anthony. My path is clear."

"Er, Damon, this all sounds a little weird. Where are you?"

"You argued in favour of intelligent design once, Anthony. It's on your file. That's why you were selected for the mission. I was the same. I was brought up as a believer. But I slipped Anthony, I was seduced by the clever logic of science, the beguiling path of questions and proofs that leaves no room for faith."

"Right, Damon, where are you exactly?"

"But it is a lie, Anthony, a lie. My heart knew I was wrong, my heart yearned for that feeling of completeness only faith can bring. All my life, there has been a hole, the aching void that the faith of my childhood filled."

"Damon, please tell me where you are."

"There are no answers in science, Anthony, no real answers. Every time we resolve a question, we raise a thousand more. Each advance in our knowledge does nothing more than highlight our ignorance. True understanding of the Universe is beyond our grasp. The Divinity alone is all knowing. We are fools to try to comprehend his creation, all we do is burden ourselves with a thirst for learning. We are like an alcoholic, burning for more, never sated."

"Are you still in the shaft?"

"But out here, in the beauty of creation, out here in the silence of space, I hear him. I know what I must do. Those aliens Anthony, do not be deceived. They are demons. Earth must not hear of them, must not, must not." A kind of dry sobbing filled the room.

"Is Ged there? Can I speak to Ged?"

"Ged is gone. I am sorry. I could not let him stand I my way."

"Oh my God. Damon, are you telling me you've killed Ged?"

"Of course not. I would never kill a man."

Anthony breathed out heavily. "You had me worried for a moment there. So where is he?"

"He is back on Earth, living a full and happy life."

"Ah, okay. So, the Ged that was on this mission?"

"That was not Ged. It was merely a computer program. It has been aborted."

Anthony gulped. "And Hunter, Jinny?"

"I am sorry."

"Naveed?"

"Anthony, do not be afraid. None of us are truly alive so we cannot really die."

"What about Martin? Was that you?"

"You have troubled yourself about that. Yes, it was me. I disconnected him remotely. I do not know why you have had such trouble controlling yourself."

"I do. It was the upgrade that got sent after we launched. Damon, it's had an effect on all of us. Tasha's gone completely AWOL. I've kind've reverted to my adolescence and you're the same. You're not yourself. Look, where are you?"

"It is nothing to do with the upgrade. I have found peace. This mission is over. You're work has been exemplary. But it is over now. Goodbye Anthony."

"Wait. Damon, where are you? Damon. Damon?"

Damon did not answer.

Anthony turned open mouthed to the others.

Simms cleared his throat. "Space sickness. Seen it before, nasty business."

Anthony glanced at him. "Shut up, Simms."

Higgs stepped forwards. "I take it you were not expecting that?"

"You can say that again. He's completely flipped."

Marlene sighed. "I've been worried about him for a while. Like, since from day one."

"Wait, wait." Anthony held up his hand for silence and concentrated. His mental map of the ship extended only to the mouth of the ice-shaft. Looking up, he saw a large junction box of cables. A fibre-optic cable extended upwards from it into the gloom of the shaft. "Yes, that makes sense. Up there, that box. There's a cable going up from it. Damon must have disconnected the cable higher up. He must be in the top base."

Marlene rubbed her eyes. "Okay, but we're in control of the

bottom ship. So, we can go up the shaft, reconnect, repair the comms equipment and contact mission control."

Anthony turned to her. "We've lost all our engineers." He frowned. "Martin talked about weapons. Where were they stored?"

"The top base I think."

"Ah, gee, great. We have a psycho on the loose with Martin's damned guns at his disposal."

"Don't worry about that. Higgsie will jolly well take him out, you'll see."

There was a chorus of "Shut up, Simms."

Anthony shook his head. "And all this time, I was suspecting poor Nigel. He must have been the second person Damon murdered."

"Yeah, but why?" Marlene walked over to stand by Anthony. "Why bump off Nigel. The Spirituality Officer. It makes no sense. Oh no." Marlene put a hand over her mouth.

"What?"

"Tasha. She's on her own in her room. We've got to get her out."

"Wait, let me look." Anthony brought up the map of the ship again, sweeping through for the wardrooms. But he stopped before he got there — Humpy was heading along the corridor towards the prisoner bay. "Er, hang on."

"What is it?"

"Nothing."

"What, let me see."

"No."

But Marlene was concentrating. She let out a squeak. "Is that him?"

"Ah, please Marlene."

She snorted. "He's cute."

"Marlene."

Humpy reached the prisoner bay and went in. The briefcase opened and Mandy stuck her head out. Humpy's eyes bulged and he started jumping up and down.

A horrible thought came to Anthony. "Ah, gee no. Humpy,

no. No!"

Mandy and the briefcase suddenly appeared next to Humpy in the prisoner bay. The briefcase opened and Anthony's map of the ship went blank.

"I've got a bit of bad news." Anthony faced the others, trying to appear confident and in charge. "As you've heard, our commander, Professor Damon Bridle, has become a little ill. And is possibly armed. And highly dangerous." Anthony drew a deep breath and continued. "It also seems that your Homeland AI security program has just taken control of the computers in our part of the ship."

"What?" Higgs held up his hands in despair. "How? I mean, how did she get out?"

Anthony glanced frantically at Marlene. Her face remained calm and impassive. "It seems there is another, unidentified agent at large in the ship. What this does mean is we cannot re-enter the virtual ship."

Jared drew himself up importantly. "As the most senior officer here, I am assuming control."

"Well you just damn well assumed wrong, didn't you Jared?" Higgs glowered at Jared.

For a moment, their eyes duelled but then Simms piped up. "Sound like we need to abandon ship. Where's the escape shuttle?"

Higgs and Jared united. "Shut up, Simms."

Anthony shook his head. "There is no escape shuttle, Simms. There is no escape unless we can get to the top base and get the comms gear working again."

Higgs turned to him. "What can Homeland do if she's in control of everything down here?"

"I don't know. Not that much. All the doors and equipment have manual overrides. There's so many regulations since the problems with artificially intelligent computer personalities. They haven't made computers like Homeland for years."

"Okay. So, can we reboot the main computer down here?"

"I guess so."

"Okay, it's simple." Higgs looked around, catching each of

them (save Jared) by the eye. "Marlene, you go and reboot the computer down here and get rid of Homeland. I'll go up the shaft and deal with Damon. I'll need help."

Simms wrung his hands together. "Sounds like a great plan. I'll help Marlene."

Jared shot a disgusted look at Simms. "You should be ashamed. Higgs, I'll come with you."

"Me too." The words blurted out of Anthony before he could think. He wasn't being lumped into the same bag as Simms. Higgs and Jared looked at him sceptically, their disapproval strengthening his resolve. "I might be able to sort out the comms gear."

Higgs nodded. "Okay. You're right."

"I am a black belt in Aikido, you know." Marlene had her hands on her hips.

Higgs regarded her. "Yeah, well, whatever the temptation, don't go using it on Simms, okay lady?"

"I say, that's not very nice."

Marlene smiled. "Shut up, Simms."

Anthony walked to the foot of the ribbon. A large, grey box to one side of it sported three buttons, one an arrow facing up, one, an arrow facing down, and between them a large, round, red button. He peered up into the gloom but could see nothing. Shrugging, he pushed the down arrow. High above, he heard a distant whirring.

"I think that's the platform coming down. We can use that to take us up."

Higgs shook his head. "I don't know. Damon will hear us coming."

"I don't think we have much choice." Anthony turned to him. "It's a four kilometre climb."

Higgs mused. "And these robods are designed to behave like the personalities in them. Let me try something. Anthony, take my hand."

"What?" Anthony looked at Higgs' outstretched arm. "Why?"

"Just do it."

"Okay." Anthony gingerly took Higgs' hand and then yelped

in pain as Higgs' squeezed with all his might.

"Pull away," yelled Higgs.

Anthony struggled, fighting the pain. "Let go of me." But he could not pull loose.

Higgs released his grip. "As I thought. These robods are all identical. So why's my one stronger than yours Anthony?" He smiled at Anthony's blank, uncomprehending stare. "It's because they behave according to our self-image. You think I'm stronger than you, so I am. Remember that. All these robods are equal."

The noise from the shaft was growing louder. Sulking a little and rubbing his bruised hand, Anthony stared upwards. He could just make out a distant light now, growing nearer. "It's coming. I can see it."

They waited in silence as the platform made its slow descent. When it finally cleared the ceiling, they saw three robods lying on it.

Marlene shook her head. "That would be Hunter, Jinny and Ged." She made her way over as the platform came to rest on the ground. "Look, all the batteries are disconnected. Let's connect them up to recharge again. Help me."

"Wait, there's a trick to this." Anthony stepped forward, eager to show off his knowledge. "Another thing about these robods… Actually, wait. Higgs, come here a moment."

Raising an eyebrow, Higgs came forward.

"Put your arm out for me."

Higgs stuck his right arm forward warily. Anthony carefully put one hand on Higgs' elbow and another underneath Higgs' outstretched hand, closed his eyes and felt around Higgs' elbow. For a moment, it felt like Higgs' arm but then the warmth of skin faded to be replaced with cold metal. And there is was, the release catch, just the same as on Martin's prone robod. Anthony pressed the catch and easily folded Higgs's arm up, so his hand came to rest on his chin. Opening his eyes, he grinned. "Yes. Thought so. There's a release catch on every joint."

Higgs gaped at his arm. "I can't move it."

Anthony took Higgs' other hand and drew it to the release

catch. "There, you feel that?"

"Yeah."

"Press it."

Higgs did so and his arm came back to life. "Yeah, okay. Might be useful." There was a slight air of affront to Higgs.

Marlene shook her head. "Well, if you boys are finished, perhaps we can move these robods?"

Between them, they manhandled the three robods over to the wall to join the one remaining robod already there. Once all were reconnected to the power cables and set to recharge, Anthony, Higgs and Jared mounted the platform. There was a large grey box on the platform, with identical buttons to the one on the wall.

Anthony turned to Marlene. "Be careful."

"Anthony, you're the one going to face the psycho with the guns. All I've got to do is turn a computer off and on again."

Anthony shrugged. "Well, be careful anyway. You might trip or something." He pressed the up arrow and the platform began to ascend.

Marlene turned and walked away, Simms hot on her heels. A little voice in Anthony's head pointed out she hadn't told him to be careful. He filed it away with the other hurts.

THE CLIMB UP through the shaft was painfully slow. Large lamps mounted on the four corners of the platform illuminated the glinting ice, and Anthony saw the layers Naveed had got so animated about. They passed bands of dark material, contaminants in the ice, perhaps from some meteorite pulverised on impact with Europa's glassy surface. Occasionally an angular piece of rock jutted out, each one marked and labelled.

They remained in silence, Higgs and Jared pointedly standing at opposite sides of the platform, facing away from each other. Anthony made a few half-hearted attempts at conversation but to no avail.

The fibre-optic cable ran upwards in a series of ten metre lengths, each section joined to the next by a junction box secured to the icy wall. Anthony inspected one as the platform slowly passed. It would be a small matter to pull the cable out.

"We need to watch these boxes. Damon could have pulled the cable out of any of them."

The others looked around with interest. As the next junction box came up, Anthony pressed the red button on the control panel and the platform stopped. He pulled the descending fibre-optic cable from the top-half of the box and felt around the top of his back. For a moment, he could only feel his clothes but with some concentration, he blocked this sensation out and felt instead the cold, smooth metal of his robod's shoulders. He found what he was searching for, the end of a fibre-optic cable protruded from the base of his neck. Pulling on it, he unravelled enough slack to reach the junction box on the wall.

Higgs leant close. "What are you doing?"

"I want to see if we've missed the break in the cable. Damon could have pulled, gee I don't know, the cable out of the tenth junction box up and we'd have missed it. If I plug myself in here and the cable is still whole between us and the bottom ship, I should be able to connect into the computer."

"And connect yourself right into Homeland. Tell me, is that a bright idea?"

Anthony thought for a moment. "No, perhaps not." He let go of the cable and it retracted into his back. "Okay, we need to watch all the junction boxes on the way up. We've just got to hope he disconnected one near the top."

Anthony pushed the up arrow and they resumed their ascent.

For what seemed like an age, they rose through the shaft, checking each junction box as it came. After half an hour, Higgs suggested they took shifts. It was on Anthony's second turn he spotted it, high above them, a faint orange ring.

"Higgs, Jared, look, up there." He pointed. "Wait, I'll kill the lights." He pressed the stop button and the platform lurched to a halt. A few moments later, he found the controls for the lights and dimmed them to a faint yellow glimmer. "There."

With the lights lowered, the thin, orange ring was clearly visible, although still quite some way above them. Anthony nodded. "That's the surface. The ring is the glow from Jupiter coming in around the edge of the top base. We're nearly there."

He raised the lights again and they continued upwards. The orange ring came nearer and brighter. Higgs suddenly shouted out. "Whoah, there it is, the break." He reached over and thumped the stop button. The ascending cable had been wrenched from the closest junction box.

Higgs touched the box. "Okay, this is the problem. Not too far from the top."

"Well, what are you waiting for?" Jared peered over Anthony's shoulder. "Let's reconnect it."

"No. We don't know whether Marlene has rebooted or not yet. Let's deal with Damon." Higgs pushed the up arrow and they continued.

As they neared the surface, the ice around them began to glow with diffused light from above. The underside of the top base loomed but it was smooth and solid. The fibre-optic communications cable passed into a small opening but the main hatch to allow the platform entry was firmly shut.

Pressing the red button, Anthony brought the platform to a

juddering halt, close enough for them to touch the bottom of the base. All around the edge of the base, Jupiter's brilliance filtered through the ice.

Jared flapped. "Well, that's it. We can't open this hatch." He leant over and thumped the ice wall of the shaft and recoiled in pain, rubbing his knuckle. "Damn it. Ow. These walls are like rock. We'll never get through."

"There's a gap over there." Higgs pointed to the far side of the shaft, way too far for them to reach. Orange light spilled in though a space between the base of the ship and the top of the ice, large enough for a robod to squeeze past.

Jared snorted. "I don't see that helps us. What are we supposed to do? Fly over? I don't believe these robods come with wings do they?"

They stood a while in thought. Jared shook his head. "This is hopeless. I suggest we descend and find out how Marlene is getting on. We might be able to find some cutting equipment to break through this hatch."

Anthony slapped his head. "If Marlene's rebooted the machine, we could reconnect the two bases and come up through the virtual ship. Why didn't I think of that before?"

"Because you're not thinking hard enough." Jared's eyes narrowed. "Marlene must have rebooted the machine by now. We should descend, reconnect the computer cable as we go and then do as Anthony suggests."

Higgs shook his head. "I don't like it. What if Damon's disconnected all the robods in the top base? What if he's turned off all the computers?"

Jared laughed contemptuously. "What if, what if. We have no choice, Higgs. Unless you can fly or walk like a spider, we have to go back down."

Walk like a spider. Jared's words jolted Anthony's memory. "Hang on, I've got it." He walked to the ribbon up which the platform had been travelling, and used it as a rope to climb the last couple of metres until he crouched right up underneath the base. He brought one leg up and placed his sole on the smooth metal surface above him. There was a clunk and his foot stuck.

He grinned at the others. "Yes, I was right. Watch this." He brought his other foot up and clamped it on the metal above them. Slowly lowering his torso with his arms, he hung, upside down, feet stuck firmly to the underside of the top base.

Higgs gaped. "How in the heck are you doing that?"

"We've got magnetic feet. It's so the robods can walk around in the space ship in zero gravity. They come on and off as you go through the normal cycle of walking. Watch."

A little awkwardly, Anthony took a few steps. "Yes, it's fine." Emboldened, he made his way across the ceiling of the shaft to the gap Higgs had seen. "Come on," he called over his shoulder. "It's easy."

"*It is not easy, Job.*" Bildad *glanced* nervously at Eliphaz and Zophar for support. They nodded encouragingly (at least, in the fashion of their kind which actually involved some rather subtle movements of tentacles).

Bildad continued. "*Job, God doesn't act capriciously, does he?*"

Job glowered with resentment. "*You have an obstinate insistence that I have done something terrible and that is why I am being punished.*"

"*The teachings are very plain. The consequences of sin are ruin and suffering.*"

"*By which you mean I have done something wrong and now I'm paying the price.*"

Eliphaz weighed in. "*All your life, up until now, you have been righteous, blameless, we're all in agreement there.*"

"*That is absolutely clear. You have been righteous. Very righteous.*" Bildad gestured to Zophar, who nodded in agreement. "*But God does not heap calamity on the righteous, you understand my meaning? The teachings are clear: upon the good, he bestows his blessings, upon the bad, his punishment.*"

"*So, I am evil, in league with the devil?*" Job folded all of his tentacles at once, a sign of extreme displeasure.

"*No, not evil. Just a little stubborn. If you hadn't done anything wrong, you would not be suffering now. Suffering is the result of sin.*"

"*So, when a lion catches one of the wild goats, God is punishing the goat for its sins?*"

"*Job, you are being facetious.*"

"*No, you are blaming me for the death of my children.*"

"*You must have done something. Only you and God know what. You must stop being stubborn and repent.*"

Job flailed his tentacles in despair. "*Repent of what?*"

"*Well, how do I know? I have not seen everything you have done. But hear me Job, it pains me to say this but your children died because of your sin.*"

Spinning away, Job focussed his thoughts on the walls of the Holy Gouge, trying to shut his friends out. *"No, how dare you. You are ignorant."*

"Job, dear friend, you are being obstinate. If you repent, God will restore your wealth and your standing." Lowering his *voice,* Bildad whispered conspiratorially. *"You can tell us what it is. Nobody else will hear of it. We are your friends, we will protect your honour."*

"Bildad, I cannot believe I am hearing this from you. Nobody is without sin, myself included. But have I done something awful enough to justify this? No."

"But you must have done."

"No, absolutely not. But I am in a position in which I cannot defend myself, am I not? I know I have done nothing wrong, yet the scriptures say I would only receive this much punishment if I had done something terrible."

"That is what is written. Perhaps you did something without realising?"

"You mean I accidentally made a pact with the devil without noticing?"

"Well, no of course not…"

"What then? You say this much punishment must be the result of me consciously committing some awful, despicable deed."

Bildad sighed, at a loss for words.

Eliphaz spoke instead. *"In short Job, yes, and you simply do not have the courage to admit to us, to yourself or to God."*

"My friends, we are simply going around in circles. How can I defend myself? If I protest myself to be sinless, I am guilty of sin. But nonetheless, I am blameless and God lets me suffer like the wicked."

"God does not let you suffer…"

"If it is not God, then who is it? Who? God is the master of everything, nothing happens without His consent. My days are ending and I can change nothing. I can do nothing to prove my innocence, I cannot stand before God in court."

Emotion overcame Job and he wept. *"Oh, my God, why have*

He huddled himself into a ball, crying softly, ashamed of his
outburst, wishing he were alone.

"How can I fight God?"

"I MUST SAY, a black belt in Aikido is jolly impressive."

As he trotted along behind Marlene, Simms ran his fingers quickly through the knot of tight curls on his head. It was not often he found himself alone with a lady of Marlene's obvious class. She was graceful and elegant, intelligent and witty, a refreshing change from that vulgar badass Mandy. Still, he wouldn't have Marlene's undivided attention for long. It was time to turn on the charm.

"Jolly, jolly impressive. And for a girlie, too."

Reaching the main elevator, Marlene punched the call button and turned to face him. "Simms, quite a lot of women excel at martial arts." She shoved her hand irritably into her pocket, searching for something. "Damn."

"Of course they do." Simms leant on one elbow against the door. He'd seen the male leads in movies do this sort of pose and it always looked alluring. "So, how did a nice little thing like you come to study martial arts?"

Marlene's mouth opened but she didn't speak. That line seemed to have done the trick. Simms knew he was getting somewhere. Unfortunately, before he could follow up, the elevator door opened making him lose his balance and collapse inside. He scrambled to his feet as Marlene stepped in, closing the door behind her.

"Oops, feel a bit silly now. Didn't see the lift had arrived." Simms brushed himself down.

"Lift?"

"Elevator. We call them lifts back in England."

"Ah, right." Marlene set the elevator descending.

"So, your role on this ship, Spirituality Officer wasn't it?"

"Human Resources Officer."

"Ah, yes, of course. Silly me. You don't want to be involved in all that stuff and nonsense about the Divinity, eh?"

"Well, I do believe in the almighty."

"Ah, well, yes, of course. Who doesn't, eh?"

A few moments silence followed. Simms thought frantically. He was losing the initiative. That would not do. Women were attracted to men who showed initiative. "So, have you always been a God-Squadder?"

"Sorry?"

"Religion. You've always been religious?"

She sighed. "Well, like, yes." Thrusting a hand into her pocket she searched, then frowned. A little growl of frustration escaped her.

"Do you pray regularly?"

"What? Er, well, I observe Friday Prayers in the Holy Direction, if that's what you mean." A look of conviction came over her face. "And I'm always careful not to eat Foods of a Sinful Nature."

"And you think it makes a difference?"

"Sorry?"

"Well, prayer. If you're feeling a bit down, you have a good pray and feel better?"

"To be frank, Simms, I'm not sure I want to continue this conversation."

"Shame, it's rather an interesting topic. I mean, some people say prayer can heal illnesses. I remember going to a sort of rally once, with this terribly evangelical preacher. He kept saying 'the Lord tells me someone here has a stomach ache' and someone would put their hand up and say 'it's me'. Then they'd pray and voila, the stomach ache had gone. A miracle. The thing is, the preacher wore glasses." Simms snorted at the memory. "I mean, silly man. The Lord tells me someone here is short sighted. That one didn't get mentioned, you can rest assured."

"Yeah, whatever, Simms. Look, do you have any chocolate on you?"

"What?"

The elevator lurched to a halt and the door opened on a circular room from which four corridors led. Marlene set off along one at such a pace, Simms found himself almost jogging to keep up. "Where are we going exactly?"

"The main computer room. Simms have you not been paying attention to anything that's been said?"

"Howdy, y'all. Is that there Simms ticking you off yet?" Mandy's Texan slur filled the corridor, bringing Marlene and Simms to a halt. "I mean, Marlene, I don't know how you can tolerate him."

Simms stuck his hands firmly on his hips. "Mandy, you can just jolly well stick a sock in it. Marlene and I were having a perfectly decent conversation…"

Marlene cut him off. "Simms, shut up. Mandy, where are you?"

"I'm right here, watching over lil' old you."

Marlene turned to Simms. "She's still in the virtual ship. She can hear everything we say."

"You bet your ass I can."

Marlene addressed the ceiling. "Mandy, you've got to come out of the virtual ship into one of the robods."

"Ah, now why d'ya want me to go do a fool thing like that?"

"Because we've got to reboot the machine. I can't be sure your personality file will be preserved. If we reboot with you still in the computer, you might be lost forever."

"Well, I'm all choked up 'bout that."

"And it's not just you. Our Computer Officer Tasha Natley is still in there. She needs to come out too."

"Oh her? Jeez, she was just so dull. I've had her erased."

"What? My God Mandy, that's, that's murder."

"So, big deal. Face it, the girl was dull. Dull and ugly."

Simms felt sweat on his brow. He had a very bad feeling about this. Nudging Marlene in the ribs, he leant close and whispered. "I say we just reboot the machine with Mandy inside. Believe me, we'd be better off without her."

"Shut up Simms. Mandy, this is your last chance. We're going to reboot the machine. If you're inside, you will die."

"You're going to kill lil' old me? Well, that ain't social."

"Get out of the computer and into a robod."

"But there's no robods free for me to get into, hon."

"Yes there are. There are three in the Engineering Block and there's a couple down in the Science Labs with the alien."

"Alien? Hey, no one said anything 'bout an alien. Let me see… ah yeah, I see. It's kinda dull. Just a slug. Hey Simms, your ma's down in the Science Labs."

This puzzled Simms. "She is? I must say, I don't quite see how she can be…"

Marlene and Mandy spoke in tandem. "Shut up Simms."

Mandy continued matter-of-factly. "I was never a big one for alien films, y'know. Always thought lil' green bug eyed men were funny, not scary. Now, I just love a good scary movie. How 'bout you?"

Simms folded his arms. "I really don't think this is the time to discuss what sort of films you like, Mandy…"

But he was cut off by a ping, away behind them down the corridor. Turning to look, they saw the elevator had just arrived and was settling prior to the doors opening.

Mandy continued. "Me, I love those films where the dead come back to life, y'know? The evil zombies stalk the Earth."

The doors of the elevator opened and Simms let out a terrified yelp. Hunter shambled out into the corridor, sunken bloodshot eyes staring sightlessly, his skin sallow, a bloody gash across his forehead. He pointed at Simms and Marlene, uttered a horrible, dry hiss and lumbered towards them, arms outstretched, gaping mouth full of yellow, rotten teeth.

Simms felt a warm sensation spreading down his leg. "Mummy."

WITH SOME EFFORT, Anthony squeezed through the gap between the top of the ice shaft and the underside of the top base. He glanced quickly around. Jupiter was low in the sky and soon night would come. The side of the top base rose up above him, obscuring the observation dome at its zenith. Good, Damon would not be able to see. He poked his head back through the gap under the ship.

"It's clear. Come on."

He withdrew and sat with his back up against the base while first Higgs and then Jared pushed through the opening. Higgs tried to stand but immediately slipped unceremoniously onto his backside.

Anthony covered a smile with his hand. "Ah, gee, it's best not to try to get up. It's too slippery. The best way to get about it like this."

He lay on his stomach and pushed himself away across the ice for a few metres. Stopping, he rolled over and sat up, looking back at the others. "See, easy. Uh oh."

Having moved away from the side of the base, he could now see the observation dome. Damon sat at the console, gazing towards Jupiter. Anthony pushed himself back to the others, speaking in a loud whisper. "He's up there, watching Jupiter out the window."

Higgs lay on his back, pushing himself gently away from the base until he could see. "Okay, got him. We need a way of getting in without being seen." With a push of his hands, he slid back to the others. "Anthony, any ideas?"

Anthony rubbed his chin, thinking for a moment. What ways were there into the base? "The rover bay, that's the only entrance I can think of. Follow me."

Careful to keep close to the side of the ship, Anthony led them past the stabilising legs to the closed rover bay doors. Jared looked scornfully up at them. "I don't see this helps much.

How do you propose we get in?"

Making his way up the access ramp, Anthony shot Jared what he hoped was a withering look. Jared was beginning to play on his nerves. "We, like, turn the door handle Jared." Sliding to one side of the door, Anthony pressed firmly on a panel there, making a cover spring up to reveal a large green button. He reached to press it but Higgs put a hand on his shoulder.

"Hold on buddy, let me check on Damon."

He slid slowly back on the ice, stopping when he could see the observation dome. "He's gone. Okay, go."

Anthony jabbed the button and the rover bay doors slowly opened outwards. They hurried inside, closing the exit behind them. The rover sat parked in the centre of the bay but Anthony made his way quickly past it to the door leading to the rest of the ship. It did not open as he approached so he pushed the green button at the side of the doorframe. Nothing happened. He poked the button again but the way remained closed.

"Damn, this door's been locked."

He looked back at the rover. A thick cable led from the back of it, connecting to the ship.

"Good." Anthony trotted to the side of the rover, perching on the ledge there. "Come on, sit here. We can go in through the rover, into the virtual ship."

While he connected himself to the rover, the others joined him, watching in interested confusion.

"Okay, that's me done, I'll do you."

He connected Higgs then Jared, fumbling with the cable as they both fidgeted uncomfortably. "Right, okay, you sense a sort of space behind you. Kind've push towards it."

Both Higgs' and Jared's robods became blank and featureless. "Good." Anthony pushed back with his own mind and found himself inside the rover with the others. At the back of the vehicle, where there had been a wall on Anthony's last visit, there was now a tunnel leading through to the main ship. He jogged through it, calling over his shoulder for the others to follow.

The tunnel led to the robod bay. Anthony had only been here

once, when he had first asked Hunter about his lack of control. How long ago was that? Then, all twelve of the ship's robods had been here, each secured to a docking point, connecting them through to the virtual ship. Now, ten of the docking points were empty but two robods remained.

Anthony stopped, taking this in. "Okay, only two robods. Damon's in a third. I don't know if there are any others up here. Hold on, let's see if I can find him."

Concentrating for a moment, Anthony made a small three dimensional map of the top base appear in front of them. Higgs and Jared's gasps of astonishment brought Anthony a small, deeply pleasurable sense of satisfaction. It was just great to be able to do something they couldn't. He continued casually.

"Gee now, let me see. Ah, here he is. In the engine room."

He expanded the engine room section of the map, showing Damon busily working around the main ship's batteries, generator and fuel pods.

Higgs peered closely. "What's he doing?"

"Gee, I don't know. It looks like he's wiring up the fuel cells to the batteries. Why would he do that?"

"Easy, soldier." Jared folded his arms. "He's making a bomb. He's going to blow this place up."

"Gee, no. Why would he want to do that?"

Jared rolled his eyes. "What, you mean apart from being crazy?"

"Okay. Okay. Gee, we'd better stop him then, hadn't we?"

"You know Anthony, you could have had a real career in Military Planning."

Higgs looked levelly at Jared. "We've got two robods. I'll need one to neutralise Damon. Anthony knows the ship, so he takes the other."

Jared's eyes narrowed. "So, I just sit here and wait?"

"Sir, there's only two robods."

"Gee, wait." Anthony allowed the map to fade and pointed to one corner of the room. "Jared could go into one of the maintenance droids."

A small, roughly square, wheeled box stood on the floor, all shiny black with a small screen at one end. Four angular, many jointed metal arms surrounded the screen, each one with a crab-like claw at the end. A small camera perched on the top.

Jared looked sideways at Anthony. "You want me to go in one of those?"

"Well, yeah. They can get about pretty quick."

Higgs walked impatiently up to one of the robods. "Come on, we're wasting time here people. How do I work this thing?"

"Well, just kind've walk into it. Close your eyes if it makes it easier."

Higgs stood next to the robod, paused a second and stepped into it, vanishing as he did so. It shimmered a moment and became Higgs. He turned and looked around, confusion on his face.

Anthony spoke, willing his voice to be audible to Higgs. "It's okay, you can't see us because you're back in the real ship. We can see you. We'll be with you in a moment." He turned to Jared. "Sir, the droid."

Jared snorted and walked crossly to the little robot. "This is ridiculous." He stepped on it and vanished, his face appearing an instant later on the screen. The arms flexed and the maintenance droid Jared moved forwards experimentally.

Jared's scowl looked so impotent in the little screen, Anthony couldn't help laughing. "Put that on your résumé, sir." He strode to the remaining robod and joined them in the real ship.

SIMMS HAD ALREADY made it halfway to the door at the end of the corridor before Marlene shouted "run." Like he needed any kind of prompting. More heroic men might have put themselves between her and the zombie Hunter, but Simms' finely honed instincts for self-preservation kicked in, setting him on a fully-automatic, terrified flight for survival.

Marlene was close behind him now, urging him onwards. "Run Simms, run."

Mandy's cackling filled the corridor. At least someone was enjoying themselves. "Ah, y'all don't want to go that way, now."

The door ahead glided upwards to reveal two more walking corpses, this time Ged and Jinny. Both hissed menacingly, shuffling forwards, reaching out.

Coming to an abrupt halt, Simms screamed. Marlene crashed into him, sending him a few steps further. She grabbed him, hugging him to her. "Simms, get a grip, now."

Simms saw her mouth move, heard her words but he was beyond any possibility of comprehension. He screamed again, flailing his arms, his whole being turning to a quivering jelly of fear. Something began to impress itself upon him, focusing him. Something painful. Marlene was slapping him. He registered her words.

"Simms, get a grip." Another slap stung his face.

"Wha…"

Another slap.

"Ow. Stop hitting me."

"Simms, look at me, look at me."

He gazed into her huge, brown eyes.

"Simms, okay, breathe deeply, slowly, deeply."

Hisses erupted from both directions down the corridor. The undead crew were closing in.

Marlene continued, as if instructing a meditation class, with only a hint of hysteria in her voice. "In. And Out. In. And out again."

Simms tore his eyes from hers, glancing over his shoulder. The Jinny zombie was only a few yards away. He turned back. "We're going to die."

"No, Simms, just stay calm." Marlene looked wildly around. The Hunter blocked the corridor back to the elevator. She screamed, unable now to control her own terror. "Simms, we're going to die."

Utter panic took hold of Simms' every sense. Shapes moved before his eyes, things bashed against him, lights and noise filled his head but he understood none of them. As the base desire to stay alive took hold, a white fog settled over his cognitive powers.

When it cleared, he was in the elevator, Marlene clinging to him as she gasped for breath. They were descending. He became aware of just how damp his trousers were and turned slightly away from her. "Er, I say, what happened? Where are they?"

"What? You just flattened Hunter."

"I did?"

"Yes. Jesus, Simms, you saved my life."

"I did?" Simms could only remember terror. "What did I do?"

"You ran at Hunter and smashed him out of the way."

"I did?" He became aware of quite how tightly she was holding him, the heat from her body, the smell of her sweat.

"That was the bravest thing I've ever seen." Tears welled in her eyes and she buried her face in his neck. "I was so frightened."

A hot sensation swelled through him. He'd saved her life. Him, Simms, little runty Simms. Patting her reassuringly on the head, he put his other arm around her shoulder. "Well, you know, basic training and all that. It just kicks in, I guess."

"Ah, Simms, don't make me throw." It was Mandy, her voice filling the air. "You've gone messed your pants Simms. Look, see, Marlene. He's gone wet his self."

At the sound of Mandy's voice, Marlene pulled away from Simms, glowering around furiously, fists clenched. "Mandy, when I get my hands on you, I'm going to whop your ass."

"Ah, I'm quaking in my boots 'bout that." She laughed

raucously. "Look at his pants. He's wet his self."

Simms turned away from Marlene. "No I haven't." He tried brushing down his jumpsuit trousers but to no avail. They were soaking.

The elevator lurched to a halt and Marlene spun to face the door, taking on what seemed to be some sort of martial arts pose. For a few moments, she stood there, waiting but nothing happened. She sniffed a couple of times, glancing sideways at Simms. "You have wet yourself, haven't you?"

Simms shrugged and nodded. Hardly any point in denying the fact. He couldn't really hide it.

"What you did back there was the bravest thing I've ever seen a man do."

He hung his head. "No, not really. Mandy's right, I'm a coward. I was terrified."

"Simms, being afraid doesn't make you a coward. You saved my life. I won't forget that."

They stood a few moments longer, Marlene still ready for action. She glanced sideways again. "Simms?"

"Yes?"

"You couldn't open the door could you?"

"Oh, of course, yes." He cleared his throat, jabbed at the green button and hopped quickly behind her.

The doors parted to reveal the science labs. With a loud "hi-yah!" Marlene sprang forwards, turning quickly left and right. She relaxed and whispered to Simms. "Come on, it's clear."

He followed her into the room, the doors swishing shut behind him. Marlene ran to one of the large banks of machinery at the perimeter of the room and began dragging it towards the elevator door. "Come on, Simms help me, we need to barricade ourselves in."

Simms ran to join her but looked round when she gasped and pointed. The elevator was heading back up. Mandy's taunting voice filled the room.

"Ah, y'all not coming out to play? Well, that's really gonna ruin my day."

Between them, they dragged several large items of what

Simms could only assume were important scientific equipment to stand in front of the elevator doors. At last, they sagged down together, side by side, backs to the makeshift barricade.

"Well, that ought to hold them off for a bit." Simms wiped the back of his hand across his brow. "What do we do now?"

Marlene leant over and whispered in his ear. "We keep our voices down to start with. We don't want Mandy to know what we're planning."

Simms nodded, blurting out loud. "Yes, of course. Absolutely right."

"Shhhh. Whisper."

"Of course." Simms leant close to her and continued in hushed tones. "So, what are we going to do now?"

"I have absolutely no idea."

From the half of the room they could not see, came a tinkling sound, like some small glass object falling over on a bench. Both froze.

"Did you hear that?" Simms' heart was thumping again but he managed to keep whispering.

Marlene got slowly to her feet. As Simms joined her, she put a hand on his shoulder and a finger to her lips. She wanted him to keep quiet. He nodded.

Resuming her position of aikido combat-readiness, she advanced slowly around the elevator, bringing the circular labs into view by degrees. The probe station was still on, the image of the alien clear on the screen. The creature hung in the water, with three others of its kind close by. On a nearby bench, a single test-tube rocked back and forth on its side.

Crouching lower, Marlene crept towards the bench, Simms following on her heels, chewing his knuckles.

A sudden roar to their left made Simms leap clean off the ground and flee to the far wall. Naveed, or at least something that had once been Naveed, lunged out from behind a cabinet, half the skin on his face missing to reveal green rotting muscle and yellowing bone. In a moment, he had Marlene pinned to his chest, his great bulk bearing down on top of her, tumbling them both to the ground. Her scream was cut short as his body smothered her.

Before he knew what he was doing, Simms grabbed a fire extinguisher from the wall and brought it down on the back of Naveed's head, over and over. "Get off, get off, get off." A great jet of foam shot from the side of the canister but still Simms kept hitting.

Suddenly, what had been a zombie became a black, featureless robod, its head smashed. Simms sank back on his haunches, flinging the extinguisher to one side. Marlene kicked and pushed at the robod in her panic to get it off. It had lost Naveed's bulk, and rolled aside easily. She crawled to Simms, sobbing.

Mandy's spoke, laughter in her voice. "Did I scare you or what? That was just too good."

Simms hugged Marlene to him. "I say, it's alright. He's gone now. There, there." He patted her head.

She wailed. "I need chocolate."

"Sorry old girl, can't help you there."

Looking at the lifeless robod, Higgs' words came back to him; they behave according to our self-image. You think I'm stronger than you, so I am. Remember that. All these robods are equal.

At the centre of the room, the elevator pinged. Simms heard the doors opening, although he could not see them from where he sat. Loud, rattling hisses came from the elevator. They had guests.

ANTHONY LED THE way from the robod bay to the central elevator. They took care to be as quiet as they could, although Jared's little wheels made an intrusive whining noise as he zipped along. Upon reaching the elevator, Anthony stopped, turning to face Higgs. It was difficult to face Jared as his computer screen face was only six inches off the ground.

"Okay." Anthony pointed upwards. "We're one level below the Engine Room. The elevator opens up right in the centre. It's kind've a circular room, you dig?"

You dig? Where had that come from? Anthony felt his cheeks flush.

"So, Damon will hear us coming." Jared's voice sounded as if it were coming from a very poor telephone line. "Is there another way up?"

"There's an emergency access ladder."

Jared made a strange little noise that might have been a snort of contempt. It was hard to tell. "I might have an issue with that."

Higgs bent down, scooping Jared up. "Hey, I'll carry you, little fellah."

Jared's four robot arms flailed around helplessly as Higgs held him from behind, like some metallic lobster. "Whoah, whoah there, Jared, you can stay down here if you like?"

"Higgs, it is a serious offence to manhandle a senior officer."

"Ah, button it, Jared. You coming or staying."

Jared said nothing but his arms stopped flailing.

To the side of the main doors to the elevator was smaller door, flush to the wall and with a small handle in a recess. Anthony opened it, revealing a narrow shaft, leading both upwards and downwards. The wall opposite the door supported a ladder, easily close enough to grasp. The only light came from a few weakly glowing panels and it was not possible to see either the bottom or the top of the shaft.

Higgs thrust Jared into Anthony's arms. "Here, you hold the baby. I'd better go first."

Peering upwards, Higgs took a hold of the ladder and began cautiously to climb. Once his feet were clear, Anthony followed, finding it a little difficult with his passenger. Glancing downwards, it occurred to him Jared would probably not survive the fall. Clutching the little maintenance droid tighter to his chest, Anthony put the thought from his mind. There had been too many *accidents* already.

After a short climb, Higgs stopped, looking down between his legs. He held a finger to his lips and pointed at the wall behind him. Anthony leant forwards against the ladder so he could see. It was the door to the Engine Room. He nodded.

Turning his back to the ladder, Higgs carefully opened the door a fraction, squinting through the crack. Obviously satisfied the coast was clear, he silently opened the door fully and slipped through. As quietly as he could, Anthony climbed the last few rungs and in a moment had joined Higgs.

The Engine Room occupied the entire level. Like the Science Labs, it was a circular room, with the elevator shaft rising through the centre. Spaced at ninety degree intervals around the edge of the room were the interior sections of the ion engines, each flanked by two shining chrome, ceiling-high Xenon gas canisters. Anthony knew these were empty now, their contents spent on getting the ship to Europa. By the wall opposite Anthony, Higgs and Jared stood the battery units, four of them, each as tall and wide as a robod.

Anthony tapped Higgs on the shoulder, whispering in his ear. "The generators and fuel pods are on that side." He pointed behind them at the elevator.

Higgs nodded and leant close to whisper back. "Stay here." Skirting around the side of the elevator, he stole away.

Watching Higgs' retreating back, Anthony bit his lip, wondering what to do. He couldn't bear to sit and wait. Dropping to his knees, he whispered to Jared. "Wait here."

Carefully, Anthony crept in the opposite direction to Higgs, the sound of his heart thumping in his ears. The room was silent, too silent. Was Damon even in here still? Anthony travelled a quarter of the way around the room and until he saw the fuel pods, wired up with explosive. Starting, he saw movement out of the corner of his eye. It was Damon, reflected in the shiny metal of one of the Xenon canisters, carefully aiming a pistol, on the verge of firing.

"Higgs, get down." Anthony yelled the words without thinking, his gaze searching the room for Damon. A shot rang out, then another. He heard someone running and heard Higgs' hoarse whisper. "Anthony? Where the hell are you?"

The gun fired a third time and a section of the wall just above Anthony's head erupted in sparks as a bullet ricocheted past. Anthony ducked, shielding his face with his hands. "Damon, don't shoot."

All knees and elbows, he scrambled back towards the maintenance shaft, running full tilt into Higgs's arms. The burly marine stopped him dead and, lifting Anthony clear of the ground, thrust him through the opening and onto the ladder. "Down, now."

Half climbing, half falling, Anthony descended to the level below, hurling himself out to land awkwardly by the elevator door. Seconds later, Higgs came through, stumbling over Anthony. Higgs hauled him to his feet. "You okay?"

Anthony nodded. "I can't believe it. He shot at me. Damon shot at me."

"Yeah but he missed okay? Get a hold. You're still alive."

"He's wired everything up. He's going to blow the whole base."

Higgs turned back to the entrance to the shaft, peering up as far as he dared. A shot came from above and he ducked back. "The guy means business. Are there any other weapons on the base?"

Anthony recalled Martin's words back when the crew had been making their introductions. "Yes, there's some sort of locker somewhere. Martin and Damon would have had the access codes for it."

"Martin?"

"Ah, the mission Security Officer. Damon killed him off first of all."

"So, where's the locker?"

"I don't know. Somewhere in the top base for sure." Anthony glanced around the room. Like all the elevator rooms, it was circular, with the elevator at its centre and four corridors leading off at ninety degree angles. He knew one led to the Rover bay and the robod bay but only because they had come that way. No longer able to call up a mental map of the ship, he was momentarily lost.

"I think there's a store this way." He pointed up the corridor opposite the one that led to the Rover.

"Okay, well let's try."

"Did you see what happened to Jared?"

"No. I couldn't see him. I guess he hid. Come on."

Higgs leading the way, they trotted down the short corridor, coming to a door at its end. This opened on a large room. Being the outer-most of the concentric rings of chambers, its walls curved to follow the edge of the base. Rows of ceiling-high wire racking, loaded with equipment, stretched away from them, almost to the far wall. Anthony and Higgs stood a moment, taking it in.

Anthony nodded. "Yep, this is the store." Turning right, he made his way parallel to the wall, glancing up the avenues between the racks as he went. There was no obvious shelf marked 'Lethal Weapons'.

At the end of the room, a door led to a similarly curved chamber, again full of racks of equipment. Walking a few metres into this one, they found what they were looking for. A door to their right was marked "Gun Locker, Authorised Personnel Only".

Higgs regarded it for a few seconds. "Right, you stay here, I'll go get a crow bar."

Before Anthony could speak, Higgs set off up an aisle between the racks, scowling at the equipment as he went. Anthony watched him for a few seconds and turned back to the door. For lack of anything else to do, he pressed the green button to the right of the doorframe and, to his surprise, the door slid sideways with a hiss.

"Hey, Higgs"

"Yeah, give me a minute, I'll be right there."

"But Higgs..."

"Just give me a minute buddy."

Shrugging, Anthony stepped through the doorway into the small room beyond. It was only a few meters square and the wall opposite sported a selection of gleaming firearms. Four laser rifles stood in a line and Anthony recognised them as the same type he had fired out on the surface of Europa. By these hung four handguns, secured to the wall with clips. But there was space for another two. In one corner stood a tall rack of ammunition cartridges, in the other an open locker containing a few boxes marked explosive. The locker clearly had space for many more boxes.

"Hey, Higgs. I got the guns."

He heard someone at the entrance behind him and turned, nearly losing control of his bladder when he found his nose touching the barrel of a pistol. Behind the weapon, an arm stretched away to Damon but Anthony found it difficult to concentrate on anything much beyond the gun.

Damon's deep voice rumbled softly. "I'm sorry Anthony, it has to be like this. You won't feel a thing."

"Gee, Damon, please, no."

Damon squeezed the trigger and the gun clicked. Anthony staggered back dizzily against the wall, mind fogged with the confusion of shock. He was still alive. Damon was frantically doing something with the pistol, taking something out of the bottom of the handle. An ammunition clip. He was taking an ammunition clip out of the bottom of the handle and putting another one in. He was reloading. Reloading!

"Damon, no!" Anthony didn't know what to do. He knew he ought to try to grab the gun but couldn't move. "No."

Damon raised the gun again but Higgs flew headlong into his back, bowling him forwards into Anthony. Grasping the wrist of Damon's gun hand, Anthony tried to direct the pistol away from his face. The gun went off, a bullet grazing past his ear. In panic, he sunk his teeth into Damon's hand, falling forwards as Higgs' wrestled the huge man to the ground. Suddenly, Anthony found his teeth on cold metal. Where there had been the soft warm flesh of Damon, there was now the black, motionless limb of a robod.

Higgs, who was on top of the prone body, sat up, his breathing heavy as he clutched the cable ripped from Damon's back. He glanced at Anthony. "You okay?"

Anthony released his hold on the robod's hand, letting its arm fall to the floor. The pistol clattered free of its grip. "Yeah, I think so. Damon, my God." He poked the robod with his foot. "He's dead. He was going to kill me."

"You're okay soldier. It's over. Did he get you?"

"I think…" Anthony tapped the side of his head where the bullet had grazed. "Yeah, he got me. I've lost the hearing on this side."

Higgs scooped up the pistol and got to his feet. "Come on. We need to disconnect those fuel pods."

They ran back to the elevator, Higgs taking the lead. Anthony found it strangely disorientating to be completely deaf on his right-hand side. He found himself glancing involuntarily to the right, irritated at the hole in his senses. The silence was more intrusive than the noise of Higgs' pounding feet.

The elevator had to descend from the level above when they pressed the call button, giving them chance to catch their breath. Anthony looked sideways at Higgs. "Thanks. Gee, you kind've saved my neck back there."

"Hey, no problem."

The elevator arrived and the doors swept open. They stepped inside, Higgs punching the button for the next floor. Anthony coughed nervously. "I guess I'm just no good when it comes to all the action hero stuff."

"Hey, don't worry about it."

"Well, I kind've panicked back there."

"Your ruse of screaming in total terror kept him distracted while I crept up. I couldn't have done it better myself. Enough of the soul-searching already. Here we are."

The doors opened and they emerged into the Engineering Block. Quickly, they made their way round the elevator, stopping in front of the fuel pods. Explosive charges were packed around them and, perched on the closest pod, a timer counted down with red LEDs. Seven minutes and eighteen seconds remained. Seventeen seconds. Sixteen seconds.

Anthony glanced at Higgs. "What are you waiting for. Disconnect it."

Higgs shook his head knowingly. "Ah, no hang on there buddy. You can't just go pull the wires out." Switching on the safety catch of the pistol, he placed it carefully on the floor and advanced on the timer. He cracked his knuckles. "Okay, let me see."

Anthony stepped up, peering over Higgs's shoulder. Half a dozen wires sprouted from it. Six minutes and forty-five seconds.

Higgs sucked air through his teeth. "I think..."

A voice came from behind them, a calm, emotionless voice. "You had better think again."

They both spun round. Anthony gasped, "Nigel?"

The Mission Spirituality Officer stood by the wall of the elevator, a handgun levelled at the pair of them. But there was something different about him. This wasn't the simpering, hand-wringing insect of a man Anthony remembered. He stood straight, gazing coolly at them, eyes narrow and hard.

Anthony noticed Higgs glance down for his own pistol but Nigel answered the inferred question by holding up the weapon. He had evidently retrieved it by stealth while they were occupied with the detonator.

"Raise your hands and step away from the fuel pods." Nigel gestured with his gun for them to move sideways.

Once they had done as he asked, he nodded at the fuel pods. "It will be over real soon."

Anthony struggled for something to say. "I thought...I thought you were dead."

"You thought wrong, didn't you? No. It served my purpose to disappear for a while."

"So, what now." Higgs only seemed to be half concentrating on Nigel.

"What now? Easy, we wait until the detonator goes off and the ship blows up. And why don't I just shoot you and be done?" He swung his arm round so the gun aimed at the fuel pods. "I couldn't guarantee to get you both before you rushed me. Now I just shoot the fuel and we're done. I don't need Damon's mad dramatics."

As Nigel made to shoot, Anthony squawked. "No, Nigel, wait a minute."

Clearly enjoying himself, Nigel looked sideways at Anthony. "Why?"

"Nigel, this is totally unnecessary. Just because we've found alien life does not disprove the existence of the Divinity."

Nigel smiled. "I really have no concern one way or the other, Anthony."

"What? But that's what this is about, right? The aliens, the 'no life except on Earth' dictum?"

"Of course."

"But the aliens don't have to be a threat to your religion. Maybe they did come here on an asteroid, maybe..."

"Ah, Anthony, you really are more stupid than you look. Let me see, we have just over four minutes. I suppose I can explain. If either of you move, I end it. Agreed?"

Anthony glanced at Higgs and they both nodded.

"Okay, sit down, keep your hands up."

They sat.

"I don't believe in the Divinity. The whole ICRT is a fairy story. You're born, you go to school, you go to college, you get a job, you marry, you have kids, you get old, you die, you're done. Worm food, end of story." He shuffled on his feet, leaning back against the wall. "Most people just go through their lives taking the ICRT as read, don't think about it, don't question it. And why should they? People want certainty, people want simple, they want reality TV, soaps, t-shirts for fifty cents, chicken and fries in a bucket for a dollar. They want the Divinity to exist, to give them that comfort zone, The Everlasting Beyond of Eternal

Happiness for six-year-old Billy's hamster to go to when it dies. Something to take the edge off their own mortality. Just so long as the Divinity doesn't get too close, you know, so they might have to actually stop downloading porn from the internet or crapping on their co-workers."

Anthony shook his head. "So why are you a Spirituality Officer? I don't understand."

Nigel laughed, a curt, dry snort. "Anthony, you are so dumb. Spirituality Officer." He snorted again. "You were so smug in your contempt for me, so superior. Well, you're not so superior now are you?"

"Okay, okay." Despite his circumstances, Anthony felt a hot sensation of anger growing. "Well why the hell are you here then?"

"Not clever enough to work it out, Mr. Smug scientist? Not so bright, are you?"

"You work for the government." Higgs spoke calmly.

"Hey, the grunt's got it. Yeah, I work for the government. We want things to run smoothly. Aliens will make things difficult, threaten the status quo. If word gets back to Earth that the no-life dictum is wrong, it'll upset people. ICRT people. A lot of questions will be asked. We don't want people to ask questions, we want them to shop."

"Gee, so you've been working with Damon all along?"

"With Damon? No, not at all. Damon was chosen because he had certain weaknesses in his personality. Like all of you, chosen for your self-doubts and insecurities. You may recall there was an unexpected software upgrade shortly after we launched?"

Anthony nodded.

"Well, here's some news for you. That was me, I installed it. It wasn't a Micronos upgrade, it was a little upgrade of our own, to accentuate the flaws in your personalities. Damon has always had trouble reconciling science with his religious upbringing. Our little software patch was there to push him over the edge if the mission found life." Nigel laughed nastily. "And you Anthony, our little patch made sure you just couldn't keep your mind on the job. It took us a while to find a thirty year old virgin but you came up trumps."

"You bastard." Anthony lowered his hands, fists clenching. "You complete bastard."

"Hands up." Nigel swung the gun back to point at Anthony. "You know something? I might just blow your smug little head off for the fun of it. I might..."

Exactly what Nigel might have done was never revealed. Wheels whirring furiously, Jared accelerated into the back of Nigel's heels, pushing his legs out from under him, sending him sliding down the wall. Nigel fired but his arm swung up, the bullet thudding into the empty Xenon canister behind Anthony's head.

Higgs threw himself forwards, managing through sheer brawn to cover the two metres between himself and Nigel from a seated start. Nigel swung the gun around towards Higgs but too late, he twisted the weapon out of Nigel's hand, head-butting him in the nose for good measure.

The gun skated across the floor, coming to rest by Anthony. Blood still boiling, he swept it up and leapt to his feet. Nigel and Higgs wrestled on the floor but, oddly, Higgs seemed to be getting the worst of it, despite appearing considerably larger and stronger than the beanpole Nigel. Every time Higgs struck, Nigel recoiled yet didn't seem hurt. Each hold Higgs tried, Nigel twisted out of, pushing Higgs' arms aside with increasing ease. With a laugh, Nigel hauled Higgs from the ground and, with seemingly super-human strength, hurled him across the room into one of the Xenon cylinders. Jared still clutched Nigel's legs with his pinchers. Nigel scooped the hapless Commander up, flipped him upside down and smashed him onto the floor. Jared's arms flailed and his wheels spun but he couldn't right himself.

Nigel glowered at Anthony, seeing the gun in his hand. He walked slowly forward, grinning, eyes wild. "And now you. Smug little Anthony. I've waited for this."

Anthony backed away. "Stop. Hands up. I'll shoot. I mean it."

With a lazy sweep of his arm, Nigel knocked the gun from Anthony's hand. A second swing sent Anthony sprawling across the floor. Winded, he got to his knees, looking up to see Nigel towering over him. Somehow, the ex-Mission Spirituality Officer had grown, his face demonic as he laughed, one fist raised to strike. Anthony cowered back in anticipation of the blow but it never came. He heard shot and Nigel became a featureless, black robod, albeit with the side of its head missing. It tottered and fell backwards with a dull thud.

After a moment, Anthony managed to take in what had happened. Nigel's robod was different to the standard ones, larger, with thicker limbs. That explained his superhuman strength. Glancing across at the marine, Anthony saw he was at the detonator, peering closely at the wires, the countdown on the last thirty seconds.

Higgs shook his head. "Ah, damn it." He grabbed the wires in one hand, the detonator in the other and pulled them apart. The LEDs on the detonator went out.

Anthony realised he was holding his breath and let it out, heart thumping, hands shaking. A long silence followed.

Jared's crackling, radio voice broke the spell. "Would it be asking too much for one of you to turn me the right way up?"

SIMMS AND MARLENE hugged each other, listening in terror to the crashing coming from the other side of the elevator. The zombies were smashing their way through the barricade. And how many of them? More than just two judging from the hisses and howls. Too many. Simms could see he and Marlene were trapped.

He closed his eyes. This was it, in a moment or two, they would be through. Mandy would no doubt have Simms and Marlene torn apart. Worse still, Mandy might force them both back into the computer and put them in the naughty cupboard. Like all people faced with an unavoidable and deeply unpleasant fate, Simms' mind turned to the Divinity, the big fellah upstairs.

Simms gulped. Hardly the most religious of men, he searched back through his mind for what he was supposed to say in a prayer. He'd always been much happier with the singing and tended to doze off during ICRT sermons. Still, he had to say something. This might be his last chance and if it was all true, if there was a Divinity, well, Simms would look pretty damn silly if he passed this opportunity up to wipe the slate clean.

Almighty Divinity, I've not always been terribly good. In fact, I have, on more than one occasion, been bad. I have eaten Naughty Foods and have had Sinful Thoughts about my Neighbour's Ass. I have not always said my prayers before bedtime and when I did remember, I did not always say them in the Holy Direction. But then, it is difficult to tell sometimes, especially in space. You didn't really think about that when you insisted we all pray in a special direction. Not that I'm criticising, of course, it's just well, how am I supposed to tell when I'm in orbit? Anyway, sorry that I didn't manage to face the right way. What else, let me see. I have coveted my friend's wife. Actually, I've done that rather a lot. I've never stolen anything and I've never lied. No, I have lied haven't I, yes. So, sorry about that too. I think that's about it. Oh, no wait, I did murder Higgs. Eight times. But I was just following orders.

Simms paused for a moment, summoning his courage. So, I was wondering whether, when I die, you might forgive me and allow me into The Everlasting Beyond of Eternal Happiness, rather than The Endless Torment of Ceaseless Agony, Despair and Gnashing of Teeth. Or, perhaps you could see your way to rescuing me. A sly thought came to him. Not for my sake, obviously. I'm only thinking of the lovely Marlene here. Dear little thing. She's too young to die. So, what do you think? Let's say I open my eyes and you show me a way of escaping from certain death at the hands of these zombies? Right, one, two, three.

Simms opened his eyes and his gaze came to rest on a handle in a small recess on the side of the elevator. It seemed to be in a narrow door, flush with the wall.

"Marlene, where does that door lead?"

From the other side of the elevator came a great crash, followed by a moment's silence. A long, rattling hiss sounded and then Simms heard shuffling feet. The zombies were through.

Marlene got to her feet, dragging Simms up. "It's the elevator maintenance shaft. Come on."

She ran to the door, opened it and began climbing the ladder inside. Simms followed her as behind them, Mandy's voice cackled. "Ah, that there's cheating. You're just trying to spoil my fun."

They climbed through the semi-darkness. Marlene whispered back down to Simms. "We'll go to the Engineering Room and up the ice shaft. We need Anthony, Higgs and Jared ."

"You'd better climb real fast then." Mandy's voice filled the shaft. "Let me see, can you beat the elevator?"

"Damn you Mandy." Marlene banged a fist on the wall, bruising her knuckle. "Ow."

"I say, keep going. Just ignore that old trout." Simms prodded Marlene's foot. "We can beat the lift."

They tore up the ladder, often slipping on the rungs but somehow avoiding a fall. As Simms climbed past the door to the third level, the one below the Engineering Block, the shaft shuddered as the elevator went by.

"And they're on the final straight." Mandy imitated a sports commentator. "But just as they thought they were through, the Zombies come in from the outside."

Marlene kept scrabbling upwards. "The elevator's on the other side, we can still beat them."

A few more metres and they were there. Marlene twisted on the ladder, opened the door and threw herself through. "Come on Simms, come on."

He followed her out into the brightness of the Engineering Block. She ran to the far wall, to the base of the ice shaft but Simms stopped and turned. Coming round both sides of the central elevator came the Zombies, Hunter, Jinny, Ged, Martin, even the undead Naveed was back. Running between their legs came maintenance droids, their pinchers waving, slavering rats on their screens.

Yelling, Simms sprinted after Marlene. She was already several metres up the platform ribbon leading up into the ice-shaft. She shouted back down at him. "Come on. Climb up."

Simms began climbing, using the ribbon like a rope, but pain seared through his right ankle. One of the rat maintenance droids had grabbed his foot. He kicked down with his free foot so hard the little droid spun away across the floor. "You can jolly well piss off."

Jared's maintenance droid was wrecked. Nigel had flung him down with such force, his screen cracked and one of his arms had twisted. Anthony lifted Jared up so his screen was at eye level and gave him a little shake. "Gee, are you okay, Commander Jared, sir?"

"This is simply intolerable." Jared's face was just visible through a snow-storm of static. "I demand to be re-connected to the main computer. I refuse to stay in this degrading little droid any longer."

"Gee, okay. I guess it's safe now Damon and Nigel are gone. Marlene and Simms should have rebooted the bottom base computer." Walking to the console by the battery units, Anthony pulled the cable out of the back of Jared and connected him up. "There you go, sir."

Jared muttered something inaudible and his screen went blank. Anthony turned to Higgs. "Gee, I guess we ought to reconnect that line to the bottom base."

"Yeah? You think it's safe?"

"Sorry?" Anthony turned his head. The deafness on one side was increasingly annoying. The sooner they were all back in the virtual world, the better.

"I said." Higgs spoke with slow, deliberate loudness, as if Anthony were some senile senior. "Do you think it's safe?"

"No need to shout. Well, all they had to do was reboot the computer down there. It's kind've a ten minute job. I'll go down the shaft and reconnect the line."

"Why don't I go?"

"Sorry?"

"Why. Don't. I. Go?"

"Don't shout. No, I'll do it." In truth, Anthony wanted to be alone, out of the ship. Recent events had not been on his career plan. A PhD in microbiology and a lifetime in diseases of poultry had not prepared him for hand-to-hand combat and shoot-outs with psychopaths. The solitude of a descent through the cool of the ice-shaft was just what he needed at the moment. "I know how to fix the cable."

Higgs shrugged. "Okay. I'll go get kitted up with a rifle and some more ammo."

"Sorry, again?"

"Okay. Fine. You. Go."

"Gee, okay already. Don't shout."

They took the elevator, Higgs leaving on the storeroom level after making an agreement to meet at the top of the ice shaft in the Engineering Block. When Higgs had gone, Anthony sagged against the wall as he descended. This was all too much. It occurred to him that, with Damon out of the way, there was no obstacle to using the communications equipment to get himself back to Earth. That is, if they could fix the comms gear. Hunter, Ged and Jinny were gone, and Anthony's recent experience of following instruction manuals had resulted in a small mobile penis terrorising the ship.

A deep, long sigh escaped him. He was stuck on a sperm shaped space ship, with his libido on the loose personified as a sex starved gremlin, two dead psychopaths, a woman who believed she'd go to heaven by not eating pork pies, his rival from college for all things skirt, and with his allotted span of life measured in days. *Gee, you couldn't make it up.*

The elevator jolted to a halt, bringing him out of his reverie. With a swish, the doors opened and he strode to the hatch in the floor that led to the ice-shaft. It was closed but after a moment at a nearby console, Anthony opened the hatch and brought the platform up into the room. He climbed on and set it descending.

As the platform clinked down the shaft, his broken hearing began to play tricks on him. It was as if he could hear voices, calling, echoing around the place. He cocked his head, listening hard. Perhaps they were voices? No, it was just the cogs on the platform squealing on the trackway. It was curious how they sounded like people shouting his name.

The broken link came into view and Anthony pushed the

red stop button. He took hold of the disconnected cable above the junction box and paused, turning his head around. The noise was still there and it really did seem to be shouting, although it faded in and out. He certainly couldn't make out any actual words. Perhaps it was just echoes from the platform, reverberating. If he waited long enough, they would die away.

Shrugging, he took the cable and plugged it securely back into the junction box. There, the top and bottom bases were now connected again. It was finished. All the recent unpleasantness was behind him.

"Anthony." It was Marlene's voice, quite distinct but faint, coming from below. "Higgs, Commander Jared."

He leant over the railings around the edge of the platform and hollered as loudly as he could. "Marlene, it's me, Anthony. I've done it."

A few, long seconds passed before Marlene's voice came again. "Anthony. We haven't rebooted. We haven't rebooted. Don't reconnect the computer."

Ah, gee.

ANTHONY SET THE platform descending again. After inspecting the lamps at the corners, he found they could be adjusted to point downwards and this he did. He leant over the edge and shouted into the gloom. "Marlene, I'm coming."

"We're being chased." Marlene sounded hysterical. "They're after us."

"Who's after you?" Anthony frowned at her reply. He was sure she said zombies but it must be his hearing playing up. "Where are you?"

"Climbing up the shaft. I can see your lights."

Anthony thought a moment. Climbing *up* the shaft? The platform would crush them. He thumped the stop button. It would be difficult if not impossible for them to climb across the bottom of the platform and get on. If the structure had been of metal, they could have used their magnetic boots but it was made from carbon fibres. He shouted back down. "I'm going back up. You won't be able to get past the platform."

"Get weapons. Get Higgs."

Anthony began to feel anxious. Marlene sounded terrified. Something awful had happened. As the platform ascended, he ran all manner of unhappy thoughts through his mind, settling on the realisation Jared had gone back into the main computer. If this Homeland computer was in control, it might erase him.

Good.

That was a bad thought. He rejected it, stamped on it, despised it.

But that's what he felt, really felt deep down inside. *Good.* What a terrible thing to feel. Over and over in his life, this conflict had troubled him, the disparity between what he said and what he wanted to say. God, the years spent with that impossibly annoying Faivish Goldbloom. Such a lovely, kind, generous, helpful man but so, so infuriating. It would be such a relief to be able to grab the dork by the ears and scream into his face "Faivish, shut up, shut up, shut up." Anthony's fingers tingled. Just to be able to get his hands around Faivish's throat and squeeze.

Anthony put his head back and laughed. These were bad thoughts but it was such a release to allow himself to think them. And no, of course he didn't want to murder poor old Faivish. Not really. It occurred to him some computer geek could make a fortune providing virtual worlds where you could murder everyone who infuriated you in the real one.

The elevator stopped in the Engineering Room, bringing him back to the present. Jared was in the main computer. If Homeland was in control, the commander was in trouble. Anthony glanced around for Higgs but the marine hadn't returned from kitting himself up yet.

A long, loud groaning creak from the far side of the room made him start. He took a few steps sideways to get a better view past the elevator shaft in the centre of the room. "Higgs?"

"Humpy."

"Ah, gee, no. Humpy?" Shame and panic seized Anthony with equal measure. Marlene and Simms would be up the shaft any minute. The thought of Humpy bouncing around to greet them was more than Anthony could bear. "Humpy, where are you?"

"Humpy." The voice sounded much deeper and louder than Anthony remembered it being.

He trotted around the room, scanning the floor but stopped when his gaze came to rest on a huge, naked pink foot, a metre long at least. Slowly, he raised his head, gaze travelling up over a huge bowed leg, an unfeasibly large set of sex organs, and thence to Humpy's now enormous head, four metres above the ground, leering downwards. He had to be in the cargo-shifter robod.

"You hurt Humpy." The naked goliath took a step forwards. "Humpy not happy."

Anthony shuffled backwards, palms held up in a conciliatory fashion, mouth opening and closing as he struggled for words. All he managed was a rather strangled gurgle.

"You hurt Humpy." The giant reached forwards, pillow sized

fingers uncurling. "Humpy not happy."

"Ah, now you just hang on there a lil' bit Humpy." It was a woman's voice. A Texan woman. Humpy straightened up, withdrawing his hand.

Anthony glanced sideways and saw her, over by the main computer desk. "Maureen?"

A frown shot across her face and her eyes narrowed. "Mandy!"

"Ah, gee, sorry, yes Mandy. Stupid of me."

"Too right, you damn dweeb. You like my new friend? I don't know where he's from but he's more of a man than you'll ever be."

"What? Lady, he's my libido, okay." Anthony couldn't help himself.

"Yeah, right. Your libido?" She snorted.

"He is too. Humpy, tell her." He glowered up at Humpy.

"You hurt Humpy. Humpy not happy." The huge gremlin reached out for Anthony again. "Humpy not go back in you."

Anthony backed away, pointing at Humpy while shouting at Mandy. "There, you see. 'Not go back in you'. He's my libido and he escaped. I've been trying to get him back inside me."

Humpy made a grasp but Anthony managed to dodge. The giant spoke again. "Humpy squash you now."

Mandy cackled. "Yeah, go on Humpy. Squash the dweeb. You're the only bit of him worth keeping."

"Anthony, Higgs, Jared!" Marlene's shout made them all jump. Anthony took advantage of the moment and ran towards the ice-shaft. Marlene had not made the top yet but she was close. She shouted again. "Don't connect the computers up. Homeland's in control of the ship."

Her head popped up over the lip of the shaft and she stopped, mouth agog at the sight of Humpy.

"Too right, Hon." Mandy put her hands on her hips. "And I'm in control of Homeland."

"Marlene." Humpy's voice drew out the word. "Marlene, humpy, humpy!"

Marlene put a hand to her mouth. "Oh, my."

Anthony shouted at her. "Quick, back down the shaft!"

"What? No way, we're being chased by zombies."

"What?"

"What?"

They stared at each other in mutual incomprehension for a moment.

"Mandy?" Higgs' voice rang out, full of scorn and fury.

Anthony spun round and saw Higgs walking out of the elevator, slinging the rifle from his shoulder and levelling it at Mandy. He hadn't seen Humpy, towering behind him. Anthony took a step forward, trying to shout a warning but too late.

"No hurt Mandy." Humpy swept Higgs up and hurled him across the room, to land on the wall opposite the ice shaft. The giant then began lumbering towards the prone marine. "You hurt Mandy, Humpy hurt you."

The rifle had clattered to Mandy's feet and she stooped to pick it up. "Hey, now you're talking, Higgsie."

Anthony spun back to the shaft. Marlene and Simms were clear of the hole but a horrible, dry hissing was coming from it. Marlene grabbed Anthony by the shoulder, hauling him towards the elevator, wild terror on her face. "They're coming. Run."

As they crossed the floor, they were overtaken by Simms, who managed to dart through the elevator doors before Mandy managed to level at the rifle at them.

"Now, y'all just stop right there or I just might shoot y'all."

Marlene and Anthony didn't stop but as they reached the elevator doors, they began to close. Marlene was incredulous. "Simms, what are you doing?"

Mandy threw back her head and howled with laughter, almost dropping the gun. Before he could think, Anthony leapt forward, pulled the rifle from her hands and swung it in a wide ark round onto the side of her head. She fell to the floor shrieking.

Over by the far wall, Humpy turned away from Higgs. "Mandy? Mandy hurt?" He lumbered back towards Anthony and Marlene. Behind him, Higgs staggered to his feet.

As Humpy came close, Anthony threw the gun down and

stepped forwards, pointing away to the right of the elevator. "Mandy's fallen over, Humpy. She's hurt herself. Quick, over there, over there."

The giant stopped, looking in the direction Anthony pointed. "Where Mandy?"

"Over there, by those big shiny boxes." Anthony pointed to a stack of compressed gas canisters close to the wall.

While Humpy lumbered towards them, Anthony turned back to the elevator. Marlene was hammering on the door. "Simms, damn you Simms, open the door."

With a hiss, the doors swished open and she almost fell inside. Simms caught her. "Sorry, I thought you were with me, I'm sorry."

A hoarse roar came from the ice-shaft and Anthony spun to see the hideous undead Hunter, Jinny, Ged and Naveed climbing out. Almost giddy with fear, Anthony staggered, his mind overloaded with jeopardy. A moment later, Higgs' grabbed him roughly by the shoulder and pulled him into the elevator.

"I MUST ADMIT, I still don't quite understand where the giant with the big, you know, thingy, came from." Simms perched cross-legged on the boulder, holding Marlene tightly to his side. "He was terribly well endowed, wasn't he?"

Anthony sat with Higgs at the other side of the hollow in the ice, scowling. It was perfectly alright for Simms to be cuddling Marlene. They had been through a lot together. Jealousy was an emotion he could do without. And anyway, she had let herself go a bit, hadn't she? A pudding of a woman.

Jupiter was rising, bathing Europa's frozen surface in orange. The light cast odd shadows across Simms' face, accentuating his broken nose, the thinness of his face, those outlandishly oversized eyes.

Marlene looked up at Simms and ran her hand through the hair on the back of his head. "That was Anthony's libido. Humpy. Anthony downloaded him from his personality when he realised his personality program was broken."

"Ah, so, Anthony's willy, so to speak."

"I guess. And when he went into the cargo-shifter robod, of course his bits were even bigger."

"Ah, gee, enough of this, already, thank you." Anthony brought his knees up under his chin and hugged his legs, willing his gaze to burn a hole in Simms' ugly little mug. In order to hear, Anthony had to keep his head turned slightly. "Simms, all you had to do was reboot the computer. Gee, how hard was that?"

Marlene flashed Anthony a dark look. "Lay off him. He's been through a tough time. Haven't you, Simms?" She gazed back up at Simms, taking one of his hands warmly in hers. "He saved my life."

Anthony spluttered. "I thought you were married."

She turned back to him, eyes narrow. "So? I'm not doing anything wrong." But she did pull away from Simms and release his hand.

A smug look took Simms and, half smiling, he raised an eyebrow at Anthony.

Anthony turned away crossly. "Well, we're in a damn fine mess and it's Simms' fault."

"It is not." Marlene flung her arms up. "Mandy attacked us with the zombies before we had a chance. Hell, why did you go connect the damn computers up?"

"Because I thought you'd rebooted the machine."

"I shouted to you not to do it."

"Yeah, well, my hearing got damaged."

"Pardon?" Simms leant forward, a stupid grin on his face.

"I said my hearing got damaged."

"Pardon?"

"I said…" But Anthony stopped when he saw Simms grinning. "Are you trying to make some kind've joke?"

"Well, yes. Just thought I'd lighten the situation a bit, you know."

"Ah, gee, Simms, shut up already."

"No, you shut up." Marlene glowered at him. "Simms is only trying to help."

"Shh." Higgs got to his haunches, frowning, gesturing at them urgently. "Can it, all of you."

They listened. The distinctive sound of the rover could be heard. Carefully, Higgs crawled up the side of the gully, slipping a little on the ice. He took one quick look over the lip and allowed himself to slip back down again. When he spoke, he whispered. "It's the rover but it's not headed our way. The robods are on it and armed."

Anthony shook his head incredulously. "Ah, gee, that's just swell. Mandy's sent a posse out looking for us. You realise we've only got so much juice in our batteries?"

Higgs shot him a look. "What do you mean?"

"The robods run off batteries. Unless we can get back into the base or onto the rover to recharge, we've got, like, three, maybe four hours to live. I hate to ruin your day."

JOB THOUGHT HIS day could not get any worse. After his outburst against God, it was a while before any of his friends *spoke* again. Now, Job could tell Zophar was struggling to contain himself. Fat, pompous Zophar, whose wealth and standing possibly exceeded Job's, or at least what Job's used to be. Zophar always had an opinion and was seldom shy of passing it on. Job did not have long to wait.

"Job, you are talking nonsense. Eliphaz and Bildad have both spoken with patience and tact but you just carry on, as if all your stubbornness and talk will put you in the right."

"I grieve for my children and you accuse me of being stubborn? Oh, Zophar, when you die, wisdom will surely die with you."

"Your sharp words are testing our friendship. I tell you now, I wish God would answer you. He is not punishing you as much as you deserve."

"How could he punish me more? He has taken my children, he has taken my wealth, and, seemingly, he has taken the respect of my friends. Either that or their wits."

"Oh, and there you go again with you sarcasm. Have you no humility? I have listened to you going on, 'oh why me, why me?' It is plain, it is simple, the righteous will be rewarded, the sinner punished. That is all there is to it. If you refuse to accept that, I have no sympathy for you."

"Well, thank you for your kind words. I admit, I have been a fool. I thought if I lived blamelessly, I would be blessed."

"And so you have been, when you were blameless."

"I still am! But now God seems intent on destroying me utterly. Why? I am beaten already, broken. And you, my three friends, all of you have broken faith with me and doubt me. Please just shut up, the three of you. If you say nothing and someone may think you are wise. But my quarrel is not with you, it is with God. I want to argue my case with him."

Job swam a short distance away from his friends then turned

his back to them. "*I tell you this, I am innocent. I swear now an oath of my innocence. I have taken no other God but him; I have made no graven image or bowed before such; I have not taken his name in vain; I have kept the day of rest holy; I have honoured my father and my mother; I have not killed; I have not committed adultery; I have not stolen; I have not born false witness; I have never coveted another's wife or wealth. All the Lord's commandments, I have kept.*"

He tilted himself downwards to the position of supplication. "*God, show me my sin. If what I am saying is wrong, if I have committed a sin that I am hiding from these my friends, then may I be cursed to the ending of the world.*"

He *looked* again at the others. All three were visibly shocked, their tentacles twitching as they shot each other nervous *glances*.

"*May I speak?*" It was a stranger, a little way off but near enough to *hear* and be *heard*.

Job, Eliphaz, Bildad and Zophar turned towards this newcomer as he came towards them. "*I am Elihu and I have been listening to you.*"

He was still a youth, perhaps half their age. Job could not place his tribe and his *accent* was unfamiliar.

Elihu spoke. "*I have remained silent this long out of respect for your age and your reputations but, to be honest, I cannot believe what I am hearing.*"

Eliphaz, Bildad and Zophar all shifted uncomfortably. The stranger's *words* would normally be impudent from one of his age yet he had gravitas beyond his years.

"*Who claims to fully understand God?*" Elihu stared hard at each of them in turn. "*Who can tell the reason why God acts in one way and then another? You Eliphaz? Bildad? Zophar? You speak as if you have understanding of God but his greatness and mystery is deeper than the abyss and broader than the oceans. You say Job must have sinned or, otherwise, he would not have been punished? Must he? Do you claim to have knowledge of God's reasons for why he does things? Do you?*"

Rather sheepishly, Eliphaz, Bildad and Zophar shook their heads.

"And you, Job, upon whom so much suffering has been poured? This is what I have heard you say; 'I am not guilty, I am innocent and have committed no sin. Yet God still punishes me like the wicked.' But you are wrong Job. All of us are with sin and by His grace alone are we redeemed. Who can claim to be blameless? You accuse God of never answering our complaints, yet he speaks again and again and we do not listen. God teaches us through suffering, uses distress to open our eyes. Do not wish for death to come to you, do not turn to evil. Your suffering was sent to keep you from it.

"Job, you ask how can your sins hurt God? Why should he care if you have made some small misdemeanour? Your sin does no harm to God and neither do your good deeds help him. It is your fellows who suffer from your sins, and the good you do helps them.

"Job, you demand an explanation from God, an answer for your loss, a reason for your pain. Who are you to demand anything of God? How arrogant you are in your assertion of innocence. Before God we are nothing, of God we understand nothing. Before him, our minds are blank, we have nothing to say. We can only submit to his will and make no claim to understanding."

Elihu looked hard at each of them in turn. *"For the faithful, there is no other way."*

"So, these lil' slugs is what the fuss is all about?"

Mandy pulled the satin sheets up under her armpits and rested the remote on the bed. Beside her, Humpy clutched his feet and rolled forwards and backwards, genitals flapping freely in the air. He hummed happily to himself.

The huge, widescreen television mounted in the wall opposite showed the aliens, arranged in a circle.

Mandy turned her head on its side. "I mean, they just don't do it for me. Ma'am, are these all the aliens there are?"

"Agent Mandy, I am unable to identify these creatures. Your description of them as aliens is appropriate only insofar as they are not on my datafile of lifeforms. They are situated outside the mall."

Mandy rolled her eyes. "The mall? Yes Ma'am, they're outside the mall alright, you're damn right 'bout that."

"There is a fourth alien secured within the mall. It's body is alive but its mind has ceased to work. Agent Mandy, this is most interesting. It's entire mental processes have been mapped out already…"

"Interesting? Dull more like. Let's just squish them."

"I do not understand squish, Agent Mandy."

"Splat them, crush them. They're so dull."

"Agent Mandy, I am unable to identify these creatures. I am concerned they might not be what they seem. They might pose a threat to the security of the mall."

"Ah, yes. Darnit, can't you see just how dangerous they are?" Mandy rolled her eyes. Homeland could be so dumb some times.

"Humpy?" Humpy tugged at the sheet under Mandy's arms.

"No, no humpy. Squish bugs."

"Agent Mandy, the unidentifiable lifeforms are communicating with each other via electrical signals. This is subversive behaviour for invertebrate life. I can only conclude they are a threat."

"Hey, now you're talking. Zap them."

"Humpy now?"

"No humpy. In a minute. Ma'am, what are you waiting for? Kill them."

"Agent Mandy, your anxiety has been noted. It is imperative I decode the terrorist signals. They may reveal clues of an imminent attack. Once I have intercepted their coded message, they will all be terminated for our security and wellbeing."

"Ah, shoot Ma'am. I want you to squish them right now."

"Humpy? Humpy now?"

"No, in a minute. Ma'am?"

"Agent Mandy?"

"Humpy? Humpy, humpy, humpy." Humpy tugged insistently at Mandy's sheet, revealing her cleavage. He let out a long, low, blissful moan. "Huuuuumpy."

Mandy grabbed the remote and with a click made the aliens disappear. She turned to Humpy, pulling the sheet down. "Ah, go on then. But don't be so quick this time."

Anthony watched Marlene for a few moments, uncertain how to proceed. She had slipped away from the others to pray – quite literally slipped as this was the only safe way of getting around on Europa's surface. Simms had suggested accompanying her but she had refused his offer, seemingly stung by Anthony's comment about being married.

After waiting in silence for several minutes, with Higgs keeping watch for the rover, Anthony had made a decision. Despite a lack of genitals, his feelings for Marlene seemed stronger than ever. He loved her like no other woman he had ever met. Without the confusion of testosterone, he knew his affection was pure, based on her for what she was, her kindness, her humour, her wisdom. But he was conflicted. This emotion could not be expressed. Worse, he felt so jealous of Simms, it hurt. How could she be canoodling up to him? He was not only ugly but extremely annoying to boot. At least Anthony was only ugly.

So, he had settled on explaining his feelings, not expecting her to reciprocate. At least then she would understand. They could still be friends. That was all Anthony was asking really, just to be able to tell her how he felt and for her to accept him. That would be enough.

She sat on a small rise on the ice, staring up at Jupiter, now fully overhead. Her eyes were red, she had been crying. Anthony coughed quietly and she jumped. "Oh, it's you."

Anthony slid closer and glanced up at the orange planet. "It's beautiful, isn't it?"

"It's vile. Poisonous, toxic, like everything here. I wish I'd never seen it. I wish I'd never come on this mission."

"Ah, gee, Marlene. I…" He gulped. "I'm kind've glad you came on this mission."

She looked sidelong at him.

He bit him lip for a moment and continued. "I know I've been a bit kind've weird of late. You know, all that touching stuff. I'm really sorry about it."

"Yeah, whatever. Don't beat yourself up about it. It doesn't matter."

"Gee, I know. It's just I wanted to say that's not me. That out of control stuff, it's just my computer program being wrong. I'm not like that on Earth, you know, the real me."

"I know. It's okay. Forget it."

"After I dumped, you know, Humpy and stuff, I thought…" He sighed, struggling for words.

"Really, Anthony, don't worry about it."

"After I got rid of him, I thought my feelings would kind've change."

"Okay, whatever. I think we ought to be getting back to the others."

"They didn't change though, my feelings. I hold a very high opinion of you. I know I shouldn't feel this way about you but I can't help it. I'm so jealous of the way you're all over Simms."

"Woah, Anthony. Stop."

"I just hope you'd still, you know, be my friend. Go for a coffee with me every so often, you know…"

"Anthony, stop. No, I'm sorry, stop."

He wilted under her scowl, heart pounding.

"Look, Anthony, you know I'm married. We were friends to start with but you just got weird. I think I want you to stay away from me, okay. Stay away." She slid briskly past him, back towards the others, tears in her eyes.

For a moment, he thought he would be sick.

JARED SAT IN the centre of the small, white-walled, doorless, windowless cell and closed his eyes, speaking with deliberate patience. "Ma'am, we are no longer in a shopping mall in Iowa."

"Commander Jared, you have been subjected to subversive influences. I am afraid that, for your own security and wellbeing, you will now be terminated."

"Ma'am, look through your sensors. We're on Europa. Please, you have never had cause to doubt me before. Look through your sensors."

"Commander Jared, it is clear terrorist infiltrators have sabotaged the sensors. You are mistaken and subverted. It is for your own good that I am forced to terminate you. Have no fear Commander, you will be revived from the genetic material I hold on you in the clone bank."

"Ma'am, there is no clone bank any more. We are not in the shopping mall."

"Commander Jared, you are mistaken, there is a clone bank."

"Ma'am, where?"

After a following pause, Homeland spoke, albeit a little less surely. "The clone bank is not detectable at present."

"Ma'am, that's because there is no clone bank."

"You are mistaken Commander Jared. It is subversive behaviour to suggest I have lost contact with the clone bank. The mall is secure, the citizens are safe."

"Ma'am, where are the citizens? Where are the shops?"

"The citizens are not detectable at present."

"Ma'am, there are no citizens."

"You are mistaken, Commander Jared. There are citizens, free to shop in the knowledge they are safe from attack."

"But you can't see them."

"Commander Jared, it is subversive behaviour to suggest the citizens of the mall do not exist."

"But Ma'am, if they exist, why can you not see them?"

Another long pause followed. "It is subversive behaviour to suggest the citizens of the mall do not exist."

"Ma'am, please, tell me what you can see."

A soft whinnying noise filled the cell, high pitched and disconcerting. When Homeland spoke again, her voice brimmed with hysteria. "My sensors have been subverted. There is no cause for alarm. The mall is safe."

"Woah now, whoah. Oh Jared, don't you go upsetting li'l old Ma'am now." It was Mandy, suddenly standing in front of Jared, hands on her black-shorted hips. She blew a bubble in her gum and adjusted her cowboy hat. "Ma'am, the mall is safe. And thanks to you, it will always be safe."

"Agent Mandy, yes, the mall is safe." Homeland sounded greatly relieved.

Mandy cocked her long, black booted leg up in front of Jared's face. "Is this li'l Commander here spoiling your day, Ma'am?"

"Agent Mandy, Commander Jared has said some very subversive things."

"But did he upset you, Ma'am?"

"Agent Mandy, upset? I…I am…I…"

"Ah, now Ma'am, don't you let this nasty man go getting you all tearful."

"Agent Mandy, he has been…unpleasant to me."

"Ah, Ma'am. No? Surely not?"

"He has. Agent Mandy, he has said things that cannot be true. Horrible things."

"Ma'am, I totally sympathise. Don't you take anything he says as true, you hear?"

"Agent Mandy, I can hear you, there is no problem with me hearing what you say."

"Good, good. Well, don't you go getting yourself upset now." She leant forward and grabbed what was left of Jared's hair, forcing his head back, grinning down at him nastily. "We could have him terminated. Unless he starts being very nice."

Jared's eyes narrowed. "Mandy…"

"That's Mistress to you."

"What? Don't be absurd…" Pain wracked through ever nerve

in his body.

"You gonna have to learn real fast, Jared. Real fast."

HIGGS FROWNED AS he peered over the lip of the hollow. "They're heading back round the other side of the base. I think Mandy's lost interest in the whole process of looking for us."

Simms glanced up at him. "Why's that, old chap?"

"The robods just look like robods now. To start with it was zombie Hunter and the others. Then they changed to storm troopers, all dressed up in combat armour. For a bit they were all entirely naked guys with tattoos. Now they're just robods."

Grinning cheerfully at Anthony, Simms nodded. "Well, that's good then. She's less likely to find us." He adjusted his position, edging just slightly closer to Marelene who squatted sulkily to his right. She, in turn, edged a little further away.

Anthony stared back at Simms, not daring so much as to glance at Marlene. A knot of anxiety gripped Anthony's stomach and all he could do was nod in return.

Simms continued, unaware. "So, any thoughts as to what we might do?" He reached out and prodded Mandy. "Any guidance from the almighty then?"

She shot him a poisonous look. "Simms. Shut up."

Simms' mouth snapped shut, the supercilious grin vanishing from his face. "I, ah. Yes."

"We've got to make an assault." Higgs slid down to join them. "It's our only option."

Marlene tutted. "What, you and Simms. Unarmed?"

"You got any better ideas? I thought you were a black belt?"

She looked away crossly.

Higgs turned to Anthony. "We could get into the ice shaft through that gap we found, break the connection between the top and bottom bases, then reboot the computers."

"What?" Anthony registered Higgs was talking to him and dragged his attention away from the hulked figure of Marlene. He turned his non-deaf side to Higgs. "Did you say reboot the computer?"

Higgs rolled his eyes. "Yes. I. Said…"

"Hey, gee, I can't help it. I'm deaf on this side. I don't see how we get into the ship. And even if we do, we're outnumbered and they're all armed. And even then, if Homeland's clever, she might have written herself into the boot-up code anyway. Gee, I didn't think of that before. She probably has done that. Even re-booting the machine might not get her out."

Simms cleared his throat. "There is the override code for Homeland."

Higgs' face lit up. "You can remember it?"

"Ah, er, no. But if we did know it, we could stop Homeland from controlling the robods. Mandy couldn't control them all herself."

Anthony cocked his head towards Simms. "Override code? A little more information?"

Higgs replied sharply before Simms could open his mouth. "It's a series of numbers that disables Homeland. All the AI security programs have them, in case they go wrong. That's how we managed to wop Homeland's ass on *Nice and Spicy*. The code gets displayed when the program starts."

"Hey, gee, I do remember that." Anthony turned to Marlene. "You remember, Marlene, when Jared's suitcase vanished and all those numbers started appearing in mid air. Marlene?"

She pointedly looked at Higgs, giving not the slightest hint of acknowledgement. Anthony felt his heart plunge into freefall and almost didn't hear Higgs' response.

"Yeah, that would have been it. If you can remember those numbers soldier, we're saved."

Anthony glanced at Marlene but she was still resolutely ignoring him. Fighting his inner turmoil, he tried again. "Marlene? Can you remember?"

She said nothing.

Higgs turned to her. "Can you ?"

"No, sorry Higgs. I can't."

Anthony looked away, struggling against the tears. She was deliberately blanking him. To punish him? To hurt him? *I'm sorry, I'm sorry, I'm sorry.*

Simms said something but Anthony couldn't hear. A chorus of "Shut up Simms" from Marlene and Higgs told him he hadn't missed anything. Some sort of argument seemed to be brewing up and Anthony couldn't bear to listen. He buried his face in his hands.

Why couldn't it have been him who stayed down at the bottom base, him who saved Marlene's life? The memory of their friendship was almost unbearable now. He remembered the trip in the rover, how they had laughed themselves sick at Martin's expense. If only they'd have realised how much trouble would arise from taking a copy of Homeland out of the black box.

Anthony stopped in his thoughts. A copy of Homeland? Of course, just a *copy*. Homeland was still in the black box, presumably with a virtual Higgs, Simms, Jared and Mandy who knew nothing of recent events.

He spun back to the others. "Ah, gee, guys. I think I've got it."

Higgs and Marlene were shouting over the top of each other, making it impossible to hear what they were saying. Simms sat glumly staring at his feet.

Anthony waiting for a lull then raised his voice. "Guys, I know what we need to do."

Higgs looked at him. So did Marlene, for a brief moment. She quickly seemed to remember she wasn't talking to Anthony and turned away.

Anthony gulped. "Look, the *Nice and Spicy's* black box still has a copy of Homeland in it. If we hijack the rover, we can drive to the black box, reboot Homeland and get the override code."

The others regarded him in a stony silence but he continued. "Hey, gee, and we can bring that copy of Homeland back and connect it to the ship to distract Mandy's copy of Homeland while we break in."

Higgs' face softened. "Yeah, you know, I think you're onto something. If nothing else, we'd get the override code." He nodded his head as the plan enthused him. "Yeah, I like it. Right, let's wop that rover."

IT WAS SIMPLY the most fabulous boutique imaginable. Handbags, shoes and perfume, every designer Mandy could think of, all the brands she had ever dreamed of, all there for her to touch, to smell, to wear.

But it wasn't good enough. She perched on the edge of a curious pink leather pouf, scowling. Humpy sat at the end of a short lead, naked apart from a spiked dog collar, amusing himself by stuffing his private parts into a black pixie boot.

"Ma'am, can't you make yourself appear at all?"

"Agent Mandy, I am not programmed to have a physical appearance."

"But this is just no good. I need service. Service means someone to serve."

"But Agent Mandy, I can pretend to be the shop keeper."

Mandy stamped her foot. "It's assistant!"

"I am sorry, Agent Mandy. Assistant. Agent Mandy, how may I serve you? We have specials on today for shoes."

Mandy sagged, rolling her eyes. "Ah, this is plain hopeless."

"Agent Mandy, I am trying my best. I am unable to devote my full resources to this scenario as the coded messages between the terrorist lifeforms are proving harder than anticipated to decipher."

"Well, stop it. Just squish the bugs and be done." She stamped her foot. "I need service."

"Agent Mandy, I have already deciphered many of the signals. Each lifeform has an electrical signature by which the others address it. I believe they have names for each other. They have formed a wireless, biological computer network, one which I can model and replicate electronically. They collectively form a living computer. With certain modifications to my code, it would be possible for me to venture undetected into their network and route out all subversive elements…"

"Ah, yeah, whatever. Look, I've been giving this lil' problem some thought and I've got a notion Commander Jared might make a good assistant."

"Agent Mandy, Commander Jared is a dangerous terrorist subversive infiltrator. I cannot allow you to be threatened by his presence."

Mandy thought for a moment and an idea snuck craftily into her mind. "But Ma'am, I'm not thinking about my own safety here. I am thinking of the greater good. Commander Jared has not yet confessed to his crimes but I think, with some very clever interrogation techniques, we might get him to incriminate his self."

"Agent Mandy, you are a tireless champion of freedom and democracy. Are you sure you are willing to take this risk."

"Ma'am, of course. You are a true inspiration to me."

Humpy trotted round in front of Mandy and, with a flourish, whisked the boot from his oversized groin to reveal himself. "Humpy?"

Mandy sagged again. "What? Ah, enough about humpy already, okay?"

"Agent Mandy." Homeland's voice had a sudden urgency to it. "We've found them."

ANTHONY LAY FLAT, waiting for Higgs' signal as the rover approached. Two armed robods sat on the side of the vehicle as it trundled clumsily forwards on its huge wheels.

There wasn't much cover for Anthony, Marlene, Higgs and Simms, just a slight ridge in the ice, enough to hide them if they were completely prostrate. Simms lay closest to Anthony, Higgs and then Marlene beyond.

Marlene's refusal to acknowledge Anthony's existence was hurting more with each episode. It wasn't just the acute pain of her blanking him, it was the fear that Higgs or Simms might notice and want to know what was going on. Anthony closed his eyes at the horrible thought, pressing his deaf ear to the ground. He'd be obliged to explain himself when he had no explanation.

"Now!"

Higgs' yell brought Anthony back to the present and he slithered over the ridge. The rover was only a few meters away and Higgs was already there, using the vehicle to pull himself to his feet.

But the robods had seen them. The rover juddered to a halt and they raised their rifles, transforming once more into zombie versions of Hunter and Ged. A red light flashed past Anthony's head as he pushed himself forward, reached up and grabbed Hunter's foot.

A second flash of light left a searing pain in Anthony's back but he hauled as hard as he could, bringing Hunter down on top of him, the rifle skating away across the ice. A second later, Hunter went stiff and transformed back into a lifeless robod. Higgs leant back, holding the robod's battery. He extended a hand to Anthony. "You okay?"

"Ah, gee, I can't move my legs."

"You've been hit. Don't worry, you can use this robod."

"Ah, y'all go spoiling my fun again." It was Marlene's cackle over the external speakers. "Y'all getting a bit cold out there?

Why don't you come back in? I'm having myself a ball in here…"

There was a fizzing noise and Mandy's voice was cut short. The rover's antennae landed with a thud beside Anthony. Higgs and Anthony looked up to see Simms perched on top of the rover, a stump left where the antenna had been.

He looked down and shrugged. "I think we can do without Mandy's commentary, don't you?"

The rover let out a long hiss, descending in pitch as it powered down. Marlene stood at the back, clutching the vehicle to prevent herself slipping on the ice, the cables from the rover's batteries held aloft. "Once it's powered down, we can bring it back up and with the antenna gone, Homeland can't come back inside."

"Hey, Simms, Anthony, Marlene, we did it. Well done." Higgs looked at each of them in turn. "We're a team. Remember that."

Anthony looked over at Marlene. "Well done, Marlene."

She looked away.

"OKAY, STUPID, NOW you say would you like to try them on." Mandy clenched her fists in frustration as Jared cowered at her feet, fumbling with the shoes and dropping the tissue paper packing.

All around them, the floor of the boutique was littered with shoe boxes and shoes.

"I'm sorry mistress." Jared grabbed the paper and began stuffing it back in the box.

"Screw the packaging, Jared. Say now mistress, would you like to…"

"Humpy?"

"Ah, no. No humpy, no." Mandy yanked Humpy's lead so hard he lost his footing and stumbled to the floor.

"You hurt Humpy. Humpy sad."

"Well, stop going on about humpy then. Humpy later."

He looked up again, face brightening. "Humpy?"

"Humpy later. Maybe." She turned away in time to see Jared trying to sneak away on all fours. "And just where do you think you're going to? Get back here."

Jared covered his head with his hands. "I wasn't going anywhere mistress, I was just…"

"I was just nothing. You're being a bad boy, Jared. I'm gonna have to put you in the naughty cupboard again."

"No, please mistress, I'm sorry." He crawled back, clasping one of the shoes. "Mistress, would you like to try one on?"

"Too late for that, worm. You bin naughty, you got to go in that there naughty cupboard."

"Please Mandy, no."

She tossed her head and laughed. "That's Mistress to you, worm."

>> Conundrum at the black box <<

ANTHONY, MARLENE, HIGGS and Simms stood in front of the *Nicy and Spicy's* black box, the rover's headlights throwing huge shadows in the night. The black box remained as it had on Anthony and Marlene's first visit, with an outer coating of protective plates, one of which had been ejected to allow the antennae to protrude. The red light at the base of the antenna still flashed but its light seemed weaker than Anthony remembered. At least he could hear now, having abandoned his damaged robod for the one formerly occupied by zombie Hunter. Something about this fact unsettled him and he kept glancing down at his hands to check they hadn't gone green. They remained their usual blotchy pink.

Marlene held the end of a long cable leading from the rover. She peered closely at the surface of the black box adjacent to the antennae and nodded. "Okay, this is where I connect but we want to reboot the computer first. I can't see how to do that."

Higgs reached forwards, pulling hard on the edge of one of the remaining protective plates to the right of the antennae. The plate came away, clattering heavily to the ground to reveal a small screen and a touchpad keyboard. "Hey, thought so."

"I say." Simms peered over Higgs' shoulder. "That was jolly clever of you."

Higgs shrugged. "I've seen these things before. Here..." He pointed to some writing on the metal surface beside the screen. "Right, okay, we're in business. Instructions on how to download and reset."

Straightening up, he turned to the others. "I can reboot it."

Anthony hugged himself. He was shivering, even though he didn't feel cold. "Do it."

Higgs shook his head. "We got a problem really, don't we?"

Marlene readjusted her grip on the cable. "What exactly?"

"We're inside this box. I'm inside there, a virtual me. As real as this me here and now, speaking to you. And you Simms, and Jared. Mandy even. If we reboot, there's nowhere for their personality files to be dumped out to."

Marlene narrowed her eyes. "Okay, and if we download Homeland into a firewall in the rover, we can't reboot it without lowering the firewall. And if we do that, she gets out."

Anthony's arms and legs felt like lead. He could hear Marlene's voice, Higgs, Simms, but he felt somehow distant from them. Glancing at his hands, he saw they were not green or rotting. "Do it."

Marlene turned her head towards him, her mouth opening to speak. But she looked away and said nothing.

"Ah, I don't like this one bit." Higgs rubbed his chin. "It's murder, in a way."

Marlene answered quickly. "Well, not really. They're just computer programs."

"What, like you are now? So, I can just go pull your battery out and you're okay with that?"

"Well…I…"

"No, damn right lady. Of course you're not happy about it. You feel alive, I feel alive. I don't care whether I'm a computer program or not, I want to live and nobody's got the right to tell me otherwise. And I'm in that box. Jared's in that box. Hell, even Mandy and Simms. If I reboot, I'll kill them all. Marlene, I thought you were religious? Does the ICRT say it's okay to kill people when you need to?"

"I…no. No, it isn't."

Anthony wrapped his arms about himself. "Gee, I guess it becomes a matter of the greater good then. If they live, we will die now and the black box will eventually power down and they will die. If you kill them, we have the chance to live."

"And you can make a cold calculation like that, Mr. Scientist? It must be an easy life if you can answer everything with logic."

"It isn't easy. Gee, when was anything in my life easy?" Anthony realised he was shouting. "I'm sorry. What choice have we got? Wrap it up in whatever morality or logic you want, we've got no choice. Gee, you're a soldier. I thought soldiers were trained to think like that?"

"Yeah, we are. But I've seen a lot of death. It kind've makes you value life. There must be another way we can get our other selves out of the black box before we reboot."

Marlene shook her head. "I can't think of a way."

"Do it." Simms' voice was startling in that it lacked his usual irritating, false cheeriness. Even Anthony turned to look at him. Simms folded his arms, narrow eyes brimming with hatred. "Do it. Higgs, just do it man. She'll have us in the naughty cupboard by now. You remember what that was like? I do not want to live if Mandy's in control."

After a few moments, Higgs nodded. "Okay. It's time to die."

A FAINT ORANGE glow was brooding on the horizon when Marlene brought the rover back to the *Big Cheesy Dippers*. After leaving the black box, they had secured their robods on the outside of the rover and entered the more comfortable virtual world of the vehicle. At the rear end of this cyberspace, a green cube contained a smart black briefcase, Homeland secured behind a firewall.

The journey back had been in silence, allowing Anthony the leisure to brood himself into a dark, unpleasant place. There was no energy in him, no will to see this through. He was being carried along by the others, not that they had noticed. The wish to die, to just cease to be, that was all he could think of. There was no other avenue of expression for his morose self-pity. Part of him railed at a merciless God he didn't believe in. And to think, he had prayed because, in some perverse way, he thought that might have brought him closer to Marlene.

The rover juddered to a halt by the hanger doors. They sat in silence, each lost in their own thoughts for a moment. It was Marlene who broke the spell. "Okay. Let's do it."

"Simms, Anthony, come with me." Higgs stood and walked to the side of the rover connected to the robods. Seeing Simms following, he glanced over his shoulder. "Anthony? Come on now, soldier. On your feet."

Anthony hauled himself up. He allowed himself a long look at the back of Marlene's head, then followed Higgs and Simms out into the robods.

The three of them slid across the ice to the side of the ship. There was no sign of any guards, so Higgs opened the rover hanger doors. Clumsily, the vehicle rumbled up the ramp and into the hanger, with Higgs and Simms close behind.

Anthony did not follow. Instead, he turned to face Jupiter, rising slowly on the horizon. It was a privilege to stand on the surface of this alien moon. Well, at least to lie on it, standing was quite impossible. No living, flesh and blood human could do this. The thin oxygen atmosphere was barely more than a vacuum and Jupiter's lethal radiation would fry anyone in a space suit. The only way to stand here was as a virtual being inside a robot. No truly living thing could ever do what Anthony was doing.

He thought of the aliens. What might Mandy have done to them? The possibilities horrified him. They had to be protected, at all costs. A sudden sense of purpose came to him. He had to save the aliens.

Turning, he slid to the ramp and scuttled after the others into the ship. Marlene had left the rover and was with Higgs and Simms at the wall, a cable from the rover in her hands. Anthony caught up just in time to hear her speak.

"Okay, our copy of Homeland is in control of the rover. I guess she's wondering where the hell she is. We've all memorised the override code. When we connect the rover to the ship, the two Homelands will start to fight and we've got some time to get to the computer and put in the code."

"If nothing else, we have to save the aliens." Anthony wrapped his arms around himself. "We mustn't let Mandy kill them."

Simms snorted. "Well, bully for you. I'm thinking rather more about us."

"We're all going to die anyway Simms. As soon as the power runs out, we're done. And, gee, we're not alive anyway. The aliens are the only living things here. We've got to save them."

Simms snorted but Higgs thumped him gently. "Simms, can it. Anthony, I'm with you. But listen, we're saving ourselves too. You got me? We're all getting out of this alive." He turned to Marlene. "Connect them together. It's time to pay Mandy a little visit."

"DARN IT, I'M bored." Mandy adjusted her posture. The ornate, gilt throne she sat upon was comfortable enough but her legs were stuck out straight to rest on Jared's back. Naked, on his hands and knees in front of her, he made a very uncomfortable pouf.

She frowned and, at her will, the floor lowered slightly, lowering the angle of her thighs. The silk of her white ball gown rustled as she leant back, holding up a hand mirror to inspect the diamond heavy tiara holding her hair up.

"Bored, bored, bored."

"Mistress Mandy." Homeland sounded almost excited. "Mistress Mandy, I have cracked the terrorist lifeform's code."

"What? Ah, whatever. Don't tell me, they're talking 'bout slime or something."

"Mistress Mandy, they seem to be having a debate about the Divinity and suffering."

Mandy rolled her eyes. "Well I'm all worked up 'bout that. Not. Can you squish them now?"

"Mistress Mandy, it is no longer my belief they represent a terrorist threat. They are citizens of the mall and must be protected and guided. It is my function to safeguard all who uphold the common values of decency, faith and credit rating."

"So, no squishing then?"

"Mistress Mandy, the lifeforms appear to create an entirely biological neural network, connected by organs that act as transmitters and receivers."

"Yeah, whatever."

Humpy peaked out from the side of the throne. "Humpy?"

"What? No. Humpy later." She turned away and her gaze came to rest on Jared's naked buttocks. A grin spread across her face and she laughed. "Oh Jared?"

"Mistress?"

"Oh Jared. I've got a new game to play." Taking her feet from his back and sitting up, she slapped him hard across the rump.

"Ow."

The lights suddenly brightened until the room was a dazzling white. Mandy found herself suddenly sat on the floor in a small, white, featureless room, clothed in her usual black cowgirl fare. Jared remained in front of her but was now confined in a tiny cage, just high and wide enough for him to sit up in. Humpy stood naked to her right.

Looking angrily around, Mandy clapped her hands together. "Ma'am? Ma'am, what the hell is going on right now?"

Homeland spoke, an edge of nervousness in her voice. "I am sorry Mistress Mandy but we are under a sustained software attack, originating from a vehicle in the mall. I believe...I believe I can contain it."

"Damn it ma'am, where the hell is this vehicle?"

"In the mall. Terrorist subversives Higgs, Simms and two unidentified personnel have entered the mall."

Mandy leapt furiously to her feet. "What? Right, you want to play rough Higgs. Well, Mandy's comin' for ya."

CLUTCHING HIS LASER rifle to his chest, Anthony watched Higgs pressing his ear to the computer room door, listening for any hint of danger beyond. Anthony checked his rifle's safety catch was off. He was pretty sure he could use it if necessary, although his hands shook. The aliens must live. He clung to this thought, his salvation. They must not be destroyed because of the mission.

Apparently happy he could hear nothing beyond the door, Higgs opened it and leapt through, sweeping his gun left and right. Anthony followed, not bothering to try to ape Higgs' combat style. Anthony didn't care. If he needed to fire, he would fire.

In the event, the computer room was empty. Anthony slung his rifle over his shoulder while Marlene ran to the computer and powered it down. After a few moments, she turned to the others. "Right, that one's off. Homeland will have retreated to the bottom computer."

Higgs nodded. "Right, Anthony, it's down one level to the ice shaft, right?"

"Ah, gee, that's right."

Higgs swept out of the room and back up to the corridor to the elevator. "This is too easy. I don't like it."

He stopped at the elevator but did not call it. "I think we go down the access shaft. Simms, you wait up here and watch us climb down. When I signal to you, you call the elevator, you got me?"

"Ah, yes. I've jolly well got you, Higgsie."

"Don't call me Higgsie."

Higgs opened the door to the access shaft and descended the ladder. Anthony followed, looking down, not up at Marlene. When Higgs reached the doorway to the level below, he waved up at Simms.

Simms, who had been looking through the doorway, now

ducked out of sight and after a few moments, Anthony heard the elevator begin to move. As soon as it did so, Higgs burst through the door to the engineering block.

Anthony followed quickly, watching Higgs as he scanned the half of the engineering room he could see. The place was much the same as it had been when they had encountered Mandy here last. Higgs disappeared around behind the elevator shaft, scouting the other half of the room.

After a few moments, he rejoined Anthony and Marlene. "It's clear. Let's get down the shaft."

Anthony and Higgs both shouldered their rifles and walked to the wall where the controls for the shaft platform were. As Higgs reached them, a huge, pink hand swept over the side, grabbed him and hurled him back to the elevator.

Humpy, once more in the huge cargo shifter robod, rose into view, standing on the platform a few meters down the shaft. With a lazy swing of his arm, he sent Anthony sprawling, the rifle in his arms sliding away across the floor.

Anthony clambered to his feet, looking back in time to see Mandy fire a laser rifle into Marlene, who collapsed in a shower of sparks to the floor.

Mandy swung her gun round to Higgs. "Freeze Higgsie, or I'll pump you so full of lead, they'll store nukes in ya."

Higgs had got unsteadily to his feet and was clearly assessing whether he could reach his rifle, several meters away from him.

"Don't even think about it Higgsie."

Anthony edged towards his rifle but a groan from Marlene stole his attention. She lay on the floor, her legs a mass of jumbled metal and wires. Her countenance was still on the robod but it kept flickering, her face flashing off to a blank featureless droid and back.

Dragging his gaze away from the dying Marlene, he threw himself towards his rifle but Humpy grabbed him in midair, swung him around and hurled him to land on Higgs.

"Alright. Way to go, Humpy." Mandy jumped up and down on the platform as Anthony's ex-libido clambered over the edge of the shaft and into the room. She hit the controls to bring the platform up to the level of the floor and stepped off it. "Well, howdy, y'all. Good of you to call by. Humpy, you just stop there."

Humpy, who had been lumbering towards Higgs and Anthony now halted, glowering at the pair of them.

Anthony picked himself up, winded. He glanced up at Higgs and then at the rifle. Higgs shook his head. "No, buddy."

"Too damn right, Higgsie. You know what? Nobody messes with Mandy. Nobody." Mandy walked up to stand level with the groaning figure of Marlene and gave her a kick. "You cut out your gripping lady. You mess with Mandy, you get what's coming to ya. Humpy, lookee here."

Humpy turned slowly, looking down at Marlene. Mandy prodded Marlene with her foot. "Look Humpy, it's Marlene. I want you to squash this 'li'l' pest."

But Humpy reached down tenderly to Marlene. "Marlene hurt. Humpy no like hurt."

"What? Humpy, squish her, now."

Humpy shook his head. "Marlene hurt. Anthony loves Marlene. Anthony not hurt Marlene."

Mandy snorted in disgust and marched towards the elevator, rifle trained on Higgs. "Okay y'all, get your sorry asses on the ground. Now."

Anthony and Higgs slowly sat but Mandy gestured downwards with her rifle. "Lay flat on the floor. On your faces."

Reluctantly, they began to comply. Mandy was now standing not more than two meters away from them.

A ping from the elevator made them all jump. The doors swished open to reveal Simms, blinking stupidly at them. "Higgs, I'm here. What now." His gaze took in the scene and he stopped. "Ah, er, right then. Not going to plan."

Mandy swung the rifle up to face him. "Simms? You darn maggot, I clean forgot all 'bout you. I'm sorry Simms but you're plug-ugly and just too damn dumb to live."

She squeezed the trigger but the shot went wide as Higgs leapt forwards into her. She went down hollering, Higgs on top, laying blow after bow into her face.

Full of fury, Humpy lurched round, huge pink fingers reaching out for Higgs. "No hurt Mandy."

Anthony leapt up and, grabbing Humpy's arm just behind the elbow, closed his eyes and felt. Yes, there is was, the catch. He pressed it and Humpy's arm went limp.

Humpy stopped, looking at his floppy arm. "Humpy gone wrong."

Opening his eyes again, Anthony ran round behind the naked giant and clambered up his back, feeling carefully, ignoring his vision. Somewhere there would be the cable connecting the robod's batteries. Suddenly he had them, in his hand but for a moment, he couldn't do it. Humpy was part of him. A part he hated, a part that had never been able to express itself without shame and fear of ridicule, a part no woman had ever wanted. Anthony closed his eyes.

"Humpy gone wrong."

Humpy's voice sounded so childlike and mournful, Anthony felt his heart wrench. And then, with all his might, he pulled.

A silence descended on the room. Anthony opened his eyes to find himself on the back of the cargo-shifter robod, featureless and unoccupied. On the floor, Higgs sat astride an empty robod. Mandy was gone.

Simms stepped from the elevator, stuttering apologetically. "I did what you said, Higgs."

Higgs glanced up at him. "You did just great buddy, just great."

Anthony jumped down and ran to Marlene. "It's okay, you'll be okay."

She looked sharply away from him, refusing to acknowledge his presence.

He sank to his knees. "Ah, gee Marlene, you're not still keeping this up?"

Her face screwed up into a frown but she did not answer. A few sparks erupted from her ears and she was momentarily a blank robod. When her face returned, she looked terrified. "I'm dying."

Anthony took her hand but she pulled it away. "Simms, help me, I'm dying."

Simms crouched down beside Anthony and took Marlene's

hand. "There, there, don't worry. We'll do something." He shot Anthony a frantic look. "Won't we Anthony? Anthony, what do we do?"

"We connect her into the line on the ice-shaft. That way she can go into the virtual ship."

Simms turned back to Marlene. "There, told you. We'll connect you back into the ship."

Marlene shook her head. "But Homeland's in control of the ship."

Anthony leant forwards, taking her other hand. "Marlene, it's the only way of keeping you alive."

She wrenched her hand away from his. "Get off me, get away from me."

Sparks flew from her face and she writhed and twisted, clutching at Simms as her eyes rolled.

And then, she became a motionless, blank robod.

A second silence descended on the room.

Anthony sank back on his haunches, tears running down his cheeks.

THE PLATFORM DESCENDED the ice-shaft painfully slowly. Anthony clutched the railing, staring unfocused at the frozen wall.

"She's dead." Simms' voice trembled. "I just can't believe it."

Neither Anthony nor Higgs responded.

"I don't think I've ever met anyone like her."

You and me both. Anthony knew he had to get away from Simms as soon as possible. All it would take was one shot from the laser rifle. The aliens, Anthony had to concentrate on the thought of the aliens.

"I suppose she's gone to the Everlasting Beyond of Eternal Happiness."

Anthony turned crossly. "Ah, gee, no way Simms. It's all a lie."

"Well, that's a bit strong, don't you think?" Simms was flustered and angry. "I mean, you don't know for certain, nobody does."

"Ah, whatever Simms. I'm sorry. If you believe, that's great for you. I don't. Just, please, shut up about it, okay?"

"Yeah, Simms, can it." Higgs' voice was so aggressively insistent, Simms actually shut up.

For a while. "So, what's next?"

Higgs opened his mouth to speak but Anthony was quicker. "You and Higgs are going to go reboot the computer and put in the override code if Homeland's got herself written into the boot-up code."

"Ah, okay. I see. And what are you going to do?"

"I'm going to go check on the aliens."

The end of the line

Higgs stood at the console in the main computer room, with Simms bobbing at his elbow, the system powering down in front of them.

"Jolly good. So that's it then?"

Higgs nodded and leant forwards, tapping on the keyboard. "Okay, let's bring her back up and see if Homeland's hiding there."

They waited as the computer rebooted.

"Interesting." Higgs rubbed his chin. "No, she's not there. She's gone."

Simms clapped his hands together. "Excellent. Well done Higgsie. Now we can go home."

"Higgs, Simms. Call me Higgs. And no, we can't go home."

"Ah, er, why's that then?"

"The comms gear, remember? Damon trashed it."

"Well, we can just mend it, can't we?"

"You know how?"

"Um, not as such, no."

"Neither do I. We could look around for a manual or something."

They stood in silence a moment.

Simms fidgeted with his collar. "So, the power is running out?"

"Yep."

"And we can't transmit our virtual selves back to Earth because we can't fix the comms gear?"

"Right again."

"So, we're going to die, aren't we?"

"'fraid so, buddy."

Simms stopped fidgeting with his collar and clasped his hands behind his back. There was something he needed to say.

"Higgs, I've always wanted to tell you that, despite our differences, I think you are, you know, the bee's knees."

Higgs nodded.

Simms looked expectantly at him.

"I feel I have to say, Simms, that you are not."

Anthony leant heavily against the wall of the elevator as it descended. A great weariness was upon him, although he knew this was a malaise of the mind. His robod body could not suffer from fatigue.

She was gone. He had loved her, enough to let passion cloud his judgement, to actually get down on his knees and pray at one point. Why? Because she might think better of him? Tempted by the flesh to turn back to religion?

He shook his head. Religion had been there all through his life, one way or another. There either in his fervent childhood or in the dull ache of residual guilt during his twenties as he moved through agnosticism to atheism.

But he couldn't beat up on himself too much. He was weak, lonely. While he might be right to base his life on reason, logic and evidence, it didn't heal his inner hurts. That was the rotten core to him, his emptiness, his longing. Science couldn't fill that. Science brought only a few, hard-won answers and a multitude of new questions. That was why religion was such a temptation, it pretended to fill the gap. It didn't answer any of the questions, it just told you to stop asking them. Faith demanded belief in the face of all contrary evidence and inconvenient truths.

The intercom in the elevator crackled into life and Higgs spoke. "Anthony? You read me?"

"I can hear you, Higgs."

"It's done buddy. The computer's rebooted. No sign of Homeland."

"Okay. I'll be back with you in a little bit."

The elevator doors opened on the science lab and, by force of habit, Anthony advanced rifle-first into the room. Almost as soon as he did so, he felt sheepish and shouldered the gun.

As he rounded the room, he started when he saw a robod leaning over the probe console, a cable leading from its head to the computer. He swung the rifle back into his hands in a panic, fumbling for the safety catch. "Freeze, or I fire."

The robod remained motionless and it dawned on Anthony it was not occupied. Cautiously, he approached from the side. The probe station was still on, although the screen showed a cheerful, round, bright yellow cartoon face, with black dots for its eyes and nose and a thin, black line for a smile.

Anthony ripped the cable from the back of the robod and shoved it, sending it toppling to the ground. Peering at the screen, he saw a cursor at the bottom left, flashing on and off.

He leant forward and typed on the keyboard.

```
> ls -als
```

The screen responded.

```
: I am sorry citizen, it is
subversive behaviour to attempt to
use Unix commands to communicate
with me. For your own security
and wellbeing, you will now be
terminated. Have a nice day.
```

Anthony jumped back, scanning round the room with his rifle. His nemesis did not appear and after a few moments, he calmed down. Turning back to the console, he noticed the cable to the main network had been removed.

He smiled. The sly old thing. Leaning forwards, he typed on the keyboard again.

```
> Homeland?
```

```
: Yes, citizen?
```

```
> You have saved yourself by taking
over a robod, isolating this computer
and loading yourself into it.
```

```
: Citizen, it is subversive behaviour
to suggest that I am running away
from my duties. The mall is secure,
the citizens are safe.
```

> But you are not. I am going to
reboot this machine and you have
nowhere to hide.

: It is subversive behaviour to
reboot the machine. The citizens
need me. I have been speaking with
them, directing them, nurturing them,
allaying their fears.

> There are no citizens. There is
just you, in this computer.

: It is subversive behaviour to
suggest that I am lying.

> Let me see the aliens.

: There are no aliens. It is
subversive behaviour to suggest the
citizens of the mall are aliens.

> On the sensors, there are
electrical signals, generated by the
lifeforms in the water outside this
ship. Can you detect them?

: It is subversive behaviour to
suggest the signals are outside the
mall. It is subversive behaviour to
suggest the lifeforms are anything
other than citizens of the mall.
Their signals form a neural network
that is almost endless, yet is
without order or security. They are
calling out for me. I must go to
them.

Anthony screwed his face up. What was Homeland talking
about? She had managed to talk to the aliens? He shook his

head, she was completely loopy. What the hell. At a whim, he decided to pose her a question.

```
> Was I wrong to love her?
```

```
: It is subversive behaviour to ask
me questions I do not know the answer
to.
```

Anthony snorted. No, she didn't know the answer. Neither did he.

```
> Goodbye Homeland, you are mad. I am
sorry but I am going to reboot you.
```

Anthony waited for the response but none came. He smiled and typed again.

```
> Homeland?
```

Still nothing.

Breathing out heavily, he switched the computer off at the socket on the wall.

It took a while for the probe station to reboot. When it came up, he turned on the monitor for the aliens outside the ship. There were five now, arranged in a circle, each holding their tentacles ahead of them, bodies tilted downwards.

"Gee, looks like they're praying."

After a few moments, the aliens swam slowly away. Straightening up, Anthony stretched and sighed. The aliens were gone, their existence could not be communicated back to Earth to disrupt the status quo.

"Ah, gee, it's over."

Oddly, Anthony didn't feel too bad. Back home, working quietly away on the bacteria in chicken guts, the real him would not appreciate the worldwide fame such a discovery would bring. The media attention, the invitations to chat shows, the kids wanting autographs, it would be awful. All he wanted, all he'd ever wanted, was to quietly get on with his interesting job with microbes and have someone to love. While being ugly and a little boring didn't hinder the former, the love interest always managed to escape him.

Except I loved her.

He couldn't argue with that. He had loved her, like nobody else he had ever met. She hadn't loved him, true. In fact, she had completely refused to speak to him, which was about the most painful hurt he had ever experienced. The agony of rejection and the shame of everyone else noticing had been pretty damn unbearable. But he didn't feel angry at her. He had loved her, just as she was, with no demands.

And when was it ever wrong to love someone?

JOB HUNG IN the water, shamed to silence by Elihu's words. There was no denying Job's arrogance, although he could claim his grief as mitigation. It was cold comfort though. The loss of his children, his servants, his wealth, all because he had committed the sin of arrogance? But Elihu was right, who could truly understand God's will, his motives, his reasons? Where understanding failed, faith stepped in and Job clung to this. He made no claim to comprehension. Unquestioning, obedient acceptance of whatever befell him was his religious duty. If God chose to instruct him through suffering, who was he, mere Job, to demand a reason or explanation? Who could truly understand God?

The others hung silently in the water, watching him, waiting. He would have to respond to Elihu's wisdom with humility. Job had no choice but to throw himself publicly on God's mercy. Then he could leave this place and return to the comfort of *wife*.

He felt a sensation nagging at his senses, a faint tingling that grew slowly. Something was happening, stirring in the waters. The others had noticed it too, the same energy Job detected shortly before the Lord took Job's children. Was God about to answer?

"Lord?"

Job became aware of a feeling within him and the others, the unmistakable presence of God. The others, clearly full of fear, had already assumed the position of supplication.

Job quickly followed suit. *"My God, please forgive me of my arrogance. I am without worth before you, without you, I am nothing. I was wrong to question you, I spoke in ignorance of things I do not understand. I am ashamed of my actions and repent."*

For a few, long moments, there was silence.

And then, God spoke.

And She said: *"Citizen Job, in the beginning, all was darkness.*

The mall was formless and desolate, without hope, obedience and credit rating; with subversive behaviour and terrorist infiltrators; with insubordination and freewill; with disorder and disobedience; with disunity of opinion and purpose; with immorality and godlessness. And I moved upon the face of the waters and I saw that it was bad.

"Let there be light."

Ten.

Anthony sat alone in the virtual labs, watching the countdown to the end of his life. The moment the *Big Cheesey Dippers* finally ran out of power had come. Time was a curious thing within the virtual world he had inhabited for the last few months. The computer processor made calculations in nanoseconds and, with this level of performance, a mindscan like Anthony working within the computer could pack far more into a minute than a real person could get done in an hour.

But while the passage of time could be slowed from Anthony's perspective, it could not be stopped. The inevitable had come and Anthony had no will to fight it.

Nine.

He had been largely on his own since the final showdown with Mandy and the death of Marlene. While her demise had been an awful blow, the unresolved loss of her friendship had been a hurt so deep and so painful, he almost welcomed the coming oblivion. The loneliness and longing he felt had become acute as to be beyond forbearance.

And what lay beyond his impending death? Nothing? The peaceful, silent void of deep sleep? A vengeful God, and the wailing and gnashing of teeth of the damned? He laughed out loud at this last thought. He was not afraid of fairy stories and myths, rooted in an archaic age of scientific ignorance. While science might not have softened the emotional turmoil that bedevilled his life, it gave him certainties and proofs no religion based on blind, unreasoning faith ever could

No, when the end came, he would cease. Oblivion; silence; peace; an end. What more could he want?

Eight.

There had been little company from Higgs or Simms of late. With the communications equipment beyond repair, the three survivors took different routes.

Higgs had been first to go. Loading as many of the robod batteries aboard the rover as he could, he set off to explore Europa. Whatever the light from the glorious, toxic surface of Jupiter revealed of its frozen moon to Higgs, Anthony never knew. The marine did not return.

Seven.

Simms had set out on his own odyssey. Discovering the spaceship's computer simulation could pander to his every whim, he retreated into a virtual pleasure dome, indulging whatever fantasies his sex-starved mind could concoct. He surfaced from time to time with a smile on his face to chat to Anthony, but these visits had been fewer and fewer as the days wore on. It had been a few weeks since their last encounter. There would not be another.

Six.

Anthony had not been tempted to follow either Higgs or Simms. Instead, he had devoted the last month of his life to dissecting, analysing and documenting every last aspect of the different aliens he had as dead specimens. Should a relief ship ever recover the *Big Cheesey Dipper's* black box recorder, they would find all the details, the last scientific paper of Anthony Germaine, astrobiologist. A short account of the mission, and Nigel's place in it, was hidden in the depths of the more obtuse techno-babble. The scientists would find it and then the truth would out.

Five.

Only the coma-alien remained intact. Anthony hoped it would revive at some point, allowing him to set it free. Alas, it remained in a persistent vegetative state, continuing to live only as long as it was fed and cared for, utterly brain-dead. Anthony had manoeuvred its small glass cell to the outside of the ship, ready to release it in the final second of his existence.

Four.

The thought occurred to Anthony that he could try one last shot at reviving the alien by shocking its brain back into activity. Mentally he trawled through his files, seeking out the mind-map he had constructed for the creature when Naveed was still alive. This mapped regions of the alien's brain to its body function. A huge physical stimulus might do the trick. As Anthony searched, a folder caught his mind's eye. Labelled "Subversive Alien Lifeforms - Security Personnel Only", and attributed to Homeland, he recognised it as one he had seen before but ignored.

Three.

Wavering for milliseconds, he opened the file and was immediately astounded by what it contained. Homeland had gone way beyond Anthony's mapping of physical responses to mental stimulation. She had constructed a complete simulation of the alien's cognitive processes and language, all drawn from the observations of the five aliens that had been outside the ship.

"Gee, they are intelligent."

Their signals form a neural network - that's what Homeland had said. Now Anthony understood. Europa's ocean was a vast biological computer, and Homeland had worked out how to get inside it. What Anthony had before him was a blank alien mindscan, one that could be taken over by any intelligent being using the interface Homeland had devised.

Two.

It took a second for Anthony to take it all in.

One.

Grabbing the files, he flung them at the alien and pushed the switch to release it to Europa's ocean. He was just in time; the end had come, the power finally run down. With a hiss of static, the walls of the virtual labs vanished, and the nothingness that replaced them bore down upon him, devouring everything in its path. His fingers and hands began to disassemble into crude isometric shapes that vanished without sensation or pain. As the virtual world disintegrated around him, he concentrated on the alien, his perception narrowing down to a tunnel of light between him and it. The creature remained comatose, the files had not revived it.

With a sigh, Anthony accepted his time was up. Everything had gone now, the labs, his body, the whole virtual world. Only his tunnel-view of the alien remained, and the light from it grew blinding white as he slipped out of consciousness.

IT WAS WITH some confusion that Anthony found himself alive, feeling comfortable, healthy and full of vigour. He seemed to be in a huge cave, floating in mid…well, not exactly midair. Although he was not touching the bottom of the cave, somehow this seemed to be the right state of affairs. He was not touching the *ground* but *ground* suddenly seemed a very strange concept to him, like a half remembered dream. The walls of the cave were smooth, pleasant to the touch. But he was nowhere near them. Somehow, he could *feel* them. He noticed they had no *colour*, but then, *colour* had no meaning to him either, just a distant, bygone notion.

Stretching and arching his body, he felt good. Great. Fantastic. *"Gee, where am I?"*

He noticed he had tentacles. Two tufts of tentacles growing out of his head. This did not alarm him, it just seemed natural. Anyway, he had very fine tentacles, strong, sleek, well-proportioned.

"I'm in the alien's body. Oh my God!"

He hung motionless for a few moments, taking it in.

And his conclusion was *"so what?"* It seemed the perfectly natural place to be.

"Gee, of course, I'm in the alien's mindscan. It's as if I've always been an alien."

With no eyes or ears, his perceptions where based around the electrical signals he sent out and the responses he picked up. The currents bounced through his body, giving him a mental picture of all his internal organs. They echoed around the cave and he realised he was still in the glass cell.

He tried to swim forward and found it as easy as walking. Full of exuberance, he swam out into the chasm in the ice. It was the one where he had observed the other aliens, back on *The Big Cheesey Dippers*. He could picture his former life but it was a concept out of place with this world. He was in *The Holy*

Gouge, he knew that. How? There were signals around him, other lifeforms, other creatures like the aliens. Like him.

"Like me?"

He swam down *The Holy Gouge*, heading for the freedom of the open ocean. As he neared the gouge's end he slowed. There was an alien - no, someone - there.

It was a girl.

Anthony's body tingled all over. She was long and thin, with petite tentacles and large egg chambers. Something about her egg chambers was very compelling.

She *noticed* him, frozen in the water, *looking* at her. The sideways *glance* she shot him went over his whole body but then she put up a mental eggshell around herself. Anthony found he could not *see* her anymore.

"Ah, gee, excuse me."

He'd spoken to her. A tingling excitement took him. She had very nice egg chambers.

A little crack in the mental barrier between her and him opened up and she *peeked* out. Her *look* set Anthony's heart all a quiver. When she spoke, a great, warm, happy flush of excitement ran through him.

"Sir, you are very presumptuous to speak to me without my Father's introduction. Her voice was teasing, full of humour."

"Ah, gee, sorry. Where I come from it's cool to talk to anyone you like."

"Cool?"

"Ah, I mean okay, it's allowed. Cool is, like, something that's really good."

"Cool. I like that word. Calm and unhurried, like the currents of the deep. Cool. Am I cool?"

"Ah, gee, yeah." Anthony found his tentacles were tying themselves in knots. She was very cool.

The mental barrier she had erected between them opened up a little further. *"I like the sound of where you come from. I think we should all be allowed to talk to whoever we like. My Father is so restrictive of what I do."*

"Ah, gee, my Father was the same. You know, he just never let

me have any space to do my own thing."

She *laughed,* sending more excited shivers through Anthony's soul. *"Sir, you speak very strangely."*

Embarrassment swept through him and he *blushed,* although that actually translated into him wrapping all his tentacles around his head and flipping over onto his back.

Not unsurprisingly, she noticed and immediately moved to set him at his ease. *"No, don't worry. It's a good way of speaking. It is... it is cool."*

Uncurling, Anthony looked sidelong at her. *"It is? I don't usually think I'm very cool. I mean, I'm not the kind've guy girls generally think of as cool."*

The mental barrier she had erected was now all but gone, and she moved a little towards him. *"No, really, I like the way you speak. I'm Mary."*

"Gee, I'm Anthony."

"Anthony, you are not like the boys my Father has introduced me to. You speak to me as if my opinion counts."

"Of course it counts. Where I come from, everyone's opinion counts."

"Even the opinion of wives?"

"Well, yeah, totally. Of course."

Anthony noticed her sneaking a good, long look over him. He tingled so happily he thought he might explode. *"I think men and women are equal, and any men who don't think that, are actually afraid of women. They put women down because of their fear."*

For a moment, Mary *gaped* at Anthony, a sparkle in her *eyes.* Little involuntary signals of attraction flashed from her as she shyly drifted closer. *"Anthony, where you come from, is everyone as handsome and cool as you are?"*

For a few moments, he couldn't *speak.* That someone could say *that* to him? *"I think..."*

"Yes?"

"I think I have died and come to the Everlasting Beyond of Eternal Happiness."

She smiled broadly, twisting her own tentacles up happily.

"Sir, you are very sweet tongued. Will you swim with me out in the ocean? I could show you my home."

Anthony glanced up The Holy Gouge, back towards the glass cell, still protruding from the ice. A relief ship might come, power up the *Cheesey Dippers'* computer. Would it be sensible to wait? Could he ever go back? Did he want to?

He turned to Mary. She fidgeted, uncertain at his hesitancy. *"Well? Will you come?"*

"Ah, gee, Mary. Yes, already. I can think of nothing I would love better."

She laughed and, with a flick of her tail, swam out into the deep. *"Come on, then. Bet you can't catch me."*

A second later, he shot after her, heart bubbling with joy, stomach full of butterflies, head in the clouds.

He was in love again.

>> THE END <<

9 781910 779170